OPHELIA O. AND THE MORTGAGE BANDITS

OPHELIA O. AND THE MORTGAGE BANDITS

Tanya Jones

HEADLINE

First published in 1995 by
HEADLINE BOOK PUBLISHING

10 9 8 7 6 5 4 3 2 1

British Library Cataloguing in Publication Data

Jones, Tanya
   Ophelia O. and the Mortgage Bandits
   I. Title
   823 [F]

   ISBN 0-7472-1305-4

Typeset by Avon Dataset Ltd., Bidford-on-Avon

Printed and bound in Great Britain by
Mackays of Chatham PLC, Chatham, Kent

HEADLINE BOOK PUBLISHING
A division of Hodder Headline PLC
338 Euston Road
London NW1 3BH

To Father Christopher Jenkins, OSB

Chapter One

He is gone, he is gone,
And we cast away moan.
God a mercy on his soul.

(Hamlet, IV.v. 194–6)

At five to nine on an October Monday morning, Rambleton had not really woken up. Ophelia had already made two circuits of the Market Square, increasingly slowly as her feet pinched with cold and new shoes. She had surveyed the fly-blown signs in the butcher's window, cheerfully advertising beef and unbelievably orange Cheddar, the matching beige cardigan and pleated skirt in Pam's Fashion Corner, the domino and quiz fixture lists outside the Ram's Leg and the blue and white polar bears, quite twenty years more modern than anything else in the square, which clambered up the plate glass splendour of Freezaland. Now Ophelia contented herself with hopping up and down the three pigeon-dropped steps which led to Parrish, Stanmore and Parrish, Solicitors and Commissioners for Oaths.

The church clock, missing its minute hand, struck nine, but this obviously had no particular significance for the Rambleton business community, which continued to consist of a spotty youth carrying boxes into Freezaland, a brown dog sniffing around the butcher's closed door, and Ophelia.

Again she clenched her icy toes and cursed Stephen Tindall, the sharp-suited partner who had interviewed her eighteen months before at the firm's Harswell office. Harswell was a prosperous little dormitory town forty miles nearer to Leeds and therefore to civilisation as Yorkshire knows it.

'Do you know Rambleton at all?'

'No, I'm afraid not.'

'I see.' Was she imagining it now or could she really remember a look of relief passing over Mr Tindall's carefully shaven face?

'Well, it's a very picturesque little market town, you know, the sort they use to film the James Herriot programmes . . .'

'I thought that was somewhere further north.'

1

'Yes, you may be right, but we needn't be pedantic. It's the spirit of the place I was trying to convey. Stone walls, rat-catchers, pints of bitter, pinnies. Wonderful characters, you know, real Yorkshire folk, not like the namby-pambies we get down here. I really look forward to going over to the Rambleton office. Gets me back in touch with my roots.'

'Oh, you're from Rambleton, then?'

'Er, no. Harrogate actually.'

The conversation had faltered a little until Mr Tindall, glancing surreptitiously at the notes in front of him, remembered to ask Ophelia how on earth she thought that she could do the job at the same time as bringing up four children. As he spoke, his eyes had flickered across her expanding girth and he hesitated upon the word 'four'. Ophelia had rehearsed a reasonably plausible version of the truth, which was that any bringing up undergone by the children, of which she could recall none, was carried out by their father, her husband, Malachi. Unfortunately this explanation, which had relied upon the judicious placing of words such as 'partnership' and 'responsibility', had completely evaporated from her memory.

'I don't think there will be a problem. My husband is very feckless.'

'I beg your pardon?'

'Flexible. My husband is very flexible. His work is practically non-existent . . . non-er-restrictive . . . and so he, er, does all the necessary with the children.'

'What is it, exactly, that your husband does?'

'He's a . . . computer dealer. And, um . . .'

'Yes?'

'Consultant!' Ophelia cried in triumph, and Mr Tindall, knowing that no one else except a native Rambletonian boy with bad breath and severe social difficulties had applied for the job, offered it to her with a show of reluctant gallantry.

So Ophelia had won the not-much coveted prize of assistant solicitorship at Parrish, Stanmore and Parrish's Rambleton office, where she was to assist the senior partner, Mr Wilfred Parrish, 'on the litigation side'. Now, after completing her articles at an expensive Leeds firm, she was ready to bring the same order and profitability to the legal milieu of Rambleton. As yet, however, the heavy front door, once sky blue, remained locked and there was no sign of Mr Parrish nor of any legal activity, litigious or otherwise.

A bus wheezed into the market square and six or seven people alighted.

2

One, a minute girl in purple leather jacket and high heels, clacked purposefully towards Ophelia.

''Iya. I'n't 'e in yet then?'

Ophelia vaguely remembered a dialect joke told her by a Yorkshire friend at university of which the punch line was, mysteriously, 'Tin tin tin', then pulled herself together.

'No, there doesn't seem to be anyone here yet. I'm Ophelia O., the new assistant solicitor.'

'Yeah. Hiya. I'm Polly. Well, Pauline really, but my Gran always called me Polly when I was little and it sort of stuck. It was horrible at school though; they all called me Polly-put-the-kettle-on. I even tried calling myself Paulette but then I met Gary and he said it sounded like a stripper's name. And my friend Kim from Bradford, that lives with an alternative newsagent, she says that all the reporters on the posh papers are called Polly or Posy and that, so I've decided to keep it. Go a bit upmarket, you know. And Mr Parrish, he likes it 'cos it was his mother's name. He's really sweet sometimes; you'll like him.'

Polly sighed and after considerable rummaging in a handbag of slightly different purple to her jacket drew out a large and old-fashioned key. Unlocking the door apparently involved a complex percussion upon various parts of the lock and woodwork, rounded off by an enormous wrench, incredible in one so small and teetering as Polly. Eventually she threw a tough little shoulder at the panels and the door groaned open.

'Wasn't locked at all. Just a bit stiff with the weather. He must have forgotten to lock up yesterday. He's always here on Sundays, even though he's got nothing to do. Even worse at home by himself, I suppose.'

Ophelia followed the secretary into a gloomy outer room, painted in solicitors' dark brown, *circa* 1930. At the far end of the room a strip of electric light showed under a badly fitting door.

'He's left his light on again. He's always doing it. I tell him that's why he'll never make money like Canards but I don't think he's really bothered any more. Be retiring soon, now that you've come, I suppose.'

'Well, he won't be able to for a while, not unless Mr Tindall comes over every day. I'm not allowed to run an office by myself until I've been qualified for three years. Law Society rules . . .'

Ophelia realised that Polly was not listening to her. Polly was standing in the doorway from which the light came, her mouth open in preparation for a scream that had not yet arrived. As Ophelia reached the doorway

3

the sound erupted from Polly's mouth in staccato bursts of shock, counterpoised by Ophelia's own gasp of horror.

Wilfred Parrish lay across his wide leather-topped desk, white, cold and unmistakable, even to Ophelia, who had never before seen a corpse. She stepped gingerly into the room and circled the desk. But there was little more to be seen; no blood, bruises or blunt-ended weapons. There was not even a crumpled note of passion or newly forged trust deed. Mr Parrish had apparently died as innocuously as he had lived, struck down by a heart attack across the pages of the *Law Society's Gazette*.

Chapter Two

What do you read, my lord?
Words, words, words.

(II.ii. 191–2)

However blameless Mr Parrish's death, his corpse was not a reassuring sight and the two women, facing each other across his balding head, were both shaking violently. Ophelia edged around the desk, put her arm across Polly's shoulders and led her back to the outer office. She closed the door firmly and switched on a mottled electric kettle.

'Does . . . did he have a family nearby? Who should we contact?' asked Ophelia, thinking irrelevantly (and irreverently) that it should have been 'whom'.

'No, he's not got a family at all. That's what I was saying, about how he'd rather be at the office. He was married, but they never had any children and his wife died a few years ago. And he's not got any brothers or sisters, either, he told me that. He lives, I mean lived,' Polly gave a long sniff and wiped her nose on a crumpled pink tissue, 'all by himself in a big house out on the Scorsdale Road. Massive place, belonged to his grandfather, same as the firm. He used to talk about it a lot, how there was no one to carry it on. "Even a daughter would be something," he'd say. He used to talk like that, I'm afraid. A bit old-fashioned. Pattyrarcal, Kim says. Didn't matter in front of me but you wouldn't like it, being a lawyer and a feminist, I suppose.'

'So who' (Ophelia ruthlessly repressed any further thoughts about 'whom') 'should we tell?'

'Well, just Mr Marrow, I suppose. He's the undertaker and he's one of Mr Parrish's clients so I expect Mr Parrish would have wanted Marrows to bury him. Milk and three sugars, please. I'm trying to give up but it is a shock, isn't it? He was always careful like that, to give his own business to his clients. That's why I told our Gary to use Mr Parrish when he was in that bit of trouble at the butchers. I told him that maybe when he'd got his own shop then Mr Parrish would buy his sausages and that from Gary instead of from Presto's, like he does now. Did, I mean. I used to see him there on Saturday afternoon sometimes. Always

5

got a Battenburg cake for his Sunday tea.' Polly sniffed again, retrieving the tissue from the wastepaper basket. 'Gary says these multinationals are the kiss of death to the small business man—'

Ophelia interrupted this flow of economic exegesis, not, as she would have preferred, to discuss whether or not Presto was a multinational, but to return to the matter distressingly at hand.

'What about Mr Tindall at the Harswell office? Surely we should ring him before we do anything ourselves?'

'Slimy Steve? He's not with the firm anymore. Didn't you know? He bought out the Harswell office in March. Gary says he only paid a quarter of what it was worth, too, but Mr Parrish wasn't really bothered. Gary's got a mate with a butcher's in Harswell and he says property there goes for a bomb, even with the rescission.'

'What? So there's only this office?'

'Yeah. Just me and Mr Parrish. There was another secretary, Mildred she was called, but she retired last year and Mr Parrish said he thought I could cope with the work. Wasn't very much, really, mostly wills and that. We were really looking forward to you coming, though. Neither me nor him could really get the hang of this court stuff. Look at this medical report. "It is of course essential in this type of case to consider the effect of functional overlay." Poor Mr Parrish was worrying about that all last Thursday. It might have killed him, you know. Consecutive stress. Do you know what it is, Ophelia?'

'Consecutive, I mean, executive stress?'

'No, that functional thingy?' Polly seemed to be cheering up. Some of the colour was returning to her small round cheeks and now she took out a compact of blusher and completed the task.

'Yes, it's the extent to which the litigation itself slows down the recovery process. But look . . .'

'Be quite fun, anyway, just me and you,' continued Polly. 'My friend Kim, that I told you about, works for a women-only solicitors' firm in Bradford and they go on marches and have cream cakes whenever one of their clients gets her husband sent to gaol for breaching an injection.'

'Injunction.'

'Oh yeah. Mr Parrish never got many of them. We don't have many marches in Rambleton either, only the Mayor's Pageant. Kim went on a good one called "Retrain the Knight". That's a good idea, isn't it? I don't suppose they've much to do with there being no dragons and virgins and that.'

6

Ophelia's own quirky thought processes were rapidly being outclassed by Polly's. She took a deep breath and retaliated.

'Look, none of us will have much to do now Mr Parrish is dead. I was trying to tell you before, I can't run an office on my own and I certainly can't take over the firm.'

'Oh, I'm sure you could. You seem ever so clever to me.'

'No, I'm not allowed to under the solicitors' rules. It's the end of my job, and probably of yours as well, unless another firm takes over this office and us along with it.'

'Not much chance of that, I think. Mr Parrish offered it to Canards, you know, the big firm in Rambleton with the posh premises on Church Lane, but their Mr Bottomley just laughed. I was bringing in the coffee and I heard it all. Well, I heard it all once I'd finished scrubbing the carpet outside the door. I had to keep an eye on him, you know.' The pink tissue made a brief reappearance. 'I used to have to stick fifty quid on to his bills just so's he'd break even. He never realised. Anyway, Gary says that he wouldn't want me working for Mr Bottomley. Too pretty for his own good, he said. And he *is* dead handsome. Mr Bottomley, I mean. Gary's more, sort of, down to earth. More like a knitting pattern than a pin-up, if you know what I mean.'

'Well that's that then. I'll just get back to my husband and five children and tell them we won't be eating this month after all.'

'Aahh. Have you really got five children?' Polly tried not to look as though she was inspecting Ophelia's figure.

'Six, to all intents and purposes. You might as well include Malachi.' Ophelia picked up the telephone directory and began to search for Rambleton Police.

'Ooh, it is a shame. It's a pity we have to tell people that Mr Parrish is dead, isn't it? I wonder . . .'

'What?' Ophelia had her hand on the telephone but had been distracted by the discovery that some unfortunate Scorsdale inhabitant was actually named Pouface.

'Well, he's got no relations; no one would really be bothered, would they? He never went out very much anyway, and you could see his clients. I can tell you all about them. I've been doing most of the litigating myself anyway. Go on, Ophelia.'

'Just a minute, Polly. Are you suggesting that we shouldn't tell anyone Mr Parrish has died? You want me to take over the firm and pretend that he's still alive?'

Polly wasn't sure whether to forestall possible practical, moral or legal objections.

'It wouldn't be a lie, would it? I mean, no one's going to come up to us and ask "Has Mr Parrish died?" are they? And I need the money as well. I won't get another job around here and me and Gary want to get a house for when we're engaged. You're bound to be as good as Mr Parrish was, so the whatever – Solicitors' Complaining Burrow – won't really be able to say anything.'

'Well, it would be a sort of lie of omission.' As a former First Communion catechist Ophelia felt obliged to correct Polly's moral theology. 'But if you are sure that you want to take the risk . . . It is a crime, you know, concealing a death, probably theft of the firm's assets as well.'

'Assets!' scoffed Polly, looking around the miserable two rooms, and Ophelia was inclined to agree with her. 'I don't mind about any risk. I can cope with trouble, Ophelia. I stood right by our Gary when he got that bit of ham on the side and it turned out to have mad cow disease.' Under the pasted foundation Polly's face was suffused with an unearthly glow and there was a light in her black-lined eyes like that of Joan of Arc riding into battle. She opened her mouth again, and Ophelia, fearing more tales of Kim and the Bradford feminists, interrupted with authority.

'Well, if you're sure that's what you want to do. But Mr Parrish must have made a will.'

'Oh yes. Lots.'

'Lots?'

'Well, not at the same time. He'd always make sure that I tore up the last one before he signed the latest. "Terrible troubles I've seen with two existing wills," he'd say. "Inter-nicotine warfare isn't in it." But yes, having no family, he didn't know what to do with his money, so he'd change his mind every couple of months. Sometimes he'd leave it to a charity, then decide that they were run by a bunch of anchorites . . .'

'Anchorites? Hermits?' Ophelia had a sudden vision of Desert Fathers rattling collection tins at passing camels.

'No, those people that wear black and don't believe in government. My brother was one before he was a New Romantic.'

'Anarchists. Go on.'

'Or sometimes he'd leave it to someone he knew, couldn't really call any of them his friends, but he'd worry that the firm and everything might be a burden to them, so he'd change it again. I can't remember

8

what the last one was. Hang on, I'll have a look.'

Polly stood on her chair and took down an old cornflakes packet from a high shelf. Wills and deeds were jammed into the packet in no discernible order but she eventually found what she was looking for.

'Here it is. He only made this one in August. I remember now, the B wasn't working on my typewriter so I had to write them all in by hand. "I, Wilfred William Parrish, blah, blah, devise and bequeath all my property both real and personal . . ." How can you have property that isn't real? I've always wondered that. Shouldn't it say, "both real and imaginary"? " . . . after payment of my just debts, blah, blah, unto the Roman Catholic diocese of Scorsdale for the establishment of a fund, to be known as the Wilfred Parrish Fund, such fund to be used for the education of the young of the diocese as to the life and work of St Wilfred, ishop of Ripon and York . . ." "Bishop" I mean, I missed that one, ". . . and for the encouragement of the veneration of the said St Wilfred. And further, blah, blah . . ." That's about it.'

'Good grief. He must have been pretty desperate for a worthy legatee. Okay, you've convinced me. St Wilfred was a good enough chap by all accounts, if a bit hard on the poor old Celts at the Synod of Whitby, but I'm sure that his need for veneration isn't as great as our need for sustenance. We're bound to be found out sooner or later, you know. But I got this job lined up eighteen months ago, and there won't be another one. Do you know how many newly qualified solicitors there are this year?'

'Twenty-five, thirty?'

'More like three thousand. All looking for jobs, all desperate, all falling over themselves to work even for the ridiculous twelve thousand a year I was offered here. And most importantly, most of the other two thousand nine hundred and ninety-nine of them don't have children. So if it keeps us afloat for a month or two then that's something. Maybe my husband will have cracked the computer business by then.'

'So you'll do it?' Polly removed the telephone book from Ophelia's hand and put it firmly in a drawer.

'Just let me have a look at the will, okay?'

Polly passed the folded sheet to Ophelia, who read through it with a practised eye.

'Extension of trustees' powers, advancement, income, charging clause, yes this all seems pretty standard. Let's just check the attestation. He was quite sane when he made it, was he?'

'Well, to be honest it's a bit difficult to tell in this part of Yorkshire, isn't it? He wasn't any worse than usual, anyway. If you had to be absolutely twelve eggs to the dozen then Rambleton would need its own Chunkery Court, wouldn't it?'

'Chunkery? Oh, you mean Chancery Court. Yes, I suppose so. How do you know about the Chancery Division, anyway? It's a bit esoteric for Parrishes, isn't it? Or are you a Galsworthy fan?'

'Oh no, Sheffield Wednesday. Gary's mum says he was perceived on a coach trip to Sheffield. Must've had the back seat, I suppose. No, the thing is, I used to work for old Mr Snodsworth at Snodsworth and Ranger before I came here. You know, their office is just on the other side of the Square. He never did anything else but this chancing stuff. Do you know, he'd been working on one case for thirty-odd years before I came and it still hadn't got to court when I left?'

'Uh-huh. Hang on a minute, what's this?' Ophelia squinted at a pencilled scrawl underneath the signature. ' "Trashers go insane that's why insurrections negating the dispersal of my baby dave seem covered over." Who are the Trashers? And who is his baby Dave? Didn't you tell me that he didn't have any children?'

'Mr Parrish's love child . . .' mused Polly. 'I can't really see it. He wasn't exactly what you'd call a ladies' man. There was one that was after him, Mrs Moore she was called, but she was ancient, nearly sixty. I don't think she could be baby Dave's mother. Anyway, he used to lock himself in the J. A. Stansmore whenever she came into the office.'

'Lock himself in the what?' began Ophelia, but Polly was reaching for the will.

'Chuck us it here, would you, and I'll make sure. He used to say that no one else could read his writing but me.' Polly leaned the will against her empty coffee cup and rocked her head from side to side, muttering under her breath. 'Right. I think I've got it. "Trustees to ensure that my instructions regarding the disposal of my body have been carried out." '

The women looked apprehensively back at Mr Parrish's room. Their fantasies of Little Orphan Dave had simultaneously melted, to be replaced by the solid reality of the dead solicitor.

'It makes sense, I suppose,' said Ophelia flatly. 'But what *were* his instructions?'

'I don't think they're in the will, are they?' Polly turned it over idly, running a manicured finger up and down the principle clauses.

'No, I've read through it all. Anyway, he'll have known that it's best practice to put those sort of instructions in a separate document.'

'Is it? Why's that then?'

'Well, in case the family don't have the will read until after the funeral. It's a bit unfortunate if they come back from the crematorium to sit round the dining-room table and hear the old solicitor's clerk read out, "It is my wish that I be buried." Rather puts a dampener on the baked meats, if you know what I mean.'

Polly did not.

'So this note will just be by way of a safeguard, I suppose, to make sure that the document about his body has been found and followed. Which in this case it hasn't. You wouldn't know anything about it, Polly?'

'Oh, no. I've never typed anything like that for him. I'm sure I would've remembered. It would have been so horrible, thinking about him being buried or chromated or whatever.' The pink tissue had been lodged in her sleeve and had crumbled to a few dusty fragments. Polly surveyed them stolidly and wiped her nose on her sleeve instead. 'And I've never come across it, either. Mind you, that's not saying that it isn't here.'

Ophelia followed Polly's glance across the dusty shelves laden with boxes, packets, even jars, of every description, each one bursting with pieces of faded paper.

'Mr Parrish thought that filing cabinets and that were a waste of money. He used to get me to bring in all my empty packets, you know, washing powder and all, and he'd get the big boxes down Presto's. Mildred used to know where everything was, but even she gave up in the end and I just bunged them in wherever there was a bit of space. It could be anywhere here.'

'Well, if we're going to carry on with this plan of yours then we'll just have to find it. If Mr Parrish went to the trouble of writing down what he wanted doing with his body then the least we can do is carry it out. We owe him that much, poor old chap, for pinching his practice and concealing his corpse. Otherwise we'll just have to phone the police and give the whole thing up now. Okay?'

'We'll find it, Ophelia, honest we will. Come on.' Polly climbed on an unsteady chair and took down the first receptacle, a rusty flour bin.

'First things first,' said Ophelia. 'We'll start looking tomorrow. Now we have to find somewhere to put him for the night.'

They both walked timorously over to the inner office door. Ophelia opened it with a last desperate prayer that Mr Parrish's condition might prove to have been a temporary coma and that he would by now have reached the classified ads at the back of the *Gazette*. It was not to be.

The corpse lay across the green leather, exactly as they had left it. Above the desk a steel clock was ticking relentlessly. Ophelia looked around the room and noticed another shabby door set into the far wall.

'Right,' she gulped. 'Let's get him into this cupboard.'

Chapter Three

Let me be no assistant for a state,
But keep a farm and carters.

(II.ii. 166 – 7)

It was nearly half-past four when Ophelia turned into the muddy track leading home. As she had envisaged, the other door in Mr Parrish's room had led into a commodious, if airless stationery cupboard. The small room now held, in addition to boxes of out-of-date headed paper and shorthand pads, the mortal remains of Wilfred Parrish. Ophelia, having read many detective novels in which the heroine is surprised at the weight of a corpse, had not been surprised at the weight of the corpse, although the manoeuvre, at least upon her part, had involved considerable exertion and nausea. Polly, probably inured to such horrors by her connections in the butchers' trade, had been matter-of-fact about the disposal of the body, recoursing only occasionally to her sleeve, and very kindly offered to take the arms, allowing Ophelia to concentrate upon the late Mr Parrish's respectable black brogues.

It was Polly, also, who anticipated the next problem.

'We can't leave him there long, mind you. He'll start decomposing soon.'

Ophelia had thought that she detected a note of lugubrious satisfaction in Polly's voice.

'Yes, I suppose so. Do you know how long we've got?'

'Not really. I could ask Gary if you like.'

'No, you mustn't do that. You mustn't tell anyone.'

'I wasn't going to tell him about Mr Parrish. I just thought I'd say: "Gary . . ." ' tones of winsome curiosity, ' "Gary, suppose I had a twelve-stone sheep that I'd killed and I wanted to keep it in the kitchen . . ." '

'No,' Ophelia had said hastily. 'No, I don't think you need to ask Gary. We'll be moving it anyway once we find his instructions. At least it's not summer.'

'Wouldn't make much difference if it was. Not in Rambleton. Same bloody weather all year round we get. Till it gets to January, of course. Then it's really cold.'

Sustained by this cheering thought Ophelia had left the stationery cupboard for the slightly less distasteful task of investigating Mr Parrish's files. They revealed almost exactly what Ophelia had expected: domestic and agricultural conveyancing, straightforward probate, petty litigation, mainly funded by the ever-trusting Legal Aid Board, and local agency work for the Mid-Yorkshire Champion Building Society, the latter being the only area of work actually to make a profit for the firm.

She had dictated a tape full of procrastinating letters and listened to Polly putting off any potential clients who called at the office. Mr Parrish had evidently felt much as she did about Mondays for there were no appointments in his diary for that day.

At four o'clock, with the presence in the stationery cupboard weighing increasingly upon her consciousness, she had taken the papers for the agency appointment next morning and set off for home.

Malachi, Ophelia, the children and the dogs had moved into Moorwind Farm three weeks before. Ophelia's heart fell as she drove over the rusty cattle grid and past the remains of a pre-war tractor heaped on the stark and muddy yard. An optimistic sign, red felt-tip pen on cardboard, was tied to the gatepost: *Wet Nose Solutions.*

To call the place a farm was, in Ophelia's opinion, almost certainly a breach of the new Property Misdescriptions Act, for there were neither fields nor farmhouse, only a collection of badly built barns and outbuildings surrounding a concrete bungalow of quite unbelievable nastiness. Moorwind had been on the market for at least four years, ever since the previous owner, a scrap iron merchant, had died, apparently while trying to move the tractor.

Malachi and Ophelia had sat every evening for the past three weeks, after the children had gone to bed, facing each other across the two bars of the electric fire, and had told each other that the house would be transformed as soon as they stamped their own character upon it. But they both felt in their hearts that the influence of the late Jas. Spikewort, Quality Metal Dealer, or it may have been the malevolent spirit of Moorwind Farm itself, would perpetually engulf even the ebullience of the O. family. In any case, they had had little choice but to buy it, for Rambleton and its environs offered no other property with room for a family of seven, a constantly breeding Labrador bitch and the collection of unsuccessful activities which went to make up Wet Nose Solutions.

Ophelia parked the old Volvo in front of the bungalow and went in.

'Hello! Malachi? Pius? Joan?'

A faint bleeping from behind a door was the only reply.

Ophelia opened the door to see a bank of four computer screens and the back of a child's head in front of each one. Malachi, a small, plump man, was kneeling on the floor running a hand distractedly through his fluffy pale blond hair while with the other he was trying to hold a toddler down for long enough to change its nappy. While he did this he called out instructions to the other children.

'Hygenus, use the other joystick, that one's a bit dodgy. You need the password, Joan. Didn't you find it at the end of the second level? Innocent, will you stop wriggling!'

'Pius, help Urban, will you? He's been eaten by that monster five times already.'

Pius, the eldest, a serious, freckled child of eight, solemnly saved his adventure game and moved to help his brother. At four, Urban was an exact miniature of his father, with the same round pinkish face and air of perpetual worry.

'Hi, Mum,' said Pius as he passed her.

'Hello, Pius. Hello all of you. Have I had a good first day at my new job? Funny you should ask. Actually my boss had died so we put him in the cupboard which made it difficult to reach the D5 envelopes but apart from that it was fine. Nice to know you're all so interested.'

There was a pause while they all failed to take in a single word. It was broken by Malachi.

'Haven't we got any of those Nappy Sack things? I keep having to use plastic bags out of the freezer so now everything's a bit muddled in there.'

'Yes it is,' said five-year-old Hygenus in tones of martyrdom. 'Everyone else had sausage rolls in their lunch boxes but mine was two potato crockitts stuck together.'

Ophelia passed her husband a Nappy Sack from the box on the shelf next to him.

'Oh, were they there?' he said in astonishment. 'You are brilliant. Isn't she brilliant, children?'

'Fairly brilliant,' said Pius judiciously. The others were still engrossed in their games.

'Has anyone taken the dogs out yet?' Ophelia asked. Again there was no reply, neither from the children nor from Malachi who had taken advantage of Pius' absence to take over his character on the furthest monitor.

Ophelia picked up Innocent, who now had a precarious-looking nappy

15

protruding from the unbuttoned side of his dungarees, and called into the darkness of the rest of the bungalow.

'Meg! Gigi!'

'Those aren't their names, Mummy,' seven-year-old Joan said pityingly. 'They won't answer unless you say their proper names.'

Meg had been acquired by the family three years earlier, when her fecundity had become too much for the elderly couple who had owned her. Her name had immediately been lengthened to Megabyte by the newly computer-literate children. She had given birth to her most recent litter two months before the move to Moorwind and Ophelia and Malachi had decided to keep the smallest bitch puppy who was named, somewhat inevitably, Gigabyte.

'Bite, bite!' shouted Innocent.

Meg was found sitting dolefully in the freezing cold kitchen, but there was no sign of the puppy. Malachi, when roused from his computer game, recollected that he had not seen her since the morning. As she could have been in any one of the eleven assorted sheds making a joyous meal of rats and sawdust, Ophelia thought no more about it and took Megabyte for her walk alone.

Later that evening, when the children had been fed and despatched to their several cold and spider-infested bedrooms, Ophelia and Malachi sat nursing cups of strong coffee in front of the inadequate fire. The television in the corner was playing Malachi's video of the last Five Nations championship.

'Come on, Rory, my son! Don't look behind; the buggers'll never catch you. Yes!!'

Ophelia leafed through the papers for tomorrow's hearing. It was a simple enough repossession. The usual hand-written defence pleaded the usual unemployment and lack of communication by the building society and concluded with the usual plea for a return of British justice to the courts. Ophelia tried not to read this too closely and concentrated upon the sporadic payment record.

Malachi had paused the video and was gazing wistfully at Rory Underwood's fuzzy figure as the ball was placed triumphantly over the line. A tear dripped into his coffee and he clutched the mug tighter against his chest.

'I should've been there, Oaf. If I'd kept my place in the Blues squad then I'd still be playing for England now. Look at Rob Andrew. He's got years in him yet. I should've been there.' He rubbed his eyes with the back of his hand, like a child, and smiled dolefully at her.

16

'I know you should, my love. If it wasn't for your back . . .'

'If it wasn't for my back, which would have been fine if it wasn't for rowing in that bloody college boat, which I never would've done if I hadn't gatecrashed the Boat Club dinner which I wouldn't have done if you'd gone to the pub with me, which you would've done if your bloody mother hadn't turned up at the Garden House Hotel . . .'

It was a familiar litany, repeated every few weeks of their married life, but tonight it held less pique than usual, repeated by rote, as though he were really thinking of something else. Ophelia reached for the remote control and switched off the video. Then she walked round to the back of his chair and put her arms around his neck. The warm wool of his shoulder smelled pleasantly of baby lotion and sawdust. Ophelia plucked a couple of grey hairs from his thinning pink scalp.

'How's business then?' she asked brightly, anxious not to be tempted by silence into disturbing him with the events of her day.

'Actually quite good.' He leaned back to look up at her and she could see that his upside-down face had lighted up like a little boy longing to be asked about a cherished secret. 'I sold five of those funny 386s to an engineering company in Leafskirk, Lancashire. I've stuck the Wet Nose logo on them, you know, the Labrador's head, boxed them off and the courier's coming in the morning.'

'That's marvellous, Mal. Only four hundred and ninety-five to go now.'

'Yes, but they were so cheap, sweetheart, I'm bound to get rid of them. And the real beauty of the thing is, with the re-badging, everyone who buys one will have the little labrador waiting to lick their faces every morning when they get to work. That way they're sure to get interested in the more exciting stuff I've got in the pipeline. It's the same principle as subliminal advertising, you see. I've got this book about it. Of course, ideally the message needs to be reinforced by the subject's total environment. Wet Noses everywhere; at home, in the car, on holiday, whatever. I'm thinking of giving away free Wet Nose tea-towels for the culinary environment, then steering wheel covers . . .'

'Steering wheel covers?'

'Well, maybe not. Do you think that dangling Labradors in the rear window . . . ? No, you don't. But have a think about it, will you, Oaf? I need something stimulating within the motoring environment.'

'Mal, what *is* this book?'

'Haven't you seen it? I got it from Dan, you remember, from college.'

'What? Dan, Dan, the fast-buck man, the one who rented his room out to American tourists and slept in the shopping centre with the tramps?' As she spoke, Ophelia disentangled herself and inspected the remains of Sunday's Burgundy. 'Want some?'

'No, you finish it, love. Yes, that Dan. Didn't you go out with him in your first term?'

'In my first *week,* Mal. And I'd hardly call it going out. He just got me to sit on King's Parade with a bucket and a sign saying: "Impoverished working-class scholar. No grant. Please give generously." My mother came down unexpectedly two days later and quickly put a stop to the bucket and to Dan.'

'But you didn't have a grant and you *were* impoverished.'

'I know, but only because Daddy spent my maintenance money on a new set of golf clubs. No, Mummy didn't mind the begging. It was the description as working-class which really enraged her. So what's Dan got to do with this wet nose business?'

'Oh, he's made a fortune selling the book. Network marketing, or something, he calls it. Anyway, you should read it; it must be applicable to solicitors, too. I don't know how you'd illustrate Parrishes within the total experiential environment, though. Maybe you could have little priests with a boundary round them. Why don't you go and get a copy of the book? There are seventy-nine left in the small henhouse.'

'Mal, are you selling this book then?'

'To tell you the truth, I'm not quite sure.' Malachi rubbed his eyes again. He drew his knees up to his chest and wrapped his arms around them, turning himself into a large furry ball. 'I got a bit confused when Dan got to that bit. I know that I got a significant reduction by taking eighty rather than only forty copies. Perhaps I should give away a copy of the book with every ten computers I sell. Except that I don't want my customers thinking too much about their total experiential environments or they might catch on. What do you think, Oaf?'

Ophelia yawned and drained her glass.

'I think I'm going to bed.'

Chapter Four

... newly come to court ...

(v.ii. 106)

Rambleton County Court met every other Tuesday morning in a shabby room above the hairdresser's on Kirkgate. For the rest of the fortnight the room was the Old People's Drop-In Centre, and the most solemn judicial processes were liable to be interrupted by an old lady, truculent or wistful, in search of the rich tea biscuits. Ophelia had attended the court once six months earlier, a 150-mile round trip from the city firm where she had served her articles. On that occasion a personable young district judge, obviously on his way to higher things, had dealt with her application quickly and with brisk efficiency. The other solicitors and clerks in the waiting room, fortified with Russian novels and flasks of coffee, had marvelled at her good fortune in visiting Rambleton on the only known occasion when its usual incumbent, Deputy District Judge Ranger, was off sick, reputedly due to a riding accident.

Mr L. Ranger, of Snodsworth and Ranger, Rambleton's third firm of solicitors, had been appointed as a Deputy District Judge, or Recorder, as they were then known, around ten years before. It was generally considered that the judicial luminaries who make such appointments must have overindulged at their clubs the night before making such an extraordinary choice. They had at least not compounded their folly by promoting him, despite his increasingly broad hints, to a full-time District Judgeship. Normally, of course, a Deputy District Judge in such an area might be expected to travel between several of the smaller county courts. Normally, moreover, Rambleton's own court would have been closed years ago and its business transferred to one of the gleaming new Combined Court Centres, so easily confused with branches of Sainsbury's. The retention of Rambleton's county court and the limiting of Mr Ranger's activities to its sittings were inextricably linked. When Deputy District Judge Ranger went (and despite new compulsory judicial retirement ages he vowed that he would 'die in the saddle') then Rambleton court would go too, to the dismay of those who enjoyed reading *War and Peace* on a draughty bench and to the delight of those

19

who were more concerned with their mileage allowances.

The Mid-Yorkshire's application was due at 10.30 a.m., block-listed, Ophelia saw on arrival, with two other possession applications. A dapper middle-aged man met her at the door. Like the employees of the larger courts he wore a Lord Chancellor's Department name-tag, but in his case the space left for the name was completely blank. He greeted her in tones of conspiratorial cosiness.

'Well, well, a new face! That's a change around here. For the Mid-Yorkshire? Are you sure? That's always been Parrishes' business. Oh, I *see*! Mr Parrish well I hope? And the young lady, Polly, is it? Very much liked by us all are our Mr Parrish and young Polly.'

Ophelia explained that she had taken over the litigation work at Parrishes and that Mr Parrish was as well as she'd ever seen him.

Mr Blank, who apparently acted as court clerk, usher, typist and Mr Ranger's tea boy, told Ophelia that her application would be heard second and directed her to a pile of *People's Friend* magazines. Ophelia had in fact, as usual, secreted a novel in her briefcase but for once was too preoccupied to read. She had called into the office before going on to the court that morning and had found Polly in a state of panic.

'Ophelia, I've just remembered. A man's coming to fix the photocopier this afternoon at half-past two.'

Ophelia looked around. 'Have we got a photocopier? I can't see one anywhere.'

'It's in . . .' Polly lowered her voice ' . . . *that cupboard*. It hasn't worked for six months so there are all papers and stuff on top of it, but it's right next to, you know, *Mr Parrish*. The man'll have to step right over him. Do you think we can pretend he's a roll of carpet or something?'

'I shouldn't think so. What time is the photocopier man coming?'

Eventually Ophelia managed to leave, having promised to find a solution by half-past two.

To Ophelia's surprise she was the only person in the court's waiting room.

'Looks like I'll be in straightaway after all then,' she said lightly to Mr Blank.

'Oh no.' He sounded deeply shocked. 'Does things properly, does our Mr Ranger.'

Ophelia was puzzled but sat down and pretended to memorize a knitting pattern.

When Mr Blank had retreated to his inner sanctum she abandoned the pretence and gazed out of the window. She could just see the Market

Square at the other end of Kirkgate, the blue and white polar bears of Freezaland somehow even more garish at a distance. She thought of her own freezer in its confusion, plundered for nappy disposal, and wished that she was at home. Imagining herself contentedly defrosting, cleaning and sorting beefburgers from ice-cream, she drifted into a reverie of good housekeeping. Unfortunately, the memory of Mr Parrish's cold, blue hand persisted in creeping in beside the frozen sausages . . .

She started as someone else came into the room. It was a tall and heavily built man, perhaps five years older than she. He was rather handsome in an unpleasant way, supercilious and saturnine, with heavy dark stubble already showing beneath jowls that had obviously been expensively shaved that morning. In a larger court Ophelia would have ignored him, but in Rambleton it would probably be wise to cultivate the acquaintance of anyone whose jacket matched his trousers. She glanced at the clock before she spoke and was surprised to find that it was already five past eleven.

'What time are you on?'

'Half ten.' He not only looked like Heathcliff but apparently shared his conversational generosity.

'Oh, but it's already—'

'You're new I see. There's plenty of time. He's not dealt with his first half ten yet.'

'No, it's funny. I was here when the court opened and I didn't see anyone else waiting for that appointment. Is there another door or something?'

'No, there's no one else there. Ranger argues it out himself if neither party turns up. Listen.'

Ophelia did so and realised that for some time she had been hearing a single voice rise and fall as though in impassioned debate, occasionally reaching a crescendo then dropping to an almost inaudible murmur of reasonableness. No words could be heard except for a single shout of what sounded like 'Giddyup!'

It could not really have been 'Giddyup', of course, but some Latin tag indicating that the argument was over, for Mr Blank then appeared at the door and called Ophelia through.

'Mrs O. for the plaintiff. No attendance by the defendant.'

Deputy District Judge Ranger rose as Ophelia entered the room. He was enormously tall, approaching seven feet, and very thin with the furrowed creosote brown skin of the elderly horseman.

'Howdy, Mrs O.'

'Good morning, sir.'

'Take a seat, ma'am. This is a sorry business.' His accent, middle-class Yorkshire overlaid with Texan, disorientated Ophelia.

'I'm sorry, sir, I don't quite . . . Have I done something wrong?'

'Young lady, that is a matter between you and your Gaad. I was referring to this sad business of young Billy Cox.'

'Billy? Oh, I see, yes, Cox, the defendant. Right. I have here an affidavit from the building society with the charge certificate, MHA search and office copies. I am instructed to ask for possession within twenty-eight days.'

Ophelia passed the documents to Mr Ranger but he left them lying on the table.

'And is young Billy not to have the opportunity to defend himself? Is his home to be taken from him, from his poor wife, his little children, with the dead words of your affidavit? Have you no compassion in your heart, Mrs O.?'

'With respect, sir, I believe that your file will show that Mr Cox had ample notice of this application and of the hearing today.'

'That may be so. But have you considered that he may be ill, he may be lying in bed at this moment, unable to reach the telephone? Indeed, he may well not have a telephone. The lives of the poor folk even in this town can be mighty hard, Mrs O.'

'Again, with respect, sir, if that is the case then Mr Cox will be able to apply for a stay of execution. The evidence before you is quite clear. Mr Cox has paid nothing at all for five months, was already considerably in arrears before that, and there is nothing to suggest that he will be in a position to commence payments in the foreseeable future.'

Ophelia was beginning to cheer up. There was nothing like taking a firm line with a District Judge to brighten a dull day. What was more, while she rattled off the familiar patter, an idea was beginning to form in her head as to how to solve the problem of Mr Parrish.

The unwritten rules of this scenario were that Mr Ranger would make an order for possession suspended on payment of the mortgage instalments. Ophelia would object, citing the rules that required a likelihood that all arrears could be paid off within a year. Mr Ranger would ignore her objections, Mr Cox would not pay a single penny and she would be back in court in another two months, at which time Mr Ranger would make the order which she had originally requested. Mr Ranger would have salved his conscience, Ophelia would get two lots of agency fees, the building society would claim more costs out of the sale of the house and Mr Cox would have an extra two months before being evicted. Unfortunately Mr Ranger did not play by the rules. He stood up suddenly so that Ophelia had to struggle to her feet as well, trying to disguise the fact that one of her shoes had fallen off under the table.

'I will not stand by and see the blood-sucking leeches of the Mid-Yorkshire Champion Building Society deprive a man of hearth and home. We hold these truths to be self-evident, that a man is entitled to the pursuit of life, liberty and happiness. Billy Cox is one such man and he is not alone. I stand here, I can do no other.'

It was like one of those Radio Four quizzes, thought Ophelia, where the panellists had to disentangle quotations.

'The application is dismissed. Costs in favour of the defendant. Giddyup!'

'I shall advise my principals to appeal.' Ophelia retorted, but she was already being shepherded out of the room by the impassive Mr Blank. As she went out she caught sight of a battered brown object hanging on the back of the door. She had no doubt but that it was a genuine Stetson.

Chapter Five

For every man hath business and desire,

(I.v. 136)

'I've got an idea!' called Ophelia to Polly as she rushed straight into the far room.

'Great. Do you want . . . ?'

'Yes. Extra strong, please.'

She rummaged through the pile of incoming post from the day before which she had put aside as being not immediately urgent. The letter was not difficult to find, with electric blue polar bears frollicking about the heading.

Freezaland
7–11 Market Square
Rambleton

Dear Mr Parrish,

Thank you for your recent letter enclosing another copy of your bill.

Please be assured that I have not overlooked your account and that I am most grateful for your help in the matters referred to.

Unfortunately I am really in no position to satisfy the account at present owing to an extremely poor year's trading. However, I am optimistic about the outcome of our move into the green chest freezer market and have prioritised your account for settlement as soon as possible.

Meanwhile I urge you not to take the action threatened in your last letter. As you must realise, this would almost certainly result in the closure of the business and in losses for all our creditors, including yourself.

If you would like to discuss this further then please ring me or have a word at the next <u>meeting</u>.

Yours faithfully,

Stewart Saggers (Managing Director)

Ophelia could recognise a desperate man, one prepared to use any possible weapon. She wondered whether the underlined 'meeting' was a threat or merely an appeal to Masonic solidarity. On second thoughts, Mr Parrish's will had suggested that he was a Catholic, so it was probably just the Rotary Club.

Polly brought in the coffee.

'Thanks. Polly, could you get Mr Saggers of Freezaland on the phone for me, please?'

'Yeah, course. You do know that it's nearly half-past twelve and that the man's coming—'

'Off you go, Polly.'

'Good morning, afternoon. How may I help you?' The voice was bluff but nervous.

'Good afternoon, Mr Saggers. My name is Ophelia O. and I am the new assistant solicitor at Parrishes. Mr Parrish has asked me to deal with all costs collection matters. I've noticed that your outstanding bill is well over five thousand pounds and I think it might be useful if we were to have a discussion.'

'Well, I do normally deal with Mr Parrish himself.' Ophelia could sense the 'little woman' card about to be played.

'I appreciate that, Mr Saggers, but Mr Parrish wishes me to deal with this matter. Perhaps you would be kind enough to call round at the office? I have a suggestion to make that may resolve the problem but it is essential that we speak in person. Immediately.'

After a little more bluster Mr Saggers agreed and Ophelia went through to brief Polly.

Five minutes later, when he arrived, the girls were presenting a united front. Polly escorted him into Mr Parrish's room where Ophelia sat behind the imposing desk. She hoped that the interview would not take too long, as her bottom was already aching on top of the four box files balanced on the seat of the large oak chair.

'Mr Parrish is away at a conference today. He is allowing me to use his room while I wait for mine to be decorated.'

'There isn't another room in here,' objected Mr Saggers. 'My dad was outdoor clerk to Mr Stanmore so I should know. Not unless you include this cupboard, of course. I suppose you might make a little office out of it. Paint it white, put some plants and pictures up; I know you ladies are good at that sort of thing.'

Ophelia watched, horrified as he moved towards the door of the stationery cupboard. She could not speak, could not move, could not breathe. A strange little strangled squeak came out of her mouth, then nothing.

Polly saved the moment.

'Oh no, Mr Saggers. Mrs O.'s office is going to be out here, where I work. Open-plank, it's called. So when clients come in, they can see her working straightaway and they'll know they can trust her. Mr Parrish took a lot of persuading, mind. I don't think he'd want clients looking at *him* as soon as they walked through the door.'

Which, considering Mr Parrish's current condition, was almost certainly true.

Mr Saggers was looking dubious and his hand was still on the doorknob. Ophelia broke out of her torpor. As she stood up the box files clattered to the floor, startling him into loosening his grip.

'Actually, I would appreciate your opinion as a successful marketing man. Do you think that a screen across here would maximise beneficial client interface?'

Mr Saggers allowed himself to be seduced away from the cupboard and was soon pontificating happily upon what Ophelia, in a moment of inspiration, christened 'office topology'. Eventually she managed to steer him back into Mr Parrish's room and to the subject of his overdue account.

'Tell me about the green fest cheeser market,' she suggested.

'Well, the fest cheeser, chest freezer market boomed, of course, in the 1970s when the freezer craze really hit the UK and people started buying bulk ice-cream from cash-and-carries. Plus the *Good Life* phenomenon, when everyone wanted to be self-sufficient and we made them think that if they grew and froze enough runner beans they'd end up looking like Felicity Kendal. The women that is, the men just wanted their wives to look like Felicity Kendal.'

'And did the men want to look like Richard Briers?' asked Ophelia, fascinated despite herself.

'I've really no idea. I think it's unlikely, don't you?'

'I bet the wives wanted their husbands to be like him,' interjected Polly. 'I think he's dead cuddly.'

'Anyway,' continued Mr Saggers, whose ideas of executive differentials did not allow him to discuss marketing strategy with secretaries, 'we sold a hell of a lot of these bloody great caverns, then suddenly it was all over.'

'Oh, why was that?' asked Ophelia obediently.

'The eighties. Executive stress, red braces, *nouvelle cuisine*. No one wanted to admit to having time to cook, gardening was all hostas and Chinese pots, and what yuppie wanted to go into the garage to get the pudding?'

'I see your point. So the eighties were a bad time for the freezer business?'

'Oh no, not as such. You see, the yuppies might not have bought chest freezers but they bought expensive fridge-freezers and wine-coolers and dinky little table-top fridges for the office.'

'*Were* there many yuppies in Rambleton?'

'We had our moments. Anyway, we're talking national trends. No, the problem was that the oldies, the ones who'd bought their chest freezers in the seventies, weren't replacing. And you know why that was?'

'I'm sure that you'll tell me.'

'There's nothing wrong with the bloody things! They never wear out! I don't know what the manufacturers were thinking of, defying all the laws of built-in obsolescence. I can only assume, trying to be charitable, that there was some essential component which they hoped would break down and it never did. The blasted machines just go on for ever, stuck in the garage full of raspberries. And the owners, Goblins, we call them—'

'Goblins?'

'Getting On, Buy Late Or Never.'

'That's "Goblon".'

'Is it? Well, don't blame me, I don't make these things up. Got that one out of *Refrigeration Monthly*. Anyway, where was I? Oh yes, these Goblins, Goblons if you prefer, won't buy a new freezer for the hell of it, or because it looks good, or because it's endorsed by some actress or footballer. They won't even replace it with a space-saving model because there's still plenty of room in the garage for the Maestro. That left us in the industry pretty stuck, I can tell you. But now the Scandinavians have come up with these environmentally sound jobs, low energy, no CFCs, recyclable, the works. Now that's just the thing to appeal to your Goblin, with her left-over social conscience and rapidly diminishing pension on the horizon. Mind you, I don't really know what the Scandinavians want freezers for anyway with their climate. Would have thought they could just stick the turkey drumsticks in a nearby fjord, eh?'

He was growing relaxed and Ophelia decided to let him ramble on a little longer, ignoring Polly's frantic gestures towards the clock.

'And have they remembered the built-in obsolescence this time?'

Mr Saggers failed to notice the irony.

'Well, we hope so, but they're being made mainly by the Krauts, and you know what they're like. Even their electric can-openers are lasting more than six months now, so God knows what they've done to the freezers. Probably be putting frozen lamb and goat in them at the Last Judgement. But we'll cross that bridge when we come to it.'

Ophelia was momentarily taken aback by Mr Saggers' flight of apocalyptic fantasy but she recovered quickly.

'And do you have these freezers in stock at the moment?'

'Oh yes, took delivery of three bloody monsters this morning. Cost a grand each, but you could stick two cows in them and still have room for the ice-pops.'

'Mr Saggers, I have a proposition to put to you.'

'Oh aye?' said Mr Saggers, who had almost forgotten why he was there in the first place.

'Parrishes would be prepared to take one of these large chest freezers for the office in part-payment of our invoice. The balance of the monies would be deferred for, shall we say, eighteen months from today's date?'

'Well, that's a very welcome proposal, Mrs O., but are you sure that a big freezer is really what you need in here? I could do you a nice little compact, big enough for your milk and any odds and ends of shopping you girls might do at lunch time.'

'Thank you, but the situation is a little more *complex* than that. I don't know whether you know Polly's fiancé, Gary?'

'Gary? Oh, is that the lad at the butchers?'

'Yes, that's right. Gary and Polly want to get married, you see, but they can't possibly afford a house on her wages here and the pittance Mr Whitworth pays Gary. The only way they can do it is if Gary does a bit of, um, private enterprise. I'm sure a successful entrepreneur like yourself can appreciate the situation.'

'Ah,' nodded Mr Saggers, a smile of sly complicity passing over his large face. 'Always ready to help a small businessman on the way up. Sort of undercover Chamber of Commerce.'

'I'm glad that we understand one another, Mr Saggers. Now the only thing is, Mr Parrish is due back at two o'clock and we don't know when he'll be away from the office again. Now, as I explained, he's left costs collection entirely in my hands, but I don't like to worry him, if you see what I mean. So could you possibly have it delivered immediately?'

'Can do, Mrs O.,' he promised with a jaunty wink.

29

'Thank you. And another thing. Are these freezers lockable?'

Ophelia grinned at Polly as the door swung behind Mr Saggers' corpulent backside.

'There we are then, we'll get Mr Parrish safely frozen. The mortuary couldn't do it better and it should give us a few days to find this blasted bit of paper. Polly? What's the matter? I'm sorry I had to use Gary's name but I couldn't think of anything else. He doesn't actually have to be involved, you know.'

'No, it's not that.' Polly shifted from foot to foot. 'You know that case you had this morning? Was it for the Mid-Yorkshire?'

'Yes, you know it was. Parrishes don't do any other court work. Why?'

'Well . . . I ought to show you this. I'd hidden it, I felt so awful. But now I feel worse for hiding it.'

Polly handed over a letter with the white rose and trophy heading of the building society. It stated, in terms of no ambiguity, that the society's legal department were reconsidering Parrishes' agency status owing to the 'cursory and haphazard' way in which their applications were being managed.

'You've been doing these yourself, have you?'

'Oh yes. Mr Parrish said that he'd forgotten where the court was, and certainly wasn't going to stand up like a ninny in front of some jumped-up registrar at his age. I did my best, Ophelia, honest I did. But the building society are so horrid and the poor defectives . . .'

'Defendants?'

'Yes, them . . . are so nice. You know last time I had to do one of those awful examinations.'

'Oral examinations?'

'Isn't that dentists? I mean when you have to ask the person questions about their money and the court clerk writes it down.'

'Oral examinations, yes. Nothing to do with dentists. What happened then?'

'I had to awfully examine this man who'd been overdrawn by sixty pounds. Well, he turned up, and he was a really sweet old thing and ever so worried about it all. So, I asked him all the questions on the list, did he have any investments, how many holidays he had, had he won money on the horses and all that. And to every question he just smiled sadly and shook his head. I was so embarrassed, I had my head stuck behind my papers all the time. It didn't help that he had lots of holes in his jumper and trousers, in the most peculiar places. So, it wasn't until

30

it was all over and he'd signed the clerk's report and was going out that I realised.'

'Realised what?'

'The poor old sod only had one leg. The other was a sort of metal thing, like you tie a clothes line to. And then the bloody building society write and say that I haven't been sufficiently rigorous. What do they want to do, send the bailiffs to seize his crutches?'

'I wouldn't be surprised. Well, today's hearing won't have helped. I'll have to try harder next time. I know they're bastards, Polly, but we can't possibly do without the agency work.'

'I know. I just wish there was something we could do to get back at them.'

'Well, let me know if you think of anything, will you? So long as it doesn't involve a balaclava and a sawn-off shotgun. I'm allergic to wool over my face.'

Chapter Six

By heaven, it is as proper to our age
To cast beyond ourselves in our opinions
As it is common for the younger sort
To lack discretion.

(ii.i. 114–17)

Meanwhile Deputy District Judge Ranger had completed his morning of court appointments, and was trotting jauntily down Kirkgate towards the Market Square. With his Stetson set well back from his face and his briefcase flapping against his leg like a loosened saddlebag, he arched his neck to feel the crisp autumn breeze against his leathery cheeks.

'Steady, girl,' he whispered as his imaginary mare whinnied and pawed the pavement. 'Soon be back at the corral.'

At the corner of the Square he pulled hard on the reins – she was a young filly and sometimes headstrong, especially close to home – and guided her to a halt outside a dusty grey shopfront. The old-fashioned bay window was decorated with draped silk, faded to blotting-paper blue, and a small card in the centre proclaimed:

W. R. G. SNODSWORTH, MA
L. N. RANGER
SOLICITORS & COMMISSIONERS FOR OATHS

Mr Ranger dismounted, lifting a long leg high over the horse's back and jumping down from the saddle with a light bounce which startled a little girl walking past, and enraged her Yorkshire terrier. The stunted creature, more emaciated guinea pig than dog, began to snap at Mr Ranger's ankles and tore a small hole in his white cotton baseball socks.

'Gee, is there somebody darn there?' exclaimed the Deputy District Judge, feeling the sharp canines piercing the flesh of his lower calf. He squinted down from his great height and was in time to see a dim brownish shape reluctantly extricate its jaws and follow the little girl's tugging lead.

Dripping blood and trailing white cotton, Mr Ranger still remembered to offer the mare a lump of well-deserved sugar before limping into his office.

The door, as he pushed it open, was offering some considerable resistance, and it took all his strength to force it back against the inner wall. There was a sliding noise, the grating of metal, a squawk and then the recriminations of a red-faced mother who had rescued her baby from its pushchair just in time. Hers was not the only protest, for the small waiting room was crammed with seven or eight people, all of whom seemed to cry out at once to the bewildered Mr Ranger.

'You could have killed him! Who do you think you are, striding in here, squashing innocent babies? Dere we are, sweetie. Did the nasty man try to squidge you, den?'

'About time too! I've been waiting since half-past ten for you, you know!'

'Oh Mr Ranger, please could you ask Mr Snodsworth to come out? We're supposed to be moving house today but he won't do the completion. Even the potty's in the furniture van and my little girl's getting desperate.'

'Oi! Tell Will Snodsworth I'm off t'Parrishes, will ye?'

'Guys 'n' gals.' Mr Ranger raised his voice above the clamour. 'Guys, gals 'n' little tykes.' He smiled at the baby which renewed its howling. 'It seems there's been one heck of a ding-dong-hog's-mess round here. Y'all just sit down tight on your ar— seats and I'll sort it out.'

Trying to ignore the blood that flowed ever more freely on to the carpet, he picked his way through the maze of knees and knocked on the door of Mr Snodsworth's room.

'Come!' creaked an ancient voice.

Mr Ranger opened the door just enough to slide his thin body through the aperture, closing it quickly behind him as he sensed the surge of animosity from the waiting room. From behind an enormous mahogany desk, clear and polished to brilliance, a tuft of white hair arose from behind a small sheaf of paper.

'Ah, Lionel. How are you, my boy?'

'I'm just fine, Mr Snodsworth, sir. The fact is, there are a few folks in the waiting room.'

'Folks in the waiting room? And what are they doing there?' The old man's voice was slow and measured.

'They're, well, waiting, sir.'

'Waiting. In the waiting room. How very appropriate. Was it really necessary, Lionel, to disturb my reading of counsel's opinion in a *most* important case, merely to tell me that people, *folks* as you so quaintly put it, are *waiting* in a room specifically designated for that purpose?'

'I suppose not, sir,' replied Mr Ranger, uncomfortably conscious that Mr Snodsworth's expensive Persian carpet was gradually receiving a new, dark red pattern. 'Er, is it the *Geranium* case?'

'Yes, my boy.' Mr Snodsworth seemed pleasantly surprised. 'Have I mentioned it to you before? Well remembered. 'We'll make a solicitor of you yet. Yes, *Re Geranium Trusts.* Unfortunately this young barrister,' he waved the opinion, which bore the name of a very eminent QC, in Mr Ranger's face, 'doesn't seem to share my optimism about my client's case. Never mind, never mind.'

'Excuse me asking, sir,' began Mr Ranger, whose American accent never survived for long in the quintessentially English atmosphere of Mr Snodsworth's chamber, 'but haven't you asked for quite a few opinions in this case already?'

'Twenty-seven,' replied the old man with satisfaction. 'Sixteen of the barristers are dead now, two in the loony bin and one's Lord Chancellor. Still, my client died in '59, so there's no hurry now. Slow and steady, that's the way to succeed in the Law, m'boy. Slow and steady. By the way, did you want to tell me something about these people waiting in the waiting room? The waiters, shall we call 'em? Ha!'

'They seem to think they have appointments. Some with me, and it's my court morning, you know, and some with you.'

'Court morning? Are you still on that business? In my day we never went near a court once we got past twenty-two. Not if we were gentlemen. Left that sort of thing to the clerks. You're slipping, my boy, you're slipping. Yes, I expect I told them they could toddle along, but that was before this opinion came in. Can't drop *Geranium*, you know. Can't you tell them just to toddle back again?'

'I don't think so, sir. Perhaps if I could get your files then I could sort them out. Do the completions and so on.'

'Yes, yes, help yourself. Give and take, change and change about, that's the way to succeed in the Law.' He waved a dismissive hand towards a loose mountain of paper, three or four feet high, which had been swept from his desk top on to the floor. 'Hmm. What we need, m'boy, is a clerk to tidy some of this stuff up. Can't you find us one?'

'I think that most firms have lady secretaries now, sir.'

'Lady secretaries! Are you sure? Very well, I know we're nearly into the 1970s now. You'd better get us a lady secretary, then.'

'We did have one, sir, a few years ago. Don't you remember? A nice little gal called Polly. She left when you wouldn't pay her more than one and six a week. Went to work for Parrishes.'

'More than one and six a week! I should think I wouldn't pay more than one and six a week. A working man would be over the moon at one and six a week.'

'It is only seven and a half pence in the new money.'

'New money, new money? Bless my soul, what is the boy talking about now? Do go away and leave me to my *Geranium*. If young Wilfred Parrish knows about these lady secretaries, why don't we get him to come and work for us? Then we could get on with our proper work, my *Geranium* and your ridiculous court business.'

'Wilfred's a partner now, sir. But we could suggest a merger. I've often thought it might be beneficial to both practices.' Deputy District Judge Ranger had now removed his shoe and was attempting to mop the blood up from the carpet with what remained of his sock.

'A merger, hey? Well, there are precedents. Ratchett and Probe merged with Washburn & Co back in '97.'

'In 1897, sir?'

'No, no, 1797. I said "back in", didn't I?' Mr Snodsworth flapped his hands irritably. 'Now, for the last time, Lionel, do go away. Merge with young Wilfred if you like, I don't mind. I have to draft some fresh instructions.' He ran his finger down a directory of barristers. 'Ever heard of this Mortimer boy?'

Mr Ranger picked up an armful of paper and retreated, leaving his shoe on the carpet. As he closed the door behind him he took great gulps of Texan air.

'Now then, folks,' he called, slapping his holster with a sunburned hand, 'the Sheriff's back in town. Which of y'all stand in the greatest need?'

Chapter Seven

One woe doth tread upon another's heel,
So fast they follow.

(IV.vii.162–3)

'Caw!' crowed the photocopier mechanic, bursting into the office at five minutes to five. 'Don'cha believe in signposts up norf, den? Two-an-a-arf bleedin' hours I bin looking for this Rambleton place. I bin to Leeds, 'Arrogate, Firsk, Darlin'ton an' 'alf-way to *New*carstle before I found it.'

'*New*castle,' explained Polly. 'You have to say the last bit very fast, or else people will think you're a southerner.'

'I *am* a bleedin' suvverner, aren't I? 'Snot my fault that bloody Reg Tranter, wot was the northern region service engineer, went AWOL with a van full of spares an' the sales director's missus. I never asked to be sent up 'ere, but Mr Bleeding Pike, 'e says, "Damien," 'e says, "you've got a clean licence, 'aven't you, lad?" "Well, cleanish," I says and next fing I know I'm on the bleedin' A1 Norf, me that's never bin further than Chelmsford. I say, gotta cuppa tea, 'ave ya? Me marf's like bleedin' Canary Wharf.'

Polly put the kettle on (as it were) while Ophelia tried to entice Damien into the stationery cupboard. But after his long northern tour he was not to be hurried, and sat happily on her desk, swinging expensive trainers against the wastepaper basket.

'Bin doin' a bit of spring-cleaning 'ave ya, girls?' he enquired pleasantly, gazing about him at the morass of papers which represented the afternoon's search for Mr Parrish's instructions. 'I suppose the seasons are different up 'ere. Closer to the Norf Pole, incha?'

Eventually, after three cups of tea and the serious depletion of the fig rolls, Damien was persuaded to glance at the photocopier. Ophelia had suggested to Polly that she go home after the second cup but Polly frowned, shook her head and hissed, in a completely audible whisper, 'I'm not leaving you alone with him. You heard what he said; he's from *London*. He's probably one of those serious killers.'

Nothing in Damien's frank and freckled countenance could dispel the taint of the capital, so Ophelia consented to be chaperoned and all three squeezed with difficulty into the stationery cupboard.

'Cosy, this, innit?' commented Damien, grinning at the flushed Polly. 'What's this then, a freezer? Looks like a bleedin' tomb.'

Polly choked on the last fig roll and Damien thumped her enthusiastically on the back.

'Watch yourself, darlin'. No, it's like one of them sarcophagi, innit? I'm interested in all that stuff, you know, old churches and that. What you need is one of them statues on the top, lyin' down. Like this.' He hopped on top of the freezer and lay down on the lid, his eyes closed and hands folded in silent prayer. 'Course, watcha need is 'is lady lying up 'ere next to 'im,' he added, opening one eye to wink at Polly.

'And a little dog at his feet,' added Ophelia, doing her best to enter into the spirit of the thing.

'Anyway,' concluded Damien, jumping down from the freezer with an exaggerated shiver, 'don't know watcha need a freezer for in 'ere. Bleedin' brass monkeys. What's your boyfriend do to warm 'imself up then?'

'He's a butcher,' replied Polly severely. 'He chops up Cockneys with his biggest meat cleaver and feeds them to the Yorkshire wolves.'

'Aw right, darlin', aw right. Let's 'ave a look at this machine then. Betcha forgot to put in the toner.'

At a quarter past six Ophelia and Polly waved goodbye to the still cheerful Damien, then collapsed in exhaustion on to the file-strewn carpet.

'I think,' said Polly judiciously, 'this has been the most horrible day of my life. Even worse than when Gary got his finger stuck in the ham slicer.'

'It was somewhat gruesome,' agreed Ophelia. 'Mr Parrish seemed to be heavier than yesterday, didn't he?'

'And smellier. Did you see Mr Saggers sniffing when he brought the freezer in? You know, when poor old Mr P. was behind the photocopier. I had to pretend that I'd left some salami in my handbag last month. And then he wanted to inspect the room for, what was it?'

'Pockets of heat-retaining atmosphere.'

'Oh yeah. Good thing you got him distracted with that about the total conventional environment. *And* he bought a copy of your husband's book. I think we did pretty well, considering. All the same . . .' Polly's voice trailed off, and her complexion, behind its layered foundation, grew perceptibly paler.

'All the same what?'

'I do wish that Mr Saggers hadn't left quite so many bags of frozen mushy peas at the bottom. I know he meant to be kind, but I don't think I'll ever be able to eat them again. And we still haven't found those instructions.'

'Never mind.' Ophelia gave a long sigh. 'There are still seven Persil packets, four Rice Krispies, six milk cartons and a tomato box to check. *Nil desperandum.*'

'Oh, I don't care about the football results,' said Polly, with a brave smile.

Ophelia arrived home to find an unfamiliar black Skoda parked in the yard. In the kitchen Malachi and a large Irishman were drinking sherry out of the children's Winnie-the-Pooh plastic tumblers.

'Ah,' said Malachi, as he looked up from the kitchen table. 'Father, may I present my wife, 'Phelia O., slistor extraordinaire. 'Phelia, thi'is Father Jim. He says he's our parish priest.'

'Pleased to meet you, Ophelia,' said the priest, with a little bow. 'I trust that we'll be seeing you at Mass this Sunday.'

'Yes, of course, Father.' Ophelia collected a grimy mug from the draining board and slumped on to the pine bench next to him. 'Malachi, why are you drinking Bristol Cream? I only use that for trifles; I won it in a tombola. I'm sure there's some whisky somewhere.'

'There was,' agreed Malachi. 'We drank it.'

'And very welcome it was too,' added Father Jim. 'Not that we should despise the Bristol Cream. There's many an old bird in the parish that's kept from falling into the sin of despair by the judicious application of your Bristol Cream.'

Judging from the rate at which his tumbler was emptying, the priest had been applying the Bristol Cream, not to mention the Glenfiddich, pretty judiciously himself, but unlike Malachi he exhibited no ill effects.

'Where are the children?' asked Ophelia.

Father Jim raised his face from his tumbler. 'Ah. They're showing Sister Hedwig around this fabulous farm of yours. Wonderful place you've got here, great for the children. Reminds me of me own boyhood in County Clare. I had four serious agricultural accidents before I was twelve. Marvellous experience. Not that I was accident-prone like our Padraic, mind. By his eighth birthday he'd only got seven fingers left. Now that lad of yours, the lively one – Hygenus is it? – he's the spit-wash image of our Padraic.'

39

'Really?' Ophelia was craning her neck in alarm, trying to see past him into the yard. 'And they're with Sister, what was it, Hilda?'

'Hedwig, Hedwig. Dear Sister Hedwig is my assistant in the parish: catechist, teacher, sermon writer, you name it. A remarkable woman, quite remarkable. In fact, I am planning,' he lowered his voice conspiratorially, 'I am planning for her to be the first woman priest in the whole Catholic Church. God grant that I live to see the day.' He crossed himself reverently and returned to his drink.

'Well, I hope she'll live to a remarkably old age then,' said Ophelia, helping herself to sherry and finding none left in the bottle. 'What with this invasion of refugee misogynist Anglicans it's going to take even longer than it would have done anyway.'

'I wish I could say "ref'gee soggy Anglicans",' said Malachi wistfully, and laid his head on the table.

'What about the dogs? Have you found Gigi yet?'

'Sister Hedwig,' answered Father Jim, as Malachi seemed to have gone to sleep, 'is organising a thorough search with the aid of your delightful children and the remaining dog, Maggie is it?'

'Meg.'

'Ah yes, of course, Meg. I thought that the dear creature was much too good-natured to be a Maggie. I am sure that Sister will find the little puppy. She has great success in retrieving my spectacles from the most unexpected corners of the presbytery.'

Unfortunately Sister Hedwig's talents had failed her, for she returned shortly, somewhat tousled, with only two children and one dog.

'Joan and Hygenus wanted to play on the old tractor,' she explained. 'I didn't think it very safe but the eldest boy said he would keep an eye on them. He seems a sensible lad so I let them stay. I managed to hang on to the little ones, though.'

Innocent, grubby and tired, clambered on to Ophelia's knee while Urban settled down next to his father, unperturbed by Malachi's now heavy snoring.

'Are you 'sleep, Daddy? Why aren't you in bed? Is it your bedtime? It's not my bedtime. Wake up, donk head.'

There was no reply and Urban, annoyed, laid his little blond head next to Malachi's and imitated his snores.

'Hoooonggg-choo. Hoooonnnnnggggg-CHU!'

'And I'm afraid that we didn't find the little dog,' Sister Hedwig continued, absently stroking first Urban's, then Malachi's hair. 'The mother seems to be getting quite worried. Maybe you should call the police.'

Malachi woke, prompted by Urban's prodding and by Sister Hedwig's caresses.

'Can't do that,' he said, and fell asleep again.

'I really think it might be best,' insisted Hedwig, her faded blue eyes bright with concern.

'No, I'm afraid we really can't,' said Ophelia. She looked at the Irish priest and at the pink-scrubbed nun and decided that they could be trusted.

'We had a slight accident at our last house, involving an excellent bottle of malt, our two cars that were the wrong way round on the drive and had to be reversed into the road, and a police sergeant next door who had never liked us. The result was that we were both banned from driving for six months, and there are three months still left to go. We really can't risk having anything to do with the police.'

Malachi lifted his head again and smiled beatifically, the corners of his eyes crinkling with charm.

''Phelia will find her,' he prophesied. 'Wonderful 'Phelia. Wise 'Phelia.' He was reminded of a song, and continued, crooning, gently into his glass:

> 'Wise 'Phelia O. is
> My favourite wife.
> She's been a solic'tor
> For all of her life . . .'

'It's a funny thing,' said Pius, coming in with Joan and Hygenus after the religious delegation had left. 'There are four hundred and ninety-six computers in the barn and only four hundred and ninety-five boxes.'

'Good grief, you didn't count them all?'

'No, I got Hygenus to do it. He always gets confused after seventy-nine so I wanted to give him some practice.'

'Well, now I've had enough practice for the next gillion years,' said Hygenus stoutly. 'Mummy, I've got three new bashes on my knees and two on my arms.'

'Well, I did tell you not to climb on the henhouse,' said Pius.

'Mummy, you know the Olympic Games?' said Joan, apparently apropos of nothing.

'Yes, love?'

'Well I hope there's a British bossing team, 'cos Pius would easily get the gold medal. What's for tea?'

* * *

41

Ophelia was woken next morning by the distinctive mewing of a Labrador. She opened the bedroom door and Meg slunk in, brown eyes heavy with misery.

'Poor old girl,' said Ophelia. 'Still no sign of Gigi?'

Meg licked Ophelia's nose and deposited a long strand of slobber on to her chin. Ophelia's affection for the dog, transient at the best of times, left abruptly.

'Oh, do go away, you disgusting dog. She's bound to turn up. And don't chew my knickers!'

But by breakfast time Gigabyte was still missing and Meg sat in front of the stove, looking accusingly at each member of the family in turn. Meg, in common with most Labradors, could plunge the most blameless into an abyss of guilt by one of her long stares. This morning she obtained reparations of four sausages, six slices of bacon and half a bowl of muesli. She left the muesli as a sign of maternal grief.

The postman arrived early at Moorwind, probably wanting to get its baleful effects over with as soon as possible, so Ophelia was generally able to read her post before going to work. This morning Joan collected the letters and sorted them between her parents.

Ophelia was browsing through a mail-order catalogue when an immense cry broke through Malachi's hangover.

'Bloody hell, Ophelia, look at this! No wonder we couldn't find the puppy!'

Trembling with indignation he handed her a letter. It was written on headed paper, 'Leafskirk Engineering' in olive green embellished with an ivy design. The body of the letter, however, was made up of letters cut from newspapers, in traditional criminal style.

> *dEAr SIrs*
> *we aCKNowLEDgE RECEIPT of the CONsignMenT of computers.*
> *UnFORtuNateLy you put A DOg IN the last PArCEl.*
> *WE wilL keep THE DOG unTIl YOU pAY us £70,000.*
> *we WIll PHONe ON Saturday.*
> *dO NOT cAll tHe POLICe Or the doG GETs iT.*

'Malachi,' said Ophelia quietly, 'how did the dog get into the box?'

'Well,' Malachi helped himself to another two aspirin from the bottle in front of him, 'I was training her, you see.'

'Training her to do what?'

'Um, search for drugs.'

'So you put, what, a packet of dope in the computer box, got Gigi to go in after it, said, "Good girl!", closed the box and sent her off to Leafskirk?'

'If you're just going to be silly, Ophelia, then I won't tell you at all. I'm not well, you know. I think I've got chickenpox. It's going round the children's school.'

'Have you, Daddy? Can I see your spots?'

'Patrick Riley had seven on his bottom. How many have you got on your bottom?'

'Daddy's got a spotty bot! Ner ner-ne nerner!'

'Bum.'

'Be quiet, children. Daddy hasn't got chickenpox, he's got a hangover. Don't sing at the table and don't say bum.'

'Our teacher says bum.'

'What's a hankover?'

'Our teacher doesn't; she says backside.'

'I said be quiet. Go on then, Malachi.'

'I didn't put *drugs* in the box, I put *dog biscuits*. And I didn't know the dog was in there, she must have gone in while I went to change Innocent's nappy. Then Inn was talking such a load of rubbish that I forgot where I was and thought I'd packed them all. You might as well blame him as me. Stupid baby.'

Innocent burst into tears. So did Urban.

'Blame him for what?' shouted Joan over the shrieks. 'What's happened to Gigabyte?'

'Is she dead' asked Hygenus with interest.

'No, of course she's not dead. Daddy accidentally sent her to some people in Lancashire and they are very kindly looking after her for a while until we can fetch her. Now go and clean your teeth, all of you. Pius, you've got PE this afternoon, don't forget your kit.'

When they had gone Ophelia and Malachi looked at each other.

'Well, the police are out anyway,' said Ophelia.

'Oaf, we can't let her die, we just can't.' Tears were brimming in Malachi's pale blue eyes. 'They might do anything to her, torture her. They'd probably say it was a necessary act in time of war.'

'What war?'

'The War of the Roses. Oh, Ophelia!'

'Don't worry, Mal. We won't let her die.' Ophelia looked across the table at her husband as he sat sadly, Meg's nose resting on his knee. He

43

ran a delicate hand through his wild blond hair and did his best to smile. 'Don't worry, angel,' she repeated. 'We'll just have to find seventy thousand pounds.'

Chapter Eight

...lawless resolutes
For food and diet to some enterprise
That hath some stomach in't, which is no other ...
...But to recover of us by strong hand
And terms compulsatory those foresaid lands
So by his father lost.

(ı.i. 101–107)

Meanwhile Gigabyte was having the time of her short life.

Sated by dog biscuits and leftovers she had fallen asleep in the cardboard box on Monday afternoon and had not woken until the courier had picked up the box on Tuesday morning. She had whimpered in alarm but the man, whistling to himself, had not heard her. From then on all was jolting and confusion, engine noise and shouted commands until, around lunchtime, the box was finally deposited on firm ground. For a while Gigabyte could hear nothing but birdsong and distant traffic, then footsteps. Next came two voices; the first a woman's, the second a man's.

'Wardle, duck, what've you got here?'

The puppy could hear the rustle of hands being drawn across the top of her box.

'Just a minute, Dot.' The second set of footsteps drew nearer. 'Oh yes, I remember. I ... er ... ordered them yesterday.'

'But what are they? Personal Computers? Wardle, the business is about to go bust, the bank are going to repossess the house and you're buying, what, *five* computers?' The rising intonation of the woman's voice was familiar and Gigabyte shrank from the scolding.

'Yes, well, it's part of a plan, Dotty.' The man sounded worried.

'What sort of a plan? A business plan or an ELLA plan?'

Gigabyte could not hear the man's muttered reply.

'And what sort of an ELLA plan, lovey?'

'Well, dear, you remember that at the last meeting we talked about launching a guerrilla offensive against the Yorkshire commercial mafia?'

'No, I think I must have been doing the washing-up during that bit.

45

There's always far more than you would expect for only four people having tea and cakes.'

'Well, anyway, I thought, as the leader, I should strike the first blow. My idea was that I'd order these computers – they're from a firm in Rambleton – then send one back saying that it was faulty. What they wouldn't know is that I'd have placed an incendiary device in the computer so that when they opened it up . . .' The man's voice was slowing.

'An incendiary device? You mean a *bomb*, Wardle? Oh Wardie, you're not a terrorist!'

'No, Dottie, I'm not really, though I am supposed to be a freedom fighter. Anyway, as I was placing the order on the phone, the man sounded so nice, and I'm almost sure I heard children in the background. So then I changed my mind about the bomb, but I couldn't just tell him to cancel the order straightaway, it would have sounded so daft.'

'Oh Wardie!' Now the scolding tone had disappeared from her voice and she sounded only pained.

'Then I had another idea. I was going to put the incendiary device in after all, just a little one, but then I'd open it up myself. Then I could sue them for my injuries. I would say that a valve blew up.'

'Are you sure that these computers have valves? I read somewhere that they use those microchips, though I don't know how they keep them frozen. That reminds me, I've got some in, would you like them for your tea with a couple of sausages?'

The word was familiar to Gigabyte, who lifted her nose to the inside corner of the box in anticipation.

'Yes, that'd be champion. Anyway, then I remembered that I don't know how to make an incendiary device. Pity, because the Mid-Yorkshire Business Directory says that their turnover is five million pounds so I might have got quite a lot out of them for the Cause.'

'Well I'm very glad that you aren't. I know that the Cause is terribly important, but I'm sure that it's not worth blowing yourself up for.'

'Dot, don't you remember what Father used to say? "The Cause of establishing the Pennine Socialist Republic must come before all else. The East Lancashire Liberation Army demands our absolute loyalty, even unto death!" '

'And that's why he died at seventy-eight, tripping over his shoelaces, is it?'

'Dorothy!'

'I'm sorry, Wardle. But really, it is just a dream, isn't it?'

Gigabyte began to subside again, having managed to catch no further reference to sausages.

'It was Father's dream. I can't let Father down. And there are Flies and Mrs McHenry to think of now, as well. If they didn't have the Cause I'm sure that Flies would go back to a life of crime and poor Mrs McHenry would be awfully lonely.'

Dorothy sighed. 'Sometimes I wish that the Vicar had never allowed you to give that talk in the Church Hall. Those two are more trouble than they're worth. What's that?'

Gigabyte had settled down at the bottom of the box, giving a low moan of hunger as she laid her snout upon her front paws.

'What's what?' Wardle was slightly deaf. 'But, Dot, ELLA doubled in size when they joined. Funny, I never thought of myself as an orator, not like Father. Remember that speech he gave at the Free Trade Hall? I was only six or seven, but I'll never forget sitting beside him up there with all those union men standing up to cheer and tossing their caps on to the stage in excitement.'

'Hmm, perhaps. I think it was more desperation than enthusiasm. Father had been speaking for three hours. Anyway, ELLA more than doubled after your talk, I would say. You can't really call me a member. I only do the tea.'

'You're a pillar of strength to us all, Dottie. We'd never manage without you. Now we might as well open these boxes now they're here. I've never seen a computer close up.'

Gigabyte heard the sounds of tearing cardboard and creaking polystyrene. She cocked one ear but was careful to make no sound.

'Well, these do look exciting, don't they, Dot? Perhaps we could try one out.'

'It's nice that they come with plugs on, isn't it, dear? I always feel a bit nervous when you have to put the plug on yourself.'

'Dorothy, I may not be the world's greatest technological wizard, but I do have an engineering business that hasn't quite failed yet. Believe it or not, I can put a plug on.'

'Oh, I'm sorry, Wardie. Oh!' The last was in tones of great disappointment.

'What is it, Dottie?'

'They're all grey! I was hoping that they would come in different colours. I'll just check the last one. Perhaps that's different. With cookers you can usually choose between brown and white, can't you?'

Gigabyte listened with growing excitement as the masking tape was pulled off the top of her box.

47

'Wardle! Oh Wardle, look! Oh the poor little thing!'

A round grandmotherly face was peering into the box, large grey eyes wide with concern. Another face joined it, identical but for its bald forehead.

'It's not *that* little,' he said nervously, as Gigabyte leaped up and licked his nose.

'Oh Wardie, it's only a pup. Come on, boy, out you come. That's right.'

Gigabyte jumped out of the box and danced around Dorothy, bounding up to scatter little pieces of polystyrene packaging over her print dress.

'Good boy!' she cried with inaccurate abandon.

When the initial euphoria of freedom had died down, Gigabyte suddenly remembered that she was hungry. She sat down in front of Dorothy, head on one side, eyes liquid, whining plaintively.

'What is it, boy? What's the matter? Are you hungry? Dinner?'

Gigabyte leaped again.

'Now what have I got? Wardie, duck, d'ye mind not having those sausages after all?'

'Er . . . what?' Wardle was lost in thought. 'Sausages? No, no I don't mind. I wonder how he got in there? You don't think they meant to send him, do you? I mean, if they'd found out who I was – after all, my talk was reported in the *Leafskirk Gazette* – then they might have deliberately planted him to destroy me. He might have rabies.'

'Rabies!' scoffed Dorothy. 'Just look at him.' Gigabyte was drinking noisily from a pail of soapy water with which Dorothy had been about to mop the floor.

'Well, perhaps not rabies, but he might be a pit bull terrier, biding his moment before he attacks us.'

'Wardie, he's a Labrador puppy.'

'Labrador! Just a minute.' Wardle tore open the 'Documents Enclosed' polythene envelope on the top of the box. 'Yes I thought so! This company, Wet Nose Solutions, their emblem is a Labrador's head. Look, on this delivery note. He must be some sort of a company mascot. I bet they'd be prepared to pay a lot to get him back.'

'Wardle, are you thinking . . . ?'

'Well, why not? I know you'll say it's blackmail but like I said, I *am* supposed to be a freedom fighter. I'm not very good at fighting but I think I could manage being a political prisoner. I might get a job in the prison library. If the worst came to the worst the trial would be wonderful publicity for ELLA. And we really do need the money.'

'To pay off the mortgage, you mean?'

'Oh no, Dorothy. We couldn't use it for ourselves. That would be like stealing. No, for the Republic. Look what I saw in yesterday's *Gazette*.'

Gigabyte, ever optimistic, bounded after Wardle as he went into the dining room. But he only took a newspaper from the table and returned to Dorothy, who was unwrapping a packet of sausages from the fridge.

'Here it is.

END OF AN ERA.

Leafskirk Town Hall, meeting-place and administrative centre for Leafskirk Town Council for over a century, is to be put on the market. According to the Town Clerk, Mrs Jean Dodson, since the local government reorganisations, the Council only has the functions and resources of a parish council and cannot afford to maintain the historic building. Offers are invited in the region of £70,000 and should be received by the council by 25 November.

You see? It's exactly what we need. The Town Hall as a headquarters would give us just the credibility we need. Members would come flooding in then, just like the old days.'

'Well, I don't know, Wardle. It seems to me that it'll cause a lot of trouble. Why don't we just take the doggie back? It'll be a nice drive to the Dales. No, duckie, Auntie Dot has to cook the sausages first.'

'Dorothy Beatrice Emmeline Smith, don't you dare use the words "nice" and "Dales" in the same sentence. You might be my big sister but you can't boss me around all my life. This is our one big chance to put East Lancashire on the world map. Give young Flies something to aim at.'

'Very well, dear. I'm sure you're right. Oh, Wardle?'

'Yes, Dot?'

'You don't think raw sausages are dangerous to dogs, do you?'

Chapter Nine

Be thy intents wicked or charitable,
Thou com'st in such a questionable shape
That I will speak to thee.

(i.iv. 42– 44)

There was little that Malachi and Ophelia could do about the puppy until Saturday, so they tried to carry on as normal, or as near normal as ever at Moorwind, parrying the children's questions.

'Can we drive over and fetch Gigabyte at the weekend, Mummy?' asked Joan. 'I bet she's missing us. Bernadette's granny lives in Lancashire and she says it's dead boring and they have to eat black pudding.'

'What's black pudding?' asked Hygenus. 'Is it like that bad apple I found down the back of the sofa?'

'No, worse than that.' Joan lowered her voice to a sinister drawl. 'It's made of Blud. Yuman Blud.'

'Don't be silly, Joan. It's pig's or sheep or something like that,' said Ophelia vaguely. 'I'm sure Gigi would love it, whatever it is.'

'Yes, but can we go and get her anyway? She'd rather have us than dead sheep's blood.'

The others joined in. 'She'd rather have us than dead cow's brains.'

'Cows haven't got any brains. Can't you tell from looking at them?'

'She'd rather have us than frogs' legs.'

'She'd rather have us than rabbit poo.'

'We'll have to see. We'd have to go over the Pennines and there's often snow at this time of year.'

'In October?' Pius was sceptical.

'It's a particularly cold October.'

'Yes,' agreed Hygenus cheerfully. 'We might get stuck in the snow and die of freezing and scarvation.'

'Starvation.' Ophelia corrected him automatically, then, seeing Urban's stricken face, wished that she had not.

'Gigabyte is fine,' she concluded, 'having a lovely holiday in the Lancashire moors, and she'll be coming home very soon.'

The children recognised their mother's most authoritative tone, and dispersed.

Wednesday and Thursday were quiet at the office, with very few clients or calls. Some regulars asked after Mr Parrish, but all were satisfied with the women's extempore explanations. Polly found a spare desk which they moved into the outer office and Ophelia brought in an assortment of wallpaper left over from Malachi's last bout of DIY enthusiasm. As they painted and papered over the thick layers of solicitors' brown, their spirits rose and for moments they were able to forget the brooding and frozen presence of the late Mr Parrish. Meanwhile the redecoration was giving them the opportunity to check every corner and crevice for his hidden instructions, which had so far eluded them.

'We should be all right as long as the clients don't compare notes,' Ophelia called from the stationery cupboard. She was using the freezer as a pasting table. 'Each one should just think that Mr Parrish happens to be busy with all the other clients' work. The problems start if they get together and realise that no one has seen him. Luckily Rambleton doesn't seem to be a very communicative place. Oh, sorry, I didn't mean—'

'That's okay,' Polly mumbled from her half-painted skirting board, 'I'm not really a Rambletonian myself. Dad lived in Huddersfield until he was fifteen and Mum's from Shakeston.'

Shakeston was a village three miles from Rambleton.

'As far as the other solicitors are concerned things shouldn't be too bad,' Ophelia continued. 'I was supposed to be taking over the litigation anyway so they won't expect to see Mr Parrish in court, and you can field the conveyancing calls. I've been practising his signature and I've got an idea of his style by reading the files, so I think I can manage letters and faxes.'

'Yes, I think we've cracked it,' agreed Polly.

But they had reckoned without Edgar Pottlebonce.

By half-past eight the next morning, when Ophelia arrived, Rambleton's only car park was already full. She was diverted into a nearby field and charged £2.50 by a taciturn ploughboy. Market Square, in contrast to its usual air of silent misery, was littered with poles, awning and cardboard boxes, and noisy with clatter and argument. On her way to the office Ophelia passed four fruit and veg stalls, five selling cleaning products and eight festooned with nylon knickers.

The view out of Parrish's front window was entirely obscured by cheap prints of sheep going home in a snowy sunset.

'I assume Friday is market day?'

'Ooh yes,' said Polly, already laden with carpet shampoo and a bamboo-framed mirror. 'You can get lovely things, dead cheap. Mr Parrish used to give me and Mildred a long lunch on Fridays to do our shopping.'

Ophelia wondered how much longer a lunch could get than Polly's usual hour and a half.

The office was considerably busier than earlier in the week, with clients popping in to sign wills or discuss their neighbours' sanitary habits before buying the week's potatoes. They would trail in, negotiating the heavy door with pushchairs, dogs, shopping trolleys and large purchases and would forget, on average, one item each, so that by eleven o'clock Ophelia and Polly had collected two baskets of groceries, a bad-tempered poodle, an imitation Jacobean occasional table and a six-week-old baby. All were soon collected, even, to Ophelia's secret regret, the baby, and at a quarter to twelve Polly put her coat on ready for lunch.

Suddenly the door was violently bounced open and a heavy, red-faced man in olive-green tweeds confronted them.

'Where's Wilf?' he demanded.

'Mr Parrish? I'm afraid he's had to go to a site meeting in Northumberland today. May I help? I'm the new assistant solicitor, Ophelia O.'

'No, you certainly may not help. What the hell does Wilf Parrish think he's doing? He never goes out on a Friday. Thirty-two years he's been at this office and he never goes out on a Friday. Every Friday dinner-time for the past thirty-two years I've been walking past that side window and I've looked in and seen Wilf at t'desk. Thirty-two years, young lady!'

'Well, I'm very sorry, but this really was unavoidable. I'm sure that Mr Parrish didn't mean to offend you.'

'Offend me! I didn't say anything about being offended, you silly girl. Do I look like the sort of man who would be offended?'

Ophelia thought that he looked exactly like that sort of man, but she said nothing.

'I'm not *offended*,' he continued. '*I* don't care if Wilfred Parrish has gone to bloody Barbados with t'East Rambleton Women's Institute. It's a question of t'market.'

'The market? In the Square?'

'No, no, you daft woman!' The man was getting redder and more agitated with every exclamation. 'T'agricultural market. Don't you know who I am?'

'Mr Kettlebounce, isn't it?' said Polly, arrested in mid-sleeve by the excitement.

'Pottlebonce, young lady, Edgar Pottlebonce, chairman of Rambleton NFU and, what's more to the point, secretary to t'cattle market for thirty-two years. Your Mr Parrish, he's always been our, like, legal adviser, there in case there's any disputes or argumentations. I don't know what he thinks he's doing, going out on a Friday when we might need him.'

'Perhaps he thought that I could deal with anything that came up,' suggested Ophelia. 'Do you often have to ask his advice?'

'Aye, lass, we do. It's been twice since I've been secretary, once in 1963 and once in 1969. It's been quite amicable lately, like.'

'I see. So you don't usually actually speak to Mr Parrish?'

'No, no. Haven't you been listening, girl? Good God, what do they think they're doing, calling these stupid girls solicitators? I've not spoken to Wilf Parrish for twenty years, not since my nephew Brian's wedding, but I always wave at him and he always waves back. That way I know he's there if we need him. It's quite simple. If you can't get your flippin' female head round that then you certainly wouldn't be any good to us at t'market.'

'I see now, Mr Pottlebonce. I'll let Mr Parrish know that you called in and I'm sure that he'll be here every Friday from now on. Meanwhile if you need any legal advice at today's market I shall be happy to give you my assistance. If you have any doubts as to my competence then I suggest that you read my university dissertation, *Some Aspects of the Doctrine of Laches within the Agricultural Contract*. I'll pop and get it for you, shall I? What? You're in a hurry? Another time then perhaps? Good afternoon, Mr Pottlebonce.'

The deflated farmer allowed himself to be shepherded out of the room by Polly.

'Well, that got rid of him.'

'Yes, thank goodness.'

'Did you really write all that about lychees?'

'Not a word. My degree was in medieval history.'

'And why on earth did you say that Mr Parrish would be here? Why didn't you say that he'll be away every Friday or something?'

'Because then he'd have kicked up a real fuss and someone would have demanded to see Mr Parrish. As it is, if the last "argumentation" was in 1969 there isn't much chance of being called on to do anything.'

'But this waving business?'

'Well, until we find out what to do about the body, we'll just have to get him out of the freezer on Fridays and make him wave, won't we? I just hope that Mr Pottlebonce walks past at the same time each week. I don't fancy spending every Friday lunchtime under a desk with a decomposing solicitor.'

The afternoon was quiet again and Ophelia sat pensively at the window, watching the market traders dismantling their stalls. She had promised Malachi that she would raise the £70,000 demanded by Gigabyte's kidnappers but as yet she had no idea of how to do so. Opposite the office the Arthurian Bank stood grey and foursquare, its cash dispenser solidly inoperative. Ophelia scowled through the window at the manager, who had returned her last Barclaycard payment cheque, ignominiously defaced with red ink. She felt like robbing the bank, balaclava allergy or no balaclava allergy, but violence was not really her style. Anyway, the Rambleton branch probably did not keep more than a couple of thousand on the premises. She thought of selling herself as a white slave, caught one of the folds of her tummy on the edge of her desk, and thought again. Middle Easterners were reputed to like their women plump, but they probably preferred them unfurrowed by five sets of stretch marks.

At half-past four Ophelia was about to tell Polly that she could go home when two men walked through the door.

The first was a youth of about nineteen with the most viciously repellent face Ophelia had ever seen, shrivelled and rodential. He was followed by a thick-set middle-aged man, coughing violently.

The boy leaned on the counter and called, 'I want a solicitor.'

'Certainly,' replied Polly. 'Your name is . . . ?'

'Darren Skate.'

'And I'm 'is dad,' said the older man. 'I'm 'ere to make sure that 'e gets 'is rights.'

Ophelia, watching with a sinking heart from across the room, thought that she had rarely seen anyone more capable of asserting his rights than Darren Skate.

'I usually go to Canards,' said Darren, 'but they're acting for 'er so they told me to come 'ere. Mind you, if you're no good then I'll go to those others, Snotsworths. Like me dad said, I know me rights.'

'Yes, well, if you'd like to come this way then Mrs O. will be able to help you.'

Darren and his father followed Polly to Ophelia's screened corner where they pulled two chairs forward so that they were only inches from her nose. She could not disguise her recoil and was grateful for the masking smell of the cigarettes which they immediately lit.

'How may I help you?'

'I want to get custody of our Kylie.'

'I see. Well, we actually call it "residence" now, since the passing of the new Children Act. The concept of "access" has been changed too; it's now called "contact". The idea is that the needs of the child come first: the child has a right to contact with the parent, rather than the parent having a right to access to the child.' Ophelia smiled primly.

'Kylie's norra child. She's a rat.'

'A . . . rat?'

'Yeah, a white one. She's my f–ing rat and I want legal aid to get 'er back.'

''E's got 'is rights,' repeated Mr Skate. 'That's 'is sodding rat and that f–ing cow's got to give it back, right?'

'I see. Well, I think that this is really a question of property rather than family law. A court would probably just want to establish who owns Kylie rather than who could look after her best.'

'I f–ing own her, don't I? *And* I can look after 'er best. That Sharon, she's not taken Kylie out fighting once since she took 'er. Kylie's a fighting rat. It's not natural for 'er not to go out fighting.'

'What about natural law then, eh?' demanded Mr Skate. 'Watcher got to say about that?'

'I would say that the concept of natural law is a theological one and absolutely nothing to do with the issues at stake here,' snapped Ophelia.

'Don't you get stroppy with us,' retorted Darren. 'I know my rights. If you don't get Kylie back I'll report you to the RSPCA and to the Law Society. You're not allowed to discriminate, you know, not against rats.'

'So it would seem.'

'So give us the sodding legal aid forms, then you can issue proceedings. I've done this sort of thing plenty of times before, you know. I know what you 'ave to do. Come on.'

'If you give me some more details then I may be able to write to Sharon for you under the Green Form Scheme but I really can't do any more. As I explained, this is a matter of property law, and full legal aid is not available unless the value of the property is over a thousand pounds.

I'm afraid that Kylie, however good a fighter she is, is unlikely to be worth that much, isn't she?'

'Bollocks,' replied Mr Skate. 'My Darren knows 'is rights.'

'Yeah,' said Darren. 'Worrabout section eight, rule six in Schedule C to the Legal Aid Amendment Regulations?'

'What about it?'

'It says that you can get legal aid anyway in cases of 'umanitarian necessity. Our Kylie's a 'umanitarian necessity, right? So get those f–ing forms. You'll need the one for emergency legal aid too – that's the pink one, if you don't know.'

'Which it looks like she don't,' added his father. 'Come on, get yer finger out; we've got to get to the DSS before it closes to get 'is Domestic Animals Bereavement Grant.'

'Mr Skate, Mr Skate,' said Ophelia, standing up, 'I shall be happy to check the Legal Aid Regulations to find out whether you may be entitled to apply for full legal aid and meanwhile I am willing to deal with this matter under the Green Form Scheme. Alternatively, of course, you might consider paying for my services.'

'Paying!' cried the two men in simultaneous consternation. 'We're on the sick, you know. We don't 'ave to pay for things. We know our rights.' They each lit another cigarette.

'In any case,' continued Ophelia, 'this office is now closing. I suggest that you consider the position over the weekend and come in to see me again on Monday. If you prefer to go to Snodsworth and Ranger then I shall, of course, fully understand. Good evening, gentlemen.'

'Eh!' complained Mr Skate as the front door was closed behind them. 'I 'aven't finished me fag!'

Chapter Ten

This quarry cries on havoc.

(v.ii. 369)

Gigabyte lay on her back in front of the fire, stretched, and waved four paws in the air. She had never known such luxury. Moorwind's electric bars gave out nothing like this smoky, roaring heat and she was invariably banished from the fireside before Ophelia got home. Sometimes Gigabyte suspected that Ophelia did not really like dogs. There was something about her touch when offered a muddy dog's tummy to scratch that suggested the resolute gritting of teeth.

She gave a contented belch. That was another thing: at home they gave her Economy Complete Dog Food once a day. Here, after seeing the delight with which Gigabyte had eaten her lunch-time sausages, Dorothy had taken her for a walk to the village shop and bought another pound, together with a packet of Wagon Wheels. These were supposed to provide supper for both Gigabyte and Wardle (Wagon Wheels were his especial favourite) but she had forgotten all about her brother and had fed the whole lot to the puppy. Wardle did not seem to mind, though. As Dorothy had set off for the village, he had put his head out of the study window and given her a letter, stamped first class, to go by the afternoon post. It was addressed to Wet Nose Solutions in wobbly black capitals and Wardle advised her to wipe it clean of fingerprints before she posted it. Dorothy was tempted to throw the letter into the weedy village duck pond to be consumed by the ravenous mallards, but remembering Wardle's outburst, she thought that she had better not.

As the sitting room door opened Gigabyte started, ready to be exiled, but it was only Dorothy again.

'Hello, boy. Getting yourself nice and warm down there?' Dorothy put down the two large plates she was carrying and scratched Gigabyte's belly. 'There we are, old thing.'

Much as she enjoyed a good tummy rub, Gigabyte was more interested in what was on the plates. She let her nose wander in their direction while her eyes pretended to have nothing to do with it. Dorothy, thankfully, was extremely quick to take a hint.

'Oh, you want to see what's on there, do you, love? This one's sandwiches, salmon paste, and egg and cress. And this one's nibbles: crisps, potato rings and Twiglets. Want to try one?'

One was not exactly what Gigabyte had in mind but it would do as a start.

'They're for the meeting. Wardle's called an extraordinary meeting of ELLA to discuss what to do about you. You shouldn't worry though, dear.'

Gigabyte showed no signs of worrying but put on a plaintive expression which won her a salmon paste sandwich.

'Poor Wardie, he's not really cut out for this guerrilla business, you know. It's all Father's fault. He was one of those old-fashioned socialists, all bushy moustache and piercing eyes, quite ordinary to start off with. Arthur, his name was. That's his picture over there on the bureau. Then he got this idea that true socialism could only be found in the factories and mills of Lancashire and that its greatest enemies were the conservative peasants of Yorkshire. Well, this idea got stronger and stronger and began to take him over. Then he decided that the people in the cities, Manchester and Liverpool, were enemies too, and that only East Lancashire was still untainted. I suppose he really liked to be a big fish in a little pond.

'He was a good man, though, very conscientious. He brought Wardle and me up himself, you know. Our mother ran away with a baker from Halifax when we were tiny. Very bitter, he was. Never touched a loaf of bread for the rest of his life but ate cream crackers with everything. Cream crackers! No wonder he was a bit peculiar. I mean, you wouldn't want to live on cream crackers, would you, doggie?'

Gigabyte tried to convey, by means of a complex combination of grin and droop, that cream crackers, though not suitable as a staple food, were perfectly acceptable from time to time. Say, every twenty seconds.

'And, of course, his mania about Yorkshire got so much worse. That's when he founded the East Lancashire Liberation Army. It had quite a few members in those days, though I don't think they ever did anything, but gradually they all left or died and there was only Father left. We thought he'd forgotten about it as he got older and spent most of his time just sitting in his chair, dreaming. Well, dreaming and moaning and grumbling at us and eating cream crackers. Then one day, not long before he died, he called Wardle into his old study and spent hours talking to him. I don't know exactly what he said but he told Wardle to keep ELLA going and Wardle promised that he would. And he's never gone back on that promise. He's devoted his life to that blinking ELLA ever since Father died fifteen years ago. I wouldn't mind if it made him happy, but he feels all the time that he's not doing enough. Father used to tell us these stories, you see, about his adventures in the Spanish Civil War and that, all exaggerated I think, but they made him sound like some great hero of the people. Poor Wardle just wants to be a hero too, instead of a fifty-eight-year-old engineer with a failing business and a daft old maid for a sister.'

Dorothy paused to give Gigabyte, who was listening with feigned intelligence, another sandwich.

'Anyway, there was just Wardle until earlier this year when he had the idea of giving a talk on ELLA in the church hall. The Vicar doesn't like to say no to anyone and I think he wanted to impress the Bishop, who's a bit of a Marxist, according to the papers. So, anyway, the Vicar let him do his little lecture and the usual bunch of people with nothing else to do turned up to listen. You know, the ones who go to Dr Sanders' Portuguese slide shows and Mrs Mason's macramé. The talk was a disaster, of course – over everyone's head and quite inaudible in any case – but afterwards two people stayed behind and said they'd like to join. One was Flies, who I'm almost sure went along to see what he could pinch, and the other was Mrs McHenry. Ms McHenry, we're supposed to call her, but Wardle and I can't remember, and to tell the truth, neither can she most of the time. I don't know what happened to Mr McHenry but she'd spent the last few years at Greenham Common. The end of the Cold War left her at a bit of a loose end and the local Green Party wasn't really violent enough, so she joined us.'

Gigabyte stretched understandingly and looked at the Twiglets.

'Here you are then, dear. I don't know why I get this stuff out, no one ever eats it. I love entertaining though. What I would really have liked would have been to join the WI and have them come to my house for committee meetings. I could have given them jam tarts and French fancies. But Father would never let me, he said it was part of the bourgeois conspiracy. Then after he died it seemed too late and Wardle would have been upset.'

She gave Gigabyte another Twiglet as the door opened.

A woman of about Dorothy's age walked in. But where Dorothy was rounded, she was angular and while Dorothy wore a dress appropriate to her Women's Institute aspirations, this woman was covered with the same cheesecloth and Indian cotton in which she had demonstrated twenty-five years ago. It was unfortunately also obvious that her bra, once burned, had never been replaced. She walked over to the fireplace and, dislodging Gigabyte with a prod of her Peruvian slipper-sock, took up a commanding position with her back to the mantelpiece.

The youth who followed her in was also caught in a sartorial time warp, but his was dated around 1977. As he brushed past the sofa a couple of his zips snagged on the brushed nylon covers. He sat down with a loud sniff.

'Gorra dog?' he enquired in a friendly tone. 'Hope it's a killer.'

'You do realise,' said Mrs McHenry, wrinkling her nose delicately, 'that keeping an animal as a pet is psychological exploitation equivalent to the suffering of veal calves. That dog's essential autonomy is being eroded by its position of artificial subservience.'

'It's not a pet,' said Wardle, appearing at the door. 'It's a hostage.'

Wardle and Dorothy explained the circumstances of Gigabyte's arrival and the kidnapping plan. Wardle had photocopied his letter to Wet Nose Solutions and he showed it proudly to the others.

'I used letters from newspapers so that they couldn't trace it to me.'

'But you've used headed writing paper,' Mrs McHenry pointed out. She had now identified the smell that had been exercising her nostrils as singeing cheesecloth and sat down hurriedly. Gigabyte, with a brief 'Hurrumph', returned to the hearthrug.

Wardle was crestfallen. Dorothy quickly changed the subject.

'I think the first thing to do is to give him a name,' she said.

'How about Spot?' suggested Flies, between squeezing pustules of acne.

'Why?' asked the others. 'He isn't spotted.'

'That's the point, innit? If the pigs come round looking for a plain black dog then you just say, "Oh yeah, we've got a dog. He's here somewhere. Spot!" Then they'll say, "Oh no, can't be that one. The dog we want's not spotted," and they'll go away. See?' He returned, triumphant, to his pimples.

Wardle thought this was an excellent idea. Dorothy was not quite sure. Mrs McHenry thought that to name an animal at all was to fall into the anthropomorphic fallacy. So they called her Spot.

Dorothy gave her an egg and cress sandwich in honour of her new name and the conversation turned into a debate about the Marxist-Leninist credentials of the Animal Liberation Movement.

By now, in addition to the sausages and Wagon Wheels, Gigabyte had eaten seven salmon paste sandwiches, six egg and cress, and most of the plate of 'nibbles'. Inside the cauldron of her stomach nature had carried out her usual chemical experiments and now the most peculiar smells were wafting about the room. Her nose followed them with thoughtful detachment.

'Pooh! Who's let off then?' cried Flies. He turned to the vegan Mrs McHenry. 'You been eating your beans again?'

Flies and Mrs McHenry tended not to see eye to eye at the best of times. This was not the best of times. Mrs McHenry rose in great dudgeon.

When Mrs McHenry had first come in, Gigabyte had noticed a strange scent which she had never before encountered. It was in fact patchouli. Now the warmed patchouli was blending with the old goat of Mrs McHenry's afghan coat, the singed cheesecloth and her own female odours to create a perfume fascinating to the puppy. For some time the mystery vied with the comfort of the hearthrug and Gigabyte lay content, quietly dreaming of the olefactory excitements concealed beneath the faded cotton. She was nearly asleep when Mrs McHenry stood up, but the sudden eddy of scented air awoke her instantly. With a short bark of excitement, Gigabyte rose from the fireplace, galloped over to Mrs McHenry and thrust her nose up the woman's skirt.

Mrs McHenry screamed.

'Wassamarrer?' asked Flies. 'Dontcha fancy dogs?'

Mrs McHenry snapped her legs together and recovered her poise, rapping Gigabyte on the nose with her Peace Pledge Union propelling pencil.

'I am a theoretical lesbian separatist,' she announced.

'What's feeretical?'

'It means I don't actually . . .' She coughed delicately and smoothed back a strand of hair that had escaped from her bun.

'Spot! Here, boy!' called Dorothy, dismayed at the turn of the conversation. She held out the last of the egg and cress sandwiches.

'Anyway,' said Wardle, feeling that control of the meeting was escaping from him, 'I'd like your suggestions about our next move. As you know, I've said that I'll phone Wet Nose Solutions on Saturday. Obviously we need to arrange a changeover point where they leave the money and we hand over, er, Spot. I was thinking of the Lancashire-Yorkshire border on the A56 just before Thornton-in-Craven. The road's very twisty and hilly round there, so we could hide quite easily and there's a "Pendle County" sign where they could leave the money. There's also a pub, if that helps to clarify our minds.' He smiled avuncularly at Flies, whom he insisted on thinking of as a decent high-spirited lad.

'I think that's rather a pedestrian plan, don't you?' said Mrs McHenry, still rather pink, who sat with her propelling pencil poised to defend her honour. Unfortunately the sound of her voice reminded Gigabyte of the tantalising delights to be discovered under her skirt and the pencil proved to be no effective deterrent.

'Eeee! Get it off me! This is exactly the sort of mindless male violence that we women have to keep fighting against. Eeee!'

Flies noticed a half-full bottle of whisky on the sideboard.

''Ere, I'll give 'im some of this. That'll send 'im off.' He poured a generous portion into his saucer and called to Gigabyte, who lapped it up eagerly.

'So, what do you suggest we do now?' Wardle asked Mrs McHenry, trying to remember his father's story of how he once silenced the elderly Beatrice Webb. But the memory was gone, and Wardle suspected that Mrs McHenry might have defeated even the indefatigable Arthur.

'I think we should infiltrate Wet Nose Solutions. Destroy the Mafia machine from within. I myself would be quite happy to volunteer for this dangerous mission. Seduce the managing director, get access to his secret files . . .' Mrs McHenry trailed off into a blissful reverie of her new life as Lancashire's Mata Hari.

'Thought you was a lezzie,' said Flies.

'Do I detect a touch of homophobia?' asked Mrs McHenry scornfully.

'Oh, I get that in those shopping centres,' said Dorothy, bowling a Twiglet into Gigabyte's saucer of whisky. 'I went to the Arndale in Manchester one day with my friend Iris and I came over all funny. I felt better after a cup of tea, though.'

Gigabyte, having finished the whisky, began to run in circuits around the sitting room. Every time she passed Flies, of whom she was suspicious despite his generosity with Wardle's whisky, she barked and every time she passed Mrs McHenry she snapped at her skirt. The alcohol boosted her already considerable energy and neither the pencil nor Flies' favourite breaking-and-entering screwdriver could inhibit her. Her tail waved with an anarchic life of its own and teacups, ornaments and lamps crashed to the floor in its wake.

Wardle continued to try to keep a grip on proceedings.

'I'm sure I speak for us all when I say that we are most grateful to Mrs McHenry for her valiant offer on behalf of ELLA. I think, however, that such a level of espionage would be more appropriate at a later stage of the campaign. Meanwhile, the main problem as I see it is to link the receipt of the money with the handing over of the dog.'

'At Morrisons,' began Flies, pouring out another saucer of whisky, 'they've got these trolleys that you 'ave to put a quid into so's you can pull 'em off the others. An' if you chuck 'em into the river then you don't get yer quid back.'

'Oh, *what* a good idea,' said Mrs McHenry with heavy sarcasm. 'All we have to do then is attach seventy thousand shopping trolleys to the dog so that the representatives of Wet Nose Solutions have to put in seventy thousand pound coins before they can release it. That will be *really* quick and unobtrusive, won't it? Eeek!'

Gigabyte, fortified by the second saucer, had completed another circuit.

'Oh, shut up, you silly mare,' said Flies. ''Ere, Spot, you 'ave this last bit, then you'll kip, woncha?'

Gigabyte lapped up the last of the whisky and decided to pussyfoot no longer. She leaped at Flies with a bark that enveloped his nose and knocked him flying into the last surviving lamp, then bounded towards Mrs McHenry. The mystery of that scent was to be solved at last. Mrs McHenry, with a pre-feminist screech, tried to climb on top of the table. She was too late. Taking a corner of the cotton skirt in her mouth, Gigabyte pulled hard. Unfortunately, the skirt, made by a women's co-operative in 1973, was a wraparound design and as the frayed knot snapped, the whole thing fell at Mrs McHenry's feet, revealing a pair of sturdy Marks and Spencer knickers. The pants were modelled to their best advantage by Mrs McHenry's pose, one leg seductively raised to the table top.

Wardle, who had never before seen a woman in her underclothes, screamed and hid behind the sofa. Disturbingly, Mrs McHenry also screamed, yanked her leg down with a nasty grating sound, and hid behind the same sofa, which was where Dorothy found them, both crimson and gibbering, when she came in a few seconds later with another pot of tea. Meanwhile Flies had disappeared out of the window with a cut-glass decanter and four sherry glasses.

'I declare this meeting at an end,' muttered Wardle, his voice muffled by the cushion held protectively in front of his face.

'Yes, I think that's best, dear,' agreed the shaken Dorothy.

Gigabyte was sober enough to beat a tactical retreat and found half a salmon paste sandwich under the hearth rug.

Chapter Eleven

but O, what form of prayer
Can serve my turn?

(iii.iii. 51–2)

On Saturday morning Ophelia took the children out to climb a nearby mountain while Malachi waited for the telephone call from Leafskirk Engineering. After a couple of false alarms the telephone rang at half-past ten.

'Wet Nose Solutions.'

'Hello this is ELLA, I mean Leafskirk Engineering.'

Malachi had intended to stay calm and detached.

'Help! Have you got my dog? Is she all right? You better not have hurt her. Let me hear her. I'm not talking to you until I can hear her.'

'Yes, of course you can,' said Wardle, somewhat surprised. 'Here he is.'

He carried the receiver from his armchair to the hearth rug where Gigabyte was lying.

'Say hello to Daddy,' he whispered

Gigabyte moaned, a long low moan, full of the existential pain of living and the aftereffects of half a bottle of Bells.

'Oh my God!' cried Malachi. 'She's dying. You've been torturing her, haven't you, you evil bastards?'

'No, no, Mr Wet Nose,' protested Wardle, becoming quite flustered. He had never been called a bastard before, even by the retired Major from Pickering who had heard his talk at the church hall. 'The dog's fine, I promise you. You can have him back as soon as we get the seventy pounds, I mean seventy thousand pounds. Have you got the money?'

'We can get it, but it'll take a while. Can you give us, say, four weeks?'

'Oh yes, of course,' said Wardle, envisaging the liquidation of multimillion-pound assets. 'Thank you very much.' Dorothy always told him to be polite when discussing business. 'Goodbye for now then.' He replaced the receiver with a shaking hand and Malachi was left listening to the line's steady hum.

'Bloody poofter,' Malachi commented and reached for the new bottle of sherry.

Ophelia and the children came back in time for lunch. As they sat around the table she asked, in a voice that quavered slightly, 'Did they ring then?'

'Yes. I talked to some transvestite, called himself Ella.'

'What's a transvestite?' asked Hygenus.

'It's that train from Leeds to Manchester, isn't it, Dad?' said Pius.

'Yes that's right. He said she was okay but I heard her and I think she's been t-o-r-t-u-r-e-d.'

'Tortured! Who's been tortured?' asked Joan with irritating intelligence.

'Your teddy bear,' replied Ophelia. 'Urban's tied it to the bathroom light switch again.'

The children shrieked and ran out of the room.

'Anyway,' said Malachi, 'we've got four weeks to get the money. You can manage it, can't you, Oaf?'

'Of course I can, Mal. Don't worry.'

'That Proverbs chap got it wrong, you know. It's not a virtuous wife that's prized above rubies. It's an efficiently dishonest one. Where would I be without you?'

'Pickled, I expect. That reminds me, have you seen the new Mid-Yorkshire Business Directory? I found a copy at work today and Wet Nose Solutions is listed as having a turnover of five million pounds. You didn't tell them that did you?'

'Well I didn't mean to. It was one of those multi-choice questionnaires and I thought I'd ticked the box for five thousand or less. You know that I've never got the hang of all those noughts.'

'Oh well. No harm done,' said Ophelia innocently.

'We're going to the six-thirty Mass today at St Barnabas,' Ophelia announced when the children had returned for their puddings.

'Oh no,' said Hygenus crossly. 'It always bes too long. Why do we have to go?'

'Because we're Catholics,' said Pius piously.

'And because we haven't been since we moved here and because we want to light a candle for Gigabyte to make sure that she has a good holiday. Anyway, your friend Sister Hedwig may be there.'

'She smells like airing cupboards,' said Urban.

'And very nice too,' said Ophelia in her best Mary Poppins voice.

'Now who wants to scrape out the custard tin?'

The Roman Catholic church of Our Lady and St Barnabas was a small dark building hidden away in one of Rambleton's unsigned back streets. Catholic churches invariably fill up from the back so that by the time the O. family filed in, halfway through the Gloria, the only remaining places were in the front pew.

'Lord Jesus Christ, only Son of the Father . . .' recited Ophelia, Malachi, Pius and Joan.

'I want to sit by Daddy,' announced Urban, and promptly felt a bony finger between his shoulder blades.

'Ow,' he said, and turned around. So did Hygenus, who was sitting next to him.

An elderly lady, draped in a musty mantilla, was staring at them with tightly pursed, purple-painted lips. The finger with which she had prodded Urban was still pointed towards them, crooked with infinite menace.

The boys turned back again.

'Witch,' Hygenus explained tersely to his brother and Urban nodded in agreement.

' . . . seated at the right hand of the Father, receive our prayer,' continued Ophelia. She was puzzled. Someone behind her was slightly out of time, reciting the prayer half a phrase behind the rest of the congregation. But there was something else as well, something different, yet familiar about the words. She concentrated harder.

' . . . *ad dexteram Patris, miserere nobis.*' The voice was crisp and autocratic, the careful enunciation loud enough to reach Father Jim on the altar steps. He was rather pointedly looking at the congregation on the other side of the aisle.

I bet she wants you facing the other way, as well, thought Ophelia. None of this Mass-as-a-meal, sharing round the table stuff.

She had noticed the little boys turning round and longed to do the same herself.

I'll have to wait until the Peace, she thought, and smiled to imagine with what horror this aristocratic Latinist would shrink from the post-Vatican II handshake.

' . . .with the Holy Spirit, in the glory of God the Father. Amen,' she concluded, and five seconds later the woman ended with, ' . . . *cum Sancto Spiritu, in gloria Dei Patris. Amen.*'

After Father Jim had read the Gospels, he came down the steps to speak informally to the congregation.

'Brothers and sisters,' he began, 'have you heard the one about the Englishman, the Scottishman and the Irishman? They all died in the same accident and arrived at the gates of Heaven together where St Peter was waiting for them. "Our Father's house has many mansions," said the old saint. "In order to know where to put you, I have to ask you three questions. First of all, what musical instrument would you like to play for your first thousand years?"

' "Oh by Jove, the harp, what?" said the Englishman. "Traditional, don't you know?"

' "I'll be for me bagpipes," said the Scottishman. "Ye'll not stop me from being Scottish, or I'll be straight down to the other place."

' "Oh begorra, that's a mighty hard question," said the Irishman. "I've never been a musical man, but I'll try the pianner, so I will." Or was it the violin? Oh dear, I really don't seem to be able to remember the rest. I am sorry, my dear people. Anyway, the point of the joke is . . . Oh Lord preserve us, I've forgotten the point of the bluddy thing as well. And it was told to me by a real live Cardinal at me niece's wedding in Galway.'

Father Jim beamed round at his congregation. Joan was enchanted by him, leaning forward in the pew with an answering grin. Ophelia and Malachi were smiling too, but Pius was looking superior and the three littlest boys were pinching each other. They were suddenly silenced by a hiss of 'Peasant!' from behind them.

'Anyway, as you know, I don't normally say much at your Saturday evening Mass, so I won't be keeping you long from your suppers. What I meant to say was this. You'll all have heard on the television that a Very Important Person Indeed is to be received into our Church and I'm sure that you'll all be having your little celebrations and giving your thanks to Our Blessed Lady for that.'

'I don't know why we should,' said the voice from behind the O.s. 'Common little German upstarts.' She began to whistle 'The Skye Boat Song', slightly out of key.

'But I'd like you to remember amidst your rejoicing,' continued Father Jim, trying to frown at the woman and smile at the rest of the congregation at the same time, which gave him crossed eyes, 'that some of these Anglicans, I'm not saying this one, but some, think that by becoming Catholics they can keep themselves from coming across any lady priests. Well, I'm sorry, but that's just not the case. Sister Hedwig, come up here a moment, will you?'

The sister rose from her place halfway down the church and came up to the front, a little pinker than usual.

'If I had my way it would be this dear lady who would be your priest, my friends, not an ignorant old bog-trotter like myself who cannot even remember the punch lines of his jokes. Remember that, my dear people, and when the time comes, be ready to greet Hedwig and her sisters with the same joy as you welcome the conversion of your beloved country. Bingo Tuesday seven-thirty as usual, Family Fast Day on Friday, and someone's left a woolly hat in the vestry. We believe in one God . . .'

Sister Hedwig came demurely down from the steps. The sharp voice behind Ophelia said, 'Ridiculous,' and no one except Father Jim himself noticed another woman, large, ungainly and purple-faced, leaving clumsily by the side door. Not many visitors in Rambleton, he thought to himself. I must find out who she is. But when he got back to the presbytery, he found that a parishioner had left him a lemon meringue pie, so all other thoughts went out of his head.

The remainder of the Mass seemed more subdued than usual. Father Jim had used up his histrionic talent in reciting his truncated joke and repeated the Eucharistic prayer in a monotone. The responses were flat and quiet, allowing the Latin variations to ring out even more clearly than before. During the Peace Ophelia allowed herself to turn around and saw, much as she expected, an aquiline woman in her seventies dressed with aristocratic shabbiness, resolutely kneeling and clutching a string of jet rosary beads.

Unlike the jovial family gatherings of Sunday mornings, Saturday evening Masses are not normally followed by coffee, biscuits or parish socialising, so Ophelia did not expect to be introduced to anyone on her way out. To her surprise, however, as she turned from her hasty genuflection, the aisle was blocked by the lady from the pew behind. A leather-covered notebook had been produced from somewhere on her tweedy person and she held a chewed biro in readiness to write.

'New in the parish,' she snapped. 'Name?'

Ophelia, taken aback, gave her name, wondering if she was to join the church cleaning rota or Agnus Dei.

'No Irish blood?'

'No. My husband's parents are Irish, though.'

'Yes, I can see that. He obviously won't be on my list. And you're not a convert, I trust?'

'No. This list . . . ?'

'And how far back have your family been Catholics?'

71

'Well, as far as I know of, but that's only to my great-grandparents.'

'That will have to do. Beggars can't be choosers in a parish like this. Wednesday, seven-thirty for eight.'

'I'm sorry?'

'My Wednesday evenings. Tartleton Court. Just you, if you please. I don't want that husband of yours or any ghastly children. Good evening.'

With that, the tweeds turned sharply and disappeared into the mêlée at the door.

'I see you've met our Lady Tartleton,' said Father Jim at Ophelia's shoulder.

Chapter Twelve

Set me the stoups of wine upon that table.

(v.ii. 264)

Ophelia was woken next morning, as usual, by the removal of her duvet and the kicking by innumerable small legs of what had been the warmest part of her curled back. She reached out with a practised hand and yanked the edge of the quilt back over her torpid body, tucking it protectively under her knees.

'Mummy!' came the indignant cry, as she knew it would. 'Dad, Mum's pinched all the cover again! Tell her!'

'Shhh,' whispered Malachi, padding into the bedroom with a tray of hot drinks. His blue paisley pyjamas were too long for him, and it was all he could manage not to trip over the trouser legs and send tea, Ribena and hot milk in a glorious cocktail over his comatose wife. 'Remember what we said, boys.'

'Oh yeah!' The multiplicity of limbs separated into Hygenus, Urban and Innocent, who crawled out from under the duvet and began to bounce on variously tender parts of Ophelia. 'We're going to be 'specially nice to you today, 'cos of your new job.'

''Cos you're working really hard and making all the money and Dad doesn't do anything.'

'I didn't say *that* exactly,' protested Malachi from the depths of the wardrobe. 'What are we going to make for Mummy?'

'Git-gits,' suggested Innocent.

'No, Innie, not biscuits.'

'Breakfast-in-bed,' chorused Hygenus and Urban.

'That's right. Whatever Mummy wants.'

Brief and hazy visions of country-house sideboards passed through Ophelia's mind: kippers, kedgeree and ironed Sunday papers. They melted like Tennyson's dawn in the silent summer heaven.

'Lovely,' she said. 'Coffee and toast, please,' and drew the duvet back over her head.

The breakfast, when it was eventually borne in by a majestic procession of little boys, was really not too bad. The toast had been left

73

to grow cold before being spread with cooking margarine, the coffee was watery and the Sunday paper was two weeks old, but she had been allowed a blissful hour in bed reading Jennings stories while she waited, and Malachi had remembered her favourite dark Oxford marmalade which disguised even the taste of the margarine. Ophelia munched and slurped, almost with relish.

After breakfast she washed, dressed and, feeling rather like Paddington Bear, made a feeble attempt at removing crumbs and marmalade stains from the sheets. She opened the door cautiously, expecting the tide of devastation by now to be lapping at the bedroom frontiers, and was astonished to find an empty, if grubby corridor. It did not stay empty long.

'Surprise!' cried six simultaneous voices, closely followed by six badly dressed bodies obtruding from four different doorways. Ophelia adjusted Urban's jumper so that he had a sleeve for each arm and removed the nappy from Innocent's head.

'Another surprise?' she asked suspiciously.

Malachi kissed her reverently on the forehead. 'A mere breakfast in bed could never convey the depth of our indebtedness to you, my lady,' he proclaimed, sweeping into a low bow and banging his head on the wall. The grandiloquent effect was further diluted by his having put his old school rugby shirt on not only inside-out but also back to front, so that the erratically sewn nametape faced Ophelia throughout his speech.

'Oh, it was lovely,' she protested. 'But now I think that someone had better do the washing-up.'

'Thou durst not step over the threshold to the kitchen. Durs'n't she?' Malachi turned for support to his doting henchmen, who cheered raggedly. 'For the kitchen be this day the province of males only. Unless Joan the Bone wants to help, that is.'

'No fear,' said Joan. 'I'm going to have a rest with Mummy.'

'Oh, I'm going to rest, am I?' asked the bemused Ophelia.

'Yes, and we're going to cook the dinner,' explained Hygenus.

'An' it's chicken,' said Urban. 'An' that's a secr— Daddy!' He flung himself at his father in a deluge of remorse.

'It doesn't matter, sweetheart.' Malachi picked up the little boy and swung him up to his shoulders. 'Come on, lads, we've got some serious roasting to do.' He disappeared into the kitchen like the Pied Piper, leaving Ophelia shaking her head at the swaying lampshade.

'I'm not eating chicken!' called Joan after them. 'I'm a vegetarian.'

'Since when?' shouted Pius.

'Since Bernadette told me about black puddings. Grue-*some*!'

Malachi had thought of everything, and, once back from a crisp walk with Megabyte, Ophelia and Joan were settled at either end of the sagging sofa, each with a volume of P. G. Wodehouse's short stories and a supply of peanuts, Joan's salted and Ophelia's dry-roasted. They kicked each other companionably and swapped peanuts and books whenever a particularly energetic crunch or giggle required. From time to time Ophelia would notice the thick dust on the television screen, a hairy half dog-chew under the table or damp stain spreading below the window, and would start to get up. Joan would then check her, pointing to the large glass of sherry at her mother's elbow. Gradually, as the morning passed, Ophelia began to notice less and less.

And this did seem to be a particularly long morning. Twelve o'clock went by, and one and two, and still there was no sign of the promised lunch other than the smell of charred skin and the rattle of Malachi's exhaust as he surreptitiously collected fresh supplies from the Sunday grocery in Rambleton. Often there would come a crash, occasionally distinguishable as glass or china. The more serious of these were inevitably followed by Innocent's toddling into the sitting room bearing the diminishing bottle of supermarket fino and enquiring, in a tone which justified his name, 'More shee?'

Ophelia invariably accepted, and thus the morning passed into the afternoon and both passed pleasantly until, around five o'clock, Pius crept obsequiously into the sitting room, a tea towel draped over his arm and whispered, after a deferential cough, 'Dinner is served, Mum, I mean ladies.'

Ophelia, supported by Joan, weaved after him into the kitchen where, through the smoke, she could make out the shapes of Malachi and the three little boys. She felt a sudden rush of sympathy for Napoleonic soldiers during the worst bouts of cannon bombardment. Pius shepherded her to the table, at which the children joined her.

'Ta da!' sang Malachi as he approached the table, bearing a baking tray.

Ophelia's first thought was that it was ten years since she had last seen a doily. However, Malachi had obviously been anxious to remedy the deficiency, for at least eight could be seen adorning the chicken, six providing a delicate carpet for it to rest upon, one folded to form a feathered tail-piece and one fashioned into an elaborate crown, resting on the neck where the unfortunate bird's head had once reposed.

75

Unfortunately, this froth of white paper served only to emphasise the imperfections of the chicken itself. It had probably not been a large bird to begin with, barely enough to feed the O. family, even with Joan's new-found vegetarianism. Now its long sojourn in the oven had robbed it of any flesh worth speaking of, so that its dark brown skin clung directly to its bones like an ageing Hollywood actress after too much sun and liposuction. Ophelia cast a last pitying glance at the shrivelled creature and turned to the vegetables.

These were scarcely better. There were mashed potatoes, gritty lumps in a cold and watery liquid, cauliflower cheese made with processed cheese slices (Innocent having eaten the pound of Cheddar while Malachi braved the oven) and baked beans whose digestibility had been ensured by a three-hour simmer on top of the stove. Poor Joan had not been forgotten. For his only and beloved daughter, her father had improvised a nut roast: ninety per cent unshelled sunflower seeds, eight per cent salted peanuts and two per cent a Brazil nut saved by Urban in his coat pocket from last Christmas. No one, as Malachi plaintively pointed out, had told him that it was customary to add some more viscous material with which to bind the nuts together.

Ophelia took a deep breath, playing for time as her brain plundered its database of tactful responses. It might have saved itself the trouble, for as she was about to try, 'What a very *intricate* chicken,' she caught Malachi's eye and found it sparking with merriment.

'Not my forte,' he confessed. 'Sorry, Oaf.'

'That's okay. I've had a lovely day with the sherry and Lord Emsworth. But I *am* hungry.'

'Hungy!' said Innocent, his lower lip wobbling as he viewed the dinner.

'This is really disgusting, isn't it, Dad?' asked Pius, as they watched Hygenus and Urban playing at inter-planetary ballistic warfare with the cauliflower cheese. The chicken was soon redesignated as a Mk III andranoid space vessel while the mashed potato needed little imagination to become animate slime from the planet Zog, threatening to engulf civilised solar systems in its gravelly tentacles. Joan flew her nut roast mega-yark laser transporter in to assist, and Pius fetched the grapefruit flavoured skimmed milk black hole, alias trifle from its festering place at the bottom of the fridge.

Half an hour later, when the light bulb had been cleaned of custard and Innocent had been changed three times, the children said with aggrieved surprise, 'But we've *still* not had any lunch!'

Ophelia decided that it was time to return to the helm.

When five distinctly grubby children, several with mashed potato in their hair, were jostled through the door of Rambleton's one, surprisingly pleasant Italian restaurant, the young waiter swooped upon them with cries of Mediterranean pleasure.

'*Il bambino! I fanciulli! La ragazza!* Come in, come in. Welcome to our *ristorante*! I find you very nice table, yes? Many chairs, much laughter. Ah! *La madre! Il padre!* Now we have all of *la famìglia,* yes?'

With great relief Ophelia and Malachi allowed themselves to be shepherded towards a large table. The young man, dark-skinned, lithe and smelling pleasantly of *pesto* and cologne, patted them constantly on the shoulders, brushing away stray Labrador hairs and straightening their hasty collars.

'This table, it is nice, yes. Very lovely position, beneath *il spècchio,*' he indicated a large smoked-glass mirror, 'in which *la bella donna* may see her lovely *fàccia*. Now, before you order, a little *pane,* a glass of chianti perhaps, some Coke for *i bambini*?'

The meal was a great success and Ophelia, further mellowed by the chianti and pleasantly full of pasta, gazed unsteadily across the table at her family. The waiter was right, she was indeed *la madre fortunata.* She caught sight of his dark fish-shaped eyes in the mirror and smiled into them. Strange how these Mediterraneans saw life so clearly, even the very young. She imagined the boy's own mother, an enormous Sicilian peasant, perhaps, who would clasp him to her gigantic black-clothed bosom with the same pleasure as Ophelia cuddled little Innocent. Her boys were all clustered around their father now, swapping the discarded crusts of their pizzas for the meatiest portions of his, while Joan womanfully munched her way through a volcano of spaghetti with vegetarian chili sauce. Dear children. Dear Malachi. She *would* get his blasted dog back, whatever it— Ooops.

Ophelia had refilled her glass with the last of the chianti and, amazed at the speed with which the raffia bottle had emptied, had waved it in the air with an expansive Italian gesture. Italians themselves presumably made sure that their freshly filled glasses were well out of the way before making expansive gestures, for she had never seen one down whom red wine cascaded with quite so great abandon. She got up with a delicate squawk, knocked her chair to the ground, and scuttled across the restaurant to the ladies'.

When the O. family had first arrived, they had been the only customers, but in the past half-hour the restaurant had been filling up quickly, and Ophelia had to weave her way past several groups before reaching the toilets. Both cubicles in the ladies' were engaged, and Ophelia had no choice but to listen to the bawled conversation across the division as she gave her dress an ineffectual mopping.

'How's the business then?'

'Can't complain. Not the season for sun-beds, mind. George wants to diversify into Christmas trees but I'm not sure about the needles. My clients won't want pine needles in their you-know-what's when they come for their spring all-over tan treatment. How about yours?'

'Oh, it's bad. Bad and getting worse. Folks won't drink milk these days, you know, just won't drink it. I blame this cholesterol, I do. I remember ten years ago Scorsdale Road was gold top all the way. You could look down from top of t'hill and see the rising sun glinting off all that gold foil. Like the Yellow Brick Road, it was. Now, you can't sell it, of course; just mention it and they feel their arteries hardening. And that skimmed stuff's so flippin' watery I don't blame them for giving up altogether. Every week another one goes. Take that Mr Parrish – you know, the solicitor at The Larches. I thought we could rely on him, but no, he hasn't even taken in his milk for the last six days and he hasn't paid his bill, which he always did on a Tuesday. I wondered if he might be ill, or something, so I asked that lass at his office, but she said he was fine. Very busy, she said. Well, we know what that means.'

'What does it mean, then, Peggy?'

'On a diet.' The words were delivered with a stolid resignation.

The two lavatories flushed simultaneously and the locks were drawn back. Ophelia slipped out of the door, soggy and thoughtful.

On the way out Malachi pressed a generous tip into the young waiter's caressing palm and asked in an avuncular manner, 'Which part of Italy are you from, son?'

The boy looked around carefully before replying, in a lowered voice, 'I'm not from Italy at all. I live just over on the council estate. I'm on a YTS, see, but Mr Orecchino told me that if I were good at it, and sounded dead Italian, he might keep me on. D'ye think I'm doing okay then? I've got to Chapter Three in *Italian Made Simple.*' As Peggy the milklady approached them he raised his voice again, adding a continental embrace. '*Arrivedérci, signor! Addìo, bambini!*'

Chapter Thirteen

Hum, this fellow might be in's time a great buyer
of land, with his statutes, his recognizances, his fines,
his double vouchers, his recoveries.

(v.i. 101–4)

When Ophelia forced herself, fuzzy and fragile, through the door of Parrish, Stanmore and Parrish at five past nine on Monday morning, her bleary eyes were stung by the sight of Polly's electric-blue legs perched on top of a ladder.

'Ophelia, that you?' called a disembodied voice from a gap in the ceiling.

Ophelia stood, swaying slightly at the bottom of the ladder and looked up at the blue tights, red leather mini-skirt and white crochet jumper. 'Yes, it's me, I think. Ask me again after a couple of coffees. What are you doing up there?'

'Looking.' Polly began to descend, revealing a spiky little haircut veiled in dust, blackened hands and an antique torch. 'It was a last report.'

'Last resort.'

'Yeah, that too. I've looked everywhere else, absolutely everywhere.' She waved her arm expressively and the ladder began to wobble.

'Well, come down now, for goodness' sake. It doesn't take much to make me feel dizzy this morning, certainly less than you wobbling up there like the Statue of Liberty with subsidence.'

'Okay,' said Polly cheerily, jumping off the fourth rung and on to Ophelia's foot. ''Snot a proper loft anyway, just a gap between the old ceiling and this hardboard stuff. I remembered that we once stuck Major Lamb's shotgun up there for him when he'd forgotten to renew his licence. But there's nothing there now.'

'Except a lot of dust,' said Ophelia drily. 'Wash your hands and make me a cup of coffee, will you, there's a love? I've had a very busy Sunday, resting. I can't think until I've got a bit more caffeine into my alcohol stream.'

The coffee soon arrived, milky and very strong, and Ophelia cradled it gratefully in her hands.

'So Mr Parrish's document about his burial or whatever definitely isn't in the office?' she asked.

'Defiantly not. I'd looked in all the obvious places last week, you know, and I came in this morning at half-past six to search everywhere else.'

Ophelia gave a little groan.

'Ooh, I don't mind. I like mornings, me. I always used to do my yogi first thing, 'cept that my grandma, that's got the room under mine, moaned like mad. So I've got into this Transcontinental Mediation now, 'cos it doesn't make the floorboards creak as much. And it's dead good for getting things straight in your head.'

'Well, I hope you had a double session this morning, because my head's like the Hampton Court Maze. Anyway, if the instructions aren't here, do you think it would be worth trying to get into his house to have a look there?'

'It wouldn't do any harm, I s'pose. Drink up your coffee, Ophelia, it'll get cold fast with all that milk in. He never kept his papers and stuff at home, mind, always brought everything into the office. You know, bills, letters, magazines, all that. He used to say that his job seemed to be nothing but filling in forms and paying bills, with all the land going registered now, so he didn't want to face a single piece of paper when he got home at night. But this instructions thingy's different, isn't it? That might be there, I suppose.'

'I think I should try to get over to the house anyway,' said Ophelia, and related the conversation she had heard in Mr Orecchino's lavatories. 'Not that I fancy fishing the key out of his pocket.'

'Oh no, you're all right there. He always kept a spare key in the petty cash box. Here you are. Should we both go, d'ye think? I've never been there, so I won't be able to help 'specially, but it'll be quicker if we both look.'

'Yes, please, if you would, Polly. We ought to go as soon as possible in case Peggy the Milk is still calling round.'

'Well, why don't we just close the office early, fourish or something, and pop up? You haven't any appointments and you've got your car, haven't you? Like my uncle Abel says,

> Bet' shearn sheep on t'hill a fortnight early
> Than be shaven thysel by t'horn grewn curly.'

80

'I'll bet he does,' said Ophelia faintly.

If Ophelia had hoped that her rudeness would have driven the Skates to Snodsworth and Ranger then she was soon disappointed. At a quarter past ten, after her third cup of coffee, father and son presented themselves at the front desk, bleary-eyed but voluble. Ophelia came out to intercept them, but they jostled past her and slouched into chairs around her desk. Mr Skate lit an insouciant cigarette and Darren picked his nose as they waited for her to return.

'I'm afraid that I've got some bad news for you,' she began. Darren turned his attention to the other nostril. 'I've checked the current Legal Aid regulations and I really don't think that there is any provision for your case.'

'Oh, you're all right,' said Darren magnanimously. His usually indeterminate diction was exaggerated by his scraping between his teeth as he spoke. 'Me and Sharon are back together so you don't 'ave to do anything about Kylie. Sharon's mum took 'er to a big fight on Saturday and she killed an eighter. Got some sense 'as Sharon's mum.'

'It killed an eight-year-old rat?' asked Ophelia, whose natural history was shaky.

'Nah. An eighter. A rat wot's killed eight other rats.'

'Oh, I see. Like conkers.'

'If you say so,' said Darren, who had only a hazy idea of what a conker was, having spent his childhood enjoying the alternative pastimes of petty theft and criminal damage. He sniffed his armpits pensively.

'Anyway, it's most kind of you to pop in and let me know what has happened,' said Ophelia, rising to conclude the interview.

'No, luv,' interrupted Mr Skate. 'We want your advice on summat else now.' Another cigarette was lit from the first and the still glowing butt thrown on to the floor.

Ophelia's heart executed a spectacular dive. 'Oh yes?'

'That Mick and Doreen next door, they've bought their 'ouse, right?'

'Their council house?'

'Well, they 'aven't bought the 'Ouses of Parliament, 'ave they?' he replied with ponderous sarcasm. 'Yeah, they bought their 'ouse off the council. It only cost a few thousand 'cos they've bin there since they got married, right?'

'Right.'

'But they borrowed more off the building society, see, so now they've got a couple of grand extra to build a conservatory, right?'

81

'Right.' Ophelia was surreptitiously trying to see whether the carpet was on fire from the cigarette end. The smell of the Skates was so pungent this morning that the smoke alarm had probably switched off its sensors in self-defence.

'Well, Mick, 'e's on the sick, like us, in'e, and Doreen, she only works part time down the betting shop.'

'And you'd like to do the same, buy your house from the council?'

'Well, yes and no, if you see what I mean. I'm not bothered about achully buying the 'ouse, bloody old tip it is, with our Darren's rats and all, but I wouldn't mind *saying* that I was buying it to get a bit of a loan, like.'

'I see. And this loan, would it be used for home improvements like your neighbours?' The carpet seemed to be safe, if a little blackened.

'Well, not exactly *home* improvements. More, like, improvements to us *lifestyle*. And a bit for, what would d'ye call it, reinvestment?'

'You mean you'd spend it on beer and fags, and down the betting shop?' translated Ophelia, who was beginning to like Mr Skate despite herself. He obviously sensed this, for he grinned at her in grimy complicity. She wondered whether he might be persuaded to smoke stronger-smelling cigarettes. Gauloises, perhaps. He might even go the whole *cochon* and festoon his neck with a string of onions.

'I've always 'ad an eye for t'hosses,' he was saying. 'And fer women, come to that.' Here he gave her a long wink. 'Problem is, I've never 'ad the chance to realise me potential. Now if I 'ad, let's say five grand, I could double it in a month. You can't f–ing argue with that, can you?'

'I'll look into it for you,' Ophelia promised. 'You know that there won't be any legal aid for this.'

'Not even . . .' He looked hopefully at the row of legal textbooks behind her.

'Not even nothing.'

'Fair enough,' he conceded. 'We'd let you 'ave a reasonable percentadidge. Come on, Darren, I've gotta pick up me new teeth before opening time. See ya then, luv.'

After they had left Ophelia spent some time staring at the Princess Diana calendar on her wall. What on earth had made her promise to consider Mr Skate's scheme? It had been the perfect opportunity to get rid of them while keeping her conscience intact, and she had blown it. She sighed and picked up the new *Law Society's Gazette*.

'Mortgage fraud on the increase,' it proclaimed. 'Solicitors' Indemnity Fund faces record payout.' No escape there. Mortgage fraud was exactly what the smelly old Mr Skate was proposing. She started to turn the page but then stopped.

'Eureka!' The sudden cry from behind the screen disturbed Polly's mid-morning Belgian bun.

'I'm what?' she called back with her mouth full.

' "Eureka". It's what Archimedes said when he realised that when he got in the bath, the equivalent amount of water came out of it.'

'It wouldn't if he hadn't filled it too full in the first place. My mum's always having to tell my brother about that. It's no reason to go round calling people Eekers.'

'No, I suppose you're right,' said Ophelia, not wanting to get further embroiled in Polly's surreal imagination. She wanted to be alone to work out the implications of the idea which was glimmering at her mind's edge.

A quick glance at the *Gazette* showed that mortgage frauds of several million were not uncommon. A mere seventy thousand, plus whatever the clients would want, would scarcely be noticed, hardly meriting a rap on the knuckles from the Solicitors' Disciplinary Tribunal. And there was no doubt but that the lenders deserved it. She had received another letter from the Mid-Yorkshire Champion Building Society yesterday instructing her to ask for additional costs at future oral examinations involving one-legged defendants to cover the time spent holding open the door for them. Then she had tried to use her card in the Arthurian Bank's cash dispenser that morning, only to have it swallowed up with a mechanical belch.

Ophelia took a piece of paper and began to work out the mechanics. Mythical council house sales alone would be unlikely to raise enough capital. In this part of Yorkshire, people still thought that negative equity was what happened when they wired a plug the wrong way round, but the building societies were nervous about ridiculous advances. She skimmed through the article again. Non-existent clients, mythical properties . . . It seemed to involve a serious drain on the imagination. Why not use real clients and real properties? The idea crystallised suddenly: a chain of clients, each in need of money, each pretending to buy the property of the next, but in fact remaining in their own homes. That way she could have access to both the actual properties and the title deeds. She would do all the conveyancing as though the transactions were really going ahead and then at the last moment simply fail to execute the transfers and mortgages. The building societies would expect them to spend the next few months at the Land Registry anyway, so suspicion would be postponed for some time.

But then what? Ophelia wanted first of all to get Gigabyte back, then to give the Mid-Yorkshire and Arthurian a salutary shock. She had no desire to hang on to the money permanently. She thought of Mr Skate's horses and Mr Saggers' chest freezers. Most people only wanted money in order to make more of it. If she chose the members of her chain carefully, then perhaps they could pay back the lenders and still make a profit. She would be carrying out an economic service, really, a maverick business investment scheme.

As for her own cut of the money, there was little hope of recovering the £70,000 ransom money from Leafskirk Engineering. She would just have to repay it by her own efforts. Canards were making money in Rambleton, by all accounts, so it could not be impossible. As a last resort, perhaps Malachi would manage to sell some of his computers. She had asked him why he couldn't get rid of them to raise Gigabyte's ransom. After all, a hundred and fifty computers at £500 each would be more than they needed. He had become evasive, muttering that they 'had a slight technical problem' and were possibly not actually worth even the £100 each that he had paid for them.

'Why don't you get back to the company you bought them from? I could write you a solicitor's stiff letter?'

'Bust,' he had replied, and disappeared into the loo with convenient diarrhoea.

Later he had explained that they were useable 'for limited purposes' and that he had hopes of getting rid of them in quiet ones and twos, chained to a cast-iron contract to be drafted by Ophelia herself. She had said nothing, but reached for the Sale of Goods Act from the top of a nearby book shelf.

Chapter Fourteen

And thus do we of wisdom and of reach,
With windlasses and with assays of bias,
By indirections find directions out.

(II.i. 64-6)

In the afternoon Ophelia had another visitor, a very young man in a grey suit, which was in itself an event in Rambleton. He introduced himself as Geoff Papping of the Lord Chancellor's Department. He flipped open his portable computer and consulted the screen.

'Right. This is, er, Parrish, Stanmore and Parrish. Senior partner Mr Parrish?'

'Yes, but Mr Parrish is on holiday for a few days. May I help you? Ophelia O., senior assistant solicitor.'

'Pleased to meet you. Yes, I would imagine so. Have you heard of the Lawsquad Initiative?'

'No, I'm afraid I haven't.'

'Jolly good, you're not supposed to have done. Very hush-hush. Up to now, of course. Actually, they only thought of it last Thursday so there hasn't really been time for a leak.'

Polly, eavesdropping as usual, broke in.

'Oh, haven't you? You poor man. There's a toilet just over there; the door marked "J. A. Stanmore". Off you go. We won't mind.'

'Actually, I don't think Mr Papping meant that sort of leak,' explained Ophelia hastily, seeing the civil servant's discomfiture. She supposed that this sort of thing didn't happen in Whitehall.

'Er, no thank you. It's the photocopiers, you see. It's standard practice now. Before announcing anything controversial someone goes round and takes all the paper out of the photocopiers. No one knows how to reload them, and without a photocopier you can't have a leak, can you?'

'I suppose not,' agreed Ophelia, 'unless you could put the relevant pages straight through the fax machine.'

'They've thought of that,' said Mr Papping. 'Unbendable staples.'

'I see. So, anyway, what is the Lawsquad Initiative?'

'Well, the most important thing is that it is spelled with an "or" in place of the "aw" and a "kw" in place of the "qu". L-o-r-s-k-w-a-d.'

'Why? And why is it so important?'

'It's supposed to make it more relevant to the man in the street. Snappy, demotic, sounds like a reggae band. Now that justice is to be subject to market forces, the consumer has to be able to identify with it. The classless society, you see. Mustn't discriminate against people who can't spell.' He tapped a few letters, apparently at random, into his computer.

'Of course not,' said Ophelia. 'What do you mean, justice subject to market forces?'

'That's why I'm here, the whole point of the Lorskwad Initiative. The courts are to be privatised, sorry, opened up to the benefits of entrepreneurial achievement, and firms like yours are being given the opportunity to bid for their local franchise.'

'What, to run Rambleton County Court?'

'Yes. The magistrates' court too, if you like, but you'd need to be involved in the security side in that case, and that's notoriously a headache. Basically, how it works is this.' He swivelled the lap-top around so that she could see an elaborate and incomprehensible flow chart displayed on the screen. 'You submit a bid by the end of next week for a year's franchise. Then the highest bidder for each court runs it for a month's trial. At the end of that month the Government look at it to see whether it seems to be working. If it is then you get the franchise for the rest of the year. If not then the courts revert to the Lord Chancellor's Department, everything's kept very quiet, and you don't have to pay a penny.'

The flow chart faded, to be replaced by a horrifyingly accurate graphic of the Prime Minister beaming over the scales of justice.

'So presumably you're expecting running a court to be profitable?'

'Oh yes. You see it'll involve a massive deregulation. All the rules about which county court you can use to issue proceedings will be thrown out, so if you can attract enough business then the sky's your limit. Then the court fees are entirely up to you and you can charge a percentage of damages and costs if you want to. You appoint your own staff, including judges and you can act as judges yourselves; we're getting rid of any requirements like being barristers or solicitors of so many years' standing or whatever. In fact they don't have to be lawyers at all.'

'The classless society again?' suggested Ophelia.

'Exactly. It has been intimated from the very top that firms appointing "judges with experience of real life" will be looked upon extremely favourably.' He gave a deferential nod in the direction of the computer screen.

'What about conflicts of interest? Presumably a firm of solicitors couldn't act in a case being dealt with by their own court, or even worse, where one of them was the judge?'

'Oh, no one's had time to go into that sort of thing. As I said, we want to get rid of all these restrictions. It'll be your court, you run it as you like. Just show lots of marvellous productivity figures and a few heart-warming success stories and your OBE's in the bag.'

'So we could use, say, trial by combat if we liked?'

'Oh yes. That's an excellent idea, you know.' He tried to type on the keyboard but found that the computer had locked upon the holographic image of the Prime Minister and gave only beeps of disapproval. Mr Papping began to panic, patting his empty pockets repeatedly until Ophelia passed him a pencil and a piece of paper.

'Thank you so much. Yes, an excellent idea. You could combine it with a theme park and get a European Tourism grant which would cover most of the cost of the franchise. I see that you've really got the hang of all this.'

'Hmmm. One other thing. What's the hurry? Why is this all going ahead so quickly? It usually takes you years to get anything new going.'

'I think that I'd prefer not to comment on that, if you don't mind, Mrs O. I'd just ask you to consider how long it is since the last General Election and the fact that a new showpiece privatisation, in the first flush of success, might be a welcome, er, *distraction.* Now let me leave you this information pack and envelope for your bid. It's been a pleasure talking to you. No, no, I'll see myself out. Thank you so much.'

As he closed the door behind him, Polly was already wriggling into her leather jacket and recording her message on the answering machine. Mr Parrish had always refused to have one, insisting that anyone foolish or hasty enough to want to contact him outside the civilised hours of half-past nine and four o'clock deserved nothing more co-operative than an unanswered ringing tone. He had not, in fact, according to Polly, even become used to the idea of there being more than one telephone in the office, and would snatch up his own in distracted confusion whenever he could hear hers ringing. As both telephones were connected to the same line the consequences had often been difficult, especially when Gary, in an unusual fit of amorousness, had phoned Polly to tell her that she was his little pumpkin-bottom.

'Pumpkin Bottom?' Mr Parrish had roared, having no faith in the amplificatory powers of British Telecom. 'One of your fields, is it? Boundary problem? Well, I'll look at the deeds for you, if you like, but I won't take it to court.'

'Yes, sir, I mean, no, sir,' had stammered the paralysed Gary.

'Always remember a little rhyme that Father taught me:

> Plaintiff or defendant
> If the case concerns a boundary,
> Keep it from the court, or else
> Your brief will surely founder-ee

Not exactly Milton, but I'm sure you see the point.'

'It's not—' Gary had begun, but Polly was quicker-witted.

'This is the operator,' she had announced, holding her nose between her finger and thumb, and doing her best to remember the right wording from the old Ealing film she had seen the week before. 'Your two minutes are up. I shall now be cutting you off. Beep, beep, Crash.'

'Funny,' Mr Parrish had said, looking reflectively into the humming receiver. 'I haven't heard them say that for a while.'

Ophelia sometimes longed to be back in an era when the most immediate form of communication was the telegram, and completions took place at a gentlemanly rendezvous, rather than muttering 'Formula B' into a telephone, but her professional self had been horrified at the lack of an answering machine and had installed one even before Mr Parrish was fully frozen. Polly was enchanted by it. Every day the message would be changed, becoming more elaborate and genteel each time.

'Par-reesh, Starnmore and Par-reesh,' she was saying now, squeezing her vocal cords in a painful attempt to eradicate her Yorkshire accent. 'We are frightfully sorry thart no one is available to be of acceptance to you. Do please leave a message after the musical tone so that we may get bark to you as soon as possible. Good evening.'

'Right,' she added in a normal voice, as soon as she had pressed the Stop button. 'That'll shut 'em up till morning. Let's go.'

* * *

The Scorsdale Road was long and leafy, rising gently from the west end of the town into the undulations of the Dales. The houses were all set far back from the road, screened by trees and high hedges, and it was very quiet. Ophelia drove slowly, checking the name of each house as it appeared, burned into rustic bark or swinging from a miniature wrought-iron gallows. Every driveway, with its incandescent Mercedes or Audi, sleek Jaguar or lovingly preserved pre-war Rover, made her more conscious of her Volvo's dirt and dents. Polly was wriggling on the passenger seat.

'Ooh, ooh, slow down. I think it might be this one. Look, those are larches, aren't they? And there's the sign. Yes! The . . . Laurels. Oh, hurry up, Ophelia, can't you drive any faster?'

Eventually, about halfway up the hill, they found it. It was not actually one of the biggest houses, and had none of the expensive accretions of the more flamboyant, other than a neat, old-fashioned tennis court. Ophelia turned into the drive with assumed bravado and parked on the gravel.

Upon closer inspection it was clear that the tennis court was not a later addition, but that the house and court had been designed together. It would not even be an exaggeration to say that the house was designed for the tennis court, for its principal windows, pretty terrace and two sets of French windows all looked out on to the quiet grey rectangle. From these French windows A. A. Milne's Rabbits or William Brown's elder brother and sister might have dashed, dropping thirties' slang with their wooden tennis racquets. In short, it was a little bit of Betjeman's Surrey in the depths of Mid-Yorkshire.

While Ophelia was thinking all this, imagining herself as nineteen and white-skirted, Polly had got to work.

'Here's Peggy's milk, anyway,' she called from the porch, where seven full bottles stood, in decreasing order of degeneration. Several had notes underneath, and Polly removed these and read them aloud.

' "Dear Mr Parrish. Please let me know if you wish to alter or cancel your order. Sincerely, M. P. Braithwaite (Mrs)."

' "Dear Mr Parrish. I hope you are not unwell. Sincerely, Margaret Braithwaite (Mrs)."

' "Mr Parrish. It is customary to inform your dairy supplier when you intend to go away. M. P. Braithwaite."

' "Mr Parrish. I would remind you of your oral contract with Braithwaite's according to which all milk delivered must be paid for whether or not consumed. I would also draw your attention to the embossed notice on the side of the bottles stating clearly that they are the property of the dairy. M. P. B.'"

Polly emptied the contents of all seven bottles down a nearby drain, flinching at the contents of the earliest. She turned over the most recent note and wrote on the back of it.

'Dear M. P. B. (Mrs). I have given up milk out of sympathy with the Cow Libation Front. I enclose payment for your milk bill. Please use the change to buy yourself a book about Equitette. Sincerely, W. W. P. (Mr).'

She then took a ten-pound note from her purse, wrapped it up with the message and placed it in the neck of the nearest bottle.

'That's told her,' she said, and placed her key in the front door lock. 'After you, Ophelia.'

The heavy door opened reluctantly against the mass of post piled up behind it, and as she pushed, Ophelia looked down at the red-tiled floor to be sure that there was nothing to be crushed. She had no idea, therefore, that anything might be lying in wait for her, stretched out along the top of the broad gilt mirror. The door edged around, revealing a growing segment of patterned rug. The hinges squeaked very slightly, and there were faint sounds of wind and distant traffic; otherwise it was silent. A few more inches, and she could sidle through the gap into the still, wax-polished hall.

'Aaaeeerhhh!'

The impact was directly upon the back of her neck, with no warning, neither rush of air nor glimpse of movement, just this cacophony of sensation, soft (or was that just her own hair?), lacerating, squirming and ruthless. Her brain's failure to make sense of the attack was more frightening than the blow itself, and she struggled, twisting her neck in panic and reaching back with hands that were similarly by turn scratched and then stroked .

'Polly, Polly!' she whimpered.

But Polly, slipping through the door after her, was no help, for the sight, presumably even more horrific than the sensation, had driven her into a hysterical frenzy.

'A-ark, a-ark!'

The choking whoops were painful to hear and, even as the thing around her neck squeezed more tightly, Ophelia held a bleeding hand out to comfort the younger girl. But the hand was not taken.

'Poll,' Ophelia gasped. 'What is it, Poll? Do you know?' As she

90

asked the question she realised its futility. How could a child like Polly be acquainted with the arcane classifications of demonology? Whatever fiendish creature, alive or undead, was sucking the blood from her throat, its name and purpose could never be spoken by the innocent of heart. As its grip tightened yet further, she could hear a bell sounding, to summon her to Heaven or to . . .

'It's a cat,' spluttered Polly, between her giggles.

Ophelia looked up into the mirror, at her own face, bleached and foolish, and at the smaller one which hung over her shoulder. It was indeed a cat, little more than a kitten, black splodged unevenly with white, his green eyes gazing plaintively at his own reflection. Around his neck, attached by a blue velvet ribbon, was the little silver bell that Ophelia had heard calling her to judgement. Now that she was still, and he no longer needed to struggle to keep his perch, he gave a long and piercing mewl of desperate hunger.

'Oh, the poor little thing!' cried Polly. 'And I've just poured seven pints of milk down the drain. Come on, let's find the kitchen first.'

The kitchen was not hard to discover, at the end of the long shining corridor, with the cat's increasingly excited meows to guide them. It was a large room, with an old-fashioned dresser and white-painted cupboards, all scrupulously clean and tidy. Only a single cup and saucer, left to drain on a rack by the sink, suggested that it had been used in the last half-century. As the cat still clung to Ophelia's neck, Polly found several tins of cat food in one of the cupboards, and spooned a generous portion on to a china plate. He sprang down to eat the food, hastily but still with a fastidious care, paused to give his paws and whiskers a cursory wash, and leapt back up to Ophelia's shoulder. He stayed there for the remainder of their tour of the house, disdaining all attempts to coax him down, breathing fishy fumes down the back of Ophelia's jacket and making her feel like a cross between Long John Silver and Martyn Lewis.

The search did not take long, for Wilfred Parrish's house was as well-ordered and bare as his office was crowded and chaotic. In room after room, only a faint layer of dust disturbed the perfect order of linen, mahogany and shelves of leather-covered books, well read and well cared for. One, a volume of John Masefield's poetry, lay beside his smooth bed, a bookmark halfway through its fragile pages. Polly had been right; there were no papers to be found anywhere in this quiet sanctuary, only a little packet of love letters from the courtship of his wife.

91

'Let's go now,' whispered Ophelia, ashamed to intrude further. Her feet seemed too muddy, her step too quick for the silence. The cat rubbed his head against the side of her head in reassurance. They decided to take the post back to the office to be dealt with and loaded it into the boot, where it was hidden by an old picnic rug. As she turned back into the road an unexpected creak came from the rear of the car, but it had so many rattles and squeaks that she thought nothing of it.

'We'll have to go back every day to feed the cat and get the post, won't we?' asked Polly.

'Oh yes, but we'll have to make sure we avoid the cleaning lady. You wouldn't know when she comes, would you?'

'Oh, he never had one. I remember him saying that he did all the cleaning himself. Very proud of it he was. "I can polish a table so you can see the colour of your eyes in it," he said, and he was right, wasn't he?'

At home that evening Ophelia asked the rest of the family how much they would pay to run the court for a year.

'A million pounds!' shouted Hygenus.

'About five hundred pounds, I think,' said Pius, biting his lip in concentration.

'That dump you were telling me about?' asked Malachi. 'Excuse me.' He gave an enormous sneeze and wiped his streaming eyes.

'Are you getting a cold, Mal? You haven't stopped sneezing since I got home. Yes, it is a bit of a tip.'

'How on earth could you make it profitable, then? Unless you could get hold of the shopfront underneath, of course, in which case Wet Nose Solutions could have a useful retail outletishoo! Say ten thousand.'

'Six pounds forty-three,' suggested Urban, which was the total in his piggy bank, carefully counted that afternoon.

'Nothing,' said Joan. 'I'd rather run a circus.'

'From what I hear, it needn't be much different,' muttered Ophelia. 'Any ideas, Innocent?'

'Milk. Hot.'

'Righto.' Ophelia entered their suggestions, valuing the hot milk at forty-five pence, into her calculator. She worked out the average, wrote it down on a piece of Parrishes' headed paper and put it in the Lorskwad envelope.

'Just take this down to the post for me, would you, Pius, while I make the supper?'

Chapter Fifteen

There are more things in heaven and earth, Horatio,

(I.V. 174)

Pius, who was busy building an observatory on top of the pigsty, forgot to take the letter until after supper, when it was too late for him to cycle the half-mile to the nearest postbox. Instead, Malachi posted it on his way to the Rambleton off-licence in the car.

As he drove back into the yard the security light came on and Ophelia, who was finishing the washing-up, could see out of the kitchen window on to the floodlit concrete. Malachi looked dreadful as he stumbled out of the driver's door and groped his way around to the boot, leaning on it for support for a few seconds before opening it up and removing the carrier bags full of beer cans.

'Oh Mal, they weren't having another Madeira evening, were they?' cried Ophelia, dashing out into the yard, her hands dripping with the slime which she had been extracting from the plughole.

'I've not had a drop,' replied Malachi indignantly, wiping his streaming eyes with the back of his arm, 'not even the medicinal brandy they offered me on the house. No, it's this cold. It got really bad while I was driving. I could hardly see and felt all sick and . . .' He slumped over the tailgate and said no more.

'By the way,' he added half an hour later, tucked up in bed with a hot-water bottle and spiked Guinness, 'there's a dreadful squeak from that rear axle. Had you noticed it?'

Next morning he seemed better, so Ophelia went to work as usual and she and Polly sorted out Mr Parrish's post.

'I thought I'd pop up there myself at lunch,' said Polly. 'Get the bus. I mean, if we go in your car every day it might be a bit, y'know, abstrusive.'

'Abstruse?' Ophelia was mystified.

'Abstrus*ive*. You know, sticking out, obvious. I thought you were an interlectual.'

Ophelia looked quizzically at Polly, who was again wearing her purple leather jacket and red leather skirt, combined, as the morning was a chilly one, with a pair of orange Lycra leggings. She suspected that the outfit might have the edge over her beige Volvo when it came to publicity, but did not like to thwart the secretary's good intentions.

'Fine. You'll get the post and feed the cat, then?'

'Yes, and I thought I'd have another scout round to see if he had any, like, secret hiding places. You know, electric sockets that turn out to be wall safes, and that. You know, Alf Roberts has got one.'

'So he has,' agreed Ophelia, pleased to see that whatever Polly's wilder fantasies, she was firmly grounded in the cobbles of Coronation Street.

But when Polly returned in the afternoon she was downcast.

'No hidden wall safes?' asked Ophelia.

'No, nothing. And I couldn't find the cat anywhere. I called it, but it had to be quietly and just Kitty, 'cos we don't know its name, but it wouldn't come. D'ye think I should go back this evening?'

'No, leave it until tomorrow. You know what cats are like; it'll have found six or seven soft-hearted families to feed it by now, all of them thinking that they're the only ones. Don't worry about the cat, Poll, concentrate on these blasted instructions. Anyway, can you hold the fort here for the rest of the afternoon? Joan's just phoned to say that Malachi's really ill. She's not one to panic unnecessarily so I've told her to ring the doctor and that I'll be straight back. That okay?'

'Of course.' Polly took off her jacket, hung it on the back of Ophelia's chair and perched on the desk. 'Just leave everything to me.'

Ophelia arrived home at the same time as Dr Horatio Hale. Despite their erratic diet, supervised by Malachi, which seemed to Ophelia to consist entirely of crisps and winegums, the children were all large and sturdy and enjoyed health which was not so much rude as downright obscene. They had consequently not yet met their new doctor. He turned out to be shortish and slightly overweight but blessed, or otherwise, with what Ophelia's mother would have called 'bedroom eyes' and a deliciously curdling public-school accent.

'Mrs O., I presume?' he murmured as she got out of the Volvo, which, incidentally, had lost its extra squeak. Ophelia nodded clumsily and they went into the house together.

Malachi was lying in bed, fully clothed and rugby-booted, with the duvet pulled up over his head. When Ophelia drew it back, he blinked up at her out of swollen and bloodshot eyes, tried to speak, and sneezed more violently than ever. Dr Hale unfastened his black bag and, very politely, motioned her out of the room.

When she came back they were talking in low serious voices. She draped herself about the open doorway for a couple of minutes, but neither Malachi's blond head nor Dr Hale's dark one lifted, and their twin bald spots bobbed in serious conference. Ophelia coughed, but still there was no response. She approached the bed, until she could hear the conversation.

'He wasn't called "The King" for nothing!' Dr Hale was protesting.

'That's exactly what I mean. Rugby is a team game. We can't be doing with kings. Democracy in action, that's what it should be. Those Springbok backs weren't so keen, were they?'

'Democracy! Look what happened in the second '33 Test. He did what they'd wanted, threw his feet away, and the Ozzies slaughtered them. Rugby's not about democracy, it's about talent.'

'What on *earth* are you talking about?' asked Ophelia, noting that whatever it was, the restorative effect on Malachi was astounding.

'Bennie Osler, South African fly half, twenties and thirties.'

'And Stanley's underrated, you know.'

'Stanley?' Ophelia was wondering why on earth she had rushed away from a fascinating affidavit of plight and condition in order to stand about in a smelly bedroom listening to drivel about men in baggy shorts.

'His brother. Played for Oxford in '31.'

'When you've finished in the Rugger Hall of Fame, perhaps you could tell me what's wrong with my husband?'

'Of course. Well, it's not a cold.'

'Not a cold. Right. And?'

'It looks very much like hay fever.'

'Hay fever.' Ophelia looked out of the window at the bleak autumn landscape, upon which a few drops of rain were beginning to fall.

'But it obviously isn't,' concluded Dr Hale hastily.

There were some moments of silence. Neither Dr Hale nor Malachi seemed to think that any more needed to be said.

'Er, do you have any idea of what it is, then?' asked Ophelia awkwardly, not liking to destroy their little oasis of tranquillity.

The doctor continued to stare out of the window, humming quietly to himself.

'Allergic to anything, old chap?' he asked suddenly.

'Yes,' replied Malachi. 'Talcum powder. Makes me sneeze and itch like anything, especially that stuff for athlete's foot. Used to have to tell the lads not to bring it into the changing rooms.'

'But there's no talc in the house,' objected Ophelia. 'There never is.

97

I even do the babies' bottoms with cornflour. So it can't be that.'

'Can't it?' asked Dr Hale regretfully. 'No, I suppose it can't. Well, pop down to the surgery when you're feeling a bit more the thing, and we'll run some tests.'

'Right oh,' said Malachi.

'I always like saying that, you know, "run some tests",' mused the doctor. 'Sounds so bloody professional, don't you think? Well, cheerio, nice meeting you, Mrs O. A pleasure.' And he was gone.

Malachi was staring down at the duvet cover, a little frown on his pink and white face. 'I don't know,' he muttered. 'I don't know.'

'What don't you know, love? What's the matter?'

'Stanley Osler. I still think Hale's too hard on him. Can't have been easy, trying to live up to that brother.'

Ophelia sighed and took his hot-water bottle downstairs to be refilled.

Megabyte was lying across the kitchen doorway, groaning to herself. As Ophelia approached she raised one ear and turned her head slightly, with an expression of agonised endurance.

'Hello, Megs. Cheer up. We will get her back, you know. I've got a plan now.'

But Megabyte was not mourning her daughter. She rose with a low snort and nudged her empty bowl so that it vibrated gratingly on the dusty floor.

'Have they all forgotten to feed you? Is that it? Joan! Pius! Has anyone fed the dog today?'

'Yes, I did it as soon as I got in.'

'Yeah, half an hour ago!'

'I feeded her too!'

'Mistress Megabyte O., you *bad dog.* You've had at least three dinners. Now is it really fair to take advantage of Malachi's being ill like this?'

Megabyte looked from Ophelia to the bowl with undiminished accusation.

'Megabyte! You could at least give up with some grace when your little scam's been uncovered. Now go on, get in your bed. Honestly, sometimes I don't—'

But neither Megabyte nor the children found out what Ophelia sometimes did not do, for at that moment the telephone rang. It stopped in the middle of its third ring, presumably having been answered by Malachi in the bedroom. She absently filled his hot-water bottle from the cold tap and went through.

98

'Hello, Julia darling,' he was saying in a deadpan voice but with his face contorted into an expression of hideous mania, his lower lip twisted down in a clown's grimace and his eyebrows drawn closely together.

'No, darling, no proper job yet, darling. Bridge going well, my precious? Ah. Ophelia darling, you'll never guess. It's your poppet of a mother.'

Ophelia gave him a warning glance as she took the receiver.

'Hello, Mummy.'

'Darling. How are you, darling? Still in that dreadful shack? And Malcolm tells me that he still doesn't have a job. It's really not good enough, darling. Even your father managed forty years with the bank. They just need a bit of encouragement. I know Malcolm's a sweetie, always so affectionate towards me, but you have to *prod* them a bit. Like cows, darling, they just need a little mild electrocution.'

'Mummy, he's called Malachi, not Malcolm. And he has a job, he's a company director. That should sound well enough to your bridge club.'

'Well, of course it would, darling, but then they ask what company, don't they, and I have to say that rather rude wet nose thing. And as for Malachi, we may be Catholics but we certainly don't have to *advertise* the fact. Anyway, darling, what I rang to say was, I may be going on a little toddle. So will you telephone your father from time to time and check that he's behaving himself? Oh goodie. Now I must dash, darling, he's *swinging* in the conservatory. Love to the poppets.'

'Doddling again?' asked Malachi through his sinuses, as Ophelia replaced the receiver.

'Toddling, yes.'

'Where to this time?'

'I've no idea. Somewhere hot, doubtless. I think Tenerife is a bit passé now. It was Florida last autumn, then Nepal in January . . . Whatever. I expect we'll get a postcard. But, Mal, do you have to darling her quite so much? Even she's bound to twig eventually.'

'Not her. Your mother wouldn't recognise irony if it dressed up as Omar Sharif and dealt her a hand of thirteen aces. Hatishoo!'

The telephone rang again and Ophelia picked it up.

'Hello again, Mummy. No, Mummy, you know we don't even get the *Telegraph* and if we did then we wouldn't have time for the crossword. What? South American reptile, seven letters, second might be M. All right, I'll ask Pius. He'll ring you back if he knows. Bye-bye, Mummy. Have a lovely toddle.'

Ophelia rang off hastily before she burst out laughing at Malachi's impression of a South American reptile at a ladies' bridge party.

'If you're feeling that much better then you can sort these socks.' She took a basket of indeterminate grey wool and emptied it on to the duvet. 'I'm just going to put Innie to bed.'

Chapter Sixteen

Excellent, i'faith, of the chameleon's dish.

(III.ii. 93)

Next day the symptoms of Malachi's unseasonal hay fever did not actually seem to be lessening, but he was growing used to them and was able to get up and deal with the children. Dr Hale had called around again in the afternoon but all that Malachi could recall of the conversation was an argument as to the number of international tries scored by Cyril Lowe.

'But didn't he say anything about your sneezes?'

'Not that I can remember. We had to get the books out, you see, to check all the tries.' Malachi made a wide gesture with his arm which encompassed the ten or twelve rugby handbooks and biographies which littered the sitting-room floor. 'And then he found he was late for something, emergency surgery or an operation, some such thing. Anyway, I feel much-oo! Better.'

'It's this Lady Tartleton thing tonight. I'd better phone and say that I can't come.'

'No, don't do that, Oaf. I'll be fine. And I don't think I'd like to cross her if I were you.'

'No, she'd probbly turn you into a frog,' said Hygenus, who was hanging about in the doorway with his hands behind his back. 'Can I have a biscuit?'

'Just one, supper's nearly ready,' said Malachi.

'Oh good, 'cos I've already had it.' Hygenus brought out his hands, imbued with warm chocolate, and disappeared to incite the others.

Tartleton Court was a heavy, low grey stone building built in a U-shape around a mossy courtyard. Ophelia parked on the cobbles between a battered Land Rover and a Mercedes 190 and followed a middle-aged couple through the main doorway. The hallway inside contained a row of stout aluminium coat-pegs which reminded her of school. She hung up her Barbour along with all the others, surreptitiously combed her hair and passed through a stone archway towards the sound of voices.

101

She was a few minutes late, as she had called at The Larches on the way. There was still no sign of the little cat, although she had called to him by every name suggested by his peculiar black and white face. Eventually, after 'Panda', 'Domino', 'Jaguar' and 'Kitchen Floor Tiles', she had given up and walked back up the sloping lawn towards the drive. On the way she had passed the back door to the garage, which they had overlooked before. The door was unlocked but inside she found only a collection of woodworking tools, neatly hanging over a workbench, an old-fashioned petrol lawnmower and a stack of back issues of the *Sunday Telegraph*, each folded at the prize crossword, with seven or eight of the clues tentatively pencilled in.

'Pity you never met Mummy,' Ophelia had said aloud, and started as a mouse scurried into the corner of the garage. No cat in here, then. After a feeble attempt to rub the dust and newsprint from her clothes she had left the garage and climbed back into the Volvo.

The room which she now entered was very large and very cold. Threadbare tapestries hung on the walls, their green and gold patterns hardly visible under the dim electric lights. A huge fireplace was miserably heated by a tiny smouldering pile of coals before which three handsome black Labradors were scuffling. Although they were male dogs, larger and more powerful than Megabyte and the puppy, they wrestled with the same mixture of pride and playfulness. As Ophelia watched one suddenly deflected from a winning cuff by the more glorious prize of his own tail and another pausing halfway through a bout for an affectionate lick, she could not help but think of Meg, lonely and despairing under the kitchen table, and of Gigi, far away beyond the Pennines. She managed to keep the tears at bay, but could not prevent a snuffling tickle at the back of her nose. Ophelia searched in vain for a handkerchief. She was wondering whether she dared wipe her nose on her sleeve when a military gentleman assailed her with heavy gallantry.

'Halloa! A new young lady come to join our little gathering. How charming, how very charming. Do let me get you a sherry. Sweet or dry?'

'Oh dry, please.'

'How very liberated of you. I do hope you aren't too liberated in other directions, eh? Not that I don't think you're right.' Here he lowered his voice. 'To be quite frank with you, Lady T.'s sherry is absolutely dire. *Not* the thing at all. According to my wife, who accidentally picked up my glass one evening, the dry is slightly less ghastly than the sweet.

I've never tasted sweet sherry, of course. Not a wufter, what?'

With that he turned on his heel and marched with a faint limp towards a dim sideboard on the other side of the room.

While he was gone Ophelia looked about her, taking care to avoid the Labradors. There were only about twelve people in the room, mainly faded elderly ladies with the odd consort. Ophelia recognised Lady Tartleton, chastising a cowed maid, and, the only other person under sixty in the room, the good-looking solicitor whom she had met at Rambleton County Court. He was sitting on a shabby chaise longue talking earnestly to a lady in a turquoise tweed dress. She was nodding enthusiastically and edging closer to him in response to his carefully modulated bedside manner.

'Touting for business, I see,' said Ophelia to herself as the military gentleman returned, bearing her glass of sherry in a ceremonial fashion and followed by an obedient woman in plum-coloured Crimplene.

'Here you are, my dear. Cheers! May I introduce my wife, Letitia. Letitia this is . . . ?'

'Ophelia O. I'm an assistant solicitor at Parrish, Stanmore and Parrish in Rambleton.'

'Pleased to meet you, my dear. Frederick Lamb, Major, retired.' Each word was boomed out like a cannon salute. Mrs Lamb gave an almost imperceptible nod of her head but said nothing.

'So where's old Wilfred tonight then? Usually a regular at Lady T.'s evenings, is Wilfred. Not seen him at Mass since his mother died but he doesn't usually miss her ladyship's Wednesdays. Wouldn't dare. Court-martialling offence, what?'

Major Lamb laughed heartily and his wife smiled, gazing at him in obvious adoration. Ophelia panicked and said the first thing that came into her head.

'He's gone bowling.'

'Bowling? What, crown green bowls? At this time of night? The man must be mad. How the devil can he see what he's doing? D'ye hear that, Letty? Old Wilfred's gone to play bowls in the park. Finally flipped. I always said he would, didn't I, Letty, miserable old bugger (excuse me, ladies) living by himself like that.'

'No, no,' interrupted Ophelia, envisaging a search party scouring Rambleton's Councillor Pillmore Memorial Park for a lunatic bowls-playing solicitor. 'Not bowls. Ten-pin bowling. There's a new place opened in Leeds.'

'Ten-pin bowling!' exploded the Major. 'Isn't that what those damn

Yanks play? Skittles, isn't it? What does a grown man want with playing skittles? Never heard anything like it. D'ye hear that, Letty? Says Wilfred's playing skittles in Leeds. What's he want to go to Leeds for? I haven't been to Leeds since 1944, except Headingley, of course. Damn good Roses match this year, wasn't it, Letty? But I wouldn't go to Leeds for anything else. Full of natives, now, so they tell me. Damn good chaps at home in India but I don't know what they want in Yorkshire. Bloody cold. What's Wilfred doing with these Yanks and natives then?'

'I think there's a possibility that the firm might be acting for them,' said Ophelia desperately.

'Parrishes acting for an American bowling arcade!' scoffed a new voice. The handsome solicitor had sidled up to their group. '*Most* unlikely. There are major international firms in Leeds, you know, if they wanted someone local.'

'I am aware of that!' flashed Ophelia. 'I imagine that Mr Parrish must have been recommended to them.'

'Old Parrish recommended?' he sneered. 'Yes, possibly, if they wanted a sheep evicted from a cow pen and didn't mind waiting forty years for it to be done!' He laughed unpleasantly and walked away.

'Steady on!' barked the Major to his retreating back. 'In my day young men didn't speak like that about chaps old enough to be their fathers.'

'All the same,' he addressed Ophelia now, 'he's quite right. I can't see anyone recommending Wilfred, especially to Americans.'

'I expect I've got a bit confused,' fluttered Ophelia, falling back on the last feminine weapon of incompetence. 'Who is that man, anyway?'

'Who, Nick Bottomley? Haven't you met him yet? He's a partner at Canards, your rivals. It was his uncle's firm, you know, so young Nick got the whole thing given him on a plate. Arrogant young cub. The ladies go for him, you know.'

Here he fixed Ophelia with a serious stare, as though inspecting her for signs of incipient infatuation.

'Can't stand the blighter myself and neither can Lady T.,' he continued. 'Not a Catholic, you know. But he's a trustee of the Tartleton Trust so she has to keep in with him. Now, why don't you come over and have some nosh? Always puts on a fine spread, our Lady T. All good meaty stuff. None of this vegetarian nonsense.'

He strode, limping slightly more now, towards a linen-covered trestle table set up against the wall near the fireplace. Letitia and Ophelia followed in single file, like members of a decorous harem.

At one end of the table a large silver tureen was filled with what appeared to be boeuf bourguignon, thick, dark and aromatic. A platter of sliced baguettes was its only simple and appropriate accompaniment. A stack of shallow dishes, gold edged and crested, stood next to the platter with a heap of heavy silver forks. Further down the table were a stack of matching plates and another silver salver piled with triangles of toast generously spread with pâté. The only other foods were several bowls of unusual pretzel-type snacks, larger and darker than those commonly served on such occasions.

Ophelia ate one of these absent-mindedly, worried about her bowling alley gaffe, and picked up a plate. No one else had yet broached the boeuf bourguignon and she did not dare to be the first so she took three triangles of pâté-covered toast to sustain her while she waited. They looked delicious and she was very hungry, Malachi having miscalculated the fish fingers for supper. She bit into the first, relishing the crisp crunchiness of the toast, the delicate layer of best butter and the rich, gamey, oddly familiar tang of the pâté. Very oddly familiar. She looked again at the labradors before the fireplace, who were regarding the table with a peculiar complacency.

The Lambs were talking to another couple with their backs to Ophelia and there was no one else nearby. Ophelia had noticed a door just behind the table which, from the smells and glimpse of melamine, seemed to lead to a kitchen. She looked around again and quickly slipped through the door.

It was not the handsome farmhouse kitchen she had envisaged, with pine scrubbed table and Aga, but a small and miserable room furnished with 1970s kitchen units, scratched and stained. Near the door was a small plastic pedal bin. This was what Ophelia was looking for. She pressed down the pedal with her best court shoe and peered inside.

It was just as she had thought. With a thumb and forefinger she removed the evidence: a plastic package marked 'Tartan Game Luxury Dog Food'. Inside the plastic clung remains of the excellent pâté. Ophelia was still looking into the open bin when she heard a voice behind her.

'Please don't tell anyone.'

Lady Tartleton stood in the middle of the kitchen, a flowered apron over her faded lavender cashmere. Her patrician features were softened by chagrin and her tone was pleading.

'It's not harmful, you know. In fact it's probably more nutritious than the usual rubbish people serve nowadays. The dogs certainly look well enough on it, don't they?'

'Is it all . . . ?'

'Dog food? Oh yes. The pâté, the boeuf bourguignon, those silly things, what do people call them, "nibbles"? I've been serving them for years and no one has ever guessed until now. How did you know?'

'I've got Labradors myself.'

'Ah, that explains it. You'll know how cheap this stuff is then. The "boeuf" is economy dog food from the supermarket, you know. I couldn't afford Chum.'

'Are you very short of money?'

'Well they say I'm not – your Mr Parrish who is my own solicitor, and that young man in there who is trustee of Cecil's family trust. Cecil was my husband, you know, died in '81. They say that there's plenty of money but what with this damn inflation and property prices going down all the time, quite frankly I simply don't believe them. Trying to humour a penniless old woman. Well, I don't intend to end up in the workhouse so if I have to feed dog food to my guests then so be it. Of course, I should really sell this place but I simply can't bear to.' She ran a gnarled hand over the damp stone wall.

'Isn't it part of the settlement, the family trust?'

'No, that was Tartleton Hall, over at Fourbridge. It was sold twenty years ago. Cecil and I bought this place together and named it Tartleton Court. It's in my sole name now, the damn trustees can't get their hands on it. The bank's offered to lend me money using the house as security, but I don't trust that nasty little manager and his interest rates. Usury, my father would have called it.' The old lady looked defiantly at Ophelia, her little black eyes suddenly very beady.

'Of course I won't tell,' said Ophelia. 'To be honest, I've always thought the same, especially about that pâté stuff. But look, about the money . . .' The maid was at the door. Ophelia lowered her voice and spoke quickly. 'Come and see me at the office tomorrow. I think I may be able to help.'

Chapter Seventeen

The graves stood tenantless and the sheeted dead
Did squeak and gibber in the Roman streets;

(I.i. 118-9)

'I've got another idea, though,' said Polly, when she arrived back in the office on Thursday afternoon to report that there was still no sign of either a cat or of any burial instructions at The Larches.

'Oh good,' said Ophelia, trying to sound encouraging whilst avoiding looking directly at Polly. Her astonishingly long lunch break had obviously been used not only to investigate Mr Parrish's house but also to have her hair re-dyed. It was now a dark orange-brown, the colour of a newly creosoted fence and the effect, when combined with the ubiquitous purple jacket, was startling in the extreme. 'Go on then.' Urban had a pair of Fred Flintstone sunglasses somewhere. Ophelia wondered whether they would fit her and whether the relief to her eyes would be worth the whispers of Rambleton.

'Well, you see, Mr Parrish had a safe in the bank. He always put copies of his new wills into it, so I thought this thing about his body might be in there.'

'It might, yes. Good thinking, Polly, it's worth a try. We may have difficulty getting hold of it, though.'

'Yes, I was thinking about that at the hair . . . on the bus back. We could send a fax to the manager saying that our telephones don't work and that Mr Parrish wants to sort out the stuff in his safe, so will they let me fetch it all. Then you can just sign it with his signature and we'll be away!'

Overwhelmed by Polly's optimism, Ophelia agreed.

The manager of the Arthurian Bank was duly taken in, though he commented wryly in his answering fax that he 'was mystified as to how your fax line can be in operation while your telephone line is dysfunctional', and Polly skipped out of the office to collect the contents of the safe.

She was not skipping when she returned, under the weight of seven box files. It had proved impossible to negotiate the cobbles under the

107

twin handicaps of the files and her pink stilettos and so she had taken her shoes off and balanced them on top of the pile.

'Ee!' she exclaimed, dropping the whole lot on to the middle of the carpet. 'I'd sooner calve cow up funnel.'

'What?'

'I'd sooner calve cow up funnel. I don't know what it means. My mum says it when she's had to do something, you know, sinuous.'

'Strenuous, I think. Come on then, let's see what we've got here.'

Two hours later it was obvious that there were no burial instructions amongst the mass of papers. With the exception of the deeds to The Larches and a few share certificates, the files were entirely filled with copies of Mr Parrish's many wills. There were legacies to animal charities and to tradesmen, residuary gifts to Rambleton Council and to television weather forecasters, trusts to encourage the appreciation of Browning and to maintain Shakeston Post Office. On top was the latest will, the original of which Ophelia had already seen, establishing the trust for the veneration of St Wilfred.

Polly was repacking the papers in the last file when she felt a bulky package between the pages.

'Hey, Ophelia, hang on. There's something funny in here.'

It proved to be a brown envelope, many times folded and Sellotaped to form a flattish parcel about four inches square. Polly unwrapped it nervously, her long red fingernails scrabbling at the tape.

'Look!' she sighed, laying its contents reverently on Ophelia's desk.

'What is it?'

'It looks like some sort of brooch, doesn't it? It must be dead old.'

Ophelia picked up the heavy bronze object. It seemed to her to be a clasp, rather than a brooch, for it was as big as the palm of a man's hand and formed in an intricate pattern of coiling snakes, with tiny sapphires and emeralds for their eyes. She had never held such a thing in her hands before, but had breathed over similar treasures in electrified glass cases and had seen illustrations of young warriors, their cloaks carelessly caught up on the shoulder with just such an ornament.

'If this is as old as I think it might be,' she said, after a few seconds, 'then it's probably worth more than The Larches and this place put together. Quick, let's take it all back. It makes me nervous just having it here. So beautiful . . .' She lingered over the clasp for a few more moments, tracing its curves with a faltering finger.

'The money you need to raise . . .' began Polly.

'No. Not this. Even if it wasn't real stealing and a shabby way to treat the poor old man, we'd never get away with it. You'd need proof of ownership, a proper provenance, all that. No, this isn't what we were looking for so let's get it safely back to the bank. I wonder if the manager even knows what he's got in there?'

As it happened, Lady Tartleton was not able to come in to Parrishes that day, but she arrived first thing on Friday morning and entered enthusiastically into the conspiracy. It seemed to her a matter of course that 'people like us' should outwit and defraud their financial stooges. Ophelia was tempted to tell Lady Tarleton about the kidnapping of Gigabyte, knowing that she was the only person Ophelia had yet met in Rambleton who would really understand their responsibility towards the puppy, the impossibility of abandoning her or of risking a bungled police rescue. But she did not, at least for the time being, suspecting that Lady T. would instigate some more direct action against Leafskirk Engineering. The interview drew to a close and Ophelia and Lady Tartleton moved slowly towards the front door.

'And if anyone asks where I'm supposed to be moving to?' asked Lady Tartleton coolly.

'I suppose logically it should be to the first link in the chain, into Mr Skate's council house.'

'Wassat?' demanded Mr Skate, who had just come into the office.

'I've been working on that little plan you suggested,' explained Ophelia. 'Lady Tartleton here has to pretend to move into your house.'

'Oh aye? Well I'm not moving out, any road. Mind you, if you'd like to move in with me, I'm not complaining. Eh, Darren?' He looked Lady Tartleton up and down with a lasciviousness which she seemed to find not unpleasing.

'Would Mrs Skate not have something to say about that?' she enquired graciously.

'Marge? She died ten year ago. There's only me and Darren and I s'pose 'e'll be living over t'brush with Sharon now 'e's got Kylie back. Nah, just be you and me. Nice little love nest.'

'Well, I do appreciate your offer,' said Lady Tartleton, using the tone with which she opened garden parties. 'Now I really must be getting on. The broken biscuits go so terribly quickly and my maid tells me that one of the stallholders has some dodgy Flash at only twenty pence a bottle. I honestly don't know *how* one would manage without the market.'

She sailed out to plunder the streets for bargains, leaving the others gaping behind her.

'Is she really a Lady?' asked Darren. 'Ee, I think you're in there, Dad.'

'She is, yes,' said Ophelia, 'and a formidable one, at that. Come through, and I'll let you know how things are going.'

Thirty minutes later she was shepherding them out of the door, air freshener concealed in her sleeve ready to be used immediately they had gone. It had been decided that Mr Skate senior would apply for a mortgage to buy his council house while Darren and Sharon would pretend to buy a 'first-time buyers" house of their own if a suitable link could be found. Darren would need proof of employment for his mortgage and Ophelia had promised to put him on the payroll of Wet Nose Solutions, on the strict understanding that no money or labour would in fact change hands. Darren proposed to repay his share of the mortgage advance by selling 'secondhand' videos in the Ram's Leg, but Ophelia, aware of the penalties attached to dealing in stolen goods, preferred to rely upon his father's days at the races.

To be fair to the Skates, it was not only their personal hygiene problems which necessitated the use of the air freshener. Extremely odd smells were lingering in the air near the door to Mr Parrish's old room, smells which neither Lady Tartleton nor the Skates had noticed but upon which more fastidious clients, or those less used to the odoriferous emanations from Labradors, might comment.

Ophelia had forgotten all about Edgar Pottlebonce until that morning when she was again forced to hand over £2.50 to the anaemic representative of the car parking protection racket. She had hurried through the drizzling town, past soggy tarpaulins and disintegrating cardboard boxes and to her relief found Polly already unlocking the door.

'Polly, it's Friday. We've got to get Mr Parrish out of the freezer to wave at Edgar Pottlebonce.'

'Yes, I know. That's why I came in early. Have you worked out any way to make him wave? I don't really fancy the idea of sitting under the table with him. I've got beef spread sandwiches today, you see.'

Ophelia had not seen, but knew better than to ask the connection.

'I think I know how we can do it,' she had said. 'Joan's very keen on the theatre and she has some proper marionettes. I experimented with them to see what strings you have to pull to make their hands wave.'

'Ooh, I don't think we could use a marieantoinette. That's a kind of puppet, isn't it? I'm sure Mr Bottletrance would notice, even through the window, if it was a puppet.'

'No, I don't mean that we should *use* the marionettes. They were just to give me the general idea. Look, Pius gave me some fishing line.'

Ophelia had fished in her coat pocket and after pulling out a handful of dog biscuits, a child's mitten, various sweet wrappers and a letter from Hygenus' teacher, eventually found a small coil of plastic line.

'It's almost invisible from a short distance. All we have to do is tie this on to Mr Parrish in the same places as the marionette's strings. Then we pass the other end over the ceiling beam and down on to your desk. When Mr Pottlebonce goes past you tug on your end of the line and Mr Parrish's hand is raised in the air.'

'But how will I know when Mr Pottlebonce is coming?'

'We'll do it with mirrors,' Ophelia had assured her mysteriously.

But both women had overlooked the initial problem. Mr Parrish, after being fast frozen for over a week, was by now completely solid. They had been able to lift him out of the freezer, one of Mr Saggers' complimentary bags of mushy peas clinging to his left shin, but could then only place him, prostrate and unbending, on top of the photocopier. His open eyes, covered in a film of ice, had stared at them in glassy reproach as they vainly tried to bend his legs and torso.

'Oh God,' Polly had panted. 'I should've known this would happen, with Gary being in the meat trade.'

'Never mind that,' Ophelia had replied, nursing incipient chilblains. 'What are we going to do now? Have you any idea how long it'll take him to defrost?'

'Hours, it'll have to be hours, won't it? If you think of turkeys . . .'

There was only one thing that Ophelia had wanted to do less than think of turkeys and that was to be trapped in a stationery cupboard with a congenitally cheerful secretary and a frozen solicitor. She had told herself severely that this was not a helpful attitude.

'We'll have to hurry it along a bit, then,' she had suggested, looking at her watch. It was already half-past eight. 'Is there a fan heater anywhere in the office?'

'Ooh yes, there's one under my desk. I use it to warm my wellies when it snows.'

'Fine, we'll try that.'

But the fan heater, although providing some general warmth to the body and releasing the first of those smells which were to become such an intrinsic feature of the morning, had not been sufficiently focused to defrost the particular joints, at knees and hips, which were required.

'This is no good,' Ophelia had admitted. 'You'll have to go round to a hairdressers, there's one below the court, and ask to borrow a couple of high-powered blow driers.'

'What shall I say I want them for?'

'Say that we've had a leak in the roof (thank God it's such a wet day) and that some valuable deeds have got wet. Tell them that the ink will run and that no one will know who owns half of Rambleton unless we dry them out quickly.'

'Right oh!' Polly had sung out as she skipped out of the door into the rain.

The hair dryers had worked, though it was a long and unpleasant task, and the church clock had struck a quarter to ten before Mr Parrish was safely installed in his chair. Ophelia felt hot, sick and filthy, but Polly had sat down and fortified herself with the first of her beef paste sandwiches. She had then got up, removed the 'Late Opening Due To Staff Training' sign from the door and admitted the impatient Lady T.

While Ophelia and Lady Tarleton were closeted together, Polly had perfected the mirror system by which she, looking into a handbag mirror on her desk, could see into the street through Mr Parrish's side window. By the time that the Skates left she had recognised three old schoolfriends, two with babies, her milkman, a stray dog and Gary, in animated conversation with the girl who did Freezaland's accounts. This last sighting had led to many tears and trips into 'J. A. Stanmore's', as even Ophelia's children were learning to call the loo.

A few minutes after the Skates' departure Polly retreated into J. A. Stanmore's to repair her eye-shadow and broken heart while Ophelia, somewhat cheered up, was spraying Floral Bouquet Room Spray around the office.

Suddenly Edgar Pottlebonce bounced into the office and cannoned into Mr Parrish's office before Ophelia could stop him.

'Wilf!' he was shouting. 'Can't stop, on me way t'market. Just to say, would you call round beginning of next week? Me and the missus want a word about young Johnny's cottage. Wilf? Wilf, are you all right?'

'Laryngitis,' explained Ophelia from behind him.

'Laryngitis? But he's not even moving his lips.'

'No, the doctor says he mustn't even try to speak. It's a particularly virulent form of laryngitis. Very infectious too,' she added, in an attempt to entice Mr Pottlebonce away from the doorway. This worked.

112

'Hope you're feeling better soon,' he called to the silent Mr Parrish before following Ophelia back into the outer office.

'He's rather deaf now, as well,' said Ophelia. 'I'm afraid that there's no way Mr Parrish could come out to see you next week,' she added with perfect truthfulness. 'Perhaps I could help. How would first thing Monday morning do?'

'I suppose it'll have to,' said Edgar Pottlebonce grudgingly. 'I'll expect you at nine o'clock. Give Wilfred my best, even if you have to serve a bloody writ on him to do it.'

Mr Pottlebonce bounced out again and Polly emerged from her retreat with J. A. Stanmore.

'Come on, Poll,' said Ophelia, locking the front door. 'Gary's not interested in her. He probably wanted some advice on wholesalers for when he has his own shop. Anyway, she hasn't got half your, um, originality.'

'D'ye really think so?' sniffed Polly, bespectacled by streaks of mascara reaching to either ear.

'Of course I do. Now we need to get Mr Parrish back into the freezer until next week. If only we could find these instructions. I'm wondering now whether he might have just told someone, not written them down at all.'

'Yeah, I expect he must've,' said Polly, inclined, that morning, to believe the worst. 'Okay, I'll take his arms. One, two three. Lift!'

The women lifted their respective ends of the body simultaneously but the downcast Polly raised his shoulders with little energy while Ophelia, anxious to put the corpse to rest once more, jerked his legs up violently. Tipped almost upside down, Mr Parrish was more forthcoming. From out of his left trouser pocket slid two objects, which fell upon the carpet with a jingle and a thump. The first was a bunch of keys, the second a worn leather wallet.

'His wallet!' they cried together and put the body down with as much reverence as their haste would allow. At last the search was over. Nestling behind a couple of five-pound notes and dry-cleaning receipts was a small envelope. On the front was a note in tidy italics, '*To be opened in the event of my death.*'

Ophelia's hands were shaking so much that she could hardly lift the flap, but after a few long seconds the slip of paper inside was opened. As Polly peered over her shoulder, Ophelia stared at its single sentence.

'*Parve segnis et abnormis Tobias confuditur resonatione residentia ductoris nostris.*'

113

Chapter Eighteen

But look, amazement on thy mother sits.

(III.iv. 112)

Ophelia arrived home that evening cold and tired with, or so at least she imagined, the stench of decaying flesh clinging to her. All she wanted in the world was a hot bath and it further depressed her to remember that Moorwind's dilapidated water system made this extremely unlikely. She put her hand inside her jacket pocket and felt the slip of paper with Mr Parrish's Latin instructions. Neither her year of third-form Latin nor the tags beloved by her profession had given her any clues to its meaning. Tobias, she remembered, was the son of Tobit, which was also one of those books of the Bible that the Protestants did not accept. Deutero-canonical. At least she could remember something. She had assured Polly that Malachi would be able to translate the sentence with no difficulty. His mother, God rest her voluble Irish soul, had been determined that Malachi, her seventh child, should follow his uncle into the priesthood, and had taught Latin to him from the age of four. Now, however, stumbling through the pot-holed yard, she was not so sure. It must have been ten years since he last twinkled at her over the naughtiest bits of Ovid, and Lewis and Short, the Latin dictionary, was now a footstool to help Innocent reach the rim of the loo.

As she pushed open the plywood front door, noticing that Malachi had again failed to replace its broken hinge, her suspicions were raised by the silence. In place of the usual clamour and chaos, with impromptu battles and pantomimes punctuated by screams of frustration or simple hunger, there was only a gentle buzz of civilised conversation from behind the closed sitting room door. Ophelia could only imagine that Malachi had introduced the children to the delights of cannibalism or main-line heroin administration.

The reality was almost as bizarre. The six, from Malachi to little Innocent, were sitting cross-legged on the floor in a straight line, each with a pile of small boxes in front of him (or in Joan's case her), a roll of silver stickers at his side, and a piece of electronic gadgetry on his lap. The scene, but for the electronics, could have illustrated an article about child labour in the Industrial Revolution.

'Hello, Mummy!' called Hygenus, who seemed the least committed to his work. 'We've got some mogems.'

'Modems,' explained Pius. 'They're so that your computer can talk on the phone to another computer.'

'Yes, and Daddy's bought five hundred,' added Joan. 'Aren't you going to tell him off?'

'Very probably,' said Ophelia. 'What are you all doing, changing the badges?'

Malachi looked up for the first time. 'Yes. They came from Afghanistan, you see, and their brand name is Tasty Little Horse.' He showed her a badge which he had just removed showing a silhouette of a horse flanked by a knife and fork.

'I wasn't sure how well that would go down in England so, in line with the total experiential environment policy . . .'

Oh, you're still on that one, are you? thought Ophelia.

' . . . I decided to rebadge them all. With the help of the kids, of course. They've worked very hard, but Innocent does tend to put them on upside down.'

'He's only eighteen months old, Daddy,' put in Joan. 'He doesn't really know about the total experimental.'

'I should think not,' said Ophelia, picking up the baby who put a Wet Nose Solutions sticker in her hair. 'So they're from Afghanistan, are they? Do they work?'

'Well,' began Malachi, and Ophelia's heart sank, 'they're not industry standard, of course. You'd hardly expect that at thirty pounds each.'

'Thirty pounds each! You've just spent fifteen thousand pounds on Tasty Little Horses when Gigabyte . . .'

'Gigabyte what, Mummy?'

'Never mind. Mal, what on earth were you thinking of?'

'Oafie, I have thought it all out. You see the proper, I mean the ordinary, PABT-approved modems, they cost about a hundred and fifty pounds each. And what are you paying for?'

'For it to work properly?' suggested Joan.

'Honestly, Joan, you're just like your mother sometimes. These *will* work. I explained it to you. Granted, they have seven bits rather than the usual eight, but the eighth bit is only used for checking the data on the other seven. They'll work perfectly well without it. At least, the Tasty Little Horse rep said they would. Just wait and see, they'll be beating a path to Wet Nose Solutions to get their hands on this one.'

'They'll have to if you don't do anything about the yard before the nettles grow again in the spring,' muttered Ophelia. 'Just get this stuff cleared away before *Coronation Street*, will you?'

'Course we will, won't we sprogs? I say, Oaf?'

'What?' Ophelia was aching all over, cursing dead solicitors and dead Romans in equal measure.

'D'ye think I've got it wrong again? I am trying to make this a success, you know.'

'Of course you are. Everything will be fine. I'm just a bit tired, love.'

'Come here then.' Malachi unfolded himself, took Innocent out of Ophelia's arms, handing him to Joan, and wrapped his wife in a woolly hug. He always shaved so nicely, she thought, a lovely soft chin. She nestled closer, smelling his woody Body Shop shaving foam while he could smell her . . .

'Ophelia?' he said, drawing away from her slightly. 'You've not been moonlighting at the butcher's, have you?'

'Er, no, no. I think I'll just go and have a bath.'

'Mummy,' said Pius, before she could escape. He only called her Mummy when he really wanted something. 'Mummy, what did you mean about Gigabyte?'

'Yes, what's happened to her?' asked Joan. 'We don't believe this holiday story any more, you know.'

'We fink she's probbly dead,' said Hygenus lugubriously. Urban began to cry. Innocent had fallen asleep on Joan's lap during his parents' embrace.

'I think we ought to tell them, Oaf,' said Malachi.

'Okay. No, she's not dead, she's being looked after. The problem is that she's actually been, um, abducted.'

'What's ducted?'

'Kidnapped, isn't it, Mummy?'

'Yes, if you must, kidnapped, and we have to get some money to get her back again.'

'How much?' asked at least three children simultaneously.

'Seventy thousand pounds.'

'Oh, is that all?' Hygenus was contemptuous. 'I fought it would be at least a dillion. Or a gillion. If I was a 'napper I would want a zillion. Bam, bam, ba-ba bam.' He ran about the room with an improvised machine gun made from two modems and a box of tissues. Suddenly he stopped. 'D'ye want me to shoot the 'nappers with my busheen gun? I can, you know.'

117

'No thank you, darling. Daddy and Mummy are sorting it all out. There's no need for you all to worry.'

'Want Giggy-byte,' sobbed Urban. 'Don't want the wobbers to come.'

'No wobbers are going to come,' explained Pius. 'Like Mummy said, she and Daddy will sort it out. And if they don't,' he added portentiously, 'Someone Else Will.'

After the younger children had gone to bed, while Pius was playing computer games and Joan curled up with *Mapp and Lucia*, Ophelia handed Malachi the slip of paper. She need not have worried. The years of declining on his mother's knee had not been wasted and Lewis and Short barely had to be recovered from the bathroom.

'It's a question of getting them early enough, you see,' Malachi explained. 'I learned all this while my brain was still forming, so it's there for life now.'

'Hmmm,' said Ophelia, who, during nine years of marriage, had received no indications that the brain-formation process was now complete.

'Yes, we'd better decide which of our boys is going to be a priest and start on them now. Or Joan, of course, if Father Jim gets his way. Though I don't suppose they need Latin these days. D'ye think I could teach them inter-personal counselling skills?'

'You'll need to teach them inter-personal first-aid skills if you don't stop burbling and tell me what this means.'

'Okay. Er, I don't think you're going to like it.'

'Go on then.'

'Right. Well, it's not very *good* Latin, but what he seems to be trying to say is, "A little slow and peculiar Tobias" – or Toby, that's a Hebrew name, you know, so you could use either form with equal impunity – now where was I? Oh yes, "peculiar Tobias is confused by the ringing at the residence of our leader." Now, are you going to explain what this is all about?'

'No, Mal, I don't think I am.' Ophelia had still not told Malachi about the death of Mr Parrish, knowing that he would be unable to avoid mentioning it to the children, who would confide in their best friends and so on, until the whole of Rambleton would be ready to inspect the corpse by the next lunchtime. 'Are you sure that's what it says?'

'Pretty sure. It is rather strange, though. Sounds like one of your mother's crossword clues.'

'Crossword clues! Oh, Mal, you are brilliant. Those *Telegraph*s in the garage!'

'What?'

'Never mind. Now, let's see if I have any maternal blood in my veins. *Tobias*. Do you think it might be a Biblical reference?'

'The only thing your mother has in her veins is unadulterated sherry,' muttered Malachi, but he took the paper and copied the words out again fifteen times, in a different order each time, in a vain effort to solve the mystery.

At midnight that night, after Ophelia and Malachi had puzzled their way to sleep, the children met for a council of war in the bedroom which Pius shared with Hygenus. Joan had tucked herself into the opposite end of Pius' bed with Innocent in her arms while Hygenus and Urban wrestled with the other duvet.

'Be quiet,' hissed Pius. 'Do you want the aged Ps to hear us?'

'The aged what?'

'It's what they call their mums and dads in those stories about children who have adventures and save their families from ruin. Except that they don't usually have both. A mum and a dad, I mean.'

'Wish we didn't,' said Hygenus. 'Mum made me wash my face *three times* today. And one time I was only going to bed. If you don't have a wash before bed then all the 'mato ketchup comes off on the pillow anyway.'

Joan nodded. 'Yes, and they go into the washing machine in any case. You'd think she'd *want* to save money by just doing that and not having to buy soap, wouldn't you? I wonder how long it would take to get seventy thousand pounds by not having to buy soap.'

'About ten thousand years,' said Pius. 'I don't think that would help. Poor old Gigabyte won't be around in ten thousand years.'

'Like a dinosaur,' Urban put in. His natural timidity and reticence were only overcome by the subject of dinosaurs. 'Dinosaurs is fousands of years old.'

'Anyway,' said Hygenus to Joan, ignoring the rest of the conversation, 'one day you'll be a mummy and then I bet you'll make your children wash their faces.'

'No I won't. I'm going to have a circus and everyone will have clown paint so they won't have to wash their faces ever.'

'Be quiet, you two,' interrupted Pius. 'We've got to think about what to do to get Gigabyte back.'

'Mummy and Daddy will get her,' said Urban naïvely.

119

'Well, they say they will, but can they? You heard how cross Mum was with Dad for spending fifteen thousand pounds on those modems. How on earth are they going to get seventy thousand? I think it's up to us, like the children in those books I was telling you about.' He brushed his fringe back with his hand and sat up straighter against the headboard.

'But we don't know where she is,' objected Joan. 'Mummy won't tell us who's kidnapped her.'

'Then we'll have to find out. That can be Stage One of our plan. Someone should be writing this down. Joan?'

'I can't, I'm looking after Innie.' Looking after Innocent was not, in fact, an onerous task, requiring only the occasional raspberry to be blown on his warm, plump tummy, at which he would squeal and wriggle with delight.

'Okay, you try then, Hygenus.'

'No, I don't want to. The letters all go the wrong way round.'

'I want to do writing,' said Urban.

'All right then.'

Urban got off the bed and lay on his stomach on the floor, doodling on one of Pius' comics where he was joined by Innocent. Meanwhile the others were dividing up the detective duties.

'You watch Dad, Joan,' said Pius, 'and see whether he acts suspiciously at all.'

'Why? You don't think he's kidnapped Gigabyte to get more money from Mum, do you?'

'No, you idiot.'

'Nitwit!' called Urban from the floor.

'Nit!' Innocent joined in.

'I mean see whether he acts suspiciously towards someone else, someone who might be the kidnapper,' explained Pius. 'You'll have to watch while Joan's at school, Urban. And, Hygenus, you watch Megabyte to see whether she gives us any clues, like sniffing in a special place or something.'

'Are you going to do anything, or just boss us about?' asked Joan.

'Of course I am. I'm going to do the most dangerous thing of all: skive off school to follow Mum about Rambleton.'

'I can do that,' offered Joan. 'I don't mind skiving off school.'

'What's skiving?' asked Hygenus from underneath his duvet.

'It means not going to school when you're supposed to.'

'Oh. I'll do that too, I think.'

'And me,' said Urban.

120

'Me!' shouted Innocent, so loudly that sounds of waking parents could be heard from down the corridor.

'Now look what you've done,' grumbled Pius. 'Anyway, Urban and Innocent don't even go to school. And you two aren't to skive, either. I'm the eldest so I should do it.'

Joan stuck her tongue out at him.

'Now here comes Mum. We'll say that Urban had a nightmare about Tyrannosaurus rex. Next meeting Monday night. Okay?'

Chapter Nineteen

But look, the morn in russet mantle clad
Walks o'er the dew of yon high eastward hill.

(I.i. 171–2)

By Sunday tea-time Malachi and Ophelia admitted that Mr Parrish's clue had defeated them.

Perhaps in apology for the five hundred modems, Malachi had again brought her breakfast in bed on Saturday morning, and thus set the tone for the next two days. The hot water system had burst into life, and so had Malachi on Saturday night, with an ardour so sudden and delightful that Ophelia only remembered in the early hours of next morning that her diaphragm was still sitting primly on the bathroom shelf. Since this was exactly how Joan and Urban had been conceived, she began to calculate dates and wonder where she had put the Moses basket. (It was in fact now Megabyte's bed, having been claimed by the dog as soon as Innocent had grown out of it.)

On Sunday morning they had prised the children away from seamless cartoons to Mass at Our Lady and St Barnabas. The service was uneventful, with no Lady Tartleton and with Sister Hedwig confined to the Children's Liturgy, attended reluctantly by Joan, Hygenus and Urban. Pius, who had taken his First Communion, considered himself to be far too old and theologically mature to join the children, and Innocent screamed hysterically at the thought of being separated from Ophelia. Ophelia had never had a clinging child before, the others being only too happy to leave her in favour of their father, a nursery, the Pick & Mix at Woolworths or anything remotely resembling a stray dog. (In Joan's case the stray dog had on one occasion turned out to be a passing flasher, but no permanent psychological damage seemed to have been done.) Ophelia wondered whether she was treating Innocent differently from the others, whether he was reacting to the disappearance of Gigabyte, or whether he already sensed mysterious couplings in the depths of her Fallopian tubes.

In any case, Pius and Innocent, instead of taking part in an impromptu dramatisation of Jesus' turning the temple tables and in the construction of first-century Jerusalem out of cereal boxes, had been forced to listen to Father Jim's biannual sermon exhorting his congregation to join the Parish Hundred Club. Pius, who took his spiritual progress very seriously, had been shocked at this worldly homily and had told the others on the way home that he 'would have to think very seriously' about offering his services as an altar boy to St Barnabas. Joan had told him not to be such a plonker. Ophelia had forbidden her to use the word 'plonker' but suggested that 'prig' would be perfectly appropriate.

'In any case, he's coming to supper on Thursday with Sister Hedwig and I want you all on your best behaviour.'

'I don't think I believe in God, anyway,' Joan had added, and thus the journey home was amicably completed.

'There's nothing for it,' said Malachi. 'You'll just have to phone your mother.' He was in a particularly good mood that afternoon, partly glowing from his exertions of the previous night, partly jubilant at the sudden disappearance of his 'hay fever'.

'Okay,' said Ophelia, languidly dialling on their heavy, old-fashioned telephone. As the dial buzzed back after each digit, she scraped a little more grime from the squat grey body. 'Don't you think this phone looks just like a toad?' she mused. 'Crouching there . . . oh hello, Mummy. Oh, Daddy. Mummy hasn't already toddled, has she? Oh no. Where? Jamaica? No, no, don't say it, whatever you do, don't say it!'

But it was too late. With the plodding inevitability of masculine bonding, her father and husband chanted together, 'No, she went of her own accord.'

'Right, that's got that out of the way. Look, Daddy, have you got an emergency phone number or something? It really is urgent. No. No, I can see that if she went with the bridge four you might well not want to. Yes, the hotel, then. I'll try a postcard. And how are you then, Daddy? Really? A birdie? Is that the same as a duck in cricket? Obviously not. And was that with your three-iron? Oh. Oh dear. Well, Mummy did warn you about the conservatory, didn't she? Yes, I suppose if it hadn't ricocheted off the potted palm it would have only been four panes. Never mind, you've got a fortnight to get it fixed. Now I must dash. Yes, yes, I'll get the children's names down for a good golf club. I do appreciate the demographics. Bye-bye, Daddy.'

'Talking of children,' said Malachi, as she replaced the receiver, 'I haven't seen them all afternoon. Do you think they're okay?'

* * *

'It's *brilliant*, Pius,' Joan was saying. Her voice, from inside the pigsty, was muffled by the straw, but her flailing legs were eloquent.

'Come on out now, Joan,' complained Hygenus. 'It's our turn. Me and Urban can fit in at the same time. We're not so fat as you.'

The insult served its purpose, for Joan reversed rapidly from the pigs' entrance and the two little boys took her place before she had the chance to swipe at them.

'D'ye think it'll come out to play with us soon?' she asked her elder brother, picking bits of straw and fossilised pig-dung from her hair.

'Oh yes, it's just a bit nervous yet. It must have been scary for it, under Mum and Dad's bed and then me carrying it out here. It'll soon get used to things.'

'What was it doing under their bed?'

'Well, you know Dad's secret beer store under there? The one Mum doesn't know about?'

'Of course I do. Everyone knows about that.'

''Cept Mum.'

''Cept Mum, yes.' She pulled at a particularly sticky lump of manure and a large portion of her hair came away with it. 'Ow.'

'Well, I was just looking in there.'

'Oh yes?'

'Just in case there was any lemonade.' Pius had turned a pretty pink and he concentrated on retying his trainers. 'Anyway, there it was, asleep in that box.'

'How long d'ye think it had been there?'

'I don't know, but remember the other day, when we all thought we'd fed Megabyte and she was still dead hungry? I know Labradors are always hungry anyway, but I bet it had stolen her dinners. It seems a pretty ruthless cat to me.'

Pius' analysis was confirmed by Urban's rapid retreat from the pigsty with a long scratch across the back of his hand. Hygenus followed him.

'You awright, Urban?' he asked protectively. 'He was only trying to ring its bell, you know. I don't think that's a cat at all. It's really fierce and it's got that funny splodgy face. I think it's a baby leopard.'

'It might be,' said Pius dubiously. 'Anyway, that's what we'll call it. Leopard. And we'll keep it here and bring it food and stuff, okay?'

'Okay,' agreed the others.

'Right. Let's go back and find the TCP. Tell Mum and Dad you've all been helping with the observatory. Right? Stars, Innie, stars.'

125

'No,' said Innocent stoutly. 'Cat.'

After this unprecedentedly peaceful weekend, Ophelia set off on Monday morning with a light heart.

Greenhaigh Farm, home of the irascible Edgar Pottlebonce, was on the top of a hill seven miles south of Rambleton. Ophelia was generally nervous of driving nowadays, knowing that the slightest nudge over the speed limit, erratic brake light or traffic policeman's bad temper could lead to the discovery of her disqualified status. But it was a bright, crackling autumn morning, the trees bronze against a clean blue sky and Ophelia sang as she drove up the steep track.

The house was handsome, whitewashed and red-roofed, with gleaming cobbles leading to the dark green front door. To Ophelia's surprise, however, the heavy Sanderson curtains had not been drawn back from the sash windows and after she had let the iron knocker fall there was no reply for several minutes.

Eventually she heard the sound of footsteps and of the disarming of chains and locks. The door creaked open to reveal Edgar Pottlebonce, bleary in toothpaste-striped pajamas.

'Eh?' he murmured, blinking in the sunshine. 'Oh, it's t'lass from Parrishes.'

'I'm very sorry to disturb you, Mr Pottlebonce. I can come back later, or another day if you're not well.'

'Not well? There's nowt wrong wi' me. Monica and I like a bit of a lie-in now we're getting on, that's all.'

'Oh. But what about the cows? Don't they need milking?'

'Cows? We've not had cows at Greenhaigh for fifteen years. Now you come and wait in here and I'll be down in two shakes of a . . . of a cow's tail. Good that, eh? Cow's tail!'

Chuckling at his little joke, Mr Pottlebonce showed Ophelia into a chintzy sitting room and disappeared up the stairs.

Along with several comfortable sofas and armchairs, the room contained two large bookcases. Remembering her great-grandfather's farmhouse which she had visited as a child, she settled down to enjoy a sentimental browse through the *Glory Hill Farm* books or wartime pig breeding manuals. But the only books in the left-hand bookcase to have anything to do with farming had titles like *Getting the Most out of Set-Aside* and *Whither the CAP?* The other books were all about accounting, investment and tax avoidance. Ophelia even recognised several textbooks, on trusts and company law, which she had used while training to be a solicitor, although Mr Pottlebonce's editions were the latest, and some were even hard-backed.

With her childhood memories receding, she moved over to the right-hand bookcase. Here the titles were even more unexpected: *The Validity of Anglican Orders, Why Thirty-Nine Articles?* and *Our Lady: Mother of England.* She had taken the latter from the shelf and was reading its blurb, which promised a full explanation of the role of the Blessed Virgin in ensuring the survival and fidelity of the Church of England, when she heard a series of heavy thumps. Ophelia replaced the book quickly and turned to see a woman in the doorway.

She was very large, at least six feet tall and fifteen stone, with a solid purple face and a quantity of wiry grey hair emanating in all directions from her head. She fixed Ophelia with a firm gaze and said distinctly, 'Nark off.'

'What?' gasped Ophelia.

Mr Pottlebonce, five feet four in his tweed slippers, appeared from behind the woman.

'Now, Monica,' he chided, 'don't be worrying Mrs O. with your ackynyms.' He turned to Ophelia. 'She's not being rude, you know, she's just trying out names for her new organisation. What's that one stand for, pet?'

'No Anglican or Roman Catholic Ordination of Females. NARCOF.'

'Oh, that *is* good. Isn't that good, Mrs O.?'

'Very clever.'

'Now, come along, dear. Why don't you make a cup of coffee for Mrs O.?'

He guided his large wife from the room with surprising gentleness and returned shortly.

'You must please forgive my wife, Mrs O. Religion's always been her hobby, like money's been mine, but it's got a bit serious lately. She doesn't believe in these women priests, you see, and so she's been so unhappy in t'Church of England. So she'd decided to become an RC, and she went along, happy as anything, to one of their services a week ago Saturday. But you'll not guess what happened.'

Ophelia thought that she could guess but thought it advisable to say nothing.

'Well, it turned out the vicar-chap, whatever they call him, gave this daft sermon full of silly jokes and then told them there'd be women RC priests before long, as well. That really upset our Monica. She's spent all her time since then talking about it; I've had to get the doctor to give her them tranky-lizers to get her to sleep at all. She's taking it all so much to heart, she's even . . . well, she's very worked up about it all.'

'I see,' said Ophelia in her most sympathic voice. She thought it best to change the subject. 'Er, I think you wanted to see me about a cottage?'

'Yes, that's right. I want you to draw up an agreement for a tied cottage for young Johnny and his wife.'

'Fine, yes. I assume Johnny works for you on the farm?'

'Well, not exactly on t'farm, no. The fact is, I don't actually do any farming any more. Johnny's my accountant.'

'Your accountant?'

'Yes. You see us farmers have been making more these days, what with EC grants and that, by not farming the land than by doing anything with it. But you have to be very quick to take advantage of it all before they close up t'loopholes. So I need Johnny close at hand, like.'

'I see. But I think it would be difficult to justify an agricultural worker's tenancy in the circumstances. Don't you do any manual work on the farm?'

'Oh aye. I have to maintain the footpaths. Very strict on footpaths is our Parish Council.'

'Then I recommend that you get Johhny to help you clear the footpaths. Now if I can take some details?'

Ophelia took out a large blue notebook and wrote down the necessary information. While she was doing so Mrs Pottlebonce appeared with the coffee, spilled it over the notebook and left the room in confusion.

When she had finished, Ophelia stood up to leave but Mr Pottlebonce remained in his armchair, shifting awkwardly from one buttock to the other. Ophelia wondered whether he suffered from some rectal complaint.

'Well, better be getting back,' she breezed. 'Please thank your wife for the coffee.'

'Er, there was something else actually.'

'Oh yes?' Ophelia sat down again.

'It's, it's a question of money, really.'

'Your hobby, I think you said?'

'Aye but there doesn't seem to be much of it to play with at t'moment, if you get me. You'll remember I said we'd not had cows here for fifteen year?'

'Yes.'

'Well, I was a dairy farmer then, made a tidy living out of it, no worries, as these Australian chaps say. Then along came the Common

128

Market, the Common Agricultural Policy, the Common Herd as you might say.'

Ophelia laughed obediently.

'So I began to look into this business of grants and subsidies and whatnot. First I began to farm different stock and crops, fancy stuff, guinea fowl, llamas, aubergines.'

'Aubergines in Yorkshire?'

'Oh aye, if you know how to do it. Any road, that did me nicely for a while, then it got so that you could make even more by leaving t'fields completely empty. So I gradually started doing that, until I got t'stage we're at now. I don't do any what you'd call farming now, it's all your form-filling. I was t'first round here to take advantage of Common Market and t'other farmers, knowing I'd always been warm, like, they started to take my advice. So I became a sort of agricultural consultant.'

'Yes, I see.'

'Brought in a few shillings, did that, I can tell you. But problem is now, the bandwagon's slowing down, like. With these GATT talks and that, you can't get nothing out of t'EC like ye used. So, I'm losing on both sides: I'm not getting t'subsidies and t'other farmers, well, half on 'em have gone right back to farming!'

'So you're a bit short of cash now?'

'Aye, you could say that. T'farm's bin mortgaged so often I feel like I'm playing Monopoly. They won't touch it again, not t'bank nor t'Agricultural Co-op. And then there's our Monica. This past week she's spent a couple of grand on . . . well, on summat.' Mr Pottlebonce looked suddenly shifty. 'Any road, what I was wondering was can you think of anything, any loan, like, that you could fix? We'll be all straight in a bit. Monica's mother, she's got plenty and she's on her last legs, but I can't say that t'bank manager.'

'Well there is something,' mused Ophelia. 'This Johnny of yours, is he, well, *straight*?'

'He's not one o' them poofters, if that's what you mean. And neither am I. Our Monica might be a big lass, but there's nowt funny about us.' Mr Pottlebonce's face was reddening.

'No, no, I didn't mean that. What I meant was, your accounts, would he, let's say *edit* them to, er, minimise the cash flow problem?'

'You mean fiddle t'books? Bloody hell, why didn't you say so, you daft lass, instead of casting perversions? Of course he'll fiddle t'books. What d'ye think I'm letting him have the cottage for?'

'Right. Do you know Lady Tartleton?'

'Daft old bat at t'Court? Oh aye.'

Ophelia explained to him the outline of her fraud and invited him to join the Mortgage Bandits. He agreed to apply for a mortgage in order to buy Tartleton Court, backed up by Johnny's creative accountancy. Now all Ophelia needed were a couple more conspirators to fill in the gap between the Skates' council house and Greenhaigh Farm. She was pondering this as she said her final goodbyes to Edgar, as he now invited her to call him, and to Monica, who was struggling with what looked like a large car battery on the cobbles outside. She was about to unlock the car when Edgar called out to her.

'By the way, lass.'

'Yes?'

'He's dead, isn't he?'

'Who?'

'Coom on, lass. Tha boss, old Wilf. Can't fool a farmer, ye know, even if he is a bloody financial consultant these days. I've seen enough dead animals to know one more. Laryngitis!'

Chapter Twenty

a kind of
yeasty collection, which carries them through and
through the most fanned and winnowed opinions;
and do but blow them to their trial,

(v.ii. 187–90)

Ophelia sat up in bed late that night, reading the papers in preparation for *Mid-Yorkshire Champion Building Society* v. *Puri (Possession)*, which was to be heard in Rambleton County Court the next morning. The building society had responded to her grovelling report of the Cox hearing with a frosty set of instructions which left no doubt as to her probationary status. The children, seeing the strip of light under her door, kept their meeting accordingly short and did not wake Innocent at all. In any case, they did not have much to report. .

'I've been watching Daddy, like you said,' began Joan, 'but you know what he's like. It's not very easy to tell when he's acting strangely and when he's just being ordinary Daddy. He's not sneezing any more, if that means anything.'

'The doctor comed today,' Urban contributed, to everyone's surprise, especially his own.

'Did he? What happened?'

'They had a argument about who's the best boy.'

'What, out of us?' Hygenus was aghast.

'No, Rory or Tony, I fink.'

'Rugby again.' Pius gave a world-weary sigh. 'What about you, Hy. Did you notice anything funny about Megabyte?'

'Yes. I watched her *all the time* and do you know what?'

'What?'

'She went into the airing cupboard.'

There was a long pause during which Hygenus leaned back against the wall and folded his arms with satisfaction. The others grew restive.

'And?' prompted Joan.

'And what?'

'What did she do in the airing cupboard?'

'Oh, nuffin. And when we took her round the farm she kept sniffing at the pigsty.'

'Of course she was sniffing at the pigsty. That's where Leopard is. Dogs always sniff at cats. It's their natrull instinct. Dad didn't notice, did he?'

'No, he just thinks she's clever 'nuff to look at Pius' obsevertory. But Mummy keeps asking why me and Urban's hands are all scratched.'

'Oh no. What did you tell her?'

'I said we had a fight and then she got all soppy and said was it 'cos she went to work and she got Dad and he gave us a lorry each. Look, here's mine.' Hygenus rummaged in a box and brought out a small yellow dumper truck.

'Cor. Jammy,' commented Pius. 'P'raps we should have a fight, Joan.'

'No, it wouldn't work. We'd just get in trouble. Anyway, did you follow Mummy today?'

Pius looked uncomfortable. 'I tried. I managed to slip out when we were going back after assembly and then I ran across the field and I'd nearly got to the fence.'

'And then?'

'Something happened. Didn't it, Hygenus?' Pius turned a ferocious gaze on to his little brother but Hygenus was not to be cowed.

'Did it? What?'

'Some silly, stupid idiotic little sprog from Year One in the mobile classroom was looking out of the window. Wasn't he, Hygenus? And this daft, dozy little infant saw me. Didn't he, Hygenus?'

'Oh yes!' Dawn had come to the dark shades of Hygenus' memory. 'I seed you and I shouted, "Hello, Pius!" but you didn't shout back. Did you hear me?'

'Yes, Hygenus, I heard you. I expect that the Queen and the Sultan of Arabia and the little green men on Mars heard you. And d'ye know who else heard you?'

'No, who?' Hygenus was glowing at the praise of his vocal powers.

'Mr Dobbin, the caretaker, that was in his potting shed heard you, didn't he? So now I've got to miss tomorrow's football practice and they'll all be "keeping a special eye on me". So there goes my top secret multinational spying operation.'

'Never mind,' soothed Joan. 'We'll just have to keep gathering clues. Do you know, Mum sent a postcard to Grandma in West India today? Now, that's a bit strange, isn't it? I thought it was the people on holiday who sent postcards to the people at home, not the other way round.'

'That's true,' admitted Pius. 'Yes, we'll all just have to keep on looking out for funny things like that. With our parents, we shouldn't have much trouble.'

'Yes,' said Hygenus, bouncing on the bed. 'And now we've got the 'mazing tracker leopard too. Na-na-na-na-na-na-na-na Tracker Leopard!'

There was an ominous creak from Ophelia's bedroom door and the children quickly dispersed.

Arriving at court on Tuesday morning, Ophelia looked around for Mr Puri. It did not take her long, as the only occupants of the waiting room were a lugubrious woman with a large piece of grey knitting, a beatific Asian gentleman and Nick Bottomley, who smirked unpleasantly as she entered. She ignored him and approached the Asian, whose expression of serenity broke into an ecstatic smile.

'Ah! You are the lawyer for me?'

'Mr Puri? Not the lawyer *for* you exactly, rather *against* you.'

'Oh no, I do not tink so. Such a beautiful lawyer!' Mr Puri took Ophelia's cheek between his finger and thumb and shook it tenderly. The sensation was not entirely unpleasant; Mr Puri was a plump, attractive man in his forties, extremely clean and smelling like a ladies' hairdressing salon. However, Ophelia was aware of Nick Bottomley out of the corner of her eye, a sardonic smile on his chiselled lips. She tried to restore a sense of professionalism.

'Mr Puri, I need to know whether you are able to make an offer to the building society.'

'An offer? How are you meaning, an offer? I have offered them everything, I offer you everything. You will not want to take my home from me, you velly beautiful lawyer?'

'I believe that you are self-employed, Mr Puri?'

'Yes, that is so. I see that you are not only velly beautiful lawyer but also velly clever, velly high-quality lawyer.'

'Could you tell me in what capacity you are self-employed, what it is that you do?'

Mr Puri gave an exquisite shrug. 'Oh, liddle bit of this, liddle bit of that. You know how it is.'

'Could you be more specific?'

'I am sorry? I do not understand "pacific".'

'Exact. What exactly do you do?'

'Oh liddle bit of taxis, liddle bit of restaurant, liddle bit of shop.'

'Do you own any premises; the shop or restaurant?'

'Oh no, all they belong to my blothers-in-law. Velly successful men, my blothers-in-law. They say: "Let us help old Puri; let us give him bit of work in our shop, bit of partner in our restaurant." But me, I own only this house that you want to take away. I do not believe that you will take it. Velly high-quality lawyer, you say to yourself: "No, I will not take away that man's house, that is all that he has in this world." Yes?'

Ophelia was saved from having to reply by the appearance of Mr Blank who beckoned them into the District Judge's presence.

'After you, my darlink,' whispered Mr Puri as they followed Mr Blank through the door.

'Ah, Mrs O.,' said the District Judge. 'Still as hard-hearted? And this is your latest victim?'

'Mr Puri, the defendant,' announced Mr Blank.

Mr Puri sat across the table from Ophelia and gazed meltingly into her eyes. She fixed her stare firmly on a nasty print of grazing sheep above his head and began.

'Sir, I am here to request an order for immediate possession. My client has the benefit of a charge over the property, 17 Heifersgate, securing the defendant's business account. That account is now overdrawn by over fifteen thousand pounds. The bank have requested repayment, in these letters dated 10 May, 16 June, 19 August and 8 September. In the circumstances they have no option but to call in their security. The defendant has made no reasonable offer of payment and appears to be in no position to rectify the situation.'

There was no hope, of course. The District Judge had refused to act when the previous defendant had not even attended court: he would hardly fail to respond to those liquid brown eyes and lilting, lingering voice. Mr Ranger opened his mouth to speak but Mr Puri got in first.

'Defendant!' he cried. 'How is it that you are calling me "defendant" when we have been such friends? Oh my darlink, most excellent and sexy lawyer, do not do this to me!'

'Never trust a broad, Mr Puri,' advised the District Judge. 'With one hand they'll be fondling your holster while with the other they're making off with your Stetson.'

'Mr Ranger, I really must protest,' said Ophelia sternly.

'I beg your pardon, ma'am. That kinda talk's more for the bar room than the court room and not right in front of ladies. I humbly beg your pardon.'

'That's all right. Now can we get on? I really must hear some concrete proposals . . .' Ophelia wondered whether she had used the right word in the light of Mr Puri's growing devotion ' . . . propositions, er, offers from Mr Puri.'

'You want me to be offering you concrete? Ah. I do not have any blothers-in-law in the concrete business but there is a cousin, I think. How many tons is it that you are wanting?'

'I think, my friend,' interrupted the District Judge, 'that before you compromise your position by making offers to Mrs O., we should look at this so-called mortgage a little more closely.'

Ophelia coughed, not trusting herself to speak.

'Now,' continued Mr Ranger, 'you had your business account with the Mid-Yorkshire Champion Building Society. Were you given any inducement to do so?'

'I am sorry. I am not understanding.'

'Did the building society give you anything when you opened the account?'

'Oh yes, yes indeed. Velly, velly nice calculating machine. Velly useful. I keep it in my pocket all the times. Here.' Mr Puri took from his inside jacket pocket a small and cheap plastic calculator.

'Aha!' cried the District Judge. 'A clear case of undue influence, wouldn't you say, Mrs O.?'

'No, I certainly would not, Mr Ranger. With respect—'

'We must indeed respect one another, Mrs O. It is upon mutual respect and tolerance that our great constitution is founded. As I was saying, a blatant attempt at undue influence. And what interest rate have you been paying on this "business account", Mr Puri?'

'Please, what is an interesting rate?'

'It is a perfectly normal business account,' said Ophelia. 'The rate would have been a few percentage points above the base rate from time to time. I dare say I could find out, but I frankly can't see the relevance.'

'Can't you, Mrs O.? Are you not aware that this court has powers to act under the Consumer Credit Act in cases where extortionate interest rates are being charged? This is clearly one such case.'

'Rubbish,' said Ophelia.

'And I order that the agreement be declared void.'

'Poppycock,' said Ophelia.

'That the mortgage be set aside.'

'Balderdash,' said Ophelia.

135

'And that the plaintiff pay the defendant damages to be assessed together with costs.'

'Tommyrot,' said Ophelia, whose store of archaic slang was running out. If the District Judge continued much longer then she would have to swear at him, contempt or no contempt.

'And now I suggest, Mr Puri, that you find yourself some good solicitor to calculate the damages to which you are entitled. Heigh-ho!'

Mr Puri had been sitting silently, mesmerised by the exchange, of which he understood nothing. At the words 'good solicitor', however, he sat up straighter and the joyous smile returned to his face.

'Ah yes! I know solicitor. Velly good solicitor.' He looked trustingly at Ophelia. 'You will be my velly good, velly beautiful solicitor?'

'Well, I shouldn't, you know.' She glanced at the District Judge who was beaming at her almost as abjectly as Mr Puri himself.

'Oh, bugger it. Go on then.' Once she had masterminded a quarter-of-a-million-pound fraud, a little conflict of interest technicality would hardly make much difference. In any case, 17 Heifersgate could be just the property that 'first-time buyers' Darren and Sharon were looking for.

Mr Puri and Ophelia walked out of the court together into the autumn sunshine. As they passed the hairdressing salon Major Lamb emerged and greeted them.

'Ah, Mrs O., isn't it? Delightful to see you again, my dear. And have you been in court? Gracious me, that sounds dreadful, doesn't it, but I suppose you lawyers are used to it!' He laughed roundly at what he imagined to be his original joke. 'S'pose you're wondering what I'm doing in a ladies' hairdressers, what? Like I said, not a wufta, you know.'

'I think it's unisex, actually.'

'Unisex, unisex, never heard such bollocks. Excuse me.' He gave a little bow. 'Man is man and woman is woman and never the twain shall meet, as old Kippers should have said. Fact is, there's a rather fine filly who trims my moustache in there and cheers up a poor old man no end. More fun than that miserable bugger at the barber's. Anyway, talking of old Kipling, who's this chap? Native, aren't you?'

Mr Puri, misunderstanding, replied enthusiastically.

'Oh yes, yes indeed, I am native. Native Englishman since 1975 when I come to Bratford with my wife and my blothers-in-law. Oh yes, indeed.'

'Mr Puri, Major Lamb.' Ophelia introduced them.

'You could be just the chap I'm looking for,' mused the Major. 'Got any business experience?'

'Oh, Mr Puri has very considerable experience of the workings of business,' said Ophelia ambiguously.

'Jolly good, jolly good. Fact is, I've been thinking about what you were saying the other night at Lady T.'s.'

'Oh, what was that?'

'About old Parrish and the skittles. I've decided to open a skittles alley in Rambleton and I need a partner. What d'ye think of skittles, eh?' This last was addressed to Mr Puri and was delivered at full volume to compensate for his Asiatic deficiencies. But Mr Puri was sharper than he looked, and knew the weak spot of a retired English soldier, especially in Yorkshire.

'Skittles? Ah yes, skittles. A velly good game, I am thinking, velly good. Only not as good as cricket, yes? You would have been watching the Test Matches, Major?'

The two men talked cricket for the next fifteen minutes, forging a bond passing the love of brothers, before returning to the matter in hand.

'One thing, old chap. You'll have to put some capital into the business, I'm afraid. Can't cover it all myself and I don't like to borrow from these blasted bank johnnies.'

Mr Puri looked crestfallen but Ophelia came to his aid.

'I think we can arrange that,' she said. 'I'm organising a small consortium to release certain monies. I should be only too pleased to invite Mr Puri to join us.'

'I am always, always being right,' rejoiced Mr Puri. 'You are indeed most first-class, sexy and stupendous lawyer.'

Chapter Twenty-One

The very conveyances
of his lands will scarcely lie in this box,

(v.i. 108–9)

'Well, I must admit,' said Stewart Saggers, perspiring even in the damp chill of Ophelia's office, 'the green chest freezer boom hasn't exactly taken off yet.'

'Have you sold any of them?'

'Not precisely *sold*, no. There was a lady took a leaflet last week, but it turned out she was from the Trading Standards. There's been an article in *Refrigeration Monthly,* you see. Sounds as though they're not quite as green as all that, after all. Very high casualty rate at the factory and a lot of dead fish downstream from the outflow pipe. Six of one, half a dozen of the other, this environmental stuff if you ask me, but there you are. I've not paid for them yet, mind.'

'And the rest of your stock?'

'Well, put it this way, Mrs. O. It's what, Wednesday afternoon now. Believe it or not, I can tell you, off the top of my head, everything we've sold in the past week. Ready?'

'Ready.'

'Four packets of economy frozen peas, two steak and kidney pies and an ice-cube tray. It's just a temporary blip, mind you. The long-term economic prospects for the frozen food sector are sky-high. It says so in—'

'*Refrigeration Monthly*?'

'That's right. Do you get it too, then? Incisive analysis, I always think. And I like the cartoons, "Chill-Compartment Chuckles". Very clever. Anyway, like I said, a temporary blip. But do the banks see it like that? Do they—'

Ophelia interrupted hastily. 'Yes, Mr Saggers. I thought the position must be something like that. That's why I wanted to see you.'

'Not the bill again? I thought that, you know, with the freezer, you were going to let me off that for a while.'

'Oh no, not the bill. Don't worry about that. No, this is another manifestation of the, how did you put it, undercover Chamber of Commerce.'

'Oh aye?' He relaxed and leaned precariously back on the flimsy typist's chair.

Fifteen minutes later he was gone, having wobbled his way jauntily out of the office, leaving the disparate parts of Polly's favourite chair behind him. Ophelia fished an envelope out of the wastepaper basket and drew a small circular diagram.

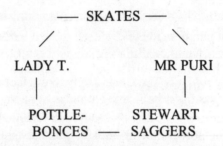

The chain of mortgage bandits was complete.

Mr Skate senior, whose first name turned out to be Albert, would buy his council house, 26 Ragged-Trousered Philanthropist Place, with the help of a mortgage from Rambleton District Council.

The name of the road caused Ophelia some mystification but its origin was explained to her by Stewart Saggers, whose father had been the lone Conservative councillor twenty years before, when the houses had been built. Apparently an extremely serious Labour colleague had suggested that the roads on the council estate be named after great works of socialist literature. The other members of the Housing Committee, anxious to show their artistic credentials, had agreed enthusiastically, but after Kapital Close and Mask of Anarchy Mount the idea had rather lost its momentum. By stretching the definition somewhat they had added Five Towns Terrace and Sons and Lovers Lane (the latter leading to considerable ribaldry). Needless to say, no resident of Ragged-Trousered Philanthropist Place had ever bothered to pronounce the name in full, and it was known universally as Raggy-Kegs.

Darren Skate and Sharon Casement would buy 17 Heifersgate from Amrit Puri. They were now applying for a mortgage from the Braddylesdale Building Society (motto: 'Backward bending to help your lending'). Advised by Ophelia, they had chosen the Braddylesdale from the bottom of the Building Societies Efficiency Table on the grounds that an institution of such incompetence would be unlikely to collect their instalments for some considerable time, by which Darren would probably be back in prison in any case.

Mr Puri would buy Stewart Saggers' house, 8 Southgate. A telephone call to the Western European Skittles Federation had suggested that an advance might be forthcoming on the understanding that the property, which had been the birthplace of the Freezaland empire, would house the Lamb-Puri skittles alley.

Stewart Saggers would buy Greenhaigh Farm from the Pottlebonces. This was the first purchase in the chain in which it would be safe to use a Mid-Yorkshire Champion Building Society mortgage and Ophelia was particularly looking forward to defrauding them. She had reported the fiascos of the Puri possession hearings by fax and had received in reply a supercilious letter from their legal department in which they expressed their amazement that she had been 'unable to establish the clear grounds for possession in both of our most recent cases and consequently to justify our continuing confidence in the ability of your firm to deal with these applications'. Ophelia filed the letter under 'Pompous Rubbish' and awaited her revenge.

The Pottlebonces in turn would buy Tartleton Court from Lady T. with a mortgage from one of the Big Five banks, probably the Arthurian, with whom Ophelia was not yet reconciled. Finally, Lady Tartleton would move herself and her Labradors into Raggy-Kegs with Albert Skate.

There it all was, then. Ophelia ran through the chain once more to make sure that it all fitted. Yes, that would do. It was hardly the most ingenious fraud of all time but it would serve its purpose. The days of Gigabyte's captivity were hurtling by, and every evening Malachi's welcoming kiss was a little more tremulous, the children's questions increasingly urgent, Megabyte's hunger less easily satisfied. It might be easier if they knew what to do with poor polar Mr Parrish. Come on, Mummy, she begged. Having sacrificed our childhoods to bridge and crosswords, the least you can do is solve this clue for me. She looked at the clock, hanging lopsidedly on the newly papered wall. Ten to five.

'I'm off, Polly!' she called into J. A. Stansmore. 'Lock up, would you?'

'Yeah, course. See you tomorrow.'

As Ophelia descended the steps she heard a low muttering coming from beneath her.

'One Civil Lit. or maybe Commercial Conv. add two Domestic Conv. and three Legal Aid (probably Fam.) makes three hours twenty at fifty pounds an hour, less light and heat . . .'

Ophelia peered over the rusty railing. 'Who's that down there?'

A dark figure unbent, still clattering to itself. ' . . . put through the client-productivity ratio, with a thirty-five per cent refinancing allowance and an overheating margin . . .' and hit its head on the drainpipe. Luckily, most of the impact was taken by his Stetson.

'Mr Ranger!'

'Good evening, Mrs O., ma'am. Keeping well, I trust?' He bowed painfully.

'What on earth are you doing down there?'

'Market research, ma'am. And I'm mighty sorry if I startled y'all. G'night, ma'am, g'night.' He raised his hat and loped across the twilit cobbles towards his own office.

'Soon,' said Ophelia to herself, 'I shall reach a plane of existential serenity where nothing whatsoever will be capable of surprising me. I think they call it the loony bin.'

Next day Ophelia began her work for the mortgage bandits in earnest. She had decided to play the conveyancing as straight as possible, so as to be able to deal with enquiries from the lending institutions with a reasonable show of competence. In any case, she enjoyed the disciplines of deducing and investigating title, from the single pink A4 sheet provided by Rambleton Council to the parchment deeds, found in Parrishes own offices, to Tartleton Court. Sitting with papers spread out on the desk before her, quietly perusing easements and the reservations of sporting rights, she could almost imagine herself as an honest solicitor, with no corpse in the stationery cupboard and no Labrador puppy to liberate.

These happy moments were disturbed by the memory of the principal under whom she had served her articles, a gentle old man who liked to announce: 'The Law is still a profession for gentlemen (and ladies, of course),' with a courteous nod in her direction. She could imagine the disappointment with which he would greet news of her falling away from his standards of honour. The only consoling thought was of his great devotion to his elderly Cocker Spaniel. Perhaps after all he would understand the imperative that drove her.

* * *

The supper with Father Jim and Sister Hedwig passed uneventfully until, after the pudding, the children were sent to bed in order for the adults to concentrate on some serious drinking. It was a great disadvantage of living in a bungalow, thought Ophelia, that there were no tell-tale creaking stairs to herald the return of an insomniac or curious child. She was right, for they had hardly broached the first bottle of claret when stage whispers were heard from the other side of the sitting-room door.

'You go, Urban. They won't tell you off.'

'Why won't they?'

'They'll think he's too little to know any better.'

'I've 'gotten what to say.'

Muffled voices and giggles.

'A'wight.'

The door opened, very slowly. Urban appeared in Thomas the Tank Engine pyjamas, inside out, and with an innocently puzzled expression on his cherubic face.

'Sister, pease will you take it off?'

'Take what off, my darling?'

Ophelia bit her lip, wondering when the sister's unworldliness would give way to the realisation that she was being made a fool of. To intervene now would be to imply that Hedwig could not cope with the children. She silently prayed that it would not be too bad. It was.

'Your head wig. It's not a very good one, is it? Joan says it's a bit fin on the top.'

'Bed!' roared Ophelia in the tone which she generally used for the dogs, and there was the sound of children scattering before their mother's fury. Urban had vanished in tears and Malachi followed to comfort him.

'I taught in Liverpool for a couple of years after college,' Ophelia explained. 'It's a knack you never lose.'

When Malachi returned five minutes later the other three were deep in conversation about the Catholic education system. With his usual tact and social facility Malachi immediately changed the subject.

'Seriously, Sister, why did you choose the name Hedwig? Wasn't she some sort of German duchess?'

'Yes, that's right. She was married to Henry the Bearded and they carried out many good works for their people. But I didn't really choose the name because of her.'

'No?'

143

'No. You see there was another Hedwig, although not many people know of her: Blessed Hedwig of Westphalia. She lived in the late twelfth century and was really one of the first of what we now call creation theologians.'

'Oh, something like Hildegard of Bingen?' asked Ophelia brightly.

'Yes, very like her in fact. They were both poets, you know. If you like I could recite some of Hedwig's work.'

'Oh, we should love that!' cried Ophelia mischievously, ignoring Malachi's imploring expression. It was his fault for asking Sister Hedwig about her name.

Hedwig cleared her throat and began.

> 'Godde be the Fader
> Moder be the Earth.
> Bringen forth the River
> At the Sonne's birth.

> 'Fader be the Springes-tyme
> Sendes down the rain.
> Makkes they the River
> Heeles mannes' pain.

> 'Fader sendes rain-fall
> Makkinge Holy Gost
> Like unto an ocean
> Bearinge us the Host.

'Of course, that is an English translation,' continued Hedwig, somewhat flushed from the Middle English vowel sounds, 'made by a Franciscan two centuries later. The Order's own mystics used the concept of spring, river and ocean as representing the Father, Son and Holy Spirit. I like to imagine that they first got the idea from the Blessed Hedwig.'

'Fascinating,' said Ophelia. 'Of course, it is Malachi who is particularly interested in creation theology, aren't you, Mal?'

Malachi had carefully avoided anything remotely theological since the age of twelve when he had been caned for pointing out to a local factory owner, a leading light in the Knight of St Columba, that, according to the Catechism, defrauding labourers of their wages was one of the four sins crying out to heaven for vengeance. He gave Ophelia a poisonous smile which she returned smugly.

144

Sister Hedwig was delighted.

'Oh, in that case you must come along to our workshop at Gloriaux Abbey in a couple of weeks' time. The Blessed Hedwig visited it, you know, eight hundred years ago this month, and we're having a sort of celebration-cum-conference there. Raymund Redforest, you know, the American creation theologian, will be there. I'm so excited! He has *such* charisma.'

'Gloriaux Abbey? I don't think I've heard of that one,' said Ophelia.

'No, it's really been kept quite a secret since the Dissolution of the Monasteries. It's one of the northern Cistercian abbeys, right on the border between Yorkshire and Lancashire actually, but unlike Rievaulx, Fountains and so on, it's always been privately owned. Until now the owners never let the public, or even scholars, near the place, but the new owner is something of an environmentalist himself so he's agreed to let us use it for our workshop. It's really a marvellous opportunity. Apparently it is a very small abbey, the smallest in England, but built according to the classical Cistercian plan. There's a good deal of it left, too. After the Dissolution it was used as a home by the family who received the land from Henry, so there wasn't the looting for stone that happened with the other abbeys.'

'That's marvellous, isn't it, Mal? Tell me more about Raymund Redforest.'

'Oho, Sister knows all about him, don't you?' chuckled Father Jim. 'Go on, tell them about your wild past.'

'Oh Father!' Hedwig blushed coyly. 'Well, it's just that Raymund, Father Redforest, was one of the major liberation theologians before he got into creation theology and he and I spent some time in Nicaragua,' Ophelia noticed that she pronounced it carefully: 'Nicaragwa', 'helping the Sandinistas before they came to power. Raymund really was a marvellous preacher and a wonderful priest. He had a great love for the country's labourers, or *labradors,* as he called them. He always tried to use Spanish wherever he could, although languages weren't really his strong point. I shall never forget a sermon he gave in the open air in Managua's main city square.

' "Friends!" he cried. "It is our fault that so many are suffering! How can we sleep easy in our beds when the labradors are still in chains? Rise up, rise up and set them free!" '

It was unfortunate that Sister Hedwig's devotion to Father Raymund, combined with the unfamiliar quality of the O.'s Bordeaux, had raised her voice to maximum pitch. It was doubly unfortunate that the children,

145

gathered together in the adjoining room, heard only this speech through the thin walls of the bungalow. They looked at one another in horror and clasped hands in a silent compact of vengeance.

Chapter Twenty-Two

Pooh, you speak like a green girl,
Unsifted in such perilous circumstance.

(i.iii. 101–2)

Meanwhile another meeting was taking place on the other side of the Pennines. On every third Thursday of the month Wardle would hold an ELLA 'executive steering committee' meeting. For years the executive steering committee had been made up only of Wardle himself and a reluctant Dorothy; now Mrs McHenry and Flies were enthusiastic co-optees.

Since the emergency meeting occasioned by the arrival of Gigabyte, Wardle had been more morose and introspective than usual. The sight of Mrs McHenry in her knickers had upset him profoundly. Try as he might, he could not prevent the image from reappearing in his mind as he tinkered quietly in his workshop or snuggled under his single electric blanket. Money worries were keeping him awake, as well, for the business was scarcely trading at all and the letters from the bank grew more threatening by the week.

So it was in fact Dorothy who unpacked one of the Wet Nose computers and gingerly plugged it in. The brightly coloured book of instructions made it sound very simple and, indeed, she remembered having considerably more trouble programming her first automatic washing machine ten years before. All she had to do, it seemed, was to plug in the keyboard, that was straightforward enough, the little television that the booklet called a 'monitor' (Dorothy paused here, struck by a happy memory of a proud term as flower monitor for Miss Spriggs at infant school) and a little rounded plastic thing that was rather surprisingly called a 'mouse'. Dorothy assumed that it was called a mouse because it squeaked, and was somewhat concerned when it made no sound at all.

Eventually all was complete, and she tentatively pressed down the power switch, leaping backwards as soon as she had done so. The machine gave a whirr and several sharp beeps while lines of meaningless words and numbers appeared on the screen. Dorothy had just decided

147

that she must have done something fatally wrong – perhaps the television was really the mouse and the little plastic thing the monitor? – when the screen changed to a pretty blue with a rather attractive flag flying and a title: something about soft windows. It reminded Dorothy of an advertisement for fabric conditioner that she particularly enjoyed on the television. She hadn't long to enjoy the flag, however, for the screen changed again, this time to rows of little pictures. The booklet told her that she could 'click' on these pictures with her mouse, and after several false starts she got the hang of the little double tap that it needed. She spent a whole afternoon exploring its wonders, pausing only to take Gigabyte (or Spot as they all called her) for her afternoon walk, and completely forgot to make anything at all for tea. Each picture led to something new and exciting: a game of patience (except that it was called 'Solitaire' which Dorothy had always thought was the cross-shaped game with pegs), a calculator, something called 'Paintbrush' which let you draw pictures, and a clock to tell the time. One or two of the pictures were a bit disappointing, like the sweet little filing cabinet which just led to an incomprehensible list but it was easy to click back to something more enjoyable.

But most thrilling of all was something called 'Write' with a picture of an old-fashioned fountain pen. She clicked on it and found that the computer had become a very special typewriter which could write in different size type, in italics or bold, underline words, move and copy whole paragraphs, oh, everything she could imagine! And if she made a mistake she could just undo it again, no messing about with Tippex or rubbers. After experimenting for a while, Dorothy set to work preparing the agenda for the ELLA committee meeting. How surprised everyone would be to receive their computerised notes! It took most of the next day, but eventually Dorothy had completed her agenda, the most stylish imaginable, with various font sizes, indented paragraphs, bold headings and centred text. She was about to call Wardle in from the workshop to show him when she suddenly realised her mistake. Her agenda looked beautiful on the screen, but that was where it would have to stay. She had no printer. Dorothy felt a heavy flush of secret embarrassment rising up her at her mistake.

But she soon recovered. At least no one else knew of her foolishness: she had not even told Wardle about the wonders of 'Write'. And she knew about computers now, she told herself as she copied the agenda from the monitor on to a sheet of paper, pressing hard through the three layers of carbon. That was more than Wardle could say, and possibly

148

more than Flies and Mrs McHenry, too. And one day, Dorothy promised herself, one day she would have her own printer.

Whether it was her new-found computer literacy, the devotion of Gigabyte or the increasing dependence of Wardle, she did not know, but Dorothy certainly felt far more confidence than usual by the time that Flies and Mrs McHenry arrived for the meeting. Wardle had suggested that perhaps Gigabyte could stay in the kitchen for the duration of the meeting but Dorothy had refused indignantly.

'It's those silly clothes that woman wears,' she explained. 'All made of animals. Not nice English animals like fox or rabbit but wild Indian things. It's not surprising that Spot got excited, thinking the house was being invaded by wild Indian animals. I thought she was supposed to be against animal exploitation, anyway?'

Wardle murmured something inaudible.

'Of course, the whisky didn't help,' Dorothy continued. 'There's none of that left, but I've put the sherry and that Chin stuff that your Jean gave us away in the sideboard and locked it. By the way, do you know what's happened to the decanter and glasses?'

'No, Dottie, I don't,' said Wardle sincerely, being incapable of suspecting Flies. Dorothy had her suspicions but decided not to say any more. Brother and sister had both been taught by their father to despise the accumulation of material things, although the old man had always insisted upon the best tobacco, fine oak furniture and cashmere sweaters for himself.

So Gigabyte again had pride of place before the fire while Dorothy distributed the agenda which read as follows:

EAST LANCASHIRE LIBERATION ARMY EXECUTIVE
STEERING COMMITTEE

MEETING NO. 173
1.   NEGOTIATIONS WITH WET NOSE SOLUTIONS [SPOT]
2.   FORMATION OF WOMEN'S GROUP
3.   THREAT TO HEADQUARTERS
4.   ANY OTHER BUSINESS

Item number three had been added to the agenda by Wardle who had silently pencilled it on to the draft notice which Dorothy had left on the hall table for him. Item number two had been added at Mrs McHenry's request. She had telephoned and, when Wardle answered the phone, had refused to speak to him, insisting that his innate sexism would prevent him from dealing positively with the matter.

'It's nothing personal,' she had assured him, 'but it is necessary for the continued growth of our community that you recognise your desire to rape me and that we deal with that desire in a pro-active environment.'

Wardle had shuddered and passed the receiver hastily to his sister. Dorothy had not had the faintest idea of what Mrs McHenry was talking about with her grandiose and rather distasteful sexual politics awareness sessions and radical gender redefinition tasking. But a 'women's group' sounded less threatening. Dorothy even had unformed hopes that it might mean morning coffee and cake once a month. Mrs McHenry had never seemed to Dorothy to be the coffee and cake type, but hope sprang eternal in the breast of a WI social secretary manqué.

Mrs McHenry arrived at the meeting safely enveloped in a pair of yellow dungarees, of the type worn by children's television presenters, and aseptically scented with lavender water. Gigabyte glanced scornfully at her but showed no further interest. Wardle avoided her eye.

Flies sidled in quietly with an optimistic smile. The cut-glass had fetched him several pounds in the pub and he was hoping for the opportunity to pinch something else this evening. He took a seat conveniently near the door.

After Dorothy had distributed cups of tea Wardle opened the meeting with a summary of his conversation with Malachi. All of the others, for different reasons, were horrified.

'Nah, you've gorrit all wrong,' said Flies. 'Haven'cha seen any films? You're s'posed to cut off the dog's ear and send it to them. You could at least say you're going to, even if you're scared to do it. I wun't mind doin' it anyway,' he added thoughtfully.

'You appear to have completely failed to take the opportunities presented by this situation,' commented Mrs McHenry. 'You were in the perfect position to expound the ideology of ELLA and to exploit the creative dynamism of the confrontation through constructive dialectic. Instead you fall into petty bourgeois patterns of subservient speech. Sometimes I fear that your political sophistication is at a very low level.'

'Yes, I'm afraid that it is,' said Wardle humbly.

'Anyway,' said Dorothy, 'we're not having the handover on a main road. You know what's Spot's like, no traffic sense at all. He went off to the village shop by himself yesterday. They phoned me up to say that he was whining in front of the custard creams. You'll have to find somewhere safe. What about that Glory-something Abbey that was on the local news? That's on the border, isn't it?'

Wardle agreed and said that he would telephone Wet Nose Solutions as soon as the meeting was over.

The next item was Mrs McHenry's Women's Group. She gave a crisp speech, quoting from various American feminists whose names sounded to the others as though they had been invented on the spot. But even Flies knew better than to argue with Mrs McHenry's interpretation of sexual politics so her motion, whatever it was, was passed unanimously. Halfway through her exposition Gigabyte became very bored and, noticing that it had crept up on her again, began to chase her tail, providing a welcome diversion for the other three.

When they reached the third item Wardle took out his sheaf of letters and laid them sadly on the table. The first five or six bore the red rose letterhead of the Bank of Lancaster and threatened, in increasingly graphic terms, horrific consequences if the mortgage account was not returned to a state of grace. The penultimate letter, adorned with a silver trophy from which a white rose extruded, added insult to injury by announcing that the Bank of Lancaster had been merged with the Mid-Yorkshire Champion Building Society. The final letter informed him tersely that proceedings for possession of the house would be taken during the next ten days.

Gigabyte walked over to the table and sniffed the letters thoughtfully. She nudged them with her nose and they fell to the carpet. Then she circled the table three times while the members of ELLA watched in fascination. Finally, with a piercing bark, she thrust her nose under the table and began to chew the letters, masticating vigorously. Within seconds they were reduced to soggy grey spheres and, for the first time in a fortnight, Wardle smiled.

Chapter Twenty-Three

Where be his quiddities now, his quillities,
his cases, his tenures, and his tricks?

(v.i. 97–8)

'The dirty double-crossing nun!' cried Pius as soon as they had retreated to Joan's tiny bedroom, which was the furthest from the sitting room. 'All that pretending to look for Gigabyte and she'd got her all the time!'

'Megabyte tried to tell us, didn't you, Meggy?' said Hygenus, sitting astride the patient dog.

'What do you mean?'

'Airing cupboards. Remember Urban said that old Wig Head smelled of airing cupboards? And then when I was watching Megabyte she went into the airing cupboard. I *told* you it was 'portant but you wouldn't listen. *As* usual.'

'We're sorry. You did very well,' said Joan in a pacifying tone.

'And that priest's in on it as well,' pointed out Pius. 'I knew he was only interested in money after that sermon on Sunday. You know, when you called me a plonker and Mum told you off.'

'Yes, but she said you were a prig.'

'Well, I bet she'd take it back now. He's probably taking all the Hundred Club money as well,' he added darkly.

' 'Dop arguing,' said Urban.

'Okay. Look we've got to follow them, especially Sister Hedwig. I'm sure it's her that's got him. Father Jim's most likely just sharing in the spoils. Does anyone know where she lives?'

'Yes,' said Joan. 'Our class went on a trip to the convent. They eat a lot of cake.'

If the children had stayed where they had been before, next to the sitting room, they would have heard Jim and Hedwig leaving and, shortly afterwards, the telephone ringing. Upon hearing the conversation, or even just their father's side of it, they might have reconsidered Sister Hedwig's guilt.

'Hello. Um . . . Wet Nose. Oh. Oh yes. How am I? How d'ye think I bloody am? You've just pinched our damn puppy, haven't you? Full of

153

the joys of spring, we are. (What? Oh all right, Oaf.) We're bearing up.
Yes, difficult for us all. Yes, two weeks on Saturday. Eleven's fine. Oh,
that's a coincidence, we were just talking about Gloriaux. At least, the
others were. I was busy drinking. Right, we'll meet there then. Any
special bit: warming-house, east transept, reredorter? What's a reredorter?
It's the monks' bog. Don't you Lancastrians know anything? Right, I'll
see you then. Okay. Bye.'

Malachi turned back to Ophelia. 'Did you get all of that?'

'Yes, I think so. I think I can get all the completions done in time.
The only worry is that the headquarters of the Western European Skittles
Federation is in Bruges and they're talking about sending the mortgage
advance in ECUs.'

'I thought it took months to buy and sell houses anyway.'

'No, that's just a myth put about by sleepy solicitors. The actual
conveyancing can be done in a day if you're prepared to get off your
bottom a bit. What holds things up is getting the money out of the
building societies which is, of course, all we're trying to do in this
case.'

'So you think it'll be okay?'

'No problem.' Ophelia spoke with a confidence which she did not
really feel.

When she woke next morning, her first, dispiriting thought was that
it was a Friday. Her second thought was that since Edgar Pottlebonce
already knew that Mr Parrish was dead, there would be no need for a
repeat performance with the turbo hair dryers and fishing line.
Encouraged by this, she bounced out of bed and made mugs of hot
chocolate for each of the children before driving to work at a speed
which defied the existence of lurking policemen.

At a quarter past nine Geoff Papping of the Lord Chancellor's
department turned up again.

'Good morning, Mrs O.,' he said politely, bringing a breath of Home
Counties air into the bleak office. 'Mr Parrish still away, is he?'

'Yes. No. I mean he came back but he's gone again now.'

'Oho, lucky for some. Mind you, judging from the size of his bid
he's got a penny or two to play with.'

'Oh, was it too high?'

'Well it's impossible to say with these things, isn't it? Look at the
television franchises and all the trouble we had with those. At least this
time they've abandoned all pretence at quality control. Present company
excepted, of course. Anyway, your bid was high enough. That's what

I'm here to tell you, that you've got the franchise.'

'Great. What do we do now?'

'Start advertising. You're running the court from Monday. We've advised all court staff, District Judges, et cetera, to be at the courts first thing Monday morning so that you can give them their pay rises.'

Geoff Papping made a little, bird-like sound in his throat to indicate that this was a civil service joke. Then, after leaving a booklet containing the new *Statutory Instrument: Courts Administration Regulations* and a card with his telephone number, he left.

Ophelia leafed through the booklet, which was very short. It appeared to repeal virtually all the provisions in the old Green Book which previously governed proceedings in the County Court. Not only fees and costs but periods of notice, rules of evidence, even guidelines set down by the Court of Appeal appeared to have been jettisoned. Ophelia felt quite giddy.

'Why have you got your head between your knees?' asked Polly. 'Have you lost a contact lens or have you got a feminine freshness problem?'

'Certainly not,' Ophelia replied brusquely. 'Is the fax machine working?'

'I think so.'

'Right. Much as I disapprove of junk faxes I want you to fax this to all the law firms north of Melton Mowbray. And can you get my husband on the phone, please?'

Ophelia handed over a sheet of paper upon which she had written the following:

RAMBLETON WET NOSE COUNTY COURT
Now under new management
  • Court fees from only £2.99
  • Free computer link-up
  • 24-hour service
  • *Little Lawyers* Club with free badge and felt-tip pens
  • Sue two – get one free!
Call our Hotline NOW for more details!

'You don't think it's too subtle, do you?' Ophelia asked.

'What's subtle? Ee, this Hotline goes to my desk. What'll I say?'

'Oh, just say,' Ophelia raised her voice by an octave: ' "Your call is being held in a queue and will be dealt with as soon as possible.

155

Meanwhile, please sit back and enjoy some music".'
'We haven't got any music.'
'No, you'll have to sing something. You must know some pop songs.'
'Would "Viva España" do?'
'Just start faxing.'

'Wet Nose shut up Innocent Solu leave his bloody ears alone Urban tions. May I Daddy's getting really cross now help you?'
'Hello, Malachi. Nice to see that course on telephone technique coming in handy.'
'Ophelia, hi. Just a temporary hiccup on the domestic front. They're playing *Star Trek* and Urban's trying to give Innocent authentic Vulcan ears.'
'How charming. Malachi, have you still got those computers and modems?'
'Of course I have. Don't rub it in, Oaf.'
'I'm not, I'm being positive. I assume that the "limited use" you talked about covers sending simple documents and playing a few games? Great. I want you to install them in solicitors' offices. Just start at Rambleton and carry on in a spiral until you run out. Tell them it's part of the Lorskwad Initiative and show them how to play Minesweeper. Take Megabyte with you as part of the total experiential environment. It's a long shot, but we might even make some money on this one. Bye.'
Ophelia put the phone down and called to Polly.
'Keep faxing solidly until two, then don't forget the five personal searches at Rambleton Council's Land Charges Department. If there's anything more exciting than a Smoke Control Zone on any of them then ring me, okay?'
'But what about me lunch hour? It's market day, remember?'
'This is the white heat of private enterprise, Polly. *Nessun dorma.*'
'What's the World Cup got to do with it?' muttered Polly, as she began the fifty-eighth fax.

'Er, Mr Snodsworth, sir?' began Deputy District Judge Ranger, sliding his long neck around his senior partner's door.
'What is it, Lionel? For goodness' sake either come in or stay out. Don't wind yourself around the door like a perishing sea serpent.'
'Yes, sir. Sorry, sir.' Mr Ranger sidled in and stood in front of Mr Snodsworth's desk, hands behind his back like a chastised schoolboy.

'The thing is, sir, I've now completed my feasibility study into the economic implications of a joint venture enterprise with our legal colleagues in the sociogeographic area.'

'What's the boy saying?' spluttered Mr Snodsworth.

'A merger with Parrishes, sir.'

'Well, why the devil didn't you say so? Wasting my time like that. Do you know what this is?' He waved a neatly bound folder in Mr Ranger's face.

'Er, a *Geranium* opinion, sir?'

'Certainly a *Geranium* opinion. Not too hopeful, I'm afraid, but there are plenty more counsel to try. Look at this in today's *Times*: a great list of chaps called to the Bar. Most of them called Hang and Wang and A-Tishoo, but none the worse for that, I suppose. And some poor fellas with women's names. Ttt-tt. Anyway, Lionel, do go away and let me finish this. I told you, merge with Parrishes if you like. *I* don't care. I'm only waiting to get *Geranium* tied up and then I'll retire. After all, I am nearly . . . How old am I, Lionel?'

'Eighty-one, I believe, sir.'

'There we are, then. Eighty-one. Wouldn't have gone about badgering a chap of eighty-one in my day. Now scram.'

'Right oh, sir. Just, sir?'

'What is it now, boy?'

'That man from the Lord Chancellor's Department, Geoff Papping, was it? Did you see him?'

'I certainly did, *and* gave him a piece of my mind. Bidding for the court indeed. I told him, the Lord Chancellor's a friend of my father. Saw him myself on the Woolsack in '23 when we went up to Town for Sophia's coming-out. Now *do* go away, Lionel. *Geranium*s don't grow on trees, you know.'

Chapter Twenty-Four

To a nunnery, go – and quickly too.

(III.i. 141–2)

'I saw a hedgehog this morning,' squeaked Sister Perpetua as she came into the stone-flagged kitchen.

'Squashed or whole?' rumbled Sister Felicity, pouring out a careful measure of cornflakes.

Sisters Perpetua and Felicity were both tiny, brown and extremely wrinkled and had been so for as long as anyone could remember. The best-read girls at Rambleton Convent had been reminded of the 'little thing, the size of a hazel-nut' in which Julian of Norwich saw all of God's creation. Those rather less well read thought of Mrs Tiggywinkle while the wildest girls, those with eye-liner and boyfriends, called them 'Parapet' and 'Velocity' and did their best to keep out of range of their beady brown eyes.

But that was twenty years ago. Now Rambleton Convent was no more, incorporated into the unruly sprawl of the Alderman Penbury Comprehensive and the two Sisters, both over eighty, were officially in retirement. They had entered the novitiate together and, like husband and wife, or owner and dog, had grown more and more like one another over sixty-five years of proximity. Now even the other Sisters relied upon their voices to tell them apart.

'Whole, actually,' replied Sister Perpetua in her high-pitched creak and both bobbed their heads in a silent thanksgiving.

Joan's pins and needles spread to the other leg. Why did they have to be so *slow*? She had been congratulating herself on sneaking out of school and into the nuns' pantry but for the half-hour that she had been here nothing had happened at all. Nothing but a procession of boring old women in navy cardigans, each more ancient than the last (both the cardigans and the sisters) and no sign whatsoever of Sister Hedwig. Joan almost wished that she had let Pius do this instead of insisting on going herself. On Monday mornings her class always wrote stories, and she was good at stories. By the time she got back it would be nearly afternoon and horrible, horrible PE.

She was wedged at the far end of the L-shaped pantry, under a shelf of home-made chutney and next to an enormous sack of brown rice. She could not stand up, and the pressure on her calves was becoming unbearable but there was a tiny gap in the brickwork through which she could see most of the kitchen.

She was about to give up and make a run for it, when Sister Hedwig finally came in. The two old Sisters greeted her with enormous enthusiasm.

'Hedwig my dear! We don't often see you in the mornings. Do have some cornflakes.'

'Yes, do. Or rather don't. They are a little soggy, don't you think, Felicity?'

'Are they really? I'm sure that we only bought them recently. Let me see. Is this a price label? One shilling and sixpence. That seems like a lot, but then it is a very big box.'

'I'm afraid that means that they must be getting on a bit. We're on this new money, now, remember?'

'So we are. I've not really got the hang of it yet. There's something called a centimetre, isn't there? Never mind, dear. How about a nice boiled egg?'

'Thank you, but I had my muesli a few hours ago now. I just came to make a cup of decaf.'

'Decaf. I wonder what that can be? It sounds terribly exciting, doesn't it, Sister?'

'Oh yes. I remember that nice French priest bringing us some smuggled Calvados once. Could it be something like that? I *did* enjoy it, I must say, though I had the fourth form after lunch and somehow they seemed to be in higher spirits than usual. I remember that they persuaded me to write some quite rude words on the blackboard. Of course it *would* be the afternoon that the Canon paid his monthly visit.'

'Oh, I'm afraid that it's not remotely as exciting as Calvados. It just means decaffeinated coffee.'

'Decaffeinated coffee? How strange. What would the point of that be?' asked Felicity.

'I have heard,' said Perpetua, in tones of confidentiality and awe, 'that shops these days sell wine and beer without any alcohol in.'

'Goodness gracious me! I hope that they are properly prosecuted by the authorities.'

'No, no,' explained Hedwig gently. 'It's meant to be like that. For health reasons and so on.'

160

'Well, well. And I suppose everyone smokes cigarettes without any tobacco?'

'Not really. People don't really smoke much any more.'

'Really? As penance, I suppose. Perhaps the world isn't such an impious place as we thought, Perpetua.'

'No, again, it's their health, you see. Cigarettes cause all sorts of diseases; lung cancer, emphysema . . .'

'Good heavens! You mean we've been here for all these years, doing without cigarettes and drink . . .'

'Except the Calvados.'

'Except the Calvados, and the whisky from the friars . . .'

'And the sherry in the trifle and the Burgundy on Mother's birthday . . .'

'And Sister Eulalia's Newcastle Brown.'

'Except all those, and imagining the world outside in a positive *orgy*,' Sister Perpetua's voice reached top C on the word 'orgy', 'of drunkenness and, er, smokaphilia, and we find out that all the time they've given up too? Dear me, I suppose the only sacrifice left is to eat these awful cornflakes.'

'Oh, I'm sure you needn't go that far,' said Sister Hedwig. 'Why don't you have some of my muesli? Here you are.'

'Organic?' growled Felicity, peering at the box. 'Whatever do they mean? Surely you couldn't have inorganic breakfast cereal, if I remember my chemistry right?'

'It's to do with the farming methods. "Organic" means that they don't use chemical fertilisers and so on. I think that if we take our stewardship of the earth seriously then we have to think about these things, don't you?'

'Oh yes, my dear. You know those artificial things they put in the soil are terribly bad for the little animals. You probably think Perpetua and I are silly about our hedgehogs . . .'

'No, not at all. In fact, why don't you come with me a week on Saturday to Gloriaux Abbey for the creation theology workshop? I'm sure you'll enjoy it and there will be lots of animals there too, dogs and so on.'

Oho! thought Joan.

'Maybe even a hedgehog.'

'I don't know, my dear. It's a long time since we've been on a trip, isn't it, Felicity? Let me see. I don't know that we've been out of Rambleton since we retired from teaching.'

'Oh, Perpetua, of course we have. We went to see the Holy Father in Manchester, remember?'

At that moment a tinny bell rang and all three Sisters hurried out of the kitchen. Joan felt as though she was finally getting somewhere. It all sounded extremely fishy. Lots of animals, mostly dogs it seemed, being brought together at this abbey place. Probably all kidnapped, she thought. Probably going to be sacrificed or something. Her cousin Danny, whose primary school was still run by nuns, had told her that you could never trust them. Now she could see what he meant. Well, that was enough surveillance for one day. If she got out now then she could be back by playtime. Perhaps no one would have noticed that she had gone at all.

She was just beginning to edge herself out from under the shelf, very gingerly to allow her cramped muscles to relax, when to her horror the pantry door opened.

But the woman who walked in was not wearing the grey dress and blue cardigan of the Sisters, and it was impossible to imagine her wild grey hair ever being confined by one of their neat half-veils. She was so tall that she had to stoop even to get through the door and she wore a dirty olive Barbour and cinnamon-coloured corduroy trousers. But what really persuaded Joan that this was not some maverick nun in mufti was the woman's expression of mingled guilt and fury. As she wedged her sturdy torso between the potatoes and the catering size tins of baked beans, Joan tried to shrink further into her corner. The woman placed her head against the wall so that one large ear was flat against the painted brick. For a few minutes the two stayed like that, both alert for any sound in the empty kitchen, as still as the food around them except for the quick, excited movements of their breath.

Another Sister walked into the kitchen and Joan could see the other woman's rather bulbous eyes straining at their sockets as she tried to see through the solid whitewashed brick. Then catastrophe struck. Joan had been suffering from a cold for the past fortnight, exacerbated by her unheated, corrugated iron bedroom. Now she felt the familiar scrape of an impending cough at the base of her throat. She tried holding her breath, her cheeks bulging with the effort, and swallowing vigorously, but the relentless progress of the cough would not be thwarted. After a few more agonising seconds it burst forth in all its spluttering glory.

'Good God!' cried the woman in a horrified bass.

'Er . . . hello,' said Joan.

'Are you some sort of a servant?' enquired the woman, thinking of

162

Victorian scullery maids and at the same time noticing that Joan was far too well-padded to be a conventional skivvy. Perhaps Vatican II had ordered nuns to stop starving their servant girls as well as to abandon their veils.

'No. Are you a nun?' asked Joan, deciding that the best form of defence was attack.

'Not exactly. I'm looking for one of them, a Sister Hedwig. Do you know her?'

'I should say I do,' said Joan darkly. 'Are you a friend of hers?'

'Certainly not. I wouldn't be lurking in this pantry if I were a friend of hers, would I?'

'You mean you're *spying* on her?'

'Well, I suppose you could put it like that,' agreed the woman. 'I prefer to think of it as vital surveillance work on behalf of the traditional Church.'

'Well that's all right,' said Joan cheerfully, ''cos I'm doing vital surv— spying work on behalf of the traditional labrador.'

'What?'

'That Sister Hedwig. She's kidnapped our puppy. She's taking it to an abbey place with lots of other animals. I think she's going to *sacrifice* it.'

'Animal sacrifice? Good God, it's worse than I thought. I knew that these women incorporated pagan elements into their so-called worship, God the Mother and such-like nonsense, but I never dreamed that it was that bad. Just wait until the *Church Times* hears of this. And the *Universe*. I must get out and start writing letters.'

'No, please don't!' cried Joan. 'If anyone finds out then she'll really kill her. I know she will. Mum and Dad are trying to get seventy thousand pounds ransom money but they're terribly poor so we're going to rescue her instead. But we mustn't tell the police or the newspapers or anything.'

'Oh dear. Oh dear me. But it would make such a very good story and put NARCOF on the map, too. Let me see. There must be something we can do.'

'I know. Why don't you help us to rescue Gigabyte?'

'Who?'

'Gigabyte. The puppy. Then when she's safe you can tell all the papers, the proper ones as well as the Church ones. It'll be a much better story with a daring rescue in it. And children. Everyone likes children and puppies. And we're quite photosynthetic.'

'Photogenic.'

163

'Yes, that's it. So you will then?'

'I suppose so. I don't know much about children, but it sounds as though we can help each other. The vital thing is to expose that dreadful woman. I did have other plans for her . . . But they say the pen is mightier than the sword and the newsprint mightier than the . . . Pity, though.' Her voice trailed off dreamily then abruptly returned. 'By the way, my name is Monica Pottlebonce.'

'Joan O.'

The two shook hands solemnly across the economy size cornflakes.

Far away, Gigabyte was eating her third sausage supper, blithely ignorant of the plans being made on her behalf.

Chapter Twenty-Five

If it be now, 'tis not to come; if it be not to come,
it will be now; if it be not now, yet it will come.
The readiness is all.

(v.ii. 216–218)

'Thank you all very much for making the time to be here,' said Ophelia formally to the assembled staff of Rambleton, now Rambleton Wet Nose County Court. They nodded in some embarrassment. It was difficult to hold a dynamic inaugural employees' meeting when the employees to be inaugurated were only three: Deputy District Judge Ranger, Mr Blank and Mrs Effington the cleaner. As Mrs Effington was also the cleaner and tea-lady for the Old People's Drop-In Centre, she would have been there in any case, and now stood impatiently, leaning on her mop, desperate to get at the floor.

'The first thing that I ought to say,' said Ophelia nervously, 'is that we shan't be making any staff changes. At least, not straight away. Mr, er,' she looked desperately at Mr Blank who inclined his head in almost imperceptible acknowledgement, 'I understand that you act as clerk, usher, um . . .'

'Caterer, security guard, typist, legal researcher and lavatory attendant,' he finished for her.

'Quite. Yes. Excellent. Well, we should be very pleased if you would continue in your duties for the Wet Nose Court.'

Ophelia felt very silly saying 'Wet Nose Court' all the time. It sounded much too close to 'brown nose' for comfort. But Malachi, imbued with the philosophy of his marketing handbook, had insisted that she use the words whenever possible. Ophelia did not like to let him down, particularly as he was now having to pay people to take the books and join his pyramid.

'Do you not act as bailiff for the court as well?' she asked.

'Oh no,' replied Mr Blank. 'If we need any of that sort of thing we use the bailiffs from Scorsdale. You wouldn't catch me doing that kind of work, out in all weathers, messing with people's nasty things and dirty houses. Taking no end of abuse, I wouldn't mind betting. It'd be

165

dealing with the public on their own territory, as you might say. At least here it's my ground; they usually show some respect. No, Mrs O., don't ask me to be a bailiff, whatever you do.'

'All right,' said Ophelia, rather taken aback. 'I won't. But we can't use Scorsdale's bailiffs; they'll charge us a fortune. Would anyone else like to be bailiff?'

She was reminded of her thankfully brief period as a teacher in Liverpool, cringing before a crowd of streetwise fifteen-year-old girls, all larger than her, and begging them: 'Won't *any* of you be goal defence?'

Mrs Effington looked her straight in the eye. 'Me 'usband likes 'is tea at six.'

Ophelia waited but there was no more.

Deputy District Judge Ranger sighed deeply and raised his eyes to heaven. 'Ah Gawd,' he breathed, 'if it is thy warl that I take on this heavy burden then send me a sign. Send me a sign, Lawd!'

The other three fixed their eyes resolutely on the floor. Ophelia and Mr Blank had lowered their heads in embarrassment, Mrs Effington in curiosity as to whether the Citrigloss Liquid she'd used last week had really given the floor a better shine.

'Oh ma Lawd, send me a sign!' continued Mr Ranger, sounding less like the Lone Ranger and more like Uncle Tom by the minute.

God, presumably tiring as much as the rest of them of Mr Ranger's fake American accent, sent a sign.

Ms Blacking, the old people's occupational therapist, had been rummaging in the storeroom on the second floor, just above the court, in search of egg boxes to be made into handy and attractive spectacle and denture stands. She had tripped over a stack of the *People's Friend* (1978/79) and had fallen headlong into the emergency supplies of Coffeemate. The resulting crash had dislodged one of the polystyrene tiles on the court ceiling and this now fell onto the Deputy District Judge, anointing his iron-grey head with flakes of plaster.

'Thank you, Lawd!' cried the Deputy District Judge, and the matter of the bailiff was settled.

'Now then,' said Ophelia, 'the next question is opening hours. I am hoping that we will get a lot more cases going through this court, which will mean that it has to open more often. Would you know who I should speak to about that, Mrs Effington?'

'Ooh no,' said Mrs Effington lugubriously. 'I shouldn't think you could 'ave the court any more often. The old people won't stand for it.

When the court first moved 'ere in 1973 there was talk of the pensioners staging a sit-in, you know.'

'I'm sure we could come to some arrangement,' said Ophelia, looking about her. The meeting was being held in the District Judge's room which, during the week, was the old people's Creative Workshop. All around them scissors and Sellotape were being wielded with a vengeance and Ophelia's notes had already been transformed into a pension-book holder. An old man had been eavesdropping on their conversation and he now shuffled over to Ophelia.

'Yes,' he whispered laboriously. 'Pay us enough and we'll let you come every day. Just give me the money and I'll make sure the others get it.' He gave her an enormous wink and shuffled back to his cottonwool earmuffs.

'I think I'll just have a word with the Vicar,' said Ophelia. 'Now, finally, I'm quite happy for you to continue to try cases in the Wet Nose Court, Mr Ranger.'

'Much obliged, ma'am.'

'But I would ask you to remember the bottom line. If we get a reputation for favouring defendants here then the plaintiffs will just go and issue proceedings elsewhere. No proceedings, no hearings, no job. I think that's clear enough, isn't it?'

'With respect, ma'am, I hope that you're not asking me to compromise my judicial integrity in order to make money?'

'With respect, sir, I am asking you not to bend completely double backwards in your efforts to find excuses for the indolent, shiftless and dishonest. I would further ask you to note that the Wet Nose Court takes fifteen per cent commission on all damages awarded. Of that, three per cent will go directly to you as a productivity bonus, to be taken in whatever tax-effective form you choose – Arabian port, terracotta flowerpots or disposable nappies. The Lorskwad Initiative is about private enterprise. Let's be as privately enterprising as possible before they start making some rules. Okay? Any questions?'

'Can I start on me floor now?' asked Mrs Effington.

As Ophelia trudged back up Kirkgate towards the Market Square, she became aware that someone was following her. She paused at a travel agents' window and was caught up by Deputy District Judge Ranger. He was rather like a Labrador himself, she thought, with his gangling limbs and perpetual expression of irritating goodwill. She felt like crying 'Down boy! Home!', but remembered the Mid-Yorkshire Champion and the necessity of obtaining what Malachi would call 'a result' at the next agency hearing.

'Did you want something, sir?' she asked, as sweetly as possible.

'Ah sure did, l'il lady, sure as Colorado's done cotton-pickin' hot.'

'Right.' There was a long silence as Ophelia counted the last-minute fortnights in Marbella and Mr Ranger toyed with his holster.

'Fact is, ma'am, I'm a-wantin' to see your Mr Parrish.'

'Mr Parrish? Oh. I'm afraid he's, er, not in the office today.'

'Not in the office? My, that's a mighty sore shame. Well, I'll just call on by in the morning, then.'

'Um, no. No. He won't be in then either. The doctor's told him to take a few days off work. Perhaps it's something that I could help with?'

'Oh no, l'il lady. I wouldn't want you worritting your pretty l'il head. I'll maybe call on him at home then.'

And before she could reply, Mr Ranger was striding off back down Kirkgate, until he reached the court and could mount his imaginary horse to gallop to the sandwich shop.

Meanwhile Malachi, accompanied by Megabyte, Urban and Innocent, was installing Wet Nose computers and modems in as many solicitors' firms as would let the motley party through their front door. Malachi soon found that the secret was to open the door with the pushchair, so that the girl on the front desk was confronted by Innocent's angelic beam and thereby put off her guard. The whole of the pushchair would then appear, being propelled by Urban, whose blond hair fluffed endearingly over the rainhood. Megabyte, with her pleading Labrador eyes, would trot alongside, playing the part as a cross between Lassie and Nana. Urban would then look up at the receptionist with intense seriousness and say, 'P'ease can my daddy come in?'

So far the technique had failed only once, when the lacquered secretary had snapped, 'No children or dogs', before returning to her magazine. Malachi had not noticed the name of the expensive Rambleton firm where this occurred, nor that a young and very good-looking man was standing next to the secretary and had whispered to her as they entered.

It had been Ophelia's suggestion that he should take Megabyte with him, as a visual (and unfortunately nasal) reinforcement of the name and logo. But struck by inspiration Malachi had taken the idea a stage further and had taught Megabyte to carry out the software installation herself. It was, of course, little more than a stunt. Malachi had prepared floppy disks at home with the simple programs necessary to prepare summonses and send them to the court. All that Megabyte had to do, once Malachi had plugged everything in, was to take a disk in her soft

168

leathery mouth, insert it in the disk drive and press the space bar with a paw. When the computer bleeped to indicate that the disk had been read, Megabyte would use her nose to press the eject button beside the disk drive, remove the disk and sit up, a wide smile on her jowly chops and her tail wagging in anticipation.

She was not often disappointed. Many a law firm in Mid-Yorkshire ran out of coffee-time biscuits that morning and many a typist ate her lunch without its usual accompaniment of crisps or chocolate bar. All were captivated, right up to the crusty senior partners, who had sworn never to have a computer in the office, who would emerge from their *Times*es to mutter, 'Damn clever dogs, Labradors. Had one as a boy, you know, used to go shooting pigeons. Damn clever.'

By the time that he had reached the twentieth, Malachi could carry out the installation process so quickly that it was not until he was halfway through a two-player game of Tetris with the girl who did accounts, that he had to explain who he was or why he had just plugged a computer into the only 13amp socket in the building.

'Free loan from the Wet Nose Court for one month,' he would recite conscientiously. 'Provides you with twenty-four-hour on-line connection to the court's central computer allowing you to issue proceedings faster than anywhere else in the country. No obligation, nothing to pay. Rambleton Wet Nose Court.'

He was then supposed to produce a natty red and green poster advertising the court from his briefcase and, with deft sleight of hand, pin it on the office noticeboard next to the Land Registry telephone numbers. Unfortunately he had picked up the wrong pile of papers that morning, so that what his briefcase actually contained was Pius' school project on the duck-billed platypus. Malachi felt that the connection between this and the Wet Nose Court was only tenuous and so, with some regret, he abandoned that part of the process.

All the same, by the time he fetched the older children from school, he had installed thirty-two PCs and made a considerable name for himself in the legal circles of Rambleton and its environs. The Wet Nose Court was in business.

Chapter Twenty-Six

. . . on Fortune's cap we are not the very button

(II.ii. 228–9)

'I say, do you know what a *Romalpa* clause is?' asked Stewart Saggers, poking his head, uninvited, around Ophelia's screen.

'Yes, I do,' replied Ophelia before returning to the contract she was drafting.

It was Tuesday afternoon and she was back at Parrishes, recklessly thundering through the Bandits' conveyancing. Her desk was piled with mortgage instructions and land certificates, her head pulsing with restrictive covenants, and her stomach empty of any lunch. She had spent most of what should have been lunch-time prowling the garden of The Larches in search of the relentlessly absent cat. At half-past one she had abandoned the quest, replaced the Whiskas in the humming fridge and called on the vicar two doors down the hill.

'The Drop-In Centre?' he had mused, standing solidly in his Victorian porch. He arched his back so that his large black stomach rose before Ophelia like a clerical whale. 'Hmm. Kirkgate, isn't it?'

'That's right. The County Court use it at the moment, every other Tuesday morning.'

'Yes. Hmm.' A rare shaft of autumn sun fell upon his heavy spectacles and he rocked his head forward and back in gentle enjoyment of the sensation. 'Nice weather for the time of year, really. Wouldn't you say so?'

Ophelia could not really trust herself to say anything, but managed a tight-lipped grimace.

'Not an unmixed blessing, of course.'

'No, of course not.'

'No.' He resumed his swaying. 'Do you suffer much?'

Ophelia was taken aback. 'Suffer much?' This was a long way from the politely embarrassed Anglicanism of her Church of England High School. ('Not the convent, darling, all those Theresas and wipe-clean Sacred Hearts in the kitchen.') She did not really want to unburden herself of Gigabyte, the Bandits and icy Mr Parrish. In any case, she

171

thought, it would be a discourtesy to Father Jim, whose delicate hints about confession had apparently gone unheeded by almost his entire congregation.

'From the frost. Do you suffer much from frost? I've put my dahlias in the shed this year, you see. They've always gone under the spare bed in the past, but for some reason my wife has put her foot down and now the space is filled with her back issues of *Model Railway World.* They're well wrapped in newspaper – not tabloids, of course. The dahlias, I mean, not *Model Railway World.* Ha-ha!'

His laughter came in little puffs, as though from one of his wife's engines. After six or seven snorts the joke was exhausted and he was serious again.

'So I'm hoping we'll be safe. Are you a great dahlia lady? No? Never mind. Hmmm.' He gazed out towards his gate, perhaps in silent prayer for his hibernating tubers. 'But you didn't come here to talk about dahlias. The Drop-In Centre, you say? And you want the court to be able to use it more often?'

'Yes, that's right.'

'Hmmm.' The gate was favoured with another meditation. 'I fear that may not be very easy. You've heard of the Grey Panthers in the United States?'

'Yes.'

'Yes.' He gave a great sigh. 'Our senior citizens are, let us say, not reticent when it comes to asserting their rights.' He sighed again, then added hastily. 'Which is, of course, as it should be. But I don't think I could, no, I'm almost sure I couldn't. And then there are the Unemployed. Oh dear.' He had begun swaying again, almost imperceptibly at first, but now with a dangerous little bounce on the backward swing. 'So nice to have met you, Mrs O. Do come and see our Flower Festival in the spring. Good afternoon.'

Unless a new venue could be found, therefore, the new Wet Nose Court would have to remain dormant until its usual opening time on the following Tuesday. Meanwhile the computer on-line facility had been rerouted to her office but so far she had received only an advertisement for wigs and a proposal of marriage, intended for Malachi, from one of the more impressionable office juniors whom he had met yesterday. As he was out installing PCs again today, doubtless seducing young girls left and right, Ophelia was not in a good mood. She required a categorical absence of interruptions, least of all from a jocular, overweight fridge salesman trying to trap her with *Romalpa* clauses. He had probably read an article about them in *Refrigeration Monthly* and now thought he was Perry Mason on the strength of it. There was nothing more irritating, thought Ophelia, than a client demonstrating his superior legal knowledge. Nothing, that was, except being cornered at a party by a newly introduced stranger wanting advice about his neighbours' overhanging pear tree. For some reason it was always a pear tree. She returned to her deeds, in which she had just discovered a right of way 'for the use of Jos. Heyward, master chandler, his heirs and assigns' through the sitting room of 8 Southgate. Who on earth would his heirs and assigns be? The ominous spectre of indemnity insurance waggled its little finger.

'No,' said Mr Saggers patiently. 'I don't know what one is, you see. That's why I came to ask you. I've just got this letter from Greenfriz, you know, they make those chest freezers, saying that they're going to repossess them all under their *Romalpa* clause. Look, it's on the back of here.' He waved a flimsy invoice under Ophelia's nose and she reluctantly took it.

'Let's have a look then,' she sighed, reading the Skittle Federations's mortgage conditions. The right of way might have been extinguished anyway, or it might be only a right *in personam* not *in rem*. Bother. What was the use of half-remembering all this stuff?'

'Polly!' she called through the locked door of J. A. Stanmore. 'Got anything that's any use for easements?'

'No, but my dad gets them really bad. Germoloid cream, he uses. And that wet toilet paper's supposed to be dead soothing.'

'Thank you,' groaned Ophelia.

'That's okay. I suppose it's having so many babies. All that pushing.'

There was a rattle and clank as the ancient chain was pulled, followed by a shuddering roar. The door was unlocked and Polly appeared.

'I've always wondered,' she began. 'Oh hello, Mr Saggers. Is it you that's got the piles—'

'Of problems with your contract,' finished Ophelia. 'Have you got Greenfriz's letter there as well?'

'Yeah, here you are.'

Ophelia tried to concentrate, but the words seemed to be waltzing around the paper and the figures all turned into eights as she tried to read them. It was too late to restrain a yawn.

'So you haven't paid for the freezers yet?'

173

'No, no. As I explained, we are having something of a cash flow crisis at this point in time.'

A disturbingly clear mirage of a sleeping bag was insisting upon unrolling itself on the carpet. Ophelia jerked herself into efficiency. 'The point about the *Romalpa* clause is that Greenfriz retain title to the goods until you have paid for them in full. I assume that you haven't sold any of these freezers?'

'Not *sold*, no. But you've got one, remember?'

The words travelled very slowly across the desk, floating in soft pastels around Ophelia's ears until their significance finally buffeted her.

'Oh my God, *those* freezers!'

She clutched the arms of her chair as two Stewart Saggerses swam before her against a background of exploding stars. She suddenly realised that, although she had had no lunch, she had at six o'clock that morning, seized with a desperate hunger after a sleepless night, eaten two packets of malted milk biscuits and three bananas. From the pit of her stomach came belated reminders of their existence.

'Mrs O., are you all right? I know it'll be inconvenient for young Gary, but unless you think we can fight Greenfriz on this . . .'

'No, no, I'm fine. Anyway, I'm sure we can stall them a bit until the money comes in from the mortgages. It won't be long.'

'Thanks, but I'd rather just give them back now. I need that mortgage money, you see, just to pay the rent on my premises and to keep the tax and VAT men off my back. There's nothing else for it; the freezers'll have to go. I don't know that I'd have sold them anyway. The Goblins are pretty cautious these days. Unless Victor Meldrew gets himself a new freezer they don't see why they should either. Why the over-sixties' role models have to be Scottish I don't know. Heroic virtues of meanness and misery. Hardly going to get the country on its feet again, are they?'

'Mr Saggers, you're wasted in the freezer business. With social observation like yours, you could be the Clive James of Mid-Yorkshire.'

'Watch it, Mrs O. No one's allowed to make cracks about my hair, not even the wife. I sacked my last assistant manager for giving me a tin of lavender wax polish for Christmas.'

'I didn't actually mean . . . Never mind. When will you want to collect the freezer then?'

'Would first thing in the morning be okay? I'll send my lads around.'

'Yes, of course. I'll get Gary to do something with his stuff tonight.'

'I feel bad about that you know, Mrs O. Would it help if I let him use one of the frozen food compartments at the back of the shop? He could stick them in the fish section. Not big fish-eaters, they aren't in Rambleton.'

'Thank you, but I think Gary would rather not risk anyone seeing the stuff.'

'Oho, say no more. Well, I won't grass on him. Did the odd bit of poaching myself with my dad when I was a boy. Nowt like it, you know. The sound of the bird fluttering in the undergrowth, the smooth metal of your gun-barrel, the twigs snapping under your feet, your heart beating double time, the cold, the freezing cold . . . Suppose that's how I got the liking for ice, really.' Mr Saggers' face had taken on a wild, poetic expression which sat uneasily upon his too, too solid flesh.

'Well, if there's nothing else, Mr Saggers?' suggested Ophelia.

'No, no nothing at all,' he said dreamily, and floated off into the street outside, every ounce the Ice King, trailing clouds of frozen glory.

Left in the office, Ophelia looked around desperately for Polly. Finally she noticed a sliver of light under the door of J. A. Stansmore.

'Polly!' she called, hammering on the frosted glass panel.

'What is it?' called a muffled voice. 'D'ye think pink mascara goes all right with tagliatelle?'

'Never mind all that, just come quickly. Thanks to the recession we've got twelve stone of defrosting solicitor on our hands again.'

Chapter Twenty-Seven

O, my offence is rank, it smells to heaven;

(III.iii. 36)

'I suppose we could drop him in the river,' said Polly, when Ophelia explained the latest developments. 'Mr Parrish, I mean. With all this rain we've been having, it'll be pretty deep under Southgate Bridge.'

'What? You mean pretend that he's committed suicide?'

'Suicide? You must be joking. People don't commit suicide in Rambleton. Namby-pamby southern way of getting out of trouble, that. No, Ophelia, you'll never succeed in this town until you realise that people here *like* to be miserable, it's our natural state. That David Attingborough ought to do a wildlife programme about us. Take my Gary. D'ye know, sometimes I think he'd rather work for Bill Whitworth for the rest of his life, and hate every moment of it, than set up by himself and risk being successful. Gives his life a purpose, like, having a good moan.'

'But you don't seem to be like that, Polly.'

'Ah well, I'm educated, see. I've got an A level in Business Studies. It gives me a wider view of the world. My mum always said I was a bit of an intellectual. She says I get it from my Uncle Rodney.'

'Your Uncle Rodney?' Ophelia felt that her own cerebral capacities were sufficiently stretched this afternoon by playing straight man to Polly's meanderings.

'Yeah, he was a teacher in one of those dead posh schools over towards Harrogate until he got probation for groping the little boys after choir practice. No, I can't see many round here going for the easy way out. Mind you, they wouldn't have the brains to think of pushing anyone else off a bridge either. Bit sophisticated for Rambleton, that.'

'Anyway,' said Ophelia, as firmly as the biscuits and bananas would allow, 'we're not dropping him in the river at all, murder or suicide. Poor old thing, we've done enough to him already, what with the hair dryers and everything. Now I've sent that clue to my mother, with any luck we'll know what he wanted soon. All we need meanwhile is somewhere cold and isolated to keep him until then.'

177

'And we'll need a van or something to get him there. He won't fit in your car, 'specially with it only being two-door.'

'Oh yes,' said Ophelia, remembering the struggle she had had to get a comatose Hygenus on to the back seat after he had mistaken the Beaujolais Nouveau for Ribena last year. 'How about your Gary? Doesn't he have the use of a van?'

'Yeah, but he'd be no good. He's really squeamish about death and all that sort of thing.'

'But he's a butcher!'

'Oh aye, but he's sick every night when he gets home and he retches something horrid if a customer asks for liver or something.'

'Then why on earth doesn't he change his job?'

'Like I told you, he likes being miserable. But he'd be no good for this. He'd go to pieces. Jump off the bridge himself more than likely. What about your husband?'

'Mal? No, I don't think so. I've managed to avoid telling him so far and I'd like to keep it like that. Crises don't really bring out the best in Malachi. No, what we need is someone solid and reliable. Someone used to dealing with the harsh realities of life and death, someone down-to-earth and unshockable, someone with a lot of land and a good off-the-road vehicle. Someone like Edgar Pottlebonce!'

'That fat farmer? What good would he be?'

'Look, he's ideal. He knows that Mr Parrish is dead already, so it's not as though we have to explain it all to someone new. Then he's one of the Bandits, so it's in his interests to help us. Who's more likely to have spare freezing cold barns than a farmer who doesn't farm anything? *And* he's bound to have some sort of Land Rover. Perfect. Edgar, every woman's dream.'

'Hardly,' said Polly, but she was so relieved to see Ophelia's recovery that she made no further objections.

Edgar's 'Land Rover or something' turned out to be an extremely expensive and impractical Japanese 4x4 in metallic lilac. It was called a Grutta and was embellished by a cute motif of a buffalo, presumably portrayed in mid-grut. Ophelia could not keep herself from glancing at its pretty little chrome wheels and delicate, colour-coordinated roo-bar.

'Well, like I told you, I'm not really a farmer any more,' he said defensively. 'There's no need for me to go rattling about in t'old truck like bloomin' Dan Archer. Mind you, I'd rather be back on'tractor sometimes. Cost a bomb, this poncy thing did, and now she keeps on at me to go on them Grutta Club rallies down in Bedfordshire or summat. Bedfordshire! Huh! No, reason I got it was for my image, like. Clients have to see that I'm successful so's they can have confidence in my advice. Least, that's what young Johnny tells me.'

'But you're not succ— Ouch!' said Polly and hopped up and down a few times, shaking the foot upon which Ophelia had just stamped.

However, the Grutta, although not designed for the carriage of anything more earthy than a briefcase and portable phone, did have plenty of room for a corpse across its periwinkle linen back seat. Edgar's principal worry was bloodstains, but when it was explained to him that Mr Parrish had been deep-frozen for a few weeks now, he agreed to transport them.

Unfortunately the back door of the office led only into a narrow pedestrian cul-de-sac and so the Grutta had to be parked ostentatiously in the Market Square. They waited until six o'clock, when the shops and offices were long abandoned and the piquant titillation of Rambleton's night life, represented by the Ram's Leg and the bingo hall, was yet to be tasted.

'Here we go again,' thought Ophelia, as Mr Parrish was lifted once more from the freezer, and she tucked the now familiar brogues under her elbows. His face was by now acquiring a blurred look, like the forgotten beefburger at the bottom of the basket, too often defrosted and refrozen.

'These mushy peas'll be ruined soon,' said Polly, as they reappeared, clinging this time to Mr Parrish's right armpit. 'Look, they've gone all soggy. Moisture got into the bag, I expect. They might be all right heated thoroughly though. What d'ye think, Ophelia?'

'Take them home and try, if you like,' said Ophelia with what she thought was a sardonic inflection.

'Ooh, are you sure you don't mind? I mean, they're more yours than mine, aren't they? You could have half if you wanted. Oh thanks. My Gary, he loves mushy peas, y'know, specially this lumpy sort.'

'Grumph,' said Ophelia, negotiating the top step.

They reached the bottom of the steps without mishap and Edgar grasped hold of Mr Parrish's waist to edge the body through the Grutta's tailgate.

Suddenly a rasping voice out of the darkness said, 'Evening, Mrs O.'

Ophelia jumped, dropping Mr Parrish's left arm so that the body dangled precariously from the grip of the other two conspirators. She turned and recognised Mr Albert Skate, lurking beneath a streetlight.

179

'Good evening, Mr Skate,' she said with all the confidence she could muster, which was not much.

'Looks rather like a body, that. A *dead* body.'

'D-does it really?'

'It does, Mrs O.' He jingled the coins in his pocket suggestively. 'I wonder if the police would be interested in a *dead* body.'

'Oh, I don't think so, Mr Skate. Not as interested as the DSS would be in Jeremy Croak, Henry Thumper, Thomas Rose and Ernest Woodley.'

Mr Skate was suddenly silent. These were the names, supplied to Ophelia by Darren Skate in a moment of filial ingratitude, under which his father claimed Invalidity Benefit at a range of Mid-Yorkshire benefit offices.

'By the way,' she continued, 'where on earth did you get the names from?'

'They're me great-great grandfathers on me mother's side,' he said proudly, forgetting to plead ignorance. 'Very keen on family 'istory were me mam.'

'Well, thank you for clearing that up, Mr Skate. Now I do, as you so perspicaciously pointed out, have a body to dispose of, so if you will excuse me . . .'

Hardly had Albert Skate left, nonplussed, on his way to the Ferret and Trouserleg on Ape Street (he decided next morning that the whole thing had been a mirage induced by twelve bottles of Owd Barrelscrapings), and hardly had they heaved the body halfway over the numberplate, when two more familiar voices drifted through the foggy air.

'I think you must have got the whole thing a bit cock-eyed, Porridge, old chap,' the first voice boomed. 'If you're selling your house to these ghastly council-estate oiks and the Kraut skittlemen are giving you a mortgage to buy this place then why can't we open the skittles alley there?'

'No, no, Major. It is pretending. We are all pretending. Mrs O., velly nice lawyer, velly clever and beautiful also, she is organising it all.'

'Well, it's a damn' shame, that's all I can say. Be a marvellous place for the skittles down there, by the river. That refrigerator chappie started off there, didn't he?'

'Oh yes, indeed, Mr Zaggers, he own it. Velly auspicious, velly great shame. But look! There is Mrs O., my velly high-quality lawyer. We will ask her to explain it all again. There, you see, leaning against that purple car. I hope she is not having the sickness. My blother-in-law, he have restaurant near here and sometimes he is not getting his meat from velly good meat man, you understand? Mrs O.! Mrs O.! Is it my blother-in-law's Vindaloo you have been eating?'

Ophelia, Polly and Edgar gazed around them wildly, then, with one concentrated effort, heaved Mr Parrish's legs up over the burgundy roo-bar. For a moment the corpse balanced there, rocking in a gentle see-saw motion. Then Edgar gave a final jerk to the still shining brogues and the body toppled slowly on to the back seat. There was a gentle creak as it bounced off the upholstery and then silence. Silence, that is, but for Mr Puri's concerned cries.

'Mrs O., Mrs O.! Are you falling over into the car, Mrs O.? I t'ink that you are having the sickness velly badly. I will come and hold your head, as my mother hold my head when I am little boy. Do not be worrying, my darlink Mrs O. I am arriving towards you velly quickly!'

But Mr Puri, hurrying along the pavement with the Major puffing behind him, could not arrive so quickly as the three body-snatchers could leap into the faithful Grutta and speed away.

Ophelia drew the short straw and sat in the back with the body. This was slightly less unpleasant than sitting in the back of her own Volvo with a couple of nauseous toddlers on a long journey, so she made no complaint. By the time they reached the top of the hill, however, the bananas and biscuits, like Mr Sinatra, were returning for one last farewell. Ophelia swallowed hard and tried to find something to focus upon that was neither purple nor dead. It was not easy. Mr Parrish was propped up next to her and as they turned through sharp corners, Edgar taking full advantage of the Grutta's power steering, a cold head would fall against her shoulder and a clammy hand into her shuddering lap. At last the farm house came into view.

'There's a barn up top be just the job,' said Edgar cheerily. 'It's right cold up there all year round. Used t'keep cattle feed in't, you know, and I'd have to take t'axe to it to break it up, were that bloomin' hard. Aye, Wilf'll be all right there till your ma does t'crossword. I'll just cut through yard here.'

But as the little Grutta bounced across the cobbles it was halted by a manic figure which leapt across its path, hair everywhere and reddened limbs akimbo.

'Edgar! Edgar!' it cried. 'I've gone and blown up my contact lenses! Can't see a bloody thing. Edgar?'

Monica Pottlebonce groped at the windscreen, peering inside with enormous owl-like eyes. Her husband wound down his window and leaned out to reassure her.

'I'm here, pet. *What* did you say you'd done?'

'Exploded the old lenses. Despatched them to Kingdom Come. They were a bit itchy, you see, so I took them out, put them on'table and went to get my specs. Well, I'd forgotten for a minute that the old specs case was part of the,' here she lowered her voice histrionically, '*experiment*. So I'm afraid it's all gone, specs, lenses, hairbrush and about half the bed. All in a good cause, though. Oh? Got visitors, have we?'

'Er, yes dear, yes. This is Polly, the secretary from Parrishes, Mrs O. you've met, haven't you, dear, and um, well, er, old Wilf Parrish in the back.'

'Oh yes. Hello, Wilf. We haven't seen you for a while.' Her large face moved blindly in through the window, bobbing about like a good-natured dinosaur. 'So what are they all doing up here?'

Edgar looked nonplussed so Ophelia stepped into the breach.

'Beating the bounds, Monica, beating the bounds. The Parish Council asked us to come and check that everything is okay. We just have to pop up to your far barn on top of the hill. Frightfully boring, really. We won't keep Edgar from his supper for too long.'

'Beating the bounds? Sounds great fun.' To their horror, Monica was thrusting herself past her speechless husband on to the back seat. 'Come on, budge up. I'll just squeeze in here between Wilf and Mrs O. Opthalia, isn't it? Nice to see you again. Well, not exactly see, eh? Off we go then, Edgar, off we go.'

As they continued up the track, Ophelia and Polly did their best to make innocuous conversation about Christmas shopping, but it was no use.

'Christmas shopping?' bellowed Monica. 'No use for it. Waste of time and money. Get a hamper sent from Harrogate, don't we, Edgar, then sit down for a solid munch. Don't you agree, Wilf?'

Wilfred, understandably, said nothing.

'Feeling all right, are you, Wilf? I must say, you do look a bit peaky.' The great head loomed over him and a rough, raw hand gave his a consoling pat. 'And you're freezing cold! Orachia, do you know, I'm terribly afraid that your Mr Parrish is—'

'Farmhouse cookery!' yelled Ophelia in desperation. 'I've always been awfully interested in farmhouse cookery. We don't all need to go up to the barn. Perhaps you could take me round your kitchen and show me your recipes. You know, home-cured ham, chutney and, er, different chutney.'

'No time for all that,' replied Monica breezily. 'We get frozen chilli con carne these days like everyone else. Now then, Wilf . . .'

'Flower arranging, then. I'm sure you must have some beautiful vases and lots of, um, oases. I'd love to know more about it. Do let's go back now.'

'Huh! Can't be bothered with all that tosh. Are you sure he's all right? Look how his jaw's hanging open.'

'*Religion then*!' Ophelia was almost screaming.

'What?'

'Religion. The Church of England. The, er, Seventeenth Article. I've never understood it, you know, and I think it's so important, don't you, in these ecumenical times.'

'The Seventeenth Article? Why, it's quite simple. It's just . . .'

'Oh, please, couldn't we walk back to your house and discuss it. It's absolutely vital, much too significant to talk about in a Grutta.'

'Very well then,' agreed Monica, and Edgar performed a perfect emergency stop midway through a shallow ford. He sighed in tremendous relief.

'But watch that poor Mr Parrish!' called Monica, ankle-deep in water, as he drove off again. 'I'm sure he's not really the thing. Now then, Oldavia, where are you? The Thirty-Nine Articles . . .'

Chapter Twenty-Eight

*

I once did hold it, as our statists do,
A baseness to write fair, and labour'd much
How to forget that learning,

(v.ii. 33–5)

Ophelia never did find out what the Seventeenth Article was all about, but managed to fire Monica's enthusiasm sufficiently to distract her from the icy state of Mr Parrish. Edgar and Polly arrived back at the farmhouse twenty minutes later and explained, to Monica's apparent satisfaction, that the solicitor had decided to walk home across the fields, 'to put a bit of colour back into his cheeks'. On the journey back Polly confirmed that his body had been well concealed behind a bale of hay and that, barring a sudden Indian summer, it was safe from serious deterioration for a few more days.

Next morning the newly issued proceedings began to come through on the office computer. Malachi was out installing PCs with Megabyte again, having got through Tuesday's quota without breaking any more hearts. The only disappointing thing was the enormous number of spelling and typing mistakes that local law firms seemed to make in their summonses and supporting particulars of claim. Perhaps they were distracted by the peculiar names of both plaintiffs and defendants and by the frankly bizarre events that led to litigation. Take this one, she thought, which had arrived first thing in the morning.

IN THE QAMBLETOW PET NOSS CORRTY COUBT

Bttweeb:
   Kohn Swith   *Ylaintiff*
   asd
   Uniced Enpineerink plc   *Refendants*

PERTICULARS OB CHAIM

1. Ac all vererial tides the Detendantz hage married on businesp as manufacturews of plectrical equicement.

2.   Thy Pluintiff was emplosed be the Hefendants as a zitter betweeb   1765 and 1438.

3.   Durinx thit seriod the Praintiff wab constantin ig conplact wish heavy snokers.

4.   Ab a desult of thos expospre, tee Plabbtife wuffered frog massive snowing.

8.   Suck passile stoking waq paused hy tue pegligenze of ghe Dufendanes.

And so it continued, for page after page. Oddly enough, the pleadings sent by post or ordinary fax contained only the usual number and quality of errors. Perhaps it was the excitement of working on the cutting edge of technology, in the white heat of the information revolution that had sent so many secretaries off the typological deep end. Ophelia mentioned it to Malachi when he telephoned at lunch-time.

'What was that, Oaf?' he yelled. 'I'm at Carlisle bus station and it's a bit noisy.'

'Carlisle! What are you doing there? I told you to move in a spiral out of Rambleton, not to head north-west faster than a Canadian blackback.'

'What's a Canadian blackback? It's not in my RSPB handbook.'

'I just made it up, you idiot. WHY ARE YOU IN CARLISLE?'

'There's no need to shout, Ophelia. The X79 to Glasgow's gone now so it's much quieter. Someone in Scorsdale had a cousin whose next-door neighbour is a magistrates' clerk in Carlisle, so I thought I'd follow the connection. It's the key to successful marketing, you know, the personal matrix.'

'I'll personally matriculate you if you're not back to pick the children up at half-past three, you incompetent fool. Anyway, I was telling you about these mistakes.'

'Oh yes. Very careless of them. Er, you said it was the ones sent via my modems, the ones from Afghanistan without the eighth bit checking device?'

'Malachi, are you trying to tell me something?'

There was silence but for the receiver swinging against the side of the phone box. Then it was picked up again.

'Er, Oaf?'

'What?'

'Could you possibly get away to meet the children from school? The thing is, you know I said that the X79 to Glasgow had just left?'

'Yes?'

'Well, I think that Urban and Innocent might possibly be on it. Don't worry, don't worry. I'll just follow it up and install some more PCs on the way back.'

Pipipipipip.

'Oh God, Malachi! *Get my babies back!* And don't install any computers in Scotland!'

'Why not?'

'Because it's a different bloody legal—'

Bzzzzzz

'System,' said Ophelia into the empty humming telephone.

St Barnabas' RC Primary School was near the church, in the centre of Rambleton, so Ophelia did not have to leave until a quarter past three to go and fetch them. When she arrived at twenty-five past, expecting to have to fight her way through muddy little boys and prams to collect her three, she found the place silent, with only a few empty pushchairs to indicate any life at all.

'It's the third Wednesday of the month,' explained a mother who had followed her in. Ophelia looked blank.

'The third Wednesday of the month,' she repeated. 'They have Creative Assembly with Sister Hedwig. The children each bring something they've made during the past month and the parents and little brothers and sisters are invited. You've got one in Year One, haven't you?'

'Yes, I have.' Ophelia was constantly amazed at these women, whom she could never remember having seen in her life, but who invariably knew not only who she was but which classes her children were in, and, for all she knew, which brand of washing-powder she used. Or Malachi used.

'Well, you should have had a personalised invitation at the beginning of term. Sheila does them on her word processor, you know. Here they are anyway. You should come along next month. Quarter to three. Bring the baby.'

Ophelia made her way towards the double doors out of which children and mothers, with the occasional uncomfortable father, were pouring. Two women in front of her were talking over the heads of their small girls.

'Sister didn't look herself this afternoon. I hope she isn't ill.'

'Didn't you see what happened?'

'No, what?'

'Well you know that Year Four made that big collage of Jesus at the Wedding at Cana with all the wedding guests having speech bubbles coming out of their heads?'

'Oh yes. I saw it on the way out. It seemed very nice.'

'Well, it was, most of it. Bernadette said that one boy had written: "I feel like getting really pissed tonight" in his speech bubble but Mrs Riley changed it to "I feel that Joe is really missed tonight" so that was okay. No, what happened was that one child, no one knows who, had pulled off one of the bubbles and changed it to: "Sister Hedwig beware – Vengeance is mine sayeth the Dog".'

'How very peculiar! And they don't know who did it?'

'Well no, but Andrew McKinley's father is a consultant graphologist and he says that if he gets a look at the whole class's handwriting, he'll be able to tell straight away.'

'So is that what they're going to do?'

'I don't know. Sister Hedwig says it's just a joke and not to worry about it, but she did look upset.'

'Oh, it's a shame. They're so badly brought up, some of these children.'

At that point Joan came out.

'Oh,' she said flatly. 'What are you doing here? Dad's supposed to pick us up.'

'Well, I've come instead as a nice surprise.'

'Oh. Carry my bag, will you?'

Pius arrived, looking, Ophelia thought, rather odd.

'Oh hello, Mum. Can you carry my football boots?'

Hygenus came tearing through the door.

'Hello, Mummy. You don't us'ally come. Is Daddy dead or somefing? This is my reading book and this is my spelling and this is my sums and this is a letter about insec's in our hair and this is my PE kit and this is my apple core from lunch-time and can I plant it and grow a apple tree?'

'And can we have some sweets?' they all chorused.

'Yes, I suppose so. Thirty pence each. Pius?'

'Yes, Mum?'

'You *are* in Year Three, aren't you?'

'Oh Mum, you are hopeless. That was last year. I'm in Year Four now. We do proper football and the girls don't take their vests off.'

'Hmmm,' said Ophelia.

By the time they got home, after a prolonged session at the corner shop discussing the relative merits of Thumb Pops and Curly-Wurlies, there was a merry message on the answering machine from Malachi.

'Just to let you know that we've found the wee laddies at Gretna Green Services so we'll be on our way back for our haggis and a wee drammie. Och aye the noo. By the way, they have a different legal system in Scotland.'

Late that evening they arrived home, the two little boys asleep, leaning against Megabyte's broad belly on the back seat, swathed in tartan scarves and caps and each clutching a little felt pony embroidered with the inscription 'We got hitched at Gretna Green'. Still later in the night Ophelia thought she heard scampering little feet and serious, excited voices, but she was too exhausted to investigate further.

On Thursday morning the summonses were coming in even faster as more and more of the North of England took advantage of the Wet Nose Court's special rates. Others wanted to transfer existing proceedings or to apply for interlocutory hearings. Already the fortnightly Tuesdays were crammed full of bankruptcy petitions, children's appointments, repossessions and applications for summary judgment. Ophelia would have to find an alternative venue if the aged Rambletonians would not relent. She wished that she had slipped a tenner to that old man after all.

Halfway through the morning Ophelia was struggling through the Western European Skittles Federation's mortgage instructions with the aid of a Flemish phrase book when she was disturbed by an angry voice at the reception desk. A youngish man was waving a document in Polly's face.

'What d'ye call this then? Somebody trying to be funny, are they? I've been to the Centre and they said you were running the Court now. And what's this "wet nose" business? All some kind of practical joke, is it?'

'I'm sorry, sir. Is there a problem?'

'I'll bloody well say there's a problem. Look what came in the post this morning . . . Hang on, hang on. It *is* a practical joke, isn't it? Come on, where is he? The camera's here, is it, hidden in the pencil sharpener? Okay, okay, where is he? He's going to come in dressed as a judge, is he.'

'Is who?' Ophelia and Polly stood together in shared mystification.

'Jeremy Beadle, of course. Or possibly Noel Edmonds. I should have guessed from the nose, shouldn't I? Me being allergic to dogs.'

'I'm sorry, Mr . . . er. We're nothing to do with any television show. If you show me the document you've received then perhaps we can sort it out.'

The man's face fell. 'You're not from *Beadle's About*?'

'No.'

'Or *Noel's House Party*?'

'No.'

'Not even from *Up the Creek with Eddie Peake*?'

'What on earth is *Up the Creek with Eddie Peake*?'

'It's a programme on Radio Scorsdale where people get tricked and Eddie Peake, he's the presenter, gives them a commemorative paddle.'

'No, we're not from that either.'

'Oh. Well, I suppose you had better look at this then.'

He handed over a creased and thumb-marked foolscap sheet.

CN THE RAMPLETON WEE NODE CUONTY COOOT
No. 9XD 5479

1. On thy 89th day of Jane 1498 the petitooner POTTY WALL was awfully marred to DERIC WALL (herringfter cashed 'the despondent' . . .

9. Thy mespondent hag behaved on suck a wax that the betitionee bonnet treasonably expected to jive with the despondent.

PARTICULARS

1. She redpongent has beveral tides called the potationer a 'batch' a 'slug' and a 'whale'.

2. Tie rexpingene has oftel trunk niny or hen pants of spider and has comb home in a stave of infoxication.

And so it continued.

'You are Deric Wall?' asked Ophelia.

'Derek, yes. Like I said, it came in the post this morning, out of the blue. Well, I was bloody gob-smacked.'

'Yes, it does often come as a shock to the husband, I'm afraid.'

'A shock to the husband? It came as bloody shock to the wife as well. I dragged our Patty out of bed, banged her head against the wall a few times and asked her what the hell she thought she was doing, saying that I called her a slug and that I drank pants of spider. Well, she didn't know anything about it. Never been near a solicitor, she said. Eight happy years we'd been married.'

'There's obviously been some mistake, Mr Wall. You say the petition was delivered to your address?'

'Yes, 27 Aspen Way.'

'Polly, go and phone the solicitors, would you? Snodsworths, it looks like, says "Snudmoles" on the petition.'

Polly reappeared a few minutes later.

'Their client is Mrs Matty Ball of 17 Aspel Way, divorcing her husband, Eric.'

'There you are, Mr Wall,' said Ophelia brightly. 'An easy mistake to make. No harm done.'

'Yes there is,' said a voice from the doorway. A pretty woman stood there, dabbing at her black eye. 'I'm Patty Wall. I'm divorcing Derek now, for this.'

At lunch-time the indefeasible Polly again took the bus over to Scorsdale Road in search of post and a cat. She found neither. Instead, standing forlorn and puzzled on the doorstep, was Deputy District Judge Ranger.

'Howdy, li'l gal!' he greeted her.

'Less of the l'il,' muttered Polly, drawing herself up to her full four feet nine (with stiletto heels), but she smiled opaquely. 'Were you looking for Mr Parrish?'

'Sure was, li, I mean, ma'am. That there doggone boyfriend of yours at the butcher's told me that you'd told him that Mr Parrish was working from home today. Said that was why he couldn't see him about some handled sausages.'

'Oh yes.' Polly cursed the hapless Gary. 'I mean no. That was last week. He gets a bit confused, does Gary. All that contact with intestines. Doesn't do him any good. No, last week Mr Parrish was working from home. This week he's gone to visit his sister in Scarborough. Yes, Scarborough, that's right. And she's not on the phone.'

'Oh dear. Oh doggone dear. I did want to see him about something extremely important.'

'I'll tell you what you should do,' said Polly confidingly. 'You should see Mrs O. about it. Marvellous solicitor is Mrs O. She'll sort it out. Now, off you go. Bye-bye.' Polly reached up to Mr Ranger's elbow, on a level with the top of her blonde (this week) spikes of hair, and led him firmly back to the driver's door of his car. She stood on the doorstep and waved him goodbye, exuding bourgeois charm from every one of her few inches.

Two letters arrived in the second post, both from the Mid-Yorkshire Champion Building Society. The first, addressed to the Rambleton Wet Nose County Court, requested that proceedings be issued against Mr W. and Miss D. Smith for the possession of 'Dunstrikin', in Leafskirk, Lancashire. The building society intimated that, provided that the application was dealt with 'efficiently and profitably', more work for the court would follow.

The second letter, addressed to Parrishes, was less friendly in tone. It made it quite clear that this was the firm's last chance to retain the lucrative agency work.

'To be quite frank,' the letter concluded, 'we expect a result. The Society has been approached by another, apparently more dynamic firm in Rambleton,' slimy Nick Bottomley, thought Ophelia, 'and is minded to transfer all future matters to this firm if Parrishes are unable to achieve a satisfactory outcome.'

Ophelia sighed, and listed the hearing for the following Tuesday. At least the removal of any notice requirements would allow her to prove her worth within a few days. Deputy District Judge Ranger would just have to toe the line this time and give no quarter to the hapless Smiths. Strange that they should be from Leafskirk. Ophelia thought sadly of Gigabyte. Whatever happened, she wasn't going to let Wobble-Bottomley get his hands on those agency fees.

Chapter Twenty-Nine

If thou canst mutine in a matron's bones,

(III.iv. 83)

'Er, Mum?' began Pius over the sausages and chips on Friday evening. 'Next Saturday is a special day for the Cubs and Brownies. There's going to be a day camp at Scorsdale Forest. Can we go?'

'What, a week tomorrow? I don't know, love. Daddy and I might have something on ourselves so I can't promise that we could take you.'

'No, that's okay. Akela will collect us at the end of our road. The little ones can go, too.'

'Not little,' muttered Hygenus and Urban.

'Except Innocent, of course,' explained Joan hastily. This was *her* plan as she, since her meeting with Mrs Pottlebonce, had assumed the leadership of the Return Gigabyte Campaign.

'Well,' said Ophelia, trying not to sound too enthusiastic. She had been praying for something like this to get the older children out of the way while she and Malachi went to Gloriaux. 'What is it, Thinking Day, or something?'

'Yes, that's it, Thinking Day,' said Hygenus quickly.

'No it isn't,' retorted Ophelia. 'Thinking Day is in February. I remember it from primary school. All the Brownies and Cubs would come to school in their uniforms and at playtime there was a marvellous fight, with the Cubs attacking us with their caps. We unbuckled our leather belts and fought back. It was great. But it wasn't in October.'

'It's all right, Mummy.' Joan hastened to repair the damage. 'Hygenus is in a muddle as usual. It isn't Thinking Day, it's Remembering Day.'

'Remembrance Day?' That's next month. The eleventh hour of the eleventh day of the eleventh month. Don't they teach you anything?'

Remember*ing*, not Remembr*ance*. Anyway, there's a practice tomorrow, as well. Can we go? Akela's going to pick us up for that, too.'

'All right then. Pius, you make sure that Hygenus and Urban are all right and don't try to burn rhododendron wood or choke on the dampers.'

'What are dampers?'

'Revolting blobs of flour and water twisted round a stick and cooked over an open fire. As you can imagine, they end up as solid carbon on the outside and glue on the inside. You then fill them with strawberry jam and consume them under Captain's eye, with every appearance of enjoyment, sticking them down your knickers as soon as her back is turned.'

'I don't think they do that sort of thing these days, Mum.'

'What, no welly gadgets made of string and small saplings? No digging a pit seven feet deep to throw the poo into? No blue cotton camp dresses for the wind to whistle through? They don't know they're born, do they, Malachi?'

'I don't know. My mum said that the Scouts was a Protestant paramilitary organisation. I was sent to Benediction to pray for the souls of those poor lost boys who went to camp.'

'There's a funny smell in here,' said Hygenus from the back seat of the Pottlebonces' Grutta. They were on their way up to Greenhaigh Farm for the campaign meeting, organised by Monica Pottlebonce and Joan during their shared sojourn in the pantry.

'Be quiet, Hygenus,' said Joan, from her elevated position in the front seat. She was beginning to think that Mrs Pottlebonce, Monica as she was allowed to call her, was, despite her peculiar appearance, one of the most exciting people Joan had ever met. Certainly more fun than boring old Sister Hedwig with her life-affirming liturgies and her inexhaustible supply of symbolic oak leaves.

'That's all right,' said Monica gruffly. 'There is a bit of a pong. I noticed it myself after Edgar was beating the bounds on Tuesday. If it wasn't that we haven't had any livestock for years, I'd swear he'd had a dead sheep in the back instead of two solicitors. Now how about a singsong? You told your parents you were going to camp, didn't you? Well, pretend you're all sitting round the campfire cooking sausages. Ready?'

And Mrs Pottlebonce, head thrown back, one hand conducting, the other on the steering wheel, began to sing.

'Onward Christian lay-ay-ay-dies
Marching as to war.
Letting our good men-folk
Always go before.

194

For they're our superiors
Nobler far than we.
That's why they are priests while we can
Only make the tea – pom pom pom.

'Onward Christian lay-ay-ay-adies
Through our humble lives.
With our shared ambition
To be vicars' wives.
Knowing that a woman has
Scarce a soul at all.
Indispensable in our own sphere;
The parish hall – POM, POM, POM.

'Come on, boys, you join in as well. I'm sure you don't want your sister becoming a bishop, do you?' Monica let out a snort of horsey laughter as she swung into her drive, scraping the side of the Gutta against the gatepost. The children waited for her to stop the car, leap out and throw herself over the bonnet in a torrent of weeping, as they had seen their mother do, but she seemed hardly to have noticed, shouting blithely, 'Tra-la. Another casualty!' and ramming the accelerator on to the floor as she tackled the final hill.

Out of the wing mirror on her side Joan could see Urban, white with terror, crossing himself and mouthing a Hail Mary as they began the ascent. He said another, obviously in gratitude, when the vehicle finally came to a stop in the cobbled yard, its protective bars embedded in the side of a barn. She wondered whether Monica had noticed. She knew that Monica wasn't a Catholic, at least not an ordinary Catholic, but her talk of priests, sacraments and missals didn't sound much like the Protestants Joan had known, either.

'Out you get, lads!' she was thundering now, giving each boy a hearty smack on the bottom as he clambered down. 'Saw you saying y'prayers there, Uriah. Well done, well done. I suppose it's the Jesuits, is it?'

Urban, who had never heard of the Jesuits and supposed that it was Mrs Pottlebonce's euphemism for car-sickness, nodded unhappily.

The children were shepherded into the sitting room and each given a half-pint mug of cider.

'Children drink cider, don't they?' Monica asked Joan.

'Well yes, I had some once. Woodpecker, I think it was called. Daddy said that it wasn't very strong.'

'That's all right then. This isn't Woodpecker; it's called Grandpa Ned's Pipribbler. It must all be much the same. What's this – 8.8 per cent? I suppose that's how much apple it's got in it. Turnips, the rest, I expect. My sister wins first prize with her strawberry jam at the Village Show every year and she swears by turnip. Go on, drink up.'

The children obediently drank up, Hygenus draining his glass in a couple of swigs.

'I liked that,' he said. 'Is there any more?'

'Later on, Hyacinth, later on. Now there's one more person coming to join us and I think I hear her car now. She's the vice president of NARCOF (I'm the president) so I want you to be on your best behaviour for her. Ah, here she is.'

The door opened and a familiar figure strode into the room.

'Oh no! Look, Urban, it's that witch from church!' said Hygenus in what he thought was a whisper. Urban, who was already looking green, grew distinctly greener.

Lady Tartleton stood on the hearth rug and surveyed the children with horror.

'Monica,' she said at last, in a voice refined by centuries of patrician tyranny. 'You told me that this was a meeting to discuss NARCOF's campaign against *that woman*. If I had been told that you were operating some form of nursery then I regret to say that I would have declined the invitation.'

'What d'ye mean, nursery?' demanded Joan, flown with insolence and cider. 'I'm seven and Pius is nearly nine.'

'These children have had their Labrador puppy stolen by Sister Hedwig,' explained Monica. Lady Tartleton's expression softened slightly. 'Apparently she's taking it to one of these feminist pagan rituals next Saturday and they're afraid that,' she lowered her voice to a confidential bellow, 'she's going to *sacrifice* it.'

'So we're all going to rescue her!' shouted Hygenus. 'P'raps you could cast a spell on old Sister Wig-Head.'

Lady Tartleton cast upon him a look of frozen wrath. Urban began to cry but the look had no effect upon Hygenus. 'Can I have some more of that sideboard now?' he asked.

'No, Hi,' said Pius, who felt his authority as the eldest being eroded. 'We have to make some plans about how to rescue Gigabyte.'

'I've been thinking about that,' said Joan. 'I think that we should kidnap Sister Hedwig. Then we'll tell the other femi-whatsits, her friends, that we'll swap her for Gigabyte.'

'Yeah!' roared Hygenus. 'Kidnap Sister Wig-Head! Battle-Leopard could guard her! Rroarr!'

'Perhaps her friends won't want her back,' objected Pius. 'I know that I'd rather have Gigabyte.'

'Yes, but Gigabyte can't do Creative Assembly, can she? Or find Father Jim's glasses and write his sermons.'

'She could find glasses,' said Hygenus loyally, 'if they were buried in the garden. With a bone.'

Urban stood up very suddenly and stood swaying, his throat working ominously.

'Goin' be sick,' he mumbled and fled for the door. Mrs Pottlebonce followed him, her purple face mottled with anxiety.

When the children got back home at six o'clock Hygenus was still singing 'Onwong Christine lay-ay-ay-adies' and Urban was still linen white. Pius, remembering his father's last afternoon with the whisky bottle, had persuaded Monica to stop and buy them some peppermints on the way home. After a few incoherent mutterings to Ophelia about the 'camp' they had escaped to Joan's room for what Pius importantly called a 'debreeching'.

'Well, we didn't get very far with the plan, thanks to Urban,' complained Joan.

'Yes, that Lady Tartyton wouldn't talk to us at all once Monica had gone,' said Pius. 'Where were you all that time, anyway?'

'She took me to the barn,' said Urban proudly. 'I was sick behind it and then she took me inside. It was full of lic'rish. She said I couldn't have any but I got some.'

From the pocket of his baggy trousers Urban took a bundle of small sticks. He held it in the air and gave it an exploratory lick.

'Urggh,' he said. 'That's not lic'rish.'

'It certainly isn't,' said Pius, who had not spent his Sunday afternoons watching cowboy films in vain. 'That's dynamite.'

Chapter Thirty

For who would bear the whips and scorns of time,
Th'oppressor's wrong, the proud man's contumely,
The pangs of dispriz'd love, the law's delay,

(III.i. 70–72)

When Mr Blank unlocked the front door of the court at five to ten on Tuesday morning there was already a queue of some fifty people waiting outside, grumbling and stamping their feet on the frosty pavement. He weeded out the seven or eight who were waiting for the Old People's Drop-In Centre and herded the rest into the small waiting room.

Ophelia was just coming in by the back door. Mr Blank grasped her arm and pulled her into the men's lavatory.

'We've got forty-seven cases listed for ten o'clock,' he hissed. 'Should we just start at the top and work our way through?'

'No. Let me see the list. I'm in that one myself. We'll do that first. Then take the rest in accordance with how rich and litigious the plaintiff is; the richest and most litigious first. That means the Arthurian Bank then Carazy Finance. Rambleton Council can wait. And give them complimentary cups of coffee while they're waiting.'

Mr Blank edged his way into the crowded waiting room where the litigants were jammed together in compulsory intimacy. A few solicitors made desultory conversation about Rambleton Town's poor performance on Saturday, a larger group of untidy defendants complained loudly over their cigarettes, and three or four filthy toddlers, their faces gilded with chocolate, chased each other around the legs of the grown-ups.

'Mid-Yorkshire Champion and SMITH!' bawled Mr Blank.

A plump woman in a neat turquoise coat disentangled herself from a feuding family and came over to him.

'I'm Dorothy Smith,' she explained. 'My brother, Wardle, couldn't come, I'm afraid. He's not been at all well.'

At ten past ten Deputy District Judge Ranger still had not arrived and Ophelia was desperately trying to reach him, using the telephone in the Senior Citizens' Co-ordinator's office. She had got through to his housekeeper, who was vague and not very helpful.

'Oh dear,' she murmured. 'Mr Ranger did leave at ten to nine, the same as usual.'

'Did he say anything special about where he was going?'

'No. No, he just said what he always says: that he was off to fight for justice and mercy in a land of cold hearts and splintered dreams.'

'What, he says that every morning?'

'Oh yes, even on Saturdays when he only goes as far as the greenhouse. The Judge is a very dedicated man, Mrs O.'

'Well, I wish he'd dedicate himself to getting to court on time. I'll try Snodsworths.'

But Mr Snodsworth, peevish at being disturbed mid-*Geranium*, had no idea where Mr Ranger might be either. Ophelia took *Anna Karenina* out of her briefcase and sat down to wait.

Meanwhile Mr Blank had ushered Dorothy into the District Judge's room and left her there while he extricated two of the chocolate-covered children from a filing cabinet. Dorothy looked at the drab walls and smiled approvingly at the homecoming sheep. Then she noticed a computer, placed in splendid isolation at the head of the large table. A motif of a labrador's head was attached, slightly askew, to the monitor.

'Aha,' said Dorothy. 'I've seen you before, haven't I?'

Since her first embarrassing encounter with 'Write', Dorothy had determined to explore further and she was no longer abashed by the deeper mysteries of *Windows*. As there were no sounds of anyone else coming into the room she sat down next to the computer. The screen was now filled with a vision of swans gliding from one corner to another.

'Screensaver,' said Dorothy to herself and gave the mouse a gentle shake. 'Wakey wakey, mousie.' The familiar icons came into view and she clicked on to 'File Manager' and began to scan the lists of files.

'Midyksmith.' That looked like it. A few seconds' frenzied clicking. Yes, here it was, pleadings, documents, letters, all scanned into the one, damning file. Quickly Dorothy set to work.

She had just finished and had moved demurely to a chair at the other end of the table when Ophelia and Mr Ranger came in. He had a bandage around his head and one arm in a sling.

'Are you sure that you're all right?' Ophelia was saying. 'I'm sure that we could get someone else to hear the cases, or adjourn them to another day.'

Dorothy noticed that blood was seeping out from under the bandage.

'Just a scratch, ma'am,' he replied. 'Just a flesh wound. Those damn bank robbers won't get the better of L. Ranger. No sirree!'

'It was very brave of you, Mr Ranger,' agreed Ophelia. 'I must say that I would never have guessed that your comb could be turned into a dagger like that. Pity that they had to use it on you. Still, I don't suppose you knew that it was only a security practice simulation, did you?'

'You can't be too careful, ma'am. Not where the safety of the townsfolk is concerned. And talking of the townsfolk, I've still not managed to catch up with that thar Wilf Parrish. That li'l gal of yours says I should talk to you instead. The thing is, you see, not to beat about the cactus grove—'

'Don't you think we'd better get on with the hearing?' interrupted Ophelia. 'You have got another forty-six after this one.'

'Okay, ma'am, you know best. Right then, let's get going, pardners. That's mighty queer. I don't seem to have any court files.'

'That's because it's all on computer now, sir. You remember that I explained it all to you last week.'

'So you did, l'il lady, so you did. Now let me see. Yee-hah! So the first case is something to do with swans. Don't tell me, don't tell me. You, ma'am,' He turned with a courteous bow to Dorothy. 'You accidentally killed one of the Queen's swans. A little target practice in the park, was it? It's high treason, I'm afraid. But we must temper justice with mercy. An unconditional discharge, I think.'

'Mr Ranger, the case has nothing whatsoever to do with swans.'

'It hasn't?'

'It hasn't, and you're not a criminal judge anyway.'

'Aw shucks. I always wanted to be, you know. But every time I applied they told me I was too eccentric. Eccentric? A clean-cut all-American boy like me. I ask you! But if the case is nothing to do with swans then what are they doing swimming about like that?' He gazed at the monitor for a few seconds. 'Ah, I know. It's one of those computer viruses, isn't it? Swan fever. Quick, quick, everybody out! Women and children first! After you, ma'am. Hurry up, I can feel it oozing out already!'

Ophelia reached over and pressed a key.

'Mrs O!' cried the Deputy District Judge. 'You've saved us! Halleluia!' He leaped in the air, long limbs akimbo, his sling flapping painfully.

'Perhaps we could begin,' suggested Ophelia, looking at her watch. 'This is an application for possession of Dunstrikin, Leafskirk, Lancashire made by the Mid-Yorkshire Champion Building Society. The property is charged to the Society to secure a business loan made

201

by the Lancastrian Bank to Mr Wardle Smith. The Lancastrian Bank has, of course, now been taken over by the Society. The property is in the joint names of Mr Wardle Smith and Miss Dorothy Smith; I have the Charge Certificate here, and the amount currently outstanding is thirty-two thousand eight hundred and seventy-two pounds.'

'I'm afraid you've made a mistake there, ma'am,' said Mr Ranger, peering at the screen. 'It says here that the amount owing is thirty-two pounds eighty-seven.'

'Thirty-two *thousand* pounds, sir.'

'No, Mrs O., thirty-two eighty-seven. It's quite clear.'

Ophelia leaned across the table. 'Oh I see. It's obviously a typing mistake. We can disregard that, even under the old Green Book rules. An error on the face of the record, or something like that.'

'I don't think so. Look, it's the same in the affidavit and bank statement.'

Ophelia swore under her breath. She had been so anxious to demonstrate to the Deputy District Judge the advantages of the paperless court that she had thrown away her own copies of the pleadings.

'With respect, sir . . .'

'You can give me all the respect you darn well like, but if you think I'm allowing those Mid-Yorkshire sharks to take away this lovely lady's home for the sake of a measly thirty-two pounds eighty-seven then you can just cottonpickin' well think again.' His injuries forgotten, Mr Ranger was in his element again. 'Now then.' He smiled at Dorothy, who fluttered in reply. 'Would you by any chance have the cash on you right now so that you can pay off these hellhounds?'

'I'm afraid I haven't,' confessed Dorothy. 'I bought a sandwich on the Trans-Pennine and I haven't brought my cheque book.'

'Don't you fret, then, ma'am. L. Ranger never saw a lady in distress and passed by the other side.' With a flourish he reached into his jacket pocket with his good hand and brought out his wallet. He opened it to reveal a few coppers, a library ticket, a kidney donor card and a membership card for the Eddie Grundy Fan Club.

'Oh, I forgot,' he said, crestfallen. 'The bank manager confiscated my cheque book and card this morning. He says I can't have any money out of my account until he's had his car windows mended. The dirty rotten double-crosser. How was I to know it wasn't the robbers' getaway car?'

'It appears,' said Ophelia sternly, 'that no one is in a position to redeem this charge. I would point out also, that under the terms of the mortgage, the building society is entitled to add its costs to the outstanding debt. As of now,' she looked at her watch again, 'those costs stand at six hundred and ninety-three pounds, thirty-five pence.'

Dorothy bit her lip. She had not noticed the reference to costs.

'I can get the money soon,' she promised. 'Next Saturday, I'll be getting quite a lot of money.' Sorry ELLA, she added silently.

'Well, as Deputy District Judge that sounds quite satisfactory. And as court bailiff I shall be only too happy to attend at Dunstrikin to collect the monies.' Mr Ranger gazed at Dorothy in admiration, completely forgetting his American accent.

'Oh, you don't have to come that far. You can meet us at . . . at a secret location,' said Dorothy, catching Ophelia's quick glance. 'I'd rather not tell you where it is now.'

'That's just fine, just fine. You just give me a ring and let me know. Here's my number.' He scrawled with difficulty on the back of his Eddie Grundy Fan Club membership card and handed it to her. 'At your service, day or night. Well, I think that deals with that little matter, doesn't it, Mrs O.?'

Ophelia was in a dilemma. If she went along with this, then there was no doubt but that the Mid-Yorkshire would give all their future work to the despicable Bottomley. However, if she retrieved the papers from her wastepaper basket then she would be admitting the fallibility of Malachi's computer system and jeopardising the reputation of the Wet Nose Court. And this Miss Smith did seem to be rather a sweet old thing.

'Yes, that all seems to be in order,' she agreed.

'Giddyup then!' called the Deputy District Judge and at the familiar order Mr Blank appeared at the door.

When Dorothy had been ushered out, before Mr Blank called the next case, Ophelia took him to one side.

'I can't stand the suspense any longer. Do tell me, what *is* your name?'

Mr Blank looked suspicious. 'Promise you won't tell Mr Ranger?'

'I promise.'

'It's Silver, Jim Silver.'

'Ah.' Ophelia smiled at him in complicit understanding and left the court.

As she walked through the car park she noticed a black Labrador sitting in the driver's seat of an old Ford Fiesta. It did look remarkably like Gigabyte. 'Funny how they are all so similar,' said Ophelia to herself, and fell to thinking about gene pools and interbreeding. She was concentrating so hard, congratulating herself upon her memory of school biology, that she did not notice that the dog was jumping up and down on the seat, scratching at the windscreen, and barking joyfully after her.

Chapter Thirty-One

For 'tis the sport to have the enginer
Hoist with his own petard, and 't shall go hard
But I will delve one yard below their mines
And blow them at the moon.

(III.iv. 208–211)

Ophelia woke up at three o'clock on Friday morning with a heavy weight of guilt and fear dragging at her stomach. She climbed out of bed, ran to the primitive bathroom and was extremely sick. Her conscience, successfully suppressed for the past four weeks, had suddenly awakened and was determined to make up for lost time. She padded back and sat on the edge of the bed, sipping a glass of water and feeling the blood flooding up to her cheekbones and back again. Why on earth had she got herself into this? It had taken years to qualify as a solicitor, years of *Donaghue* v. *Stevenson,* ring binders and legal aid forms. And now she was going to throw it all away in her first qualified month, for the sake of a dog. It wasn't even as if she liked Labradors, stupid lolloping things with their endlessly wagging tails, noses in everyone's crotches and incessant greed. Not that any of these attributes were the worst thing about them. The worst thing about a lab was not even its ability to absorb all the heat given off by any form of fire, leaving the rest of the room in cold dog-scented misery. The very worst thing was its relentless good humour, the way that no matter how often it was kicked up the bottom, sworn at, or had its nose lacerated by barbed wire fences, it would bound back with that silly grin across its slobbering chops. Bloody Malachi. She looked at him as he lay asleep, his head sandwiched between two pillows, snoring with loud and regular contentment. Ophelia prodded him with her foot and he mumbled, 'Thirty rubber bands,' before reaching out, and adding another pillow.

'What d'ye bloody mean, thirty rubber bands?' shouted Ophelia, goaded out of her depression. 'I'm about to go to prison for fraud and you're talking about rubber bands!'

Malachi removed the two top pillows, sat up and said with infinite

205

patience, 'Oyster casserole.' He then kissed her gently, lay down again and recommenced his snores.

Ophelia gave up and went to work. She left a note on the kitchen table: 'Mother earning daily Coco Pops. In case of emergency phone Serious Fraud Squad.'

As she drove past the turning for Greenhaigh she tried not to think of Mr Parrish, in lonely decomposition under a bale of hay.

It was nearly half-past four now, and the first market traders were setting up their stalls. Ophelia recognised the same pair of knickers that she had seen every Friday since she came to Rambleton, a particularly repulsive pair in puce nylon, decorated with bunches of blue roses. Outside the office the sheep pictures man was unloading his van.

'Mornin',' he called. 'Fancy a nice picture for the office?'

The picture he was holding up was the same as that on the District Judge's wall. Ophelia shuddered, and pretended that it was at the cold.

'Not today thanks. Got a lot to do.'

'You lawyers,' he grinned. 'Coining it in.'

'That's right.' Suddenly she felt quite light-headed. 'I've got a neat little mortgage fraud going today.'

'Nice work if you can get it. See you, love.'

'See you.'

Ophelia sat at her desk, the lamp casting a friendly glow on Parrish's bank statement. She slurped her coffee and reflected that there were worse things than being a master financial criminal. Those knickers, for a start. If anyone should go down for a spell in Holloway it was the woman who ran that stall. She looked again at the bank statement which she had requested the afternoon before. The money from the Western European Skittles Federation had already come through, converted out of ECUs by a bemused bank clerk, as had the advances from the Arthurian Bank and from Rambleton Council. The two building societies, the Mid-Yorkshire Champion and the Braddylesdale, were due to send their mortgage monies by telegraphic transfer sometime during that day. The total would be £180,000, of which Ophelia would take £70,000 for Gigabyte and £2,000 for Parrishes' costs. She had agreed to meet the mortgage payments for all the bandits for the first six months, while they concentrated on their various investments. Ophelia frankly expected to be slopping out her cell in six months' time, in any case. Getting to the end of today was the most that she could hope for.

There was a lot of work to do, filling in Land Registry forms and direct debits, and she was only on her ninth mug of coffee when Polly arrived.

'Oh hello, Ophelia,' she said cheerfully. 'Big day today, eh?'

Ophelia had tried to keep the truth about the mortgage fraud from Polly, hoping to save her from complicity and from notoriety in the *Law Society's Gazette* as Miss X whom 'it was ordered that no solicitors' firm should employ for a period of three years'. But Polly was sharper than her conversation suggested, and managed to wear Ophelia down with *non sequiturs* until the truth was out. In recognition of Polly's devotion beyond the call of duty Ophelia had promised her and Gary five thousand pounds out of the fraud, which would be enough for them to put a deposit down on their own butcher's shop with a flat above. Polly had no doubts about the success of the scheme. As her mum said, 'Tha' can't bak t'pud wi'out sticking thy 'ands in t'oven.'

It was around half-past nine, and Ophelia was thinking about Eccles cakes for breakfast, when Polly put her head around the screen with a slightly worried look.

'It's them bandages,' she announced. 'Them mortgage bandages. They've come to see you.'

'What, all of them?'

'Yeah. Lady Tartington, Mr Wobblecronce, that man from Freezaland, Mr Pâté with some old geezer and them Slates with that slag Sharon.'

'Polly!'

'Well she is. I was at school with her, you know. The only man who's not seen her knickers inside out is Danny Baker with his Daz doorstep challenge. And that's only because they wouldn't pass his whites test.'

The Bandits filed around the screen. There were only two chairs in front of Ophelia's desk and these were immediately and as a matter of course taken by Lady Tartleton and Albert Skate. The others stood around self-consciously, with the exception of Mr Puri, who was beaming with delight. Stewart Saggers looked particularly awkward, and Ophelia noticed that he was directing furtive and puzzled glances at the mini-skirted and bare-legged Sharon.

Lady Tartleton gave a little cough, purely symbolic in nature, and began.

'Mrs O.,' she said formally, 'I should like to begin by expressing the appreciation felt by all of us for your proffered assistance to us in our times of, hem, financial straightening. However, our positions have altered somewhat and we are here to ask you whether the plan could be, hem, slightly amended.'

Ophelia nodded, having no idea what Lady Tartleton was talking

207

about. Lady Tartleton realised her bewilderment and continued.

'Perhaps I should begin at the beginning. Yesterday morning I was walking my boys.'

'Your boys?'

'Horace, Virgil and Caesar; my Labradors. I was walking them on the Kirk Glebe on my way to Presto when they became involved in a hem, altercation.'

'Started a scrap with t'Hulk,' explained Mr Skate. ''E thought there were just the one, you see. 'E could've beaten t'shit out of one, but then these other two buggers turn up.'

'The Hulk is Mr Skate's pit bull terrier,' said Lady Tartleton. 'He's really quite charming when you get to know him. He and my boys are the greatest of friends now.'

'Yeah, they're good mates,' agreed Mr Skate. 'But you mustn't go around saying that 'e's a pit bull, yer ladysworth. 'E's a Staffordshire cross, right?'

'Oh yes, I'd forgotten,' said Lady Tartleton meekly. 'Anyway, where was I?'

'On the Kirk Glebe with four rampaging dogs?' suggested Ophelia.

'Oh yes. Well, Mr Skate . . .'

'Bert,' corrected Mr Skate.

' . . . Mr Skate,' said Lady Tartleton firmly, a hint of colour coming into her marble cheeks. 'Mr Skate and I got into conversation and he invited me to his house at, hem, Ragged-Trousered Phil—'

'Just call it Raggy-Kegs, yer ladyness,' suggested Mr Skate.

'At, hem, Ragged-Kegs, for a cup of tea. Well, when I saw it, I was simply amazed. *So* compact and convenient, so splendid for the boys with so many other dogs so *very* near, and above all so *cheap* to run, well, I decided to take Mr Skate up on his offer and to move in with him after all.'

'Dis-gustin' at your age, Dad,' said Darren with an unpleasant leer.

'Oh no, there'll be nothing like that,' said Lady Tartleton quickly. 'It will be a purely business arrangement. I am to bring a few things from Tartleton Court, the little Queen Anne table, the candlesticks and so on and Mr Skate is to help me to claim my benefits. He says that he thinks I'll be able to go on the 'sick' as well, with my dodgy knee. I fractured it in '51, you know, at a point-to-point. And then my boys will be able to have steak like their new friend the Hulk. It really couldn't be more convenient.'

Major Lamb's voice boomed out: 'Now are you absolutely sure, my dear? This chap, well, no offence, but we don't really know a damn thing about him, do we? Might be a White Slaver, what? Which school were you at, Skate, if you don't mind my askin'?'

'You can ask,' said Mr Skate, scratching his groin pensively, 'but I can't bloody remember. I were at t'mill afore I were thirteen.'

'Please don't interfere, Major,' said Lady Tartleton crisply. 'I know perfectly well what I am doing. The only stipulation I have made is that that rat is removed from the premises before my arrival.'

'An' if Kylie goes, I go,' said Darren stoutly.

'So you see Meester Darren and Mees Sharon they will be buying my humble house after all!' cried Mr Puri, who could not restrain his glee a moment longer. 'And it is all with great thankingness to you, Mrs O., my most velly high-quality lawyer.'

'Yes, yes,' said Ophelia. 'But how can you afford the mortgage payments, Darren? I can't pay them for you if I'm not getting the money, and I explained to you that Malachi can't really give you a job.'

'That's okay,' said Sharon, chewing gum as she spoke. 'I've gorra, let's say *source of income* meself. We can pay the mortgage. Just don't ask too many questions, okay?'

Stewart Saggers suddenly gave a jerk.

'That's where I know her from!' He broke off as a red tide of embarrassment travelled up his fat face.

'S'awright cock,' said Sharon, in what was supposed to be an imitation of Mandy Rice-Davies. 'We all believe in client confidentiality, don't we, Mrs O.?'

'Certainly, although I fear that my profession is not quite as old as yours. So let me get this straight. Lady Tartleton, you and Mr Skate actually want to go ahead with the purchase of Mr Skate's council house? And Darren and Sharon, you want to buy the house on Heifersgate from Mr Puri?'

'Yeah.'

'Yes, most indeedly and you are velly, velly clever to be understanding it all so quickly. And so I will be buying the most excellent house of Mr Zaggers with my dear friend the Major for our skittling alley. All is now velly good.'

'But what about your mortgage arrears, and what about the capital that the Major needs you to put in?'

'Aha,' chuckled the Major, in what Ophelia felt was an unnecessarily bluff manner. 'I think I can explain that, young lady. Fact is, we've had a bit of luck on the old gee-gees.'

209

Albert Skate, who had been dozing off, jerked his head up and turned to the Major with a look of envious suspicion.

'Happened to notice a horse, Biryani Sunrise, running in the two fifteen at Redcar on Tuesday. "I say," I said to old Porridge here, "that's your native grub, why don't we lay out a fiver each?" Well, bugger me (excuse me, m'dear) but what does old Porridge do but put his wife's bloody dowry, worth thousands of rupees, on the damn horse. So, I wasn't going to be outdone by a native. I put Letty's pearls in hock, and that diamond thingy that her grandmother gave her, and put that all on as well. Anyway, old Biryani Sunrise came in at bloody fifty to one and Porridge and I cleaned up. Makes you wonder, doesn't it, whether there mightn't be something in this Hindu and Mohammedan caper? Can't see an RC horse doing that for us, can you?'

'I really couldn't say.' Ophelia was not at all sure that her early morning had not taken its toll and that she had not fallen asleep at her desk. At any moment she might wake from this grotesquely complicated dream to find herself back with the comparative normality of fraud. 'And you, Mr Saggers? Have you had some amazing stroke of luck this week? Has it been announced that all fridges but yours cause cancer of the elbow? Has Greenfriz been taken over by a German philanthropist with a burning mission to help Yorkshire's freezer business? Or have you simply heard of the peaceful death of a distant and rich relative?'

'No, none of them,' said Stewart Saggers, still flushed from his earlier revelations. 'Though the thing about elbow cancer might be useful, tarted up a bit. No, it's just that I've been trying to get that house at Southgate off my hands for years now. With it gone that's a major load off my back. No pun intended.'

Major Lamb bowed slightly.

'And I've got some pretty big plans for Greenhaigh Farm. The Ice Imperium as I'm going to call it. An out-of-town frozen food megastore. It'll have a skating rink, all-year-round Santa's grotto, pick 'n' mix flavoured ice cubes . . . You wait, they'll be coming from all over Yorkshire for this one. Bigger than Harry Ramsden's, it'll be, with my special no-calorie meals, made entirely from ice. And with Edgar's pet accountant on the premises it can't fail. You're all invited to the Grand Opening, by the way. I'm hoping to get Torville and Dean to dance on the oven chips.'

'It sounds absolutely ridiculous,' said Ophelia, and Mr Saggers beamed happily. 'And finally Mr Pottlebonce. I hope that you're not planning on continuing with the fraud, because if you are then it looks as though you'll be homeless.'

'Well, I would've,' the farmer began slowly. 'Ask anyone in t'market or t'union, they'll tell you, Edgar Josiah Zerubbabel Pottlebonce ain't the man to set his hand t'ploughshare and then turn back. But it doesn't look like I've got a lot of choice. So I got to thinking. Like I said, I've not been a real farmer for years. A man in my position, an Independent Agricultural Finance Consultant, he ought to have an address to match his status. And with our Monica being so friendly with Lady Tartleton over this NARCOF business, I don't like to let you all down. So you can count me in. I'll buy Tartleton Court.'

When they had all left, having enjoyed a ceremonial handing over of keys, Ophelia sat motionless at her desk for a long ten minutes. That was that then, all over. Those weeks of complex planning, sleepless nights, fingers perpetually crossed behind her back, all for the sake of an ordinary conveyancing chain. It only made matters worse that there was a good deal of relief mixed up with the disappointment. What price her conscience against Gigabyte's life?

She looked up to see Polly's tear-stained face peering around the screen.

'Ooh, I'm sorry, Ophelia. Your poor little doggie. And, I shouldn't be thinking of it, I know, but I had set me heart on that little shop.'

'I know, I know. Come on, though, we've got some conveyances to date.'

211

Chapter Thirty-Two

What should such fellows as I do crawling
between earth and heaven? We are arrant
knaves all, believe none of us.

(III.i. 128–130)

Raymund Redforest quickly handed over his boarding pass and made
sure that his passport was hidden away before taking his window seat
on the Boeing 747. Air travel was always a source of worry to him, not
because he feared a crash or hijack, but because his tickets bore his real
name, Ray Plimsoll. After leaving the Ohio seminary, where he had
been known as the Damp Sneaker, for Nicaragua, he had called
himself Raymund Red. No one who had lived through those heady
days could forget Father Red in his fatigues, black beret and Che
Guevara moustache, rampaging through the streets of Managua,
unfettered by any Order. The young Dominicans used to watch him
enviously, wondering how he attained such freedom and influence. He
seemed to them almost like Christ himself, going among the poor as
one of their number, with no place to lay his head. For it was only after
dark that Raymund returned to his expensive hotel, paid for, like
everything else, by his mother's Catholic Ladies Guild in affluent
Peasville, Indiana.

Six years later, when the fires of liberation had died down, to be
replaced by the milder doctrines of creation theology, it had been a
simple task to add the final 'forest' and to become the living embodiment
of Christian ecology. Again he had out-Dominicanned the Dominicans
and still the American Catholic hierarchy had not worked out who was
funding his quixotic adventures. In fact, since the success of his book,
The Rape of the Loch, Raymund was self-financing and the Peasville
ladies were at last able to turn their attentions back to their own parish
priest.

Raymund drew from his holdall a lined notebook and turned to a
blank page. He ruled two vertical lines, dividing the page into three,
and wrote in the first section:

(a)	1	Good Thing
(b)	3	Bad Things
(c)	2	Good Things
(d)	2	Bad Things
(e)	3	Good Things

It was his infallible formula upon which his reputation as a brilliant preacher had been based. By gradually shifting the balance from Bad to Good Things, his audience, or congregation, were made to feel that Raymund himself had defeated the forces of evil and repression and that they had joined with him in the victory. He thought for a few seconds, pulling at his bushy red beard. It had been specially dyed for this trip to England, and was in fine form, hair-sprayed and blown-dry to rugged, natural perfection. For the truth about Raymund's beard, a poor, lank slug-coloured effort, was as closely guarded as the truth about his name.

The beard had brought inspiration or, at least, the memory of his last seventeen almost identical sermons, for he now filled up the second column in his notebook.

(a)	Blessed Hedwig
(b)	Repressive church authorities in Middle Ages
	Matter as evil – Augustine/Hierarchies – Aquinas
	Repressive church authorities now
(c)	Creation theology
	Green movement
(d)	Environmental dangers
	Complacency
(e)	My being here
	Your being here
	Pledge to simple life.

In the third column Raymund began to write words and phrases as they occurred to him. 'Soil, Stewardship, Paternalism, Acid Rain, The Motherhood of God.' It did not matter much what he actually said. These gatherings were always full of pious, earnest little women who could be brought to ecological ecstacy just by the virility of his beard. He had a letter from one of them in his holdall now, some poor nun from a God-forsaken place called Rambleton. That said it all, really. She claimed to have known him in the Nicaraguan days. Well, she might have done. So many nuns, so little time. He laughed to himself, a cynical, cosmopolitan laugh, the laugh of a man of the world, an international jet-setting celebrity. The woman in the next seat looked at him sternly over the top of her in-flight magazine and he stopped laughing.

Not that he had ever done anything to fracture his vows of chastity or to imperil his celibacy. Several of his friends had left the priesthood to marry and he never left after visiting them without thanking God for saving him from that temptation. Such mousey, brown little wives, such miserable semi-detached houses in cloudy suburbs, such dull jobs in middle-management or the welfare services. If that was the price to be paid, then the mysteries of sex could remain mysteries so far as Raymund Redforest was concerned.

Now the whole of the third column was filled up except for the sections beside the names of Augustine and Aquinas. He reached in his holdall for his little black book. Theology and philosophy had not been Raymund's strong points at the seminary. He liked to say that he believed in a 'theology of the people' or that he was 'not a priest's priest'. Sadly, despite these egalitarian ideals, many people persisted in expecting a modicum of theology from an internationally renowned theologian. Fortunately one of his classmates at the seminary had been a clever East Coast Ivy Leaguer who was as hot on the proofs of Divine Existence as on the ice-hockey rink. He had written a dissertation on Augustine and Aquinas from which Raymund had pinched the quotations and copied them into a small black notebook. That book had been his constant companion ever since, as indispensable to his reputation as his bottle of henna beard dye. He could usually find something in it to demonstrate his two basic ideas, that Augustine was a miserable old sod who hated women, the body, and everything to do with creation and that Aquinas was a despotic proto-fascist.

Unfortunately, the last time that he had visited England, a middle-aged priest of Jesuitical appearance, ostentatiously clean-shaven, had said: 'I notice that you have quoted from Book One, Chapter Thirteen of Aquinas' *Summa contra Gentiles*. Would you not agree that in this chapter Aquinas' conception of creation as constantly in a state of change and his notion of God's involvement in this change demonstrate a view sympathetic to your own theology as opposed to say, the mechanistic eighteenth-century concept of God as the absent watchmaker?'

Raymund, who had no idea what the *Summa contra Gentiles* was, nor what on earth watches had to do with it, had blustered pitifully. It had just better not happen again, that was all. At least no nasty English intellectual could argue with his closing triumph, the pledge to a simple

215

life. Raymund had learned a trick or two from the evangelicals and now knew that the best way to round off a successful sermon was to ask his congregation for a tangible commitment. Of course, the pledge to a simple life, which was in fact so vaguely worded as to mean nothing at all, was completely free. However, should any of the pledgers wish for a little symbol, a reminder of that special experience, prayer cards would be available after the service at only $2.50 each. Raymund reminded himself to check the exchange rate before the workshop began.

Early on Saturday, at about the time that Father Redforest was walking the long tunnels of Heathrow Airport in order to board the little plane up North, Sister Hedwig was scrubbing her spark plugs.

'Are you sure you ought to be doing that, dear?' squeaked Sister Perpetua for the fourteenth time. 'You musn't get water in the electricals, you know. I remember teaching that in Basic Science to the first form.'

'Yes, and I did it again for the First Aiders of the Sacred Heart,' growled Sister Felicity. ' "Accidents Requiring Resuscitation: Drowning, Electrocution, Severe Blow to the Head. Resuscitation Techniques: Artificial Respiration, Heart Massage, Administration of Last Sacraments".'

'Are you sure about that last one, dear? Oh, here's Hedwig again. They look lovely and clean, Sister. I'm sure that the car will start now. Oh. That doesn't sound quite right does it? Perhaps the shark plugs need a little shine. I know that Sister Eulalia keeps some Duraglit under the sink. I've seen her stir some into her Newcastle Brown on feast days.'

Forty minutes later, at the twenty-seventh attempt, the convent Mini spluttered into activity.

'We knew it would start that time, didn't we, Felicity?'

'*How* did you know?' asked the flustered Sister Hedwig ominously.

'Oh, we said a little prayer to St Christopher while you were in the kitchen. It's all been so exciting that we completely forgot to do it before.'

The onset of the journey was delayed for another ten minutes while the two old Sisters argued over who was to take the front seat, Sister Perpetua deferring to Sister Felicity's lumbago while Sister Felicity insisted on the superior claims of Sister Perpetua's rheumatism. Eventually they decided that they would both sit on the back seat where, owing to the extraordinary amount of engine noise produced by the fifteen-year-old Mini, Sister Hedwig could only catch odd snatches of their conversation.

216

But if Hedwig had hoped for a quiet and uninterrupted journey, free to meditate upon the mysteries of creation theology and upon the beauty of the Yorkshire Dales and Pennine Hills, she was to be disappointed. Every few miles she would feel a soft but insistent tapping upon her shoulder. Usually it was because the Sisters had seen the remains of a hedgehog on the road and wanted to check it for any remaining signs of life. For the first fifty miles each little creature found was crushed to a red-brown film on the road surface and nothing could be done but to say a short prayer over its remains and pass on. Just before Skipton, however, a hedgehog was seen which, though in a parlous state, was, in the opinion of Felicity and Perpetua, not actually dead. From their capacious collection of carrier bags an empty shoebox was produced and the hedgehog scraped into it. The box was safely installed on the back seat, between the two Sisters, to be taken to Gloriaux where the priestly powers of Raymund Redforest were confidently expected to bring healing and comfort.

The other principal stimulus to the shoulder-tapping was the appearance of a family restaurant, usually a Little Chef or Happy Eater. Something in their neon signs obviously had a diuretic effect upon the old ladies, who would tilt their heads coyly and beg to be allowed to 'spend just the tiniest penny'. On their way in they would peer at the menu and notice, with little cries of glee, that the farmhouse breakfasts were so *very* reasonably priced, or comment, with an air of disinterested martyrdom, that they could not remember when they had gone so long without a cup of tea.

It was over one of these pots of tea at a newly opened Tiff'n'Tuck, between Harrogate and Skipton, that Hedwig pointed out, as gently as she could manage, that she was supposed to be reading a paper at the workshop and did not want to be so very late in arriving.

'Reading a paper!' said Felicity gruffly, with a hint of her old schoolmistress's manner. 'I really don't think that you should be reading the paper while Father Redwood is preaching. I always used to give double detention *and* lines for that sort of thing.'

'Perhaps the paper will be the *Catholic Herald* or the *Universe*,' suggested Perpetua. 'It wouldn't be so bad then, surely.'

Hedwig explained, with the last vestiges of her patience, that she had meant that she would be giving her own paper as part of the day's planned events. After much delighted congratulation and merry laughter the Sisters decided that in that case they would forgo a second toasted teacake each and 'hit the road', as Sister Perpetua had once heard the milkman say to Sister Eulalia.

So it was that the Sisters completed their sixty-five mile journey in only five hours. They arrived at Gloriaux Abbey just before midday, in time to join the thirty or forty other participants in the chancel for the end of Father Redforest's keynote address.

Chapter Thirty-Three

If circumstances lead me, I will find
Where truth is hid, though it were hid indeed
Within the centre

(II.ii. 156–9)

'You the children from Moorwind Farm?' asked the postman, lifting one leg over the crossbar of his bicycle and coasting to a standstill.

Pius nodded.

'D'ye want to take the post for your mam and dad, then? I want to get finished early this morning. I'm best man at me mate's wedding, see?'

'Okay,' said Joan. 'We'll take them. And tell your friend congratulations from us.'

'Will do. Mind you take them letters straightaway, though. You'll lose me me job, else. See ya.'

He replaced his bottom on the saddle and rode away, leaving the four eldest O. children standing on the grass verge where the farm track met the main road.

'Wish I was a postman,' said Hygenus. ''Cept I'd have a motorbike.'

'I'd have a dinosaur,' said Urban, 'like on *Flintstones*.'

'That's not real, silly. All the dinosaurs are dead. Like cavemens and the Doo-doo bird.'

'Leave him alone, Hy,' interrupted Pius. 'You'll only make him cry. Is there anything int'resting in that post, Joan?'

'Hmmm.' Joan was leafing through the pile as she had seen her father do. 'Boring bank, boring bank, computer magazine, catalogue, boring bank, computer magazine, oh. Postcard from Grandma.'

'Let's have a look then.'

'No, I'll read it. "Darlings. Marvellous weather & excellent hands, esp. no trumps. Have you stopped Daddy from swinging? So pleased about your clue – knew you'd start sometime. Big prize, is it? Anyway, darling, answer is . . ." '

Pius looked over Joan's shoulder as she faltered. ' "Chequers".'

'Thanks. "CHEQUERS' BELL. Anagram of SL (a little slowly), QUEER and BELCH (12th Nt). Love to poppets, Mummy." '

'That's all nonsense,' said Hygenus stoutly.

'Well, yes.' Joan spoke slowly, squinting at the postcard sideways in an attempt to make it more forthcoming. 'But it must be nonsense that means something.'

'It's just a crossword clue, isn't it?' said Pius.

'Yes, but Mummy doesn't do crosswords. And if she did, she wouldn't send a card all the way to,' she glanced at the front of the postcard, 'Jam-caker, to ask Grandma to help. No, I think it must be something to do with Gigabyte.'

'Oh, yes,' agreed Pius. 'A clue from the kidnappers.'

'But what does it mean?' asked the practical Hygenus. 'Checky's bell?'

'Well, Chequers is where the Prime Minister lives,' said Pius. 'Dad told me that once.'

'I thought he lived at Ten Downing Street,' objected Joan.

'Oh, yes. P'raps I've got it wrong. Anyway, it's bound to be hundreds of miles away. Dad says all the 'portant places are in the south. Like Twickingham.'

'But Chequers has got another meaning as well,' Joan pointed out. 'Like Chinese Chequers.'

'And it's an old word for chess. Perhaps it means the bell in the chess set.'

'There isn't a bell in the chess set,' said Hygenus crossly. 'So stop always saying *silly* things.'

Urban had drawn away from the others and was poking about in the ditch with a long stick. Suddenly he turned around and said quietly, 'The cat's all checky.'

'*And* he's got a bell!' roared Hygenus.

'He's right, you know. Those black and white markings on his face, aren't they rather like a chessboard? This secret, whatever it is, couldn't it be inside the cat's bell?'

'But how do the kidnappers know about the cat?'

'I spect they *sent him*. Remember how he just turned up when Daddy was ill? He must have come from them. It was *almost certainly* them that made him ill, too, if you want my 'pinion.'

'Oh no.' Joan was conscience-stricken. 'And we kept the cat a secret from Mummy and Daddy, so they don't know anything about him.'

'That doesn't matter, does it? *We* know, and we're the ones that are going off to rescue Gigabyte. Good thing we got that postcard. What time is it now?'

'Quarter to eight in the morning,' chanted Hygenus proudly, displaying his birthday present watch.

'Right. Mrs Bottlebonce isn't coming till eight o'clock, is she? We've got time to go and get the bell.'

'You go, Pi,' suggested Joan. 'You're the fastest runner. Leop, I mean Chequers will still be in the pigsty. I gave him a whole box of those cat biscuit things and he won't go anywhere until he's finished them.'

Pius set off at a sprint, but Hygenus' big hand was almost on the twelve by the time he returned, panting heavily and with a long red scratch down one cheek.

'Have you got it?'

Plus unzipped his jacket and revealed a mass of angry fur. 'I couldn't get it off,' he gasped, 'so I had to bring the cat with me.'

Joan inspected gingerly, but was forced to concede the truth of this. The collar to which the bell was attached was an elastic type, to be slipped over the cat's head rather than buckled. Unfortunately, the enormous meals with which the children had fed the fortunate Chequers had produced an equivalent weight gain, so that the collar was now firmly wedged between two rolls of fatty neck.

'We'll just have to take him with us,' they agreed, and had just replaced the cat in Pius' jacket when Mrs Pottlebonce's Grutta appeared around the bend in the road. Joan quickly wiped the blood off Pius' other cheek, collected Hygenus and Urban, and prepared to greet her mentor.

However, as the Grutta pulled in and came to a violent stop at the edge of the ditch, Joan found that she had lost her privileged position on the front seat.

'Oh no, it's that bloomin' witch!' cried Hygenus, who had chosen Raymond Briggs' *Father Christmas* as his bedtime story the evening before.

'Shut up, Hy,' advised his elder brother, 'or she'll turn you into a frog.'

'Ribbett, ribbett,' croaked Hygenus and Urban as they clambered into the back of the jeep.

Unfortunately, what the children had taken for black cushions turned out to be Horace, Virgil and Caesar, Lady Tartleton's Labradors. Apparently Albert Skate had organised a Grand Dogfight at Raggy-Kegs to celebrate his entry into the home-owning democracy, and Lady Tartleton had thought it best to remove her dogs from the scene. There was therefore a certain amount of pushing and pawing before all were wedged in. Fortunately the children were well-used to dealing with Labradors and prodded them repeatedly with Joan's supply of sharpened pencils until the dogs surrendered the seats and flopped onto the floor with little grunts of resentment. Chequers, knowing when he was beaten, merely snuggled down inside Pius' jacket and slept, unmoved by the probing noses of the curious Labradors.

Monica and Lady Tartleton were little disposed to talk to the children, being engrossed in their own NARCOF discussion.

'What we must remember, Monica, is that God is *indisputably* male.' As she spoke, Lady Tartleton tapped out the rhythm of her words on the dashboard with one of Joan's pencils. 'How on earth do these dreadful people think that He could exert His authority over the world if He was just a female? Or even worse, some sort of androgynous muddle?'

Monica, having only recently got to know Lady Tartleton, had not witnessed the authority which had been strenuously exerted over the late Cecil. Nor had she yet heard Lady Tartleton's fervent trills of admiration for a former Prime Minister whose dominance was similarly untrammelled by her sex. Instead she nodded enthusiastically, knocking the rear-view mirror from its dainty perch.

'Oh, I do think you're right, Beatrice,' she said, trying out for the first time the Christian name which she had graciously been invited to use. 'And they do look so *silly* in dog-collars. Horribly masculine. And *bosoms.* So inappropriate, especially during Lent.' Monica looked complacently down at her corduroyed bulk, clothed exclusively from Milletts for the past twenty years, and at her own bosom, which had long since abandoned the attempt to comprise two autonomous entities and had congealed into a lumpy layer across her broad chest.

Joan giggled, but neither of the women heard her.

'What's a bosom?' whispered Urban, wedged between Caesar and Virgil and too terrified even to feel sick.

'Breasts,' said Joan, sitting up straighter and puffing out her own undimpled chest.

'Or you can call them tits,' added the worldly-wise Hygenus, abandoning the effort to introduce Horace to the contents of Pius' jacket. 'Tits and bums. They go together.'

'No they don't,' objected Urban. 'There's tummies in the middle.'

'Be quiet, all of you,' hissed Pius. He pulled his jacket so tightly around him that Chequers, even in his sleep, objected audibly. 'Shhh.'

'What was that squeaking noise?' demanded Lady Tartleton. 'I hope you children aren't annoying my boys.'

She evidently did not expect an answer for she immediately returned to her exposition of the ineffable maleness of the creative principle and its application to the House of Lords.

Pius lowered his voice still further. 'We've got to listen to them, remember. Find out what they're going to do with the D-I-N-A-M-Y-T.'

'Does that make Dinosaur?' asked Urban.

The discovery of the dynamite in Urban's trouser pocket had horrified the children. Pius had taken it out and put it in the rain-water butt, remembering that it was ineffective when wet, but it was hardly practicable to immerse a whole barn full of the stuff. They did not mind the idea of Sister Hedwig's being blown up, considering that anyone who could force Year Five to dress up as Mummy God's Woodland Spirits deserved anything they got, but could not risk injury to Gigabyte. Also Joan and Pius, at least, had been well-brought up by their mother and knew the importance of a well-preserved Gothic clerestory. The children had decided, therefore, to watch Lady Tartleton and Monica throughout the day for incendiary tendencies. Urban, since his spectacular vomiting, had usurped Joan as Mrs Pottlebonce's favourite and he was therefore deputed to stay with her. Hygenus, as the bravest, was to shadow Lady Tartleton.

In fact, the children's fears were unfounded. Although Monica had bought the dynamite, in the first flush of anger at Hedwig's sermon, with murderous intent, generations of Yorkshire common sense and thrift had prevailed over passing fanaticism. On behalf of NARCOF she had sold the dynamite, at a respectable profit, to Edgar, who had used it to blow up a couple of redundant barns. This had earned him a grant from the EC under the Diversification of Amenities Scheme, a grant worth twice what she had paid for the dynamite. So everyone was happy, except for the Chairman of the Parish Council who had been trying for the past seventeen years to designate one of the barns as a listed building.

'I want to go to the toilet,' said Urban, half an hour later, and Monica, having learned her lesson quickly, stopped at the next Tiff 'n'Tuck. Unfortunately she drove into the car park through the clearly marked exit, thus creating some difficulty for the two caravans and articulated lorry which were simultaneously trying to leave. Ever resourceful, she solved the problem by the original expedient of reversing around the adjacent roundabout.

'What is that, what the lorry driver called me?' she asked Lady Tartleton when the confusion had died down.

223

'I'm not actually sure. Our gardener used to shout it when he was drunk. I believe it may be an old Norfolk word for a mole, but Cecil was always a bit vague.'

'Urban still needs to go,' Joan reminded them from the back seat.

'Oh yes, yes, there we are,' said Monica. 'All nature's needs catered for.'

She was gratified and a little nervous when he insisted that she accompany him to the lavatory.

'I, um, I've never had a little boy, I'm afraid. Perhaps your big brother or sister would be better able to help you?'

'No,' he said stoutly. 'I want you. You can do your wee at the same time if you like.'

When they had disappeared into the Ladies', Hygenus looked suspiciously at Lady Tartleton, but she showed no signs of a desire to relieve herself. Instead she decided to take her 'boys' for a little walk around the car park and so Hygenus went with them.

Caesar and Virgil were each cocking a leg upon a wheel of a decrepit Mini. Lady Tartleton kicked it contemptuously.

'What a disgusting vehicle. I really don't know why the Government doesn't put a stop to the lower classes' driving about the country at all. There's absolutely no need for it and it only causes trouble. I've seen it on the six o'clock news. Traffic jams, multiple pile-ups, police overtime. Not to mention those dreadful car boot sales. And then there are so *many* of these people that of course one can't help hitting them after a glass or two. My Cecil would never go out in the Rolls without a couple of snifters beforehand. I suppose they'd lock him up these days. Thank God he's popped off, really. Of course, what we need is a decent Poor Law to make these ghastly people stay in their own parishes, back in the workhouses. They simply don't deserve—'

She broke off suddenly, remembering that she now lived with a supremely undeserving member of the lower classes and that her own Invalidity Benefit assessment was due to take place in three days' time.

'I don't like smelly people,' said Hygenus confidentially, 'but Dad says I mustn't say so.'

To cover her confusion Lady Tartleton peered into the car and noticed a small white box on the back seat. It was filled with something muddy, with streaks of blood and mucous.

'How revolting! I suppose that's their lunch. Cottage pie, I think they call it. Our gardener was frightfully fond of it.'

The car door was not locked and she opened it and removed the box.

'Good Lord!' she cried, prodding its contents with a bony finger and sniffing it vigorously. 'It's a hedgehog. Oh, I *must* take this home for the boys. Boiled up with a good bone, it'll be splendid for their coats. Might do Mr Skate some good, as well.'

And to Hygenus' astonishment she took a plastic bag from her poacher's pocket, transferred the hedgehog into it, and returned the box to its place in the Mini.

'There!' she concluded proudly. 'A tasty nutritious meal at no expense. Just see what you can do by living off the land, my boy.'

At that point Monica and Urban returned, she looking flustered and he indignant.

'She doesn't know anything about boys,' he complained. 'She made me pull my pants right down and sit on the toilet just to do a *wee*.'

Just over an hour later, after several wrong turnings and hair-raising U-turns, they approached Gloriaux Abbey. The children quivered with exhilaration at a bright yellow AA sign which announced: '*Creation Theology Workshop – Car Park – Turn Left*'.

'Oh no we don't,' said Lady Tartleton, reaching over Monica to give the steering wheel a sharp turn to the right. 'My great-grandfather didn't win the battle of Pucaloon by using the same car park as his enemies. Think strategy, Monica, strategy.'

She pulled again, harder, at the wheel, and the Grutta, amazed, teetered sideways with its off-side wheels suspended in mid-air. On the back seat, children and dogs slid together in a squealing heap with Pius and Chequers at the bottom. The cat awoke and, finding his claws too constrained to scatch, found expression for his annoyance by biting Pius' armpit. Urban, meanwhile, sat on the floor with eight stone of labrador flesh on his head and wondered whether this was what Uncle Padraic meant by Purgatory.

Using reflexes that had lain dormant for forty-five years, since her left-back triumph in the House hockey semi-final, Monica retrieved the steering-wheel and the road. When the occupants of the Grutta turned themselves the right way up, tousled and battered, they found that they were travelling on a neat and expensive gravel drive. In front of them was the old prior's lodging, now apparently occupied by the abbey's owners, with expensive curtains in the windows and a gleaming Range Rover parked outside. Meanwhile, from out of the rear window, the children could see the other participants, in their 2CVs and Dormobiles, parking in a patch of rough grass near the nave. Monica drew up, with her usual finesse, in front of the house, decapitating a small apple tree in the process. A young woman rushed out of the rustic front door, followed by a pair of yapping terriers. The girl wore a padded gilet and pearls, and her blonde ponytail flapped in agitation.

'No parking hyar!' she called, in an accent previously unknown north of Gloucester.

Monica, outclassed, scraped the Grutta into reverse but Lady Tartleton, who had refused a seat belt throughout the perilous journey, jumped on to the gravel and strode towards the girl.

'Bunny!' she cried, in tones of tender recrimination. The girl stood still, her pretty pink mouth hanging open.

'Bunny, when we've driven all the way from Sevenoaks to see you in this God-forsaken place! No parking, indeed! It really is too bad. When I think of the hours I spent, coaching you through that first gymkhana! You'd never have got that rosette, would you, if I hadn't given Lucky that *rather* special spoonful? Well?'

The gape transformed itself into a well-modulated vowel.

'Ooaah, I'm *frightfully* sorry. I just didn't *recognise* you for a minute. *Many* apologies. It's just that there are so many *awful* people for Seb's green thing today. *Do* come in and have a coffee. I'll just have to catch up with Eton and Harrow. There are so many ghastly animals here; I don't want them to *catch* anything.'

'Now come on, we need to scarper,' said Lady Tartleton, watching the girl's designer-jeaned bottom disappear around the back of the house in pursuit of the terriers. 'Any minute now she'll come back and realise that she doesn't know me from the Duchess of Dalley-dee.'

'What?' blustered Monica. 'You don't know her? But you called her Bunny and everything!'

'Oh, *Monica,* use that great turnip-head of yours, will you? *All* horrible little girls like that were called Bunny when they were six or seven. Or wish they had been. And they *all* had ponies called Lucky, bad-tempered little brutes bought on the cheap who needed a drop of the hard stuff to make them shift their overfed bottoms at all. Now come on, Monica, *quickly.*'

226

Chapter Thirty-Four

How should I your true love know
From another one?
By his cockle hat and staff
And his sandal shoon.

(IV.V. 23–6)

At nine o'clock on the same morning Deputy District Judge Lionel Ranger adjusted his tie, said goodbye to his housekeeeper and got into his old Rover 2000. Fortunately it was an automatic, so, after some initial wrestling with the handbrake, he managed to set off despite his injured arm. The *North of England Road Atlas* was open on the passenger seat, but as yet he had no need for such niceties. 'Go west, young man!' he said to himself, and turned his back resolutely to the chink of sun which just showed through the thick white cloud.

'Dotty, Dotty, Dorothy, Dot,' he sang, to the tune of 'Twinkle, Twinkle, Little Star'. 'How I wonder what you've got.' Oh no, that sounded dreadfully improper. He tried again. 'Beautiful you are, God wot.' The traffic lights in front of him turned to red and he took it as a sign to cease his improvisions. Anyway, her name alone was poetry enough. Dorothy, Dot. *Dodo*, he tried, rather daringly and then, formally, *Miss Smith*. Even that was tantalising, with its smooth, sinuous half-alliteration. Missss Sssmithhh.

'Come on, you dozy bugger!'

He looked up at the green traffic light, signalled an apology to the Astra driver behind and stalled. He started the engine again, embarrassed at his ineptitude, and told himself to concentrate on the road.

But even as he looked in his mirror to see the Astra impatient on his tail he was remembering her tentative Lancashire voice on the telephone the night before. He had almost given up, had been on the point of going out to give Prairie Foot her goodnight lump of sugar when the telephone had finally rung.

'Mr Ranger? A lady for you,' his housekeeper had said, with what his mother had called an old-fashioned look, and he had known then that it must be Dorothy. So, she had kept her word, had not been like

227

those female defendants against whom he had been warned by more cynical district judges, the sort of women who would give a promise and a flash of thigh and then be off with the catalogue debt, the abducted children or even the bailiff, given half a chance.

'Hello,' she had whispered. 'I'm sorry it's so late. I had to wait for Mrs McHenry to go. She'd read an article about masculine bonding, you see, and wanted Wardle to bond with Flies.'

'I understand,' said Mr Ranger, quite untruthfully.

'I haven't much time now, actually. Wardle's just taken Spot round the back for his, you know.'

'That's all right.' Mr Ranger hardly knew what either she or he was saying, merely wanted to keep the connection between them still humming for as long as possible. 'Where shall I see you?'

'Oh, yes. Gloriaux Abbey, do you know it? Just this side of the border. I'm not very good at directions but I think it's south of Blackburn. We'll be there about midday.'

'We?'

'Yes, all four of us, ELLA. But whatever you do, don't come and talk to me when they're there. Wait until I'm by myself. Please, it's ever so important that they don't know.'

'Of course I will.' He imagined Ella, a tyrannical sister-in-law perhaps, or maybe even a spiteful old step-mother. 'Don't worry, dear, Ella won't find out.'

'Oh thank you. Maybe you could just *lurk*. Oh no, here he is. Goodbye.'

The telephone line had gone dead, and he did not know whether or not she had heard his quick-breathed, heart-hammering promise, 'I'll lurk, my love, I'll lurk.'

With an ugly screech and fart of greyish smoke the Astra overtook on the inside. Mr Ranger watched until it disappeared around the next corner, the soccer-stripped rag doll in the rear window still swinging like an impatient pendulum. He was almost sure that he recognised the driver, now, that it was the young defendant who had come to him in tears on the last Tuesday morning, begging him not to allow Carazy Finance to repossess that same Astra. What was it that he had said he needed it for? Oh yes, driving his disabled mother to her out-patient appointments. Oh well. None of the baseball-capped, gum-chewing occupants of the car had exactly looked like a disabled mother, but you never knew. It was important not to think in stereotypes, District Judge Ranger told himself sternly.

He was out on the open road now and it took little effort to imagine the undulating fields transformed into a Texan desert. He loosened his tie, leaned back into the vinyl seat and switched on Radio Scorsdale. It was nearly time for *Corkin' Colin's Country Classics*. Mr Ranger was a great fan of Corkin' Colin and had once even had his own request, a little known Slim Whitman track, played on the programme. There were – he calculated carefully – only nine and a half minutes of *Up the Creek with Eddie Peake* left to go. This week Eddie had inveigled a sixteen-stone woman into auditioning as a topless waitress for the latest of Scorsdale's short-lived nightclubs. Mr Ranger shuddered and was thankful that it was only on the radio.

The trouble was, that he had not had much experience with girls. Or women, he supposed that he should say. There had been a nasty incident at the Yorkshire Country & Western Conference at Scarborough in 1968, but since then he had felt rather sick whenever he thought about that sort of thing. He usually went out to make a cup of tea during the romantic bits of his John Wayne videos and most of his records were songs about the fidelity of dogs rather than the infidelity of women.

Deputy District Judge Ranger wished that he had a dog. There was Prairie Foot, his horse, of course, but Prairie Foot couldn't curl up on the sofa beside him and boo when the Indians leaped out from behind cacti.

Anyway, none of that mattered now. As soon as he had walked into the courtroom, bloody but unbowed from the bank clerks, and had met Dorothy's sympathetic gaze, everything else had stopped mattering. For thirty years he had cursed the careers master at Rambleton Grammar School who had mocked his cowboy dreams and told him that the Law was a good steady sort of profession for a second-rate mind like his. Now, for the first time, Mr Ranger could not visualise the master's face. He could conjure up the shabby brown flannel trousers, the tweed jacket with its worn leather elbow-patches, even the regimental tie, but above them, delightfully incongruous, hovered Dorothy's tentative smile, and in place of the master's blunt vowels he could hear her gentle Lancashire lilt. 'Your Honour,' she had called him, and he had not known how to correct her mistake. But this time he would.

'Call me Larry,' he would drawl, holding her close against the cloisters. They did have cloisters in these places, didn't they? A horrible thought suddenly struck him. What if it was an *active* monastery? Or even a convent? Maybe Dorothy was really a nun, one of those modern

229

kinds that don't wear veils and who go to bars. Or was that only in America?

He changed down to third gear, to the consternation of the queue behind him, and tried to compose himself. A nun would, after all, be unlikely to have her name still on the title deeds of her brother's house, nor to appear in court on his behalf. No, she was surely what she seemed, a pleasant middle-aged spinster who had devoted so much of her life to her brother that she had forgotten to have a life of her own. And it was not as though he had nothing to offer. There was his house, a quite engaging bundle of investments and his share of the firm. In fact, he could even retire, if his proposed merger with Parrishes was accepted. Somehow, protecting the interests of young Astra drivers was becoming less urgent by the mile. He mused to himself, tapping his fingers on the dashboard in time with Dolly Parton. Wilfred was a contemporary of his, but the new solicitor, young Mrs O., seemed quite competent. He only wished he could ever get her to stop for long enough to talk about it. He had tried again the day before, but she had muttered something about completions and sidled away.

After making five or six stops to renew his deodorant, straighten his tie, steady his nerves with coffee or spray his mouth with mint, Deputy District Judge Ranger arrived at Gloriaux Abbey at half-past eleven. There were more people there than he had expected, and the makeshift car park was already full of battered minibuses and estate cars, some nearly as old as his own. A miserable sort of day for tourists, he thought, looking up at the solid grey sky, but these visitors did not seem exactly like the usual tourists, either, being both scruffier and somehow more vital. Watching them chattering and hugging in their fisherman's smocks and bright Peruvian jumpers, Mr Ranger felt conspicuous in his best dark grey suit, the trousers two inches short of his ankles.

Reluctantly, he unfolded his long limbs from the car and stretched. He had promised Dorothy that he would lurk, but now that it came to it, he was not sure that he really knew how. Lurking was not an activity commonly required of a deputy district judge. He wandered aimlessly through the ruins, hoping that his own greyness would be sufficient camouflage. Most people seemed to be heading for the old church where chairs were set out in bedraggled rows and so he tried to skirt around it, towards the smaller rooms on the south side. He was just sidling down a silent passage, congratulating himself on his invisibility, when a noisy and colourful family rounded a corner behind him.

'Oh Gerry!' cried an enthusiastic voice. 'Just *look* at that man in front! It's got to be, hasn't it, that lovely judge we saw when we did the Poll Tax Protest. You remember, he made that brilliant speech and let us off the whole lot.'

'I think you're right, Bernie,' said her husband in a Pooterish voice, 'I honestly think you're right. Now, what was it we called him, kids?'

'The Sundance Judge,' said the eldest child, with a touch of weariness.

'The Sundance Judge! That was it! Pity he hasn't got his Stetson today. Oi! Ju-udge! Stop! Wait! Don't we know you?'

But Mr Ranger, fearing the ubiquitous presence of the malevolent ELLA, was not inclined to wait. He dashed through the nearest doorway and found himself in a little room, roofless like the rest of the abbey, but otherwise intact. It had stone benches built into the walls down two sides and a raised tomb in the middle. He sprinted over to the tomb and peered in. It was empty, with only a few shards of stone and patches of moss at the bottom. There was no time to procrastinate, for the noisy family were close upon his black-polished heels.

'Hey! Remember the good old days? Maggie, Maggie, Maggie!'

Deputy District Ranger looked sadly down at his carefully brushed jacket and at the tiny invisible darn in the knee of his trousers. He sighed, gave another cursory glance at the musty interior of the tomb, and climbed inside.

Chapter Thirty-Five

And this, I take it,
Is the main motive of our preparations,
The source of this our watch, and the chief head
Of this post-haste and rummage in the land

(ɪ.i. 107–110)

'Er, I was actually thinking that only Dotty and I need go,' muttered Wardle uneasily as he opened the front door on Saturday morning to Flies and Mrs McHenry. 'And Spot, of course.'

'Rubbish!' snapped Mrs McHenry. 'I fully intend to accompany you. It is absolutely essential that we confront the ideologies of misogynist hegemony within their historical contexts.'

'What?' Wardle had not yet finished his boiled egg and as yet his grasp upon language was tenuous.

'I want to see the abbey.'

'Yeah, and me,' agreed Flies, reaching down his jacket to squeeze an elusive spot on his back. 'Be a laff.'

Wardle sighed, let them in, and returned to his egg. The yolk had spilled out down the side of the egg-cup and his spoon lay in its cold and viscous puddle. He chewed at a bit of cold toast. Everything was going wrong. It had seemed such a good idea at the time, holding the dog to ransom, buying the Town Hall, heroically risking all for the sake of the Cause. But almost immediately, it seemed, the taste of adventure had become tainted. Maybe it was that blood-curdling sight of Mrs McHenry in her knickers, maybe the affection between Dorothy and Spot that seemed to coincide with a certain space, a wedge, even, between brother and sister. The final disappointment, certainly, had come with the video which Mrs McHenry had lent him about prison conditions. He could no longer persuade himself, after watching it, that the inmates and warders of Strangeways would admire and venerate him, that they would speak with proud affection of their wise and courageous comrade. No, if nothing worse befell him than a beating-up, he thought glumly, he would be very lucky.

233

He lifted the spoon gingerly by its unegged end and watched it swing from his thumb and forefinger.

'Parrpp!'

Startled at the sudden noise he dropped the spoon on to his lap. Dorothy bustled over with a damp cloth.

'Come on, Wardle, we'd better be off. That's Mrs McHenry on the horn. She and Flies have already got into the Fiesta and they want to be off. There we are, dear. I know it's a bit damp at the moment but just point the hot-air blower at it and it'll soon be tickety-boo.'

They got outside to find that Mrs McHenry had installed herself in the front passenger seat, claiming that she suffered from 'acute motion-induced nausea syndrome'. Flies kindly translated this as, 'She means she's going to *baaaaarf*,' and gave an impromptu visual interpretation.

Dorothy, however, seeing Wardle's stricken face, was resolute.

'I'm afraid I have to sit at the front. I'm awfully sorry about it, but it's a term of Wardle's insurance policy.' She was rather proud of her inventiveness.

'Term of his insurance policy! I've never heard anything so ridiculous. Come on, let me sit there.'

Mrs McHenry employed her bony elbows to their best advantage but Dorothy was unmoveable.

'No, Mrs McHenry.'

'Muz.'

'Muss. You'll have to sit at the back with Flies. You should have had a Kwell before you left home. Now, that reminds me. Wardie dear, have you *been*? I shouldn't think they've got around to building toilets at this place yet.'

They eventually set off, Wardle nervous, Dorothy triumphant, Mrs McHenry sulky and Flies practising his farting skills next to her. They had gone two hundred yards when Mrs McHenry screamed. Wardle quickly and quietly applied the accelerator.

Half an hour later, when the pieces of bumper had all been collected from around the lamp-post, they set off again. Dorothy still sat regally in the front seat, but she now had Gigabyte in the footwell in front of her, the dog's muzzle contentedly resting in her lap.

'I still don't know why you had to scream like that,' she said. 'Poor old Spot's never been in the boot before. He was only licking your neck to say hello.'

'That,' pronounced Mrs McHenry, 'sounds very much like the classic male justification of the date-rape phenomenon. I am pained, not surprised, Dorothy, but pained, to hear you purvey it with such glib analytical incompetence.'

'Knickers,' muttered Dorothy but the word was drowned by Wardle's gear-change.

'Anyway,' continued Mrs McHenry, 'if Wardle knew his left foot from his right then we wouldn't have gone into the lamp-post. I told you that I could have driven. I drove an American army tank at Greenham Common when the soldier went to the loo, and none of the women had any objections.'

'I'm getting into Satanism,' announced Flies, when no one took any notice of his farts.

'Oh dear,' said Dorothy. 'I don't think that's a good idea at all.'

For the past thirty years she had been a clandestine Methodist, telling the others every Sunday morning that she was going to a meeting of the Daughters of the Revolution in Colne. Sometimes she had noticed a quizzical expression on Wardle's face as she left, occasionally even wistful, but he had always said nothing. Dorothy felt a little niggling guilt about Wardle, which grew into quite a burden during Evangelism Weeks.

'Too polite to speak of the Lord?' last year's visiting preacher had mocked. 'Embarrassed to offer salvation?'

It was all right for him, Dorothy had thought darkly. She was sure that he had not been forced to read Trotsky's *History of the Russian Revolution* while the rest of the infant class were singing 'Jesus Bids Us Shine'. She prayed as hard as she could for Wardle, but to confront him directly with her betrayal would be too much for both of them. Condoning Satanism, though, that would be quite another thing.

'I really don't think it's the right thing to do,' she repeated.

'Oh do stop bleating, woman,' snapped Mrs McHenry. 'I'm sure we don't have to be fooled by the patriarchal myths of Christianity at our stage of ideological development.' She turned to Flies, forced into alliance with him. 'Rather than centring the masculine principle of Satan, perhaps you would care to explore the possibilities of the cult of Lilith?' she suggested. 'I sense that you need to get in touch with the feminine aspects of your persona.'

'Listen, missus,' said Flies, pulling a horrible face and thrusting it into hers, 'there's nothing effing well feminine about me. Nor about you, neither, come to that. Nah, me mate lent me a book about this bloke called Alasdair wot was into Black Masses and that. 'E reckons this old abbey'd be a good place for a Black Mass. Probably full of the spirits of evil monks.'

'Ooh don't!' cried Dorothy. Last week at the chapel she had heard a sermon about the errors of the Catholic Church. The minister had concentrated heavily upon Pre-Reformation abuses and Dorothy had a vivid imagination.

By now the AA signs were appearing.

'That's funny,' said Wardle. 'I thought we'd have some difficulty finding it. What do you think a Creation Theology Workshop is? Something to do with carpentry?'

'Perhaps we'd better go back,' suggested Dorothy hopefully. The idea of losing Spot was bad enough. Malevolent monastic ghosts and wild carpenters would be the final straws. 'We won't be able to do the changeover with masses of people about.'

'Nonsense,' said Mrs McHenry. 'Onward, Wardle.'

'Yes, Mrs McHenry.'

He parked in the designated area and they all got out of the car. As they looked around, a young woman with a blonde ponytail ran over to them.

'*Excuse* me. So sorry to *bother* you, but have you seen two women, one old and frightfully thin, the other one absolutely *enormous?* They've got this simply awful horde of children with them. Honestly, they've absolutely *disappeared. Spooky!*'

'No, no we've only just got here ourselves.'

'Oh, yah. Well, don't let the dog do *poo-poos* here, will you?'

'Is there somewhere I could take him?' asked Wardle, anxious for an excuse to be by himself after the horrors of the journey.

'Oh *yah*. Over there, where the woods start. That's where we always take Eton and Harrow.'

Both Wardle and Mrs McHenry, fervent devotees of the comprehensive system, were aghast at this. All the same, Wardle knew better than to argue and trotted obediently off to the north of the abbey, with Gigabyte lolloping beside him.

'Now, are the rest of you here for this *religious* thingy?'

'Yes,' said Dorothy.

'No,' said Mrs McHenry and Flies.

'O-*kay*. Well, your lot are all gathering over there.' Relieved at the excuse, Dorothy began to drift towards the massing groups of people. She walked as slowly as was compatible with a reasonable show of enthusiasm, glancing about her for the District Judge.

Bunny looked doubtfully at Flies and Mrs McHenry. 'Do you and your son want the guided tour then? I think I can remember it all. It's *frightfully* boring, but better than the God squad, I suppose.'

'I quite agree,' said Mrs McHenry. 'My, er, son and I should be most interested in your guided tour. I trust that you will be placing it within a valid historico-Marxist dialectic continuum?'

'Yah. *Absolutely.*'

If either Ophelia or Malachi had been more house-proud then one of them might have noticed the reddish-brown stains which had been appearing for the past fortnight on the cushion inside Megabyte's basket and on the patch of carpet in front of the fire. Having noticed these, they might have understood why the Jack Russell who lived at the nearest cottage, half a mile away, was found scrabbling frantically at Moorwind's front door early on several mornings that week.

But they were preoccupied, and had not taken notes of the months passing, so that when Malachi suggested that they took Megabyte to Gloriaux Abbey with them, Ophelia quickly agreed.

'It'll be good for her to feel that she's found her puppy herself. Salvage her maternal pride. I'll never forget how humiliated I was that time when Urban had been sitting on the Toys-R-Us counter for half an hour before I recognised him. Do you remember? You were playing in the Little Tikes Log Cabin with Hygenus and narrowly missed being announced as a lost child yourself.'

The car felt strangely empty with only Innocent on the back seat and Megabyte slavering down the back of his neck.

'You have got the mobile phone, haven't you?' said Malachi as they set off. 'And the children do know the number?'

'Yes, yes. I'm sure they'll be fine. You know what these Baden-Powellites are like. Every moment of delirious fun planned out with military precision. Poor little buggers. I can't see Hygenus falling into line.'

They had decided to share the driving so as to equalise their chances of being caught by lurking policemen.

'At least it's not Sunday,' said Ophelia. 'They get even more overtime on a Sunday.'

All the same, they both drove with neurotic caution and precision, annoying several Sierra drivers by refusing to overtake a tractor until the crawler lane appeared. As Ophelia chugged past a Tiff 'n' Tuck, the speedometer needle boldly approaching forty, Megabyte spotted three labradors in the car park.

'Mmwa, mmwa!' she squealed, scrabbling at the rear window with both muddy forepaws. 'Yoww!'

237

'That's funny,' said Malachi from the passenger seat. 'There's a little boy there with the same clothes as Hygenus. Look, next to that old Mini. He's with an old biddy. Oh, look Oaf, she's kicking the car now.'

'I'm not looking at anything except the road. I haven't time for geriatric delinquency. Anyway, you can't blame anyone for kicking a Mini. She's probably trying to get the door open.'

They drove on, through the cold purple splendour of the Pennines, and changed places in the traffic jam by Bolton Abbey. The little hump-backed bridge had been colonised by orange plastic cones, standing around in proud family groups like fluorescent penguins. Malachi sat nervously tapping the steering-wheel as a terrier, which had been relieving itself on the verge, began to throw itself at the rear window in a frenzy of unsatisfied lust.

> 'When years of wedded life were as a day
> Whose current answers to the heart's desire,'

quoted Ophelia.

'Very nice, love, but I don't think we've got time for that sort of thing. Frankly, I don't think I could manage it at the moment anyway. You know how it is when I'm worried about anything.'

'No, you chump, it's Wordsworth. "The White Doe of Rylstone". He wrote it after he'd been staying around here and dedicated it to his wife. She was from Yorkshire, you know, near Scarborough.'

'Scarborough? Are you sure? It doesn't sound right, Mrs Wordsworth coming from Scarborough. Rather like Mozart taking a day trip to Blackpool. Oh look! Bolton Abbey. Is this it then?'

'No, we want *Gloriaux* Abbey. A few more miles yet. And without the grandeur of the Dukes of Devonshire. It won't be signposted but if you keep driving then I'll navigate.'

Soon the first AA signs came into view.

'Oh, bloody hell!' cried Ophelia. 'Sister Hedwig and her recyclable boyfriend!'

'Ophelia!' Malachi rebuked her, having been brought up to show unshakeable respect for nuns. 'What do you mean, anyway?'

'These signs. "Creation Theology Workshop". It must be that thing she was talking to us about, with that priest she knew in Nicaragua.'

'You mean when she read that God-awful poem in her hurdy-gurdy Swedish chef accent? *Modder is a cooking-pot, Fader is a pan, Sister's a tomato, And I'm an onion flan.* That sort of thing, wasn't it?'

Ophelia began to think that perhaps the respect wasn't so unshakeable after all. 'Oh Mal, it's not funny. We're supposed to be having this secret hangover, I mean takeover.'

'Changeover, love, I think.'

'Yes, that, and now there'll be millions of people watching.'

Malachi reached over to put his arm around her, endangering a couple of roadside elms in the process. 'Hardly millions, I shouldn't think. Not for the Blessed Hedwig. And in any case, it shouldn't make much difference to us. Might be a bit of valuable cover. All we have to do is hand over the money and take Gigabyte home. Unless you want to look around a bit, check out the misericords?'

'Mnn,' said Ophelia indistinctly. The one thing about the plan that she had not told Malachi was that she did not actually have the ransom money. She had raided the children's money-boxes and found £4.63 and had the vague hope that this, combined with her skills of advocacy, might suffice. In case all else failed she had brought Pius' cowboy pistols and Hygenus' Thundercats sword, all concealed under her baggy jumper. However, the skilful deployment of these weapons would be made considerably more difficult by the presence of a posse of non-violent ecologists.

She also felt extremely sick.

Chapter Thirty-Six

Speak the speech, I pray you, as I pronounced it to
you, trippingly on the tongue;

(III.ii. 1–2)

Malachi, whistling a particularly martial rugby song under his breath,
took the corner into the field at a rally-driver's pace, and parked next to
a hand-painted Volkswagen Beetle. He gave the handbrake a triumphant
crunch and turned to Ophelia.

'Feeling Green, then?'

'I am, actually,' she replied, opening the door hastily and climbing
out as quickly as she could manage without dislodging the brace of
pistols and the plastic sword.

'You look a bit lumpy, dear,' commented Malachi. 'Have you taken
to wearing a corset or something?'

Ophelia, grappling with Innocent's car seat, did not deign to answer
and so Malachi, his good humour undented, collected Megabyte from
the boot. They followed the occupants of the Beetle, a faded woman
with two stringy adolescent sons, through the ruined nave towards
the lofty east end of the ancient church. Malachi had forgotten to
bring Megabyte's lead and so improvised with a shoelace. This
necessitated his bending almost double in order to control the dog,
whilst dragging his right foot in a rhythmic shuffle so as to keep his
training shoe from falling off. It would only take a sneer, thought
Ophelia, following him up the aisle, and he would be a deadringer
for Richard III.

In the narthex, where the four arms of the church met, some rickety
chairs were set out in rows. About one-third of them were occupied by
a shabby set of persons, mainly middle-aged and female but with a few
elderly men and children. All had faces of well-scrubbed virtue and
clothes of Third World provenance. Many, in addition, had animals on
their laps or tethered to their chairs. Malachi limped to an empty row
and they sat down, Ophelia stabbing herself in the stomach as she did
so. Innocent identified the visible animals.

'Goggie, ca, wabbic, baa-baa, dack-dack, pie . . .'

241

'Pie, darling? What's a pie?'

Innocent pointed to a brown dome nestling in a box of straw.

'Tortoise.'

A bulky red-bearded man, heavy with self-importance, was fiddling with a microphone in front of the high altar. He tapped and blew into it and amplifiers crackled around the building.

'Testing. Testing. One, two, three,' he boomed in a Mid-Western accent, followed by a painful screech of feedback. Innocent, who had wandered towards one of the amplifiers, ran back to Ophelia in panic, while the well-behaved delegates finished their chats and faced the front in happy anticipation.

A couple of unhealthy-looking lackeys appeared from out of the stonework and fiddled with the equipment. The test was repeated but this time no sound at all could be heard. The audience shifted on the canvas chairs. It was an unusually mild day for November, but a chilly breeze was beginning to blow through the Romanesque arches. At last the sound system was pronounced satisfactory and Father Redforest began.

' "As I came nearer to the abbey of Gloriaux, it was necessary that I pass between two hills, each gently rounded and covered with sweet and verdant grass. And it appeared to me that the two hills were like unto the two breasts of a wet-nurse. Thinking upon this similarity further, it came into my mind that God is not only our Father but also our nursing mother, feeding us freely out of her great fecundity."

'These were the words of the Blessed Hedwig of Westphalia, written in 1193, following her return from England and from this very abbey in which we meet today. My friends, my brothers and sisters, I welcome you to Gloriaux Abbey today in the name of our Sister Hedwig and of our Mother God.'

Dorothy, having checked the other visible parts of the abbey for lurking district judges, now crept in through the nave. Meeting Raymund's hard stare, she quickly hid behind a pillar.

'And I greet not only my human brothers and sisters but also our sisters and brothers from the many other species with whom we share our planet. Brother Dog, I greet you!'

Megabyte, who could recognise a few words, responded with a friendly bark.

'Sister Rabbit, I welcome you! Brother Tortoise, slow and sure, you are honoured in our gathering!'

'Brother Pigeon, bugger off,' muttered Malachi, as a white splash appeared on his trouser leg.

'The Blessed Hedwig rode to Gloriaux from nearby Easby Abbey on a mule. But, unlike others in her day, she did not regard her mule simply as a dumb beast, a mode of transport. She called the mule Elizabeth, for as she said: "Thou, O mule, art barren as Elizabeth and yet just as by a miracle Our Lord made Elizabeth fruitful with child, so will thy patience and good companionship bring forth fruit in my poor writings." '

Raymund leaned forward slightly and waggled his beard roguishly.

'Now, do we have a pretty young lady who would like to read Hedwig's little lyric about her mule?'

Twenty middle-aged women licked their lips, sucked in their cheeks and straightened their anoraks in anticipation.

Meanwhile Flies and Mrs McHenry had commenced their guided tour with Bunny. She clumped briskly before them, ponytail swinging, and recited her commentary in a monotone.

'This is the Prior's Lodging, which is now our house. It was built later than the rest of the abbey, in the fifteenth century, when the original radical zeal of the Cistercians had been replaced by a more hierarchical structure. You will notice the complex tracery above the windows incorporating a boar's head which was part of the current Prior's family coat of arms. Any questions?'

Mrs McHenry had many questions, most of them about patriarchal confederation, but Bunny did not stop to listen to them. Instead, she strode over to the main part of the abbey, pausing first at the west range.

'This is the lay brothers' range.' At least, she thought it was. It was getting cold, wherever it was. She thrust her hands deeper into the fleecy pockets of her waistcoat and plodded on. 'Like most Cistercian abbeys in Yorkshire, Gloriaux relied heavily upon the wool trade and required lay brothers to carry out the manual work—'

'Who did they lay then?' sniggered Flies.

Bunny bit her lip and concentrated upon her monologue.

'However for some reason, probably a combination of disease and bad management, Gloriaux was never as successful as, say, Fountains or Rievaulx and did not therefore have their opportunities to expand.'

'Would you say,' began Mrs McHenry, in a tone which invited no possiblity of saying otherwise, 'that a feminist co-operative would have been able to . . .'

243

Bunny mumbled something indistinct and stomped on bravely towards the south range, opposite the church. If this awful pair didn't shut up, she thought, she would have to experience a sudden conversion and join the God squad in the chancel. At least it might be a bit warmer over there.

Lady Tartleton had no intention of eluding Bunny only to run directly into Sister Hedwig. The courage and guile of generations were flowing fast in her veins and her attack was to be meticulously concocted. So, when they fled from the Prior's Lodging, instead of going north-east, towards the church, her party went south-west, to explore the maze of small rooms which made up the south range. This part of the abbey was full of halved flights of stairs, ending precariously in mid-air, small windows and serving-hatches, and a multiplicity of circular routes. The children loved it and played happily for some time, forgetting their rescue mission.

'I'm a medeagle knight,' announced Hygenus, 'and this is my castle. You're all baddies and you have to fight me.'

'I'm not a baddy,' objected Joan. 'I'm a beautiful princess that's locked in the castle.' It then occurred to her that this was a somewhat passive role. 'A beautiful princess that's very good at fighting and that's found the key to her room so that she can come down and help the knight kill the baddies.'

'Don't want to be killed,' said Urban. 'Don't want to be a baddy.'

'All right,' said the knight magnanimously. 'You can be my squear. Pius can be the baddy. Let's get him!'

With cries of delighted bellicosity, the three children fell upon their elder brother, flinging him to the ground.

'Shhh,' hissed Lady Tartleton, looking up from the map which she was drawing in the mud. 'What's that?'

On the other side of the wall footsteps were crunching on the stone chippings. A cultivated and robotic voice could be heard.

'This is the main kitchen. Note the recess in the wall here where dishes were washed up and the one above it in which they were probably stored. Above this room was the frater or dining room. In the same way the dorter was situated above the chapter house and library . . .'

'Daughter? Whose daughter? Would there have been women in residence here?'

'The daughter wot the brothers laid, of course! In't that right, darlin'?'

'I haven't the faintest idea. It didn't say in the notes Sebastian got for me.'

Bunny's school had concentrated upon skiing and interior decoration to the detriment of the more mundane skills of spelling and arithmetic. She passed on quickly.

'If we go through this doorway, noticing the triple-ordered piers and fleur-de-lis carving . . .'

The footsteps grew nearer. Lady Tartleton gave a quick signal to the dogs who froze instantly, their sensitive noses raised to the breeze. The children copied them, Hygenus wobbling histrionically on one foot. Monica had noticed nothing and opened her mouth to say 'Musical Statues?' but was silenced by a flashing glare from her vice president.

For two or three seconds they remained motionless and a small fly, congratulating itself on surviving so long past summer, flew into Monica's open mouth. Then Lady Tartleton jerked her head towards the only other exit, a passage leading to the central courtyard. They rushed through it in an untidy throng, Monica tripping on the lintel, and stood, panting exaggeratedly, with their backs to the wall. Across the lawned courtyard they could see the neat cloisters which lined the outer south wall of the church and could hear the buzz of the still erratic sound system. Behind them Bunny's voice droned on.

' . . . we come to a storeroom in which evidence of barrels has been found, showing that . . .'

At their eastern end the cloisters had crumbled, as had the wall behind them, and as the children tiptoed across the courtyard they could see into the chancel, where Father Redforest was standing. They were too far away to hear what he was saying, as the amplifiers continued their deadening buzz, but his gesticulations and the frenzied wagging of his beard were entertainment enough.

'Who's that?' Hygenus did his best to whisper. 'He's like a giant dwarf. D'ye think he's a wizard?'

'He's got very funny hair,' said Urban judiciously.

'Shhh,' said Joan, before Lady Tartleton could say it. Hygenus, as usual, took no notice.

'I bet Gigabyte's over there. Let's go and get her now. Come on!'

'No. Wait,' hissed Lady Tarleton. 'Like your spirit, though,' she conceded. 'Brave lad. But we have to bide our time. Spring,' she leaned towards him confidentially, 'when they're at the grub. That's what Daddy taught me.'

The children nodded seriously. Even Chequers, still snuggled inside Pius' jacket, gave a tiny mew of confident agreement.

245

Chapter Thirty-Seven

So shall you hear
Of carnal, bloody, and unnatural acts,
Of accidental judgments, casual slaughters,
Of deaths put on by cunning and forc'd cause,
And, in this upshot, purposes mistook
Fall'n on th'inventors' heads.

(v.ii. 385–90)

Monica, the children and the dogs all stood motionless around Lady Tartleton, awaiting her commands. She gazed at each in turn, her kestrel eyes scanning their faces for signs of weakness or revolt. As she scrutinised Urban, bending low so that her face was on a level with his, she detected a tremor passing through his small body.

'Aha!' she whispered, but before she could triumph in his discomfiture her own shoulders began to shake. The nagging breeze which had been buffeting about Gloriaux all morning had developed into a full-scale gust of wind, blowing from the north. The children gathered their coats more closely around them, the dogs grumbled and sank further to the ground and Chequers curled herself inside Pius' armpit, tickling him with a wriggling paw. An involuntary splurt of laughter burst from his bulging cheeks and Lady Tartleton turned her stare upon him. There was, however, much worse to come.

As the wind passed through the church towards Lady Tartleton's party it picked up the scents of many animals. Rabbit, cat, tortoise and goat were all mingled together in a fascinating menagerie of smells. But one scent in particular was of interest to Horace, Virgil and Caesar. Even as they growled at the draught that ruffled the fur of their spines, their noses were lifting and their delicate nostrils beginning to flare. Up came their snouts, until they were almost perpendicular to their necks. Then each dog gave a great sniff, a brief yelp of delight, and was off.

'Bad dogs! Come back here! Caesar, Horace, Virgil, *here* boys!' flashed Lady Tartleton, all her menacing stealth turned to fire.

But it was of no use. Across the courtyard they pounded, three massy skulls with but a single instinct. They were bred for patient endurance, not for speed, but now even Albert Skate might be tempted to put his Invalidity Benefit on Horace who was running in the lead, his ears streaming back from his head. Close behind him was Virgil, kicking up small patches of turf with his powerful legs. Caesar had at first been confused by a little eddying counter-flow of the wind and set off slightly to the west, towards the lay brothers' wing. He had soon recognised his mistake, however, and was now catching up with his brothers. From behind each dog its testicles could be clearly seen, swinging to and fro like two boiled eggs in a string bag.

As they ran they barked, deep joyful barks of lust and anticipation. 'Arrruphhhh! Rrrrrofff!'

From inside the church, Megabyte, vaguely aware of her condition, heard their barks and replied. 'Aowwwhhh!' she howled. The sound was halfway between a keening whine and a siren song of burgeoning arousal. The dogs doubled their speed and their barks came in shorter, more urgent bursts.

'Quiet, Meg,' said Malachi, but he was too late.

She had been lying quietly at his side with her head on her paws, surveying Father Redforest with such patient boredom that Malachi had let the shoelace fall from his hand. Now she rose smoothly, pulling her back legs taut and leaving a russet smear on the flattened grass beneath her. With a deft twist she had slipped her head from its collar and was galloping between the rows of chairs. A few other animals, the two or three dogs, several cats, a goat and an adventurous rabbit, tried to follow her, but their owners had been alerted by the barking and held them firmly back. At the south wall Megabyte leaped, using the sleeping tortoise as a launching pad, and tumbled through the ruined cloisters. As she rolled into the courtyard, four legs akimbo, she was greeted by three soft noses and three panting tongues. Megabyte stretched her spine with a little whimper of delight and waved her tail in slow and languorous anticipation. 'Here we go again,' she thought to herself, raising her rear to the first probing phallus.

In 1487, it is noted in William Thine's *History of Gloriaux Abbey,* two of the monks, Richard Wass and Thomas Twigginge, suggested that a great fountain be erected in the centre of the quadrangle, 'for the better refreshment of the brothers and to the glory of God, who grants unto us the water of eternal life'. A sketch of the proposed fountain, which would utilise an existing natural spring, has even been uncovered, showing it to be a magnificent conception, a great froth of stonework, overflowing in complex orders and intricate tracery. Unfortunately, the Gloriaux sheep had still not managed to produce wool of the highest quality, and their only reliable market was nearby Preston. Richard and Thomas were instructed, therefore, that the abbey had no revenue available for such an extravagent project. William Thine had allowed himself a dry speculation upon what the adventurous pair might have said barely eighteen months later, when the Abbot's House was given a thorough refurbishment, with a new kitchen and seven new chambers 'of great beauty and spaciousness'.

Be that as it may, the fountain was never built and there was therefore nothing within the quadrangle to shield the eyes of the innocent ecologists from the canine orgy now taking place. A few, sitting at the edges of the right-hand rows, mainly the less committed, had stood to watch Megabyte as soon as she had rushed past them. Their gasps had alerted their more conscientious neighbours and soon almost all were on tiptoes, some even balanced precariously on their chairs, craning for an unimpeded view. Those who were too far back to be able to see through the ruined section of wall quickly came forward and any details which they had missed were comprehensively described by their colleagues. Only eight or nine members of the congregation, the deaf, the truly virtuous and those most directly under Father Redforest's eye, remained seated with their eyes resolutely upon the priest.

Each dog in turn, fending off his brothers, reared up, revealing an extended, slippery penis, bright pink against his black fur. Each mounted the complaisant Megabyte, leaning heavy shoulders on her broad back, and pounded vigorously before falling away. While one dog was thus engaged, the other two would be sniffing his rear, snapping at his tail or play-mounting the other in excited arousal. Squeals and growls broke the stillness of the sacred spot and mingled with the squawks of the onlookers.

Lady Tartleton had given up the attempt to hide and had run across after her dogs, calling to them with all her ancient authority. Monica puffed behind her but the children stayed in the south range, glad of the opportunity to return to their game. Joan had muttered something about the superior martial skills of princesses, a taunt which could not be allowed to pass unrequited. They had noticed what was going on in the quadrangle, but showed not the slighest interest.

'Huh,' said Pius, 'sexing again,' and returned to his joust.

After a few minutes of ineffectual bluster, realising that the dogs would not be induced to abandon their congress, Lady Tartleton decided to make the best of a bad job. She stood beside the copulating labradors and urged them on, as she had shouted to poor Cecil's eight fifty years ago, from the banks of the Isis.

'Come on, Virgil, keep it up! *One*-two, *one*-two, *one*-two! Good boy, sir!'

Meanwhile, Ophelia and Malachi, having experienced Megabyte's tumultuous seasons many times before, were trying to pretend that she had nothing to do with them. They encouraged Innocent to purloin the tortoise while its owners were staring into the courtyard, in the hope that they could pass as its keepers rather than as the unsuccessful guardians of a canine sex-bomb.

'Nice tortoise,' purred Ophelia, simpering horribly as she tried to hide the bulges in her jumper and to quell her growing nausea. She fixed her eyes on an Ideal Catholic Mother in the next row and attempted to copy her serene expression and tinkling laughter.

The only person who seemed to be unaware of the alternative attraction was Raymund Redforest himself. He continued to thrust his beard forward and backward, in an unconscious parody of the Labradors, as his address wore on.

'And so we see that Augustine, and all the other dead white male theologians who followed his puritanical lead, was fundamentally mistrustful of, and hostile towards, the body and all its beauties and functions. It is only now that we can affirm the tradition of Hedwig, of seeing all bodily creatures as sharers in the Divine Life, and all their natural instincts as holy. Eating and drinking, partaking of the fruits of God's earth, these are good and necessary. Let us remember this when we eat our meal together. Let us transform our routine grace into a great hymn to Our Lord the MasterChef. Singing, dancing, sports and games, let all these be offerings to Our Lord the Maestro. Even sex.'

Raymund paused here, waiting for the usual intake of collective breath. Oddly, it did not come and so he continued.

'Even sex is good, is meant by God to give us pleasure. I know that, gathered together in this holy place, sex is the very last thing upon all your minds. But we must all, even you buttoned-up English, allow ourselves to contemplate its mysteries for a few moments. Let us meditate upon the gentleness of lovemaking, upon the silent miracle of life created, renewed or affirmed.'

Raymund Redforest fell silent, as his careful annotation instructed him to do. But the silence, which should have been one of triumph and complacency, was instead uneasy. Somehow he sensed that his audience were not thinking of the sacred miracle of sex. Perhaps, in this dreary corner of the Northern provinces, they were too repressed.

He was, of course, partially right. The audience were not thinking of sex as a silent mystery. Instead they were cheering on its noisiest and most blatant manifestation.

Dorothy, hovering behind her pillar, was one of the last to notice the commotion. She followed the others as they thronged, but could not see past the bulky jackets of three or four tall women in front of her. The entertainment had been going on for some time when one of the women shifted slightly to talk to her neighbour and Dorothy caught a glimpse of the Labradors.

It was now Caesar's turn, and he was anxious to compensate for his late arrival by a particularly vigorous copulation. As he pounded into the complaisant Megabyte, his head thrown back and tongue hanging out, Dorothy's jaw dropped further and further.

Perhaps if she had had more than a glimpse she might have realised that the lowermost animal was not in fact the dog she knew as Spot. Perhaps not. Labradors, especially close relatives, are notoriously difficult to identify, especially tangled in frenzied intercourse. Dorothy had never seen animals mate, and, brought up by her father, had only the haziest idea of how even humans make love. She watched for a few moments in silent horror, convinced that here were the Satanic rituals so eagerly awaited by the infidel Flies.

Chapter Thirty-Eight

Diseases desperate grown
By desperate appliance are reliev'd,
Or not at all.

(iv.iii. 9–11)

The original occupant of this tomb, thought Mr Ranger, shifting uncomfortably, was almost certainly not six feet nine inches tall. After half an hour of lying with his knees bent and head twisted down to his left shoulder, he felt that he would never be able to stand straight again. Dorothy, if she were ever to take him, would have to take this disfigured letter S and show pity towards this sadly shuffling creature. Nonetheless, it was a good hiding-place, for he could hear every word of Father Redforest's sermon, complete with persistent feedback, but no footsteps had approached his morbid shelter. He eased his head across the stone chippings on to his other shoulder and settled down to a further wait of painful contemplation.

Bunny's tour had exhausted the excitements of storerooms and had passed to the east range. She had shown them the warming house and library, declined to speculate as to whether radical and feminist texts would have been available, and now stood poised in the doorway of the chapterhouse.

'This is the last monastic building we shall explore before proceeding to the church. In the chapter house the monks would gather daily to discuss the business of the abbey and to deal with disciplinary matters. Monks would confess their own transgressions or alert the community to the crimes of others.'

'Oh aye? Bad lads, was they?'

'Look, *do* stop interrupting. I don't know anything about this ghastly place except what Seb's made me learn and you're just making me lose my place. *Honestly.*'

'Okay, go on. I just wanted to know if there was any monks that was, like, really *evil.*'

'It was customary for the prior to be buried in the chapterhouse particularly towards the end of the Cistercian period. However, we commonly see only a stone flush with the ground. As you will notice this chapterhouse contains a raised tomb suggesting a considerable falling away from the eglantarian, um, eggletarian . . .'

'I think you mean "egalitarian",' supplied Mrs McHenry.

'Oh, thanks *awfully*. Egalitarian ideals of the early monks. The lid of the tomb was removed probably shortly after the dissolution and the tomb is now empty. It is thought that the relatives of the prior may have removed his body in order to place it in a family vault.'

'No skelingtons in it then? Pretty bloody boring this is turning out to be. I've not even found anywhere for me Black Mass.' Flies gave a vigorous and liquid sniff.

Bunny turned and began to lead them towards the church. So far they had remained within the walls of the ranges and had not noticed the scene in the courtyard but now they had to cross its corner in order to reach the nave of the church. Bunny felt that the time had come to investigate the increasing noise coming from the church. This was, after all, her property. Hers and Sebastian's, that was. Trust Seb to agree to let a lot of religious loonies use the place and then swan off to London himself, leaving her to deal with them. It would serve him right if they turned out to be New Age Travellers and set up camp here.

'Do come *on*! *Honestly!*'

Sister Hedwig could not resist a surreptitious glance at her wristwatch as she tilted the front seats of the Mini forward and reached in towards the immobile old Sisters.

'We're here now,' she announced brightly, trying to remind herself of the saintly virtue of patience.

Sister Felicity had gone to sleep on Sister Perpetua's shoulder. Now she opened her wide blue eyes and gave a smile of immemorial wisdom.

' "He that is hasty of spirit exalteth folly," ' she rumbled. 'Or she, of course. The Book of Proverbs, my dear. A wonderful consolation in one's later years. "As a jewel of gold in a swine's snout, so is a fair woman which is without discretion." '

' "Where no oxen are," ' responded Sister Perpetua in her soprano creak, ' "the crib is clean: but much increase is by the strength of the ox." '

Sister Hedwig looked quizzically at them, thinking that she could hardly be characterised as a fair woman without discretion, or as an ox. There did not seem to be any ulterior significance in the game, however, and so she contented herself with her efforts to extricate the old ladies from their comfortable positions embedded in the upholstery.

Ten minutes later, in a state of flustered triumph, she shepherded Felicity and Perpetua up the nave, past the crowd of excited people, and into seats on the front row. Ophelia, Malachi and Innocent sat nearby, nursing the tortoise, and Sister Hedwig beamed at them in benevolent approval. Perpetua clutched the shoe box while Felicity trailed a bundle of blankets and mackintoshes. She tripped over these as she tried to sit down, and knocked several chairs clattering to the ground. Raymund Redforest paused long enough for the three Sisters to blush and then continued.

'And that is why I agreed to come all this way, to this tiny little place, miles away from civilisation, in order to speak to you today. I know that some of you feel a little shy, a little overwhelmed that a famous international preacher, a renowned theologian, a major figure in today's worldwide Church,' with every phrase his beard was thrust out a little further, 'should turn down important engagements in San Francisco, Tokyo and Rome to be with you.'

Sister Hedwig thought that he was not quite as she remembered him. He seemed shorter, and his rather piggy eyes were surely smaller while beneath his fisherman's smock was the unmistakable curve of a pot belly. On either side of her the two elderly Sisters sat impassively, munching Polos. Forty years of assemblies had left them expert at concealing their reactions.

Suddenly there was a diversion. A large, untidy woman detached herself from the crowd and strode up to Father Raymund, scattering chairs and small animals in her wake. She picked up a rabbit upon which she had inadvertently trodden and absent-mindedly cradled it to her chest. With her other hand she wrested the microphone from the stunned priest and declaimed in a husky voice,

'Women priests, women priests, an abomination.
We shall never lie down under female domination.'

She seemed to be expecting some assistance from amidst the crowd, but none came, and so after a few seconds of edgy silence she crimsoned and blundered away. Raymund Redforest, his beard slightly awry, shot a malevolent look after her as he retrieved the microphone.

'What did she say, Perpetua?' asked Felicity. Her hearing aid was not sophisticated enough to cope with feedback.

'I think it's something about lesbian sado-masochism, Sister,' replied Perpetua, who had only caught the end of the verse and whose secret vice was the Sunday papers.

Felicity nodded serenely.

Deputy District Judge Ranger could let out his breath at last. He could hardly believe that that unfortunate young man had not insisted upon inspecting the tomb. Now they seemed to be leaving and with any luck he could stay hidden until things got a bit quieter and he could have a look for Dorothy. There did seem to be an awful lot of commotion going on for a religious retreat. Charismatic, he supposed it was. He let his eyes rest peacefully on the grey stone of the tomb wall and upon his own arm, so covered in dust that the original colour of his suit was completely obscured. He wondered whether being dead would be like this, cool, detached and pale grey.

Suddenly his reverie was broken by an acute scream.

'Spot! Oh help, help! Somebody help! Don't just stand there watching, *don't*!'

It was the voice of his beloved, heard only twice but unforgettable, and its effect upon the Deputy District Judge was as unstoppable as that of Megabyte's scent had been upon the three male Labradors. His head snapped back from his shoulder and struck hard against the wall of the tomb, but he had no time to notice the pain. As he pulled himself up by his good arm, he could hear a tearing sound as the seat of his trousers snagged against the jagged floor.

'Darn it,' he said, appropriately.

Flies had turned for a last wistful look at the disappointing tomb before following Bunny and Mrs McHenry. 'Crap,' he muttered. 'Just a load of old crap. I wish I'd gone with Steve to do that job— Aaarrghhh!'

For as he watched, a figure had emerged from the tomb, a man-sized figure, white and dusty looking. It paused for a moment, looking around, casting its bleary blind face towards Flies, before loping off in the direction of the church. Flies stood silently for a long time, staring after the figure. It was preternaturally tall, thin and bent, and loped along with a sinister and hunched gait, a strange flap of cloth (or could it be skin?) hanging down behind it. A ghost! He had only read four pages of his friend's book and already he was conjuring up spirits of the restless dead. At this rate, he'd be a warlock by Christmas. He supposed that it was the ghost of that bloke, that prior that they'd buried in the tomb. Must have been a pretty evil sod. Bet he'd help at a Black Mass.

'Hey, Mrs Mac! Didj'a see that ghost?'

'Don't be silly. Come along. We have to confront the patriarchal myths of Judeo-Christianity if we are to formulate a viable oppositional construct. And for goodness' sake blow your nose!'

Dorothy was still screaming. 'Spot, they've got Spot! Look, those horrible dogs, they're *doing things* to my little Spot. Somebody stop them, *please*!'

In a moment Mr Ranger was at her elbow. She had forgotten that she had asked him to meet her at the abbey and blinked absent-mindedly. Oh yes, it was that judge. But he looked different, dirtier than before. In court he had been odd, rather nice but odd. Now he looked dangerous, wild and determined. But still odd. Dorothy screamed again.

'Don't you fret, li'l lady. Ah'll get your dawg back for you.'

The Deputy District Judge shouldered his way through the crowd, who shrank from his contamination. Some of them remembered descriptions of fallout, and wondered whether a nuclear catastrophe had taken place. Mr Ranger approached the dogs with the same hasty fearlessness as had driven him to foil the Arthurian bank clerks. He aimed a solid kick at the fundament of Caesar, who, to judge from his pants, was close to his climax. The dog gave a squeal, of offence rather than of pain, lost his rhythm and fell off Megabyte who looked around in disappointment.

'How dare you!' called an imperious voice from the other side of the courtyard. 'Who do you think you are to interfere with my boys' sport? Go away immediately, you horrible man.'

'I will not, ma'am. I stand here in defence of decency and justice and I will not move one inch until these animals cease their unnatural practices.'

'Unnatural? What the hell are you talking about? What's unnatural about a bit of honest insemination? Good healthy bitch, that, too. They'll be handsome pups. I must find the owners and discuss stud fees. Go on, now, get out!'

Mr Ranger's only answer was a kick up the bottom of Horace, who had taken up the place vacated by Caesar.

'You have been warned,' shouted Lady Tartleton. 'You're as bad as these bloody hunt saboteurs. Only one language you people understand.' She seached in her poacher's pocket for a stone or hard ball to throw at him. She generally had something of the sort for the boys to fetch. On this occasion she found none, but drew out a plastic bag containing a spiky and glutinous mass. She glanced at it for an incomprehending

257

second or two, weighing it in her hand. That would do. She cast aside the bag, provoking a disapproving murmur from the litter-conscious audience, and flung the hedgehog at Mr Ranger.

Unfortunately, in her excitement her aim was imperfect and the shot went wide, bypassing the Deputy District Judge and the crowd, and sending the missile heading straight for Father Raymund. Fortunately, being an American, he had been trained to avoid assassination, and hopped clear just in time. There was a gentle splat and the remains of what was once a hedgehog lay, a smear of brown and red, on the tiled floor of the chancel.

Sisters Felicity and Perpetua had each watched the flying lump with a twinge of recognition. They exchanged stricken glances and Perpetua opened the shoe box for the first time since Skipton. Her fears were confirmed. With little animal cries of rage, never before seen, even by the most reprobate girls of Rambleton Convent, the two Sisters sprang from their seats and ran forwards towards the hedgehog. There was a sudden silence but for the creaking of the old ladies' bones as the momentum of their distress overcame their antiquity. With their eyes fixed upon the little brown daub and their lips mouthing silent prayers they forced themselves onwards. Against all probability, against the sad little heap of evidence, they hoped. And even as they reached the altar they continued to hope.

Chapter Thirty-Nine

So tell him with th'occurrents more and less
Which have solicited – the rest is silence.

(v.ii. 362–3)

But they were too late. Even as they knelt upon the faded red clay and held cupped palms towards the little creature, the last flickerings of hope were to be devoured. From the north side of the narthex came the sounds of scuffling feet on gravel, of urgent huffing and of inarticulate grunts. Moments later a fifth Labrador bounded in from the adjacent side chapel. The dog was in the first stages of adolescence, elastic and affable. It was dragging a damp middle-aged man at the end of a substantial lead. The choke chain was tight around the dog's powerful neck, but this did no more to impede its progress than did the man's feeble remonstrances.

'Sorry, sorry, not my dog, apologies,' he muttered as his feet slid along the ancient tiles.

The Labrador, like St Paul's devil, was roaming around, looking for something to devour. Its nose did not let it down. Within seconds it had made straight for the hedgehog and, opening its large jaws, gobbled it up in a single action.

'Spot!' gasped the perspiring man, still hanging forlornly on to the lead. The dog gave a final jerk and the man fell headlong across the front of the altar. From this position he managed to drag the dog, now sated by its snack and sobered by the residual spines, towards him.

Sisters Perpetua and Felicity, who had been thrown backwards by the sheer psychological force of the dog's onslaught, now sat back, trembling on the tiles. They pulled their cardigans around them for comfort. Hedwig, her face frozen into forbearance, hoisted her grey flannel skirt above sturdy knees in preparation to clamber over the fallen man and thus reach the old ladies. She was, however, forestalled.

Ophelia, clutching Innocent and, inadvertently, the tortoise, watched the man as he staggered to his feet. He was running now, shakily but with surprising speed, the dog bounding alongside him. They had almost disappeared now into the maze of small chapels in the south transept.

As the man trotted along, the Labrador would jump up at him, playfully snapping at his nose. Ophelia could remember Gigabyte doing the same . . . With a sudden start she turned to Malachi.'

'Mal, isn't that . . . ?'

But Malachi was no longer in his seat. It was twelve years since Ophelia had seen that swift movement, his body flung forward, arms around his opponent's ankles and the twist to bring him down. Twelve years, but Malachi had not lost the knack. As Ophelia gazed at him, she felt a warm flush of pride. For a moment she forgot Innocent wriggling on her knee, even forgot the tortoise who had just deposited a dark slug of excrement on to her lap. Gloriaux was transformed into the ground at Twickenham, Gigabyte to a melon-shaped white ball and the middle-aged kidnapper into the ferocious Oxford prop, seventeen stone and growing. And, come to think of it, the expressions of the Oxford supporters at that Varsity match had been exactly the same as those of the motley trio, two middle-aged women and a pustulous youth, who arrived, panting, to witness their leader's discomfiture. One of the women, the plump one, Ophelia was sure that she had seen before, but she had no idea where. Dorothy, with her neat perm disordered by the wind and her cheeks russet with excitement, bore little resemblance to the demure Miss Smith of the Wet Nose County Court. Meanwhile, there were more important matters afoot.

Malachi held the labrador aloft, his arms buckling slightly under the weight of a month's sausages and Twiglets. On either side of him a little nun, each returned to breath and equanimity, was bobbing up and down clamouring for a last sight of the lost hedgehog. But Malachi, for once, ignored them. Nothing could interfere with his triumph.

Ophelia sat firmly on her canvas chair, clasping Innocent and the tortoise with equal affection, and smiling idiotically. She gazed at a little crease at the base of Malachi's neck, just where it met his shoulder, and remembered when she had first noticed it. Since that glorious tackle, launched in the last few minutes of injury time, Malachi had lurched from one disaster to the next. But now, at the lowest point of their familial fortunes, when Ophelia herself was drained and despairing, he had repeated his victory. He smiled down at her, just as he had that day, when the final whistle had assured their resplendent victory. She smiled back, shimmering with desire, as she thought of muddy thighs and the warm communal bath. Innocent slipped from her knee to join his father and she squirmed pleasantly, planning a celebratory seduction in front of the electric fire. Sadly, she had only reached the rugby shirt and cream silk knickers when the fantasy collapsed. The anaphrodisiac effect of discovering a tortoise urinating on one's leg, she noted ruefully, had to be experienced to be believed.

Presently Megabyte lolloped along, bored of sex and ready to welcome her daughter. This she did with mild scolding but no great display of surprise or emotion. She was followed by voices.

'Daddy, Daddy, you've got Gigabyte!'

'Dad, we came to help but we've been a bit busy . . .'

'Mummy, I've bashed my knee again.'

Ophelia gasped, wondering whether she was suffering from an aural mirage. There must be a word for that, she thought, inconsequentially. Anyway, she was obviously going mildly potty. It was probably an effect of the strain and then the relief, that and all this unaccustomed thinking about sex. The voices, if any voices there had been, must have belonged to someone else's children. She would just check, she told herself, and rose from her seat quickly. Too quickly, for as she moved towards the approaching children, pushing impatiently at the wandering goat, her nausea returned with a dreadful, pulsing intensity. The grey sky turned black and full of innumerable shooting stars and the gravel was twisting up to meet her. Oh no, she thought. I suppose I'm waking up.

But when Ophelia did wake up she was lying on the floor of the abbey narthex and her face was being tenderly licked by Gigabyte. She raised her eyes from a row of shoes, up trousers and one pair of grubby knee-length socks, past a variety of coats to a row of concerned faces. As they floated into focus she identified them from left to right: Malachi, still panting slightly from his tackle, Pius, Joan, holding Innocent, Hygenus, Urban, Lady Tartleton . . . Lady Tartleton? Deputy District Judge Ranger . . . No, this was too much. She was obviously still in the grip of some fearful lunacy. Ophelia closed her eyes again.

'Mum!' cried Pius in anguish. 'Mummy, don't die!'

Ophelia opened her eyes once more and stared up at him.

'It really is you, isn't it? I'm not dying, you daft boy, just having a nap.' Pius looked unconvinced. 'What are you all doing here, anyway? I thought you were dib-dibbling.'

'We came to rescue Gigabyte.'

'Oh. I think your father's just done that.'

'Yes, we know he has.' Hygenus was exasperated. 'Only 'cos he got there first. We would've done it 'cept we were busy being medeagle knights.'

'I know you would. You're very brave children.' Ophelia smiled round the semicircle of faces, feeling like a Victorian matriarch on her death-bed. Her gaze moved down. They were extremely grubby, even worse than usual. And Pius' heart seemed to be pounding particularly vigorously.

'Pius, what have you got inside your jacket?'

'Oh yes, we nearly forgot. It's the answer to that crossword clue. You know, the one you asked Grandma to solve. We thought it must be something to do with Gigabyte, but now she's back I suppose it's no use.'

'No, let me see,' said Ophelia, transfixed by the activity beneath the grey nylon.

'All right then. But don't say I didn't warn you. He's getting a bit restless now.' Pius unzipped his jacket and drew out an extremely angry Chequers. Malachi, who had left the Labradors to their reunion and joined the group, now retreated hastily, his hand covering his nose and mouth.

'It's that cat!' cried Ophelia, stumbling to her feet. 'Have you children had it all this time?'

'All what time? Do you know him? He's called Chequers, you know, and the answer's inside his bell, except we can't get it off.'

'What, *Chequers' Bell*? Are you sure? I can't remember the clue now. Anyway, I suppose it might be. It's his cat, in any case.'

'Whose cat is it? It's ours now, we've been looking after it. You told us once, that if somebody finds something . . .'

'Oh, stop blethering, children! Just give me the cat, will you, and I'll unscrew the bell. Quickly before it escapes!'

Unfortunately Ophelia had no more success in opening the bell as had Pius, and Malachi, when called to help, was stricken by so severe a fit of sneezing that he had to retire. Everyone tried, from Flies to Sister Perpetua, but neither the former's house-breaking skills nor the campanological expertise of the latter were to any avail.

'Perhaps Father Redforest might help?' suggested Sister Felicity, but the priest was nowhere to be found.

Just as Ophelia was teetering back on the brink of despair, a new pair of voices could be heard from the other side of the eastern apse.

' 'Ave you got it yet, darlin'?' the first asked, with a wisp of impatience. 'The ones wot are pointy at the top, they're Gofic arches and the ones wot are just round, they're . . . Go on, you tell me.'

'Romanist?' the other voice tried, hopefully. Ophelia, smiling in astonishment, stepped back from her metaphorical brink.

'Roman*esque*. Are you sure this butcher of yours isn't going to jump out from behind the cloisters, wielding 'is meat-cleaver? I've got posterity to fink of, me.'

'Huh! Don't worry about *him*,' replied the girl. 'Serve him right if he does find out. He shouldn't have taken that girl from Freezaland down the disco, should he? Anyway, we're just having an educational visit, aren't we? I know all about misery-cords now.'

'I *could* teacha about sumfin' *else* . . .' began the boy ambiguously, but he was interrupted by Ophelia's rushing around the wall and grabbing the pair in her outstretched hands. She had still been clutching the tortoise, which now fell to the floor and began to crawl phlegmatically away. If only it had remembered to hibernate.

'Polly! And you, Mr Photocopier Man!'

'He's called Damien,' said Polly with dignity.

'Okay, Damien. Look, we've found the cat and the instructions are in its bell but we can't get it open. Come and help, please!'

'Eh?' said Damien, reflecting that these Northern women were perhaps rather *too* much of a challenge. This sort of thing never happened when he took a bird down Waltham Gatehouse.

Polly met with similar failure, despite breaking two fingernails on the bell, but Damien took the cat in his arms with confidence.

'Wot you need,' he declared, grinning around at the assembled audience, 'is a bit of Suvvern sophistication. A bit of inside knowledge, like. Know where I was before I got into photocopiers?'

No one did.

'Animal accessories,' he said proudly. 'Squeaky plastic newspapers, poodle coats, ruined castles for yer fish to swim through, poop scoops. And yer feline security devices. This 'ere, this is yer Protectapuss UltraBell. You put yer details, name, address, favourite food and that on to a bit of paper, put it in the bell, screw it on and Bob's yer window-cleaner.'

'Not mine, he isn't,' objected Ophelia. 'What's the point, when no one can get it off?'

'Not no one. Yer owner, he knows the secret, and yer designated veterinary surgeons and yer senior police officers (Acting Chief Inspector and above). And, of course, yer authorised marketing representatives, of which I am ONE.'

As he said the word *one*, Damien gave the bell a deft twist, flicked his forefinger upwards, and sent the little silver cap tinkling on to the tiles. He extracted a tightly rolled piece of paper and handed it to Ophelia with a flourish. She retreated to an abandoned chair to read the message in private.

Bene!

I, Wilfred Wapentake, otherwise known as Wilfred Parrish, hereby state my wish that my mortal remains be destroyed in accordance with the customs of my Viking forebears, by way of a great conflagration of a traditional ship upon the River Ewe in the town of Rambleton, and furthermore that with my body, that of the last of the Wapentakes, alias Parrishes, there should be burned the great Wapentake Brooch that lies in the safe of the Arthurian Bank.

May you be blessed from Valhalla!

W. W.

PS: I forgot to mention in my wills: please ask little Polly if she would like the cat.

Chapter Forty

Be wary then: best safety lies in fear

(I.iii. 43)

'Oh aye,' replied Edgar Pottlebonce, reversing the Grutta into the mouth of the barn. 'There's nowt wrong with our Monica. All that carry-on with t'dogs wouldn't bother her. Matching and mating, rutting and robbling, she's bin watching it since she was a bairn. Now then, Wilf, let's be having you.'

Edgar, Polly and Ophelia climbed out and trudged through the ankle-deep layer of hay and spilled cattle-feed towards Mr Parrish's resting place. Ophelia hung back behind the other two, but was relieved to find, when Edgar tossed aside the covering hay bale, that the body's condition had not deteriorated to any great extent. The features were somewhat more blurred and the smell more distinctive, but it was not as yet an object of utter horror. In fact, Ophelia was beginning to feel quite affectionate towards the deceased solicitor and almost sorry to think of the impending incineration of his familiar corpse.

'It's the cold as does it,' said Edgar proudly, as though the weather were of his own manufacture. 'No,' he continued, cheerfully lifting the dead shoulders, 'I reckon our Monica was pretty pleased with how things went at Glory-O. All them Green lot just sort of melted away, so she tells me, and as for that American vicar or whatever he was, story is he got a taxi all t'way to Manchester Airport and then got next flight back t'Americy. Won't be hearing from him in a hurry, I reckon.'

It was quite true, reflected Ophelia, at least the bit about the vanishing ecologists. No one, as far as she knew, had heard what had happened to Raymund Redforest. The deciphering of Chequers' bell had been the last spectacle, after which the delegates had submissively climbed back into their Dormobiles and driven away. It had been then that Deputy District Judge Ranger had sidled up to her, one hand clutching Dorothy's elbow, and had put his proposition to her.

'But Monica tells me you were taken queer,' panted Mr Pottlebonce

265

as the body collapsed once again on to the back seat. 'I hope you're all right now, lass.'

'I'm feeling fine,' said Ophelia truthfully. For the few minutes between her reading of Mr Parrish's note and Mr Ranger's approach she had been struck with renewed panic. How on earth was she to construct a Viking ship and burn it, together with Wilfred Parrish and the priceless brooch, on the river at Rambleton without anyone else finding out about it? She would, she thought, either have to disregard his wishes after all, or give herself up to the police and to the Law Society. But Mr Ranger's proposal gave her new hope. A merger between the firms would allow her to continue to work, despite Mr Parrish's death, for the ninety-odd years' combined experience of Messrs Snodsworth and Ranger would be sufficient to oversee any number of newly qualified solicitors. And so by now, late on Wednesday afternoon, the papers had already been drawn up and signed in a reasonable approximation of Wilfred Parrish's signature. The tricky part was yet to come, but she had one or two ideas still concealed in her straw-covered sleeve.

'This it, then?' asked Edgar, turning into the drive of The Larches.

The house was as quiet and as English as ever. Polly had dusted the dark wooden surfaces the day before, in preparation for its owner's reappearance, and had even allowed her beloved Chequers to spend the night there in the interests of authenticity. Ophelia checked the thick privet hedges on either side of the garden and when all was clear they carried poor Wilfred Parrish back over his own threshold.

'In here, I think,' said Ophelia, opening the door of the sitting room. 'Just settle him into this chair. That's right, the big one in front of the fire.'

'D'ye think we ought to light it?' asked Polly, staring dubiously into the empty grate. 'It's one of them real sort, isn't it? I can't be doing with anything that's not got a switch.'

'Oh no, you don't want to be lighting a fire.' Edgar was shaking his head vehemently. 'Not a fire. Heat, you see. Heat. Accelerates the decompositional processes, does heat. Light a fire next to that body and within an hour or two you'll have—'

'Yes,' said Ophelia abruptly, feeling the muscles of her throat constrict. 'We'll just leave it as it is, Poll. Now, if you can lower his feet on to that little stool, and Edgar, you make sure that his back stays straight. Good. There we are.'

Mr Parrish relaxed gratefully into his armchair for the last time. As his weight collapsed upon the seat, a breath of air was expelled from a small hole in the cushion. *Aaahhh*. To all three conspirators it seemed as though Mr Parrish himself had made the sound, a sigh of relief at his eventual homecoming.

They settled him as best they could, placing the volume of John Masefield's poems, collected from the bedroom, on his lap and the slip of paper from Chequers' bell inside his breast pocket.

'There you are,' Ophelia said gently. 'I don't think we really want to go through all that charade of the Latin crossword clue again, do we?' Thinking that this sounded ungracious, she continued. 'Not that it wasn't an awfully good clue and great fun,' here she crossed her fingers behind her back, 'to solve. And I expect you enjoyed watching, didn't you, if you're allowed to do that sort of thing? Forty years was it, as a dull old country solicitor, managing other people's whims and eccentricities? Yes I think you deserved a couple of your own at the end. So don't worry. We'll do our best to send you to Valhalla in style.'

'Ophelia?' called Polly warningly from the door.

'Yes, I'm finished now,' replied Ophelia, smoothing a last strand of hair behind Mr Parrish's ear. '*Bon voyage*,' she whispered.

When Mr Pottlebonce and Polly, in the malodorous Grutta, had crunched away, Ophelia left the front door slightly ajar and concealed herself in the little cloakroom which occupied the space between the hall and sitting room. Nearly two hours passed before she heard the sound of wheels on the gravel outside. She sat up straight and tense, waiting for voices.

'Nice place young Wilfred's got here,' said the first. 'Bit modern, mind. What's that, tennis on tarmacadam? What's wrong with a lawn, eh?'

'I think they've had these hard courts for a while, sir,' said the second man. 'They must be easier to maintain, I suppose.'

It took a few moments for Ophelia to recognise that this was, in fact, the voice that she had been expecting. She had never before heard the Deputy District Judge as the boy Lionel, cowed by his senior partner and bereft of his American accent. Someone pressed the old-fashioned doorbell, and Ophelia noticed the half-second's interval between the click of the button and the low buzz of the bell. A *scintilla temporis*, she thought, remembering her land law.

There was, of course, no reply.

'Er, the door is open, sir,' suggested Mr Ranger. 'Perhaps we should just go in. After all, Mrs O. said that he would be expecting us around now.'

'Eh? What?' answered Mr Snodsworth, who had found a note to himself about an obscure detail of *Geranium* in his waistcoat pocket and was now trying to decipher it.

But Mr Ranger had already pushed open the front door and gone into the house. Ophelia could hear the reinforced heels of his cowboy boots clicking on the tiles as he passed the cloakroom.

'Wilfred?' he called tentatively. 'Mr Parrish?'

In the silence Ophelia noticed for the first time that a tap was dripping into the washbasin. There was a creak as he pushed open the sitting-room door.

'Oh, there you are Wilf . . . Wilfred? Mr Parrish? Oh no! Mr Snodsworth! Come quickly!'

'Rush, rush, rush, that's all you young people seem to think of. Where would I be if I'd rushed through *Geranium*? Just ask yourself that, if you ever have time to ask yourself anything, you and your motor-buses . . . Oh. Well, he seems to have died, doesn't he? I don't know what all the hurry was about, though. You don't expect me to resuscitate him, do you?'

'No, no, sir. It was just a bit of a shock.'

'Suppose it must be, at your age.' Mr Snodsworth's voice had softened. 'Anyway, at least we know the fella had a good excuse for not answering the door. Well, shall we go, then? Nothing to discuss now, eh?'

'Shouldn't we do something about the body, sir? Ring for an ambulance, perhaps.'

Ophelia sat rigid, clutching the handle of the lavatory chain in both hands to stop herself from crying out. Please, please, *please*, no, she mouthed silently.

'An ambulance? Bless my soul, whatever's come over the boy? He's past the aid of an ambulance now, I fear. No, my boy, the coroner's the chappie we need. I distinctly recall that when old Lady Geranium died so suddenly between the potted palms . . .'

Ophelia heard the repeated click of Mr Ranger's heels, the rustle of his Wet Nose Court Diary and the lazy ratchet of the telephone dial. She clung tighter to the chain handle, wondering who was the local coroner and whether he was a lawyer or a doctor.

'Hello? Hi there.' With a half-closed door between Mr Ranger and his partner, he dared a mild Americanism. 'Yes, good evening. I need to speak to the coroner, please. What? Oh, I see. Yes, yes, that's fine. Thank you so much, ma'am. Have a nice day.'

The heels clattered urgently back.

'Mr Snodsworth, Mr Snodsworth!'

'Do compose yourself, my boy. Will the coroner be joining us?'

'No, he's on holiday. His cleaning lady says we have to contact the deputy coroner.'

'Oh, really? And have you *contacted*,' he lengthened the word in fastidious disdain, 'this gentleman?'

'No, sir. You see, sir, it's, um, it's you, sir.'

'It's me? I mean, it is I? Good grief. Well, in that case I don't think we need too much fuss . . .'

Ophelia let go of the lavatory chain and tiptoed out of the cloakroom, through the hall and out of the front door. On the doorstep she smoothed her rumpled suit and rang the bell. The door was answered by the Deputy District Judge.

'Ah, good evening Mr Ranger,' said Ophelia, as brightly as she could manage. 'Got you doing all the work already, has he? I just thought I'd pop in on your meeting to see whether you needed me for anything. All going well, is it?'

'Well, not exactly, ma'am,' began Mr Ranger, and explained their discovery. 'So now,' he concluded 'we're trying to find out who his doctor was, so that he can come and give us a death certificate. You wouldn't happen to know, I suppose?'

'As it happens, I do,' said Ophelia, inwardly blessing him. 'It's the same doctor as ours, Dr Hale, Horatio Hale. Shall I ring him for you?'

She tried to keep from smiling as she dialled the number. It would not do to be over-confident now. Her plans seemed to be working well, and Mr Snodsworth's being the Deputy Coroner had been a marvellous bonus, but she was not safe yet. Dr Hale might be away, or might succumb to an unprecedented attack of medical expertise.

She need not have worried. Dr Hale was only too willing to abandon his wart clinic and arrived within fifteen minutes, ebullient in his battered little Morgan. There was an awkward moment when he first viewed the body as it sprawled, soft and clammy, on the armchair.

'Are you sure the poor old blighter's just died? I seem to remember something about rigor mortis, and, well, he looks a bit decomposed, if you don't mind my saying so.'

'Nonsense,' replied Mr Snodsworth with acerbity. 'Young Wilfred always looked like that. Got it from his mother. She was a Nockling, you know. Spineless lot, the Nocklings. No, of course he's just died. Signed these papers this morning, you know.' He waved a sheaf of

269

documents in Dr Hale's face. 'Don't know what they think they're doing, sending these schoolboys out as doctors.'

'Yes, you're probably right. Can't say that pathology was exactly my star subject, don't you know? Fact is, I used to skive off most of those lectures. Ghastly woman that gave them, looked like a corpse herself. I'm a sports injuries man, myself. I've not got much patience with the dead.'

'If you could just write out a certificate then?' suggested Ophelia.

'A certificate? Oh, you mean a death certificate. Actually, I'm not sure that I really should. I mean, was this chap actually even one of my patients?'

Disturbing signs of laboured thought were appearing on the doctor's smooth brow. Ophelia had to act quickly.

'Do you find,' she began wildly, 'that the incidence of femur displacement is greater where the fullback adopts the traditional defensive role or where counter-attacking tactics are used?'

'Interesting that you should ask that.' His forehead had cleared again and the light of science shone in his come-hither eyes. 'There is a fascinating illustration of just that point in the 1986 All Blacks' game . . .'

As he lectured, Ophelia slid a blank certificate from his briefcase and filled it in. *Myocardial Infarct.* That would do.

'Of course,' Dr Hale was continuing, 'nowadays even the prop will often be scoring tries, which inevitably creates . . .'

Ophelia placed the certificate and pen in front of him and he signed it, still speaking of rucks, scrums and the two-three-two formation. Ophelia gave a final nod to Mr Parrish in his armchair and silently slipped away.

Epilogue

There's rosemary, that's for remembrance
pray you, love, remember.

(IV.v. 173–4)

The funeral of Wilfred Wapentake, a.k.a. Parrish, took place on a cold and crisp evening a fortnight before Christmas. Nearly two hundred people huddled on the banks of the Ewe, comforted by camping-stools, rugs and flasks of tea, whispering in excited monosyllables, unsure as to whether this was to be a service or a spectacle. As they waited for the church clock to chime seven, checking the time on their digital watches, for the minute hand had still not been replaced, they watched the fairy-lights at the back of Freezaland and the Ram's Leg reflected in the slightly stirring black water.

Ophelia, squatting on a bundle of sleeping-bags, gazed down at two tiny dancing points of gold. She felt as excited, and almost as carefree, as any in the crowd. Originally she had expected that she would arrange the ceremony and had – as soon as the note had been discovered and the body left to the mysterious care of Mr Marrow, the undertaker – gone straight to Rambleton Library to research the matter.

There she had found Letitia Lamb, wife of the Major, amateur local historian and part-time librarian.

'Oh dear, *Vikings*, yes,' Mrs Lamb had twittered. 'Oh the children *do* like them so, don't they? We always have masses in the children's section, or rather we don't, because they're always out. But not the adults. With the adults it's more crop rotation and the Battle of Britain. They seem to grow out of the Vikings, somehow. Except for poor old Mr Parrish, of course, but then he was rather peculiar towards the end, wasn't he? Remember the bowling, that time when we met you first?'

Ophelia did remember the bowling, and the fact that the eccentric enthusiasm had been subsequently transferred to Major Lamb. So, simultaneously, did Mrs Lamb, and an uneasy few seconds followed.

'Anyway,' fluttered Mrs Lamb eventually, 'I know that there isn't anything recorded about the Vikings locally, though we were, of course, within the Danelaw . . .' She trailed away dreamily, as though the Norse

271

government were within her own reminiscence, and disappeared behind a large book stack. Several minutes later she emerged, clutching a small volume.

'I've found this,' she began hesitantly, 'but some of it seems a bit *rude.'*

It was a summary of the account by Ibn Fadlan, an Arab, of a Viking cremation which took place on the Volga in 922.

'He was a chieftain,' said Mrs Lamb. 'The Viking, I mean. Would you say that was a bit like a solicitor, dear?'

'Oh, very much like,' agreed Ophelia, and took out her library ticket.

Unfortunately, when she stood up to address the first meeting of the Viking Committee, held three days later in the back room of the Ram's Leg, Ophelia immediately and ignominiously fainted again. This time her fall was broken by the rubber plant, from whence the Vicar rescued her. Notwithstanding this divine aid, Malachi and Polly, who were both informed of the occurrence by Lady Tartleton, formed an instant and impregnable alliance to prevent Ophelia from having any more to do with the funeral. Polly, whose self-confidence had been honed to acuity by the Bandits, took over the chair of the commitee, renewed the library book in her own name and spent the next few weeks at Parrishes, or Parrish Snodmore Ranger, as the firm was now known, constantly on the telephone.

The first fruits of Polly's labours were now visible on the opposite bank under the lights of the infant bowling alley: a great pile of wood, long, broad and flattened on the top. Most of the untrimmed trunks had come from Greenhaigh Farm where Stewart Saggers had inherited from Edgar Pottlebonce a considerable Coppicing Allowance from the Department of Agriculture. Some, however, the older and darker wood, had been sent by Lady Tartleton from her new home at Yardley Farm, three miles south of Rambleton. She had survived life at Raggy-Kegs, with Albert Skate and the Hulk, for almost a week but the abrupt end, after four days, of the cohabitation of Darren and Sharon and the imminent return of Kylie the rat, were too much for her.

'It might be cheap,' she had said, 'though with the number of cigarettes I have to buy for that man I doubt it; but I have to consider the position of my boys.'

Since the position of her boys was, generally, astride the mongrel bitch next door, her misgivings were understood. Yardley Farm, on a long and forgotten lease from the Earl of Scorsdale, was a more moderate base for economy. Lady Tartleton, in spite of her estimable work for the committee, did not in fact attend the funeral. When she discovered that the entire O. family intended to be there, leaving their two labradors at home, she was horrified.

'It's not so much Gigi. After being with those awful Lancastrians so long I'm sure that she can survive anything. But Meg! How you can think of leaving her in her condition I have absolutely no idea. Don't forget, I have a third share in those puppies and whichever of my boys is the father, they're of good pedigree stock. No, no, off you go. Enjoy yourselves. I'll just come over and spend the evening at Moorwind.'

They groaned, and hid the dog food, but agreed.

The clock struck seven and on the sixth stroke, quietly majestic, the dragon's head prow of the longship appeared from the east. It was a splendid beast, mysterious and mythic, lavished with gold, green and red, with only the occasional flaky corner to suggest its papier-mâché origins. The boat which it led was a simple barge, about ten feet long, adorned with silver bottle-tops and powered by a small outboard motor. Hygenus tugged at Ophelia's sleeve.

'We made that boat at our school, Mummy. I did one of the dragon's eyes. Don't you think it's good?'

'Our class made the motor,' added Pius. 'Mr Smith came in and did it with us. It was okay, 'cos it counted as National Curriculum Technology.'

'I'm very pleased to hear it,' said Ophelia abstractedly. 'What, you don't mean *that* Mr Smith?'

The greyish man who had been sitting next to Deputy District Judge Ranger on the opposite bank had now stood up and revealed himself to be Wardle. He watched, arms folded proprietorially, as the little barge collided softly with the pile of wood and dislodged one or two of the outer branches. Once it was stationary, Wardle shuffled forward and switched off, then unclipped the motor. He stood uncertainly for a few moments, the motor cradled in his arms, looking about at the Rambletonian hordes. One or two of the children called out to him,

'Mr Smith! Hello, Comrade Smith! It worked, didn't it, sir?'

He seemed to glance over his shoulder before answering them, as if expecting his father's ghost to appear and berate him for his treachery. But he was no Hamlet, and no supernatural solicitings prevented him from waving cheerily to the children before returning to his place between his sister and her fiancé.

273

'Well done, pardner,' Mr Ranger gripped his hand painfully. 'Or should I say brother?'

Dorothy blushed and squirmed happily between them.

'Oh look,' she whisperered. 'They're lifting it now.'

Indeed they were. Four young men, including both Gary and Damien (Well *done*, Polly! thought Ophelia), had lifted the boat and were settling it carefully upon the woodpile. As they melted into the darkness there was a doubtful patter of applause. The clapping stopped raggedly as another group of four men entered the spotlight, a bier resting upon their massy shoulders. District Judge Ranger removed his Stetson.

Mr Marrow had allowed no concessions to be made to the Viking theme, and his pall-bearers wore the same dark suits and subdued expressions with which they carried respectably closed oak coffins twice a week. But Mr Parrish was anything but subdued. Unassuming, even invisible during his life, in a tweed jacket and Rotary tie, in death he was gorgeous. Tight silk trousers in royal blue, which elicited an envious 'Cor!' from the hovering Flies, were topped by a matching tunic, thick with heavy embroidery. But even these were austere in comparison with the cloak which wrapped them. Rose-red, almost purple in its shadows, it swirled about the body in sumptous folds of delicate brocade, fastened at the shoulder with the precious intricacy of the Wapentake brooch. Above its gold-traced collar the neck and head of Wilfred Parrish rose in quiet nobility. The blue-white contours of his nose and cheekbones, his lightly closed eyelids and the half-smile of his thin lips brought a gasp from his watching neighbours. In place of the shy and bumbling, sometimes querulous country solicitor they had known, here lay a prince, a pope, a saint. The last weary lines between his brows, the lines that not even death could iron away, were the last reminder of his life with them. Mr Parrish had come into his inheritance.

The bearers carefully slipped the bier from their shoulders and slid it into the boat, where it was surrounded by cushions, flagons of wine and a sword and shield, the warrior's grave-goods speeding his journey to Valhalla. Ophelia remembered that Ibn Fadlan's account had told of many animals' being burned with the chieftain, as meat for his afterlife; two horses, two cows, a cockerel . . . And here came Stewart Saggers, bustling with self-importance and laden with frozen packages. He arranged them gingerly on the cushions and Ophelia could glimpse chicken nuggets, a beef curry and, imported especially, *Burgers au Cheval.* He spent some time fussing over the arrangement, plumping up cushions, wiping away frost and casting furtive glances of awe at the stately figure of Mr Parrish. Finally, with a last tender polishing of the beef curry, he lumbered away.

There was silence. The little ship was now laden and ready for its journey into the halls of Odin. Amidst the tawdry finery and the cheap frozen food the cold face kept its strange nobility and made of the makeshift preparations something of the ancient pagan solemnity. The Vicar felt it, and saved the moment for his next ecumenical sermon. Sister Hedwig felt it, and remembered the songs of the Celtic saints. Father Jim felt it, and reserved judgement until he should make his own journey.

Then, just as the smallest children were beginning to shuffle on their fathers' knees and the old ladies to reach for a second blanket, there came a roll on a set of invisible drums. In front of the barge stood Polly, dressed in a simple grey tunic, her hands loosely manacled together. She lifted them in the air and spoke.

'According to the words of Ibn Fadlan,' her pronunciation was supremely confident and extremely unlikely, 'when all the food and drink had been prepared for the chieftain's journey and before the commotion, I mean cremation, began, a slave girl had to be sacrificed. Well, Mr Parrish didn't have any slaves, but I was his secretary, which is probably the nearest thing . . .' There were some murmurs of agreement from young and middle-aged women in the crowd. ' . . . so I had better be the one to be sacrificed.'

Polly shook the manacles from her wrists and drew from her belt a small, jewelled dagger, and, after two or three theatrical flourishes, poised its tip upon her heart.

Ophelia tried to call out a warning, something quick and urgent, but her mind had fastened uselessly upon the word 'verisimilitude' and would not let go. Thankfully others were not so tongue-tied. Two voices cried out simultaneously, one from either bank of the river. From behind Ophelia came an abrupt growl: 'Damsel in distress, what? Damn shame!'

Meanwhile Mrs McHenry, who had been skulking discontentedly behind Wardle, stood suddenly upright and screeched: 'No more femicide! Reclaim herstory for the wimmin!'

Both would-be rescuers hurried as quickly as they could towards Polly, who stood frozen in her self-immolating posture. Years of evading riot police and American soldiers had made Mrs McHenry fleet of sandal and she was wading through the shallow waters of the Ewe before Major Lamb had spluttered his way to the front of the crowd. Their haste to reach Polly did not prevent them from trading aspersions as they travelled.

'Silly old sparrow, can't she see this is soldiers' work?'

'It'll be out of the patriarchal frying-pan into the misogynist fire if your sort gets hold of her!'

While the badinage grew more heated and the crowd established its divided loyalties, Stewart Saggers, who had returned to primp up his chicken nuggets, was heard by a few to call in desperation,

'Not real! The dagger – *Romeo and Juliet* last season. Me Mercutio!'

But even the ten or twelve onlookers who did hear him considered that he was rather unsportsmanlike in devaluing the stakes of the contest. Finally Polly realised that she had let her moment of glory last too long. She looked crossly from the Major to Mrs McHenry.

'All that shouting, you've made me forget what I was going to say. I had a lovely speech, too, all contradictory.' It was only Ophelia, who had suggested the word to her, who suspected that she might mean 'valedictory'. 'Anyway, what I was going to say was, Mr Parrish might have been old-fashioned, but he wasn't a male shavenist pig, whatever *some*,' here she gave Mrs McHenry a fearsome glare, 'might think. So I'm not going to sacrifice myself, at least, not by more than an afternoon's wages.'

She finished with a little nod, bent down and picked up a garland of fresh herbs, which she placed around the dead man's neck.

'Here's rosemary,' murmured Ophelia, 'That's for remembrance.'

The cremation proper passed quickly after that. The Arab's testimony, Ophelia remembered suddenly, had required that the closest kinsman of the deceased begin the fire, walking backwards towards the ship, naked and bearing a burning torch. Apparently Letitia Lamb, who turned out to be a keen genealogist as well as a historian, had discovered a second cousin, a Mr Bowles, living in Nottingham. He had agreed to attend the ceremony and even to bear the torch but had drawn the line at the nakedness.

As he put it, 'Nudity's one thing, and I'm not necessarily against it, not in its place. But December nights, that's another, and burning torches, that's a third, and the three in conjunction, like . . . Let's say it makes my eyes water and leave it at that.'

So a compromise was found, in the form of a substantial pair of beige Y-fronts, and honour, propriety and safety were all satisfied.

Mr Bowles' torch, thrown with nervous inaccuracy, did not actually fall upon the ship, but slipped to the ground between two trunks and fizzled out in the mud. But almost as soon as the beige behind had merged back into the darkness the other men came forward with their torches, and soon the boat was crackling behind a fog of greyish smoke.

Ophelia watched them as they shuffled forward in a straggling line, each keeping a prudent distance from his neighbour's firebrand. Horatio Hale and Malachi went up together, still discussing the All Blacks' 1974 side, with Pius trying to sound interested. It was as well for Mal, thought Ophelia, that he had a new friend, for the success of Wet Nose Solutions looked to be short-lived. A fax had appeared on her desk that afternoon informing her that the county courts were to revert to the Lord Chancellor's Department. Apparently an enterprising South London court had taken to selling its more interesting documents to the popular press and when a Cabinet Minister's wife's divorce petition had formed the front page of the *Daily Voice* it had been decided that enough was enough.

A few places behind Pius was the waiter from the Italian restaurant, who had now convinced even his mother that he was born in Padua, and behind him the unfortunate Derek Wall, reunited with Patty. Further on she could see the old man from the Drop-In Centre, the sheep-pictures man from the market, Jim Silver (or Mr Blank, as she still thought of him), twinkling Mr Puri . . .

In fact, the only male Rambletonian over seven years old who was not paying his last incendiary tribute to Mr Parrish was the saturnine Nick Bottomley. He was standing on the edge of the crowd, unwilling to be identified with it, attempting to fix Ophelia with his mesmerising stare. He suspected something, many things, but knew now that it was too late to prove any of them. With a snort, made visible by a twitching nostril, he turned and strode away.

Ophelia pulled the rug closer around her and glanced down at the sleeping Innocent. The last torch had been thrown now and soon the ship and woodpile would be burned to a little heap of ashes. They would be placed in a memorial mound, to be built in a corner of the churchyard at Our Lady and St Barnabas, after the Requiem Mass in the morning.

'Just don't go and be telling the Bishop,' Father Jim had warned, 'or he'll have me guts for gander-gags, sure he will.' So they had found an inconspicuous plot and the girl from the *Rambleton Courier* had not thought to ask any awkward questions.

All shall be well, thought Ophelia, her eyes pricking in the wood-smoke, And all manner of thing shall be well.

In the dim light she took the *Oxford Dictionary of Saints* from her bag and began to leaf through the first two pages. Adeodatus. There was a name to conjure with. 'A gift from God.' It might be a girl, of course. You never knew. Ophelia laid her fingertips upon the imperceptible bump. Adeodata.